THE SMART SET
FICTION: 1913-1923

THE SMART SET
FICTION: 1913-1923

A MODERN TIMES ANTHOLOGY

H. L. MENCKEN
GEORGE JEAN NATHAN
WILLARD HUNTINGTON WRIGHT
Editors

MODERN
TIMES

TABLE OF CONTENTS

EDITORIAL PREFACE

Despite its outsize influence on American literature, *The Smart Set* is hardly known today. Yet there was a time when the writing in its pages set the tone for the social and cultural debates of the period. Originally founded in 1900 by Colonel William d'Alton Mann as a magazine for New York's upper classes, in 1913, under the editorship of Willard Huntington Wright, *The Smart Set* became a venue for the literary avant-garde. An art critic whose star rose as quickly as it fell, Wright later made his mark as a writer of detective novels under the name S. S. Van Dine. But during his year-long tenure as editor of *The Smart Set*, he introduced a new level of literary quality that would be maintained by his successor, H. L. Mencken. Still working as a journalist for *The Baltimore Sun*, Mencken—who had been contributing literary criticism to *The Smart Set*—teamed up with the magazine's theater critic, George Jean Nathan, to establish a cultural force unlike any other in the literary landscape of the time.

Mencken and Nathan stepped up to their editorial task with a unique mix of sincerity and irony—a critical approach that was ruthless in its analysis of art and society and uncompromising in its pursuit of a modern social and artistic vision. Featuring voices known and unknown, they critiqued American culture while filling their magazine with examples of stories, poems, essays, plays, and short shorts that they believed embodied the future for the nation. Having inherited a magazine that had, in its thirteen years, published established writers like Ambrose Bierce, and Theodore Dreiser, and Jack London, as well as experimental writers like Joseph Conrad, Ford Madox Ford, D.H. Lawrence, and W. B. Yeats, Mencken and Nathan hurled themselves into the thicket of anglophone literary production, publishing well-known writers alongside young talent, and creating a unique mix of old and new, familiar and refreshing, traditional and experimental. They struck a balance that ushered in a new era in American literary production while preserving the cultural heritage in which they believed most profoundly: freedom of the individual and faith in the power of creativity.

Mencken and Nathan breathed their unique brand of meaning-making into the magazine's very title. What began as *The Smart Set* for cultural elites—the word "smart" being used in the sense of *fashionable* or *upscale*—became a magazine for people who valued what was "smart," or, in this case, *sharp*. It was intellectual, but it was not pretentious. This made the magazine relatable to younger audiences searching for meaningful debates and imaginative stories. But it also drew the wrath of the elites who believed intellectuality belonged with the upper classes. In 1920, Charles A. Beard, the American historian and Columbia University professor, used the 300th anniversary of the Mayflower's landing to take a dig at Mencken. "The Puritan may not measure up to Mencken's ideal of art," wrote Beard, "but he did build houses that are pleasing to the eye and comfortable to live in, and he never put his kitchen midden before his front door." He was right. Comfortable and aesthetically pleasing housing was not the top of Mencken's idea of what made art meaningful to people in the real world. He was brusque and sometimes recorded sentiments that were seen as problematic. But, as noted in an open letter published in *The New York Review of Books* upon the publication of his *Diary*, which was signed by Ralph Ellison and Kurt Vonnegut among others, "His hyperbole did not foreclose warm friendships with Jewish publishers, writers and doctors; no white editor of the day did more to seek out and encourage black writers; no editor did more to fight for freedom of expression for all Americans." Beard's implication that Mencken had a habit of putting his "kitchen midden," his household trash, out for everyone to see was accurate. And what it revealed was a conservative distaste for Mencken's open critiques of American literature and society. Mencken, it seemed, was too direct for Beard. He was too straightforward about what he thought was right—and wrong—with the nation.

This ironic sort of brashness, together with their sense of integrity, brought Mencken and Nathan's tenure as editors of *The Smart Set* to an abrupt end in 1923. They had written a satirical piece on the interstate funeral procession of President Warren G. Harding, whom they had often critiqued in their pages, but the magazine's new owner, Eltinge Warner, called it treasonous. This was just one example of the challenges that writers and artists faced during this period of United States history. The Sedition Act of 1918, which had limited free speech, had only been repealed two years earlier, yet the Espionage Act of 1917, which included many similar elements, was still law. And just as the Roaring Twenties were revving up, so was the First Red Scare, which was, in many ways, a dry run for the coming Cold War. The growing links between communism and intellectualism made "smartness" less socially attractive. It no longer seemed socially beneficial to be sharp. Cultural survival preferred what was fashionable.

Mencken and Nathan chose to pursue their vision outside the purview of a publisher who believed that hypocrisy was justified in service of patriotism. They started a new magazine, *The American Mercury*, published by Alfred A. Knopf, which they co-edited for a decade to much success. But the magazine never quite rivaled the legacy they had created with *The Smart Set*. Still, they had created a model that could be repeated, not just by them, but by others—not least of which were Harold Ross and Jane Grant, who, inspired by *The Smart Set*, founded *The New Yorker*.

Cultural critics of the day continued to recall the contribution that the magazine had made to the literary arts. In 1934, Burton Rascoe and Groff Conklin prepared an 840-page anthology of *The Smart Set*, featuring some of its most significant writing. Reviewing the volume in *The New York Times Book Review*, Louis Kronenberger wrote: "*The Smart Set* has become something of a legend. ... You were very conscious that it was making literary history." He wrote these words merely ten years after Mencken and Nathan had left the magazine. Yet they made clear that, as editors, the efforts that Mencken and Nathan had expended had been enshrined in what became one of the most influential literary magazines ever published in the United States.

FICTION: 1913-1923

The Modern Times edition of *The Smart Set* anthology builds on the work of Rascoe and Conklin, while making it more approachable for today's readers. It focuses on the fiction in the earlier volume, while reorganizing the material by putting it in chronological order—offering a sense of the magazine's developing interests and approaches in selecting and editing stories. A second anthology, edited by literary critic Carl R. Dolmetsch with a preface by S. N. Behrman, was published in 1966 and featured a long history of the magazine, as well as a smaller selection of its writing, none of which appeared in the earlier anthology. In a nod to this second volume, this edition includes several of these pieces as well. The Modern Times edition is also limited in scope to the editorships of Wright, Mencken, and Nathan, whose collective stewardship was the driving force behind *The Smart Set*'s cultural achievement. This offers the broadest view of the magazine's prose literary output, giving voice not only to the writers who were remembered for decades to come, but those who were forgotten and lost with time, yet who were just as much a part of what made *The Smart Set* legendary.

—David Stromberg

JESSICA SCREAMS

Floyd Dell

N o premonitory vision of Jessica flashed on Jimmy Selden's mind as he tore open Murray Swift's letter. "Come down to Hazelton," it said, "and see me masquerading as a high school principal. I finished my series of one-act plays while I was in Vienna, despite some delightful interruptions, and I have an unpublishable poem I think you will be interested in, in your academic, sociological way. Come at once, for Hazelton bores me, and I wish to talk of myself. Hazelton, by the way, is in Indiana. I'll have some real cigarettes for you, and some apricot brandy that pleases me. Very well, then, I'll look for you."

Selden dropped the letter, and with a sigh started to pack a suitcase. Murray Swift's invitations were irresistible. Yet, as he left hurriedly to catch his train, he cast a pathetic look at his bookcases, full of the sociological books with which he improved his leisure. His eye caught the title of a book by Walter E. Weyl. It was symbolic, that volume of cheerful progressivism, of all that he was leaving. To go to Murray Swift was to turn his back on civic responsibility and venture into the wilds of human nature. The City Club bulletin there on the table had a reproachful look. He shut the door with a feeling that he was playing truant.

But Selden possessed the instincts of the disciple, and he had perforce for Murray Swift the reverence, mixed with astonishment and disapproval, which one might feel for a particularly disreputable minor prophet. It was in this attitude that he greeted Murray Swift—now half disguised by a little beard—at the station in Hazelton that evening, and listened to his characteristic flood of talk, half reminiscence and half philosophy, an astonishing mixture of personalities and generalities, until they reached the old house, standing imposingly back in a large yard, where Murray Swift said he lived.

"I am quartered here at the home of Judge Wyman. A justice of the peace; a funny, solemn old gander. Come on up."

On the stairs they passed a young girl in a blue sailor suit. She smiled at Murray Swift, and demanded: "You're coming, aren't you?"

"Coming? Yes, yes. I forgot all about it."

They all paused on the stairs, and Selden looked curiously at the girl, while Murray Swift after a fashion introduced them, telling him that she was the daughter of the house and one of his pupils. Her gaze burned at Selden eagerly for a moment, and then smoldered into indifference; and Selden, half awakened to some individual quality in her, turned again and looked down at her as she descended the stairs. But all he saw was the familiar appearance of a girl of fifteen with ribbons in her hair—the ordinary young girl as he had always known her.

Murray Swift hardly gave him a sight of his room, transformed, as he transformed every place he inhabited, into a villainous hole, with a litter of manuscript, notes, letters, accounts, books, newspapers, spilt tobacco and burnt matches. "We can talk tonight," said Swift, putting on a fresh collar. "It is part of the duty of a Hazelton high school principal to be present at such affairs"—it was a school party, it seemed— "and besides I like it. I am getting acquainted with America. It is only in a town with ten thousand inhabitants and a red brick high school that one can really see the character of the American people. It should be a great thing for an amateur sociologist like you. Tonight you will see—"

"I grew up in a small town," said Jimmy Selden drily.

"Yes, of course; and therefore never regarded with curiosity any of its phenomena. Curiosity is the corkscrew that makes a man free of the wine of life."

They started down the stairs. "I swear to you," said Murray Swift, taking his friend's arm, "that in the month I have been here I have not seen an extreme of any kind. No—I am mistaken. There is an Anarchist here—the man who keeps the jewelry store. There will be no jewelry, he assured me, the day after the Revolution. I fear he is not a good Anarchist.

A mere reformer, like you. And there is a dance hall here, where I am told very scandalous scenes occur. I have not yet had time to investigate."

Somewhat out of breath with talking, Murray Swift guided his friend into the school yard. On their way up to the assembly room they passed on the stairs groups of young people who spoke to Murray Swift respectfully, as though he were a real high school principal. The assembly room itself, with its garniture of colored tissue paper festoons and a fantastic decoration in red and green chalk on the blackboard, had an air of pathetic gaiety. A few adults scattered among the younger people kept the occasion from assuming any specific quality, and it languished between ceremony and festivity.

Selden looked about for Jessica Wyman, but he did not see her. On the teacher's desk he noted a pile of "boxes," now being auctioned off. It was a rather spiritless attempt to revive an old-fashioned "box social," but every young man seemed gloomily certain of getting the box belonging to the wrong girl. Deserted by Swift, who seemed to have some official duties in connection with this affair, Selden reconciled himself to the idea of sharing a box supper with one of those strange and discomforting creatures whom he had forgotten how to talk to. But, to his relief, he drew a fat and jolly widow, who conversed with him as one sensible human being with another.

But when he had run out of things to talk about he began to feel bored. The hum of talk, so different in its rhythm from that in a restaurant with its clustered group egotisms unconscious of each other—this subdued, half-embarrassed, ineffectual attempt at conversation wearied him. The festoons looked jaded; the room seemed to have given up hope for its occupants. Selden looked over to where Swift was standing apart, pulling at his little black beard and seeming to enjoy his sheer lack of enjoyment.

And then there burst out of the cloakroom—followed by a puff of girlish laughter, like the smoke that follows the bullet—Jessica Wyman, seeming in that moment very young and bold and full of life, as, in tune with some florid music that came from a mouth harp in the cloakroom, she became a wild, whirling, twisting, fantastic figure, executing some curious combination of the steps of the latest dances. Selden, staring, recognized the peculiar movements of the "tango, " the strut of the "turkey trot, " a suggestion of the "bear" and a recurrent reminiscence of the "Boston" whirl.

She tossed her arms, she swayed to and fro, she glided and writhed, abandoning her body to a vehement and rhythmical orgy of muscular expression.

The electric lights flickered, the steam pipes began to sing, and one giddy festoon in pure joy lost its hold and fell to the floor. Murray Swift stepped back out of the way, staring with a kind of delighted dismay. But on the rest of the company there fell a silence that was not the silence of appreciation. The girl danced her way across the front of the room, too full of her own pleasure to notice how it was being taken. But when she started her backward return to the cloakroom, she looked and saw. The pleasure went out of her eyes. Her steps faltered, and after a little effort to hold herself steady to the end, she broke down, and ran swiftly to the cloakroom.

Murray Swift was after her in an instant, and led her out as the baritone might the prima donna. The cue was taken, and the room applauded, but it was applause with a moral reservation in it. "Very clever, but—" it seemed to say.

Selden followed with his eyes as Murray Swift, talking earnestly, escorted her to a seat. She was very quiet now, and Selden noted her black hair and high cheek bones. She seemed like almost any fifteen-year-old girl, demure and quiet in the presence of her elders. That burst of dionysiac energy which she had shown a moment since seemed foreign to her.

On the way home, Murray Swift talked exclusively to her—he had sent her official beau packing, and bade her come home with him and Selden. It was curious talk for the most part, strangely impersonal.

"You belong," he told her, "to the middle class, and to the middle part of that. I haven't discovered the aristocracy here in Hazelton yet, but at least it gives its daughters tennis and horseback riding. And the girls at the other end of the social scale can go to that dance hall. But the daughter of Judge Wyman can't go. The fact is, you are extraordinarily hedged in. And you happen to be the sort of girl whose superabundant energies demand unusual freedom.

"Of course, you could ride a bicycle, or go rowing, or get up amateur theatricals; but unless you were given a sort of social permission to do these things heartily, wantonly, gloriously, they would be spoiled for you. Besides, you have a specific talent. You have a right to dance."

The girl brightened up at that last sentence, and put her hand confidently in the crook of his arm. Suddenly Selden stopped short.

"Wait a minute," he said. "Why not sit down a while?"

They had arrived at a tiny park, with benches scattered here and there beside the walks. It was warm for October, and the moonlight turned the spot of greensward into a place to linger in. They strolled over to a bench.

"I now begin to understand," said Murray Swift to his friend, "why you are called Jimmy instead of James. I have been unjust to you in my thoughts. I should have thought of this myself. Sometimes I fear that I am a mere theorist, after all."

As they sat down, Murray Swift turned to the girl. Her face took on in the moonlight an unwonted maturity of expression—it seemed to express the weariness of her soul with its continual failure to find expression. "Suppose," Murray Swift suddenly said to her, "I were to make love to you." She smiled. "If you were a year or two older," he said, "I'd do it. But no—you are too carefully brought up."

"I have held hands," said Jessica candidly. "It's rather silly, isn't it?"

Murray Swift, taken rather aback, replied: "No, it is not that. I assure you it is not that. It is merely the banality of the Hazelton male which made it seem so. I congratulate you on making a start. You will find it interesting if properly cultivated. I advise you this in all sincerity. It is true that there are many other interesting things for a girl of your temperament to do, but you will not find any of them in Hazelton. That is your chief resource. Do not despise it."

Jessica was yawning. Murray Swift did not notice, absorbed as he was in talking.

"You are," he said, "what is sometimes called a tomboy. You are so unfortunate as to be neither rich nor poor, which means that you are a suppressed tomboy. You are living in a country which at best only tolerates tomboys, and at worst exploits them brutally."

Selden was looking at her, and seeing her with sharpened sight. Her black eyes, over which the eyelids drooped with languor, her petulant red mouth, were indeed the features of a child; but the mouth was just touched with a curious shade of sophistication, and the eyes had a faint expression in them of knowledge, rather than the wells of unplumbed ignorance which are childhood's. Selden looked at her face, with its high cheek bones, and the careless black hair that shaded it, at her young body that had just begun in bosom and thighs to take on the outlines of maturity, and it seemed to him that he was learning something about the "young girl" that he had never known before. He saw a strange compound, an unstable mixture of all the dangerous elements of childhood with a new and not less dangerous, though slighter, element of sex. In her blue sailor suit, with her girlish hair and pouting lips, she entered his imagination.

"Jessica," asked Murray Swift, "how, exactly, does Hazelton make you feel?"

"I want to scream," said Jessica. "*To scream!*" she repeated in a fierce whisper.

"Selden," said Murray Swift, "you and I were never made to set things right. But this girl here, whom you doubtless regard as a child, is plainly different. She will do something. It will not succeed. No, it will not succeed. But it will be a reproach to me and to you, who do nothing—who do nothing but talk. But she is yawning! Come, let us go home."

On the way home, he said: "Jessica, I accept your rebuke. I talk too much. But I shall do something. I shall write a poem subversive of the morals of Hazelton."

"This is where I live," said Jessica drily, as they reached her front gate. They went in silence up the walk, and into the house. At the foot of the stairs she bade Selden good night, smiled a faint and possibly satirical smile at Murray Swift, and disappeared.

"Now," said Swift. "I want to show you that poem of mine. Sit over there on the couch. Here are the cigarettes."

Selden left the next morning, and did not see Jessica again until the next summer. He and Swift were at an amusement park in Chicago, where Swift—having been "fired" from his position in Hazelton—was loafing. It was a June afternoon—Sunday. Selden and Murray Swift had just come out of the smoke and roar of a "naval battle," when they passed what appeared to be a new "attraction." A small building had just been put up, and was not yet painted. Swift was halted by the appearance of a woman in the doorway—a fat woman, dressed as an Oriental dancer—and by the familiar and curiously alluring music which accompanies such dancing. He quickly bought tickets, and pushed Selden in.

The hall was packed; the aisles were full of standing people, and many stood on their seats. As they pushed their way to a place where they could see, they caught glimpses of a girl dressed in red, with multitudinous red petticoats, whirling on the stage, and heard some young women of the audience who were standing near the stage applaud and cheer her familiarly. There was a good-natured flavor to the affair that could be sensed instantly. When, under Swift's energetic leadership, they reached the front, a man in Russian peasant costume, blue blouse and heavy boots, was doing a kind of dance in which he almost sat on the floor, throwing out his legs in a miraculous and very ugly fashion.

In a few moments this ended, and the show was over. Those who had not seen all the performance were invited to remain for the next period. As the audience filed out, Swift and Selden selected front row seats. Several people, dressed in more or less Orientallooking garb, came out of a little door beside the stage and started toward the outside. There was the fat woman whose fleshly promise had drawn them within. There was the man in the boots, now wearing a kind of Greek costume and carrying a drum. There was the villainous-looking Hindoo (or what you will) that they had seen outside taking tickets—all of the teeth in his wide and wicked mouth were of gold. Then came a man with a clarinet, or some such instrument; his affectation of the Orient did not go so far as to make him dispense with suspenders—he wore them along with a red sash. Then came a girl who looked like a department store clerk, with her ultra-large mass of puffs jutting back from her head; she wore a wine-colored dress and carried a tambourine. Following came the girl in red whom they had briefly seen before the curtain went down. All filed out to the entrance. And then, a little behind the rest, and running to catch up, came Jessica.

Decked out in tawdry Oriental finery, with a short skirt which showed the calves of her legs, a flush on her face under those high cheek bones, her black hair cut across the front to make an Egyptian bang, a laugh breaking from her throat, she was—though transformed—unmistakably Jessica.

She saw them, stopped with a glad laugh, and said: "Hello, hello! Say, come back and see me, will you? Soon as I get back. Bye-bye!" She waved at them, turned and dashed out through the entrance.

Selden looked at Swift.

"Well, I'll be damned!" Swift said.

"Well, what about this?" Selden demanded. "When did she leave Hazelton, and why?"

"Oh, she's been gone two or three months. She left shortly before I did. Disappeared."

"What!"

"Yes. Disappeared on her way to Indianapolis. And this is where she is! Well!"

The girls were being shown off outside, as, with faintly suggestive movements, and to "hoochee-coochee" music, they adumbrated the dances which would occur within. The house was filling rapidly.

"Good God!" cried Selden.

"Now don't be a fool," said Swift. "Wait and see what there is to see. Then make up your mind. Remember what I was going to tell her—that whatever she did would be right, even if it was wrong. This is what she's done. Let's take a good look at it before we make up our minds."

Selden was thinking of the girl in the blue sailor suit there in that peaceful Hazelton house—of her standing there, bidding him good night at the foot of the stairs. She was only a child—she looked to be hardly seventeen even now. And here in such a place as this!

"Wait!" said Swift, noting his expression. "Don't be a fool."

The seats were all full, but it seemed that they wanted to pack the aisles. The Hindoo outside exhorted the crowd; the girls—they could get glimpses of them through the curtained doorway—wriggled to the music. The band came inside, the fat lady appeared and disappeared, and the crowd filtered in.

"Ee-*yah!* Ee-ahh! E-yahh-ee!"

The man with the drum was yelling—a yell of a piece with the music. A woman's voice took it up. "Ee-yah-ee! Ah-ee!"

Then came Jessica's voice, high, shrill, youthful, full of a strange sincerity and enthusiasm: "Ah! Ee-ah! Ee-ah!"

"Nobody ever got paid for yelling like that," said Swift. And then, as if to himself: "She wanted to scream."

That sound seemed more than anything else to excite the crowd outside, and the people began to pour in. Selden and Swift looked at the audience about them. This was composed of all kinds of people—young girls of eighteen, school teachers, middle-aged women, women with white hair, men of every age—all having in their eyes a kind of candid curiosity and expectation—all eager for some erotic spectacle, and seeming frankly to admit it to each other by their smiles. Selden noted a very large German woman, beaming good nature, in the middle of the front row. Her distinguished-looking husband, leaning on a gold-headed cane, looked about at everybody, and whispered witticisms in her ear, at which she laughed helplessly. A few rows back a young mother was nursing her baby at her breast. Two girls in the row behind pierced the lowered curtain with intense looks.

This new audience, like the last, seemed imbued with good nature. It exchanged merry glances and smiles. It applauded and stamped, all in good humor. And above all the din of clapping and stamping, of drum and tambourine and clarinet, and of the damnable iteration outside, rose the girl's yells, more and more prolonged: "Ah! Ee-ah!"

She was standing just inside the entrance, looking out as through a peephole; her profile was clearly outlined, and showed a wide-open—oh, so wide-open—mouth, from which proceeded with unfailing zest this intoxicating scream, filled with the suggestion of unimaginable erotic violence. And yet it was not histrionic—it was noise for its own sake, for the sake of fun, as her face showed. She turned and struck pettishly at the man with the drum, who had been speaking slyly to her. Then she lifted her head, and her throat swelled and her bosom expanded under the volume of sound that burst forth in a last cry which might have been the primitive exultation of a young giantess. Then she ran down the aisle, past their seats, and up the steps into the dressing room. Swift was on her heels in a moment, and Selden followed. Once inside, she hailed them again, very eagerly, and then seemed to grow a little embarrassed. "So this is what you did!" said Swift. "Well, I've left Hazelton, too."

"See here," she said, looking from one to the other with a confident appeal. "You're not going to tell the folks in Hazelton, are you?"

"This man here thinks he ought to," said Swift. "But don't worry."

She turned to Selden with a look that was an assurance of complete trust in him. "You won't tell," she said, putting her hands on his shoulders.

"Here," said Swift, removing her hands, one after the other, "no fair seducing him. Let your life speak for itself."

She laughed. "I guess it does speak for itself!"

"You look happy," Selden suggested uncertainly.

She drew a breath, and stretched out her arms, and her face broke into that look they had seen on it while she was yelling—that, look of glorious fun. She dropped her arms and nodded. "Yes," she said.

The drum stopped beating outside. "Here they come. It's about to start," she whispered.

"But what about these people?" Selden demanded.

"Oh, they're all right. I don't like that black devil out there on the platform, but the others are good fun. Yusuf is a picnic, except when he's drunk—he's the man with the drum. Steve is nice, too. Bertha is a fool. And that fat old Fatima—" She made a face.

At that moment these people began to climb the stairs into the dressing room, with the exception of the black devil, who remained outside. Yusuf glared at the strangers, and the man who must by elimination be Steve looked them over critically. Steve was a lean-faced New Englander. The little room was furnished with a mirror, a chair and an unpainted kitchen table, on which lay some boxes of cosmetics; on the wall and on the floor, too, were clothes, men's and women's; the little company could scarcely all be contained in so small a space.

Jessica said, "See you later," and motioned them out.

The girl in red, to whom Jessica had given no name or comment, had lifted her skirts to adjust something, and Selden glimpsed again her scarlet underclothing as they backed out.

Their seats were gone, but they were in front. The curtain went up, showing a mongrel Turko-Greek room, with a divan, on the middle of which, her lips parted in the gayest of smiles, sat Jessica—a Sultan's favorite, no doubt. On chairs ranged against the side wall sat Yusuf, with his boots and drum, and Steve, in suspenders and red sash, holding his clarinet. On a sort of stool in the corner was Bertha, with her department store puffs and her vacuous look, a tambourine in her lap.

Yusuf raised his drumsticks, Steve put the clarinet to his lips, and Bertha lifted her tambourine. And as these all broke into music, there pranced into the room that great fat woman whom they had first noticed at the door.

Afterward they understood what Jessica meant by calling her Fatima. It was stated on the posters outside that she was the original St. Louis Exposition Turkish dancer. Probably she was. (It was also stated outside that the show was "strictly moral and clean, refined—ladies and children invited.") But the St. Louis Exposition was some years ago. It was the coarsened relic of that Turkish dancer, coarsened and augmented, that they saw before them. She was a skillful muscle dancer, and the rhythmic waves of muscle that rippled and danced over her shapeless body were impressive in one way; but if (as Swift would have pointed out) there is anything in this world which may legitimately be erotic, it is the *danse du ventre*; and a fat woman, by the mere exaggeration of these various features of her sex, may seem in such a dance the very expression of it: but this woman was so swathed in fat that it seemed no sex remained in her.

She stood almost still, a mass of undulating fat and muscle. The audience looked at her with a mingling of curiosity and derision. The music sounded wildly beside her, and on the divan behind, the girl with the high cheek bones, the little black-eyed bride of the Sultan, opened a red mouth and cried in a high voice that seemed to have in it an accent of mockery:

"La Belle Fatima! La Belle Fatima!"

After that dance was finished, and La Belle Fatima had gone into the dressing room—and thence to the front door, to eclipse her own posters—the girl jumped down from the divan, ran to the front of the little stage and commenced to dance the same dance to the same music.

She did not have a tithe of the skill of the older woman, but she had a beautiful body, and she mixed the magic of sex with the abandon of youth. Her dance was an effulgent giving of herself to her audience. And when at last, in a sort of rhythmic paroxysm, she shook her torso with a violent motion that transmitted itself to her young breasts, she turned what should have seemed an ugliness into a symbol of sexuality that intoxicated the audience. She saw her triumph, and exulted in it—but exulted with a kind of wild sexless mirth, the sheer mad effrontery of youth.

Her dance was over. Bertha was there in the center of the stage. As the music started, she whirled rapidly around—and the audience shouted with laughter, at the sight of an extraordinarily large pair of legs. From the ankles up they broadened amazingly. Selden stared a moment at them, and then he saw Jessica come down the steps from the dressing room and dart out the side door, with a glance at him and Swift.

They found her just outside, standing on the little strip of green that separated the little building from the snake charmer's tent next door. Selden was perturbed. He still had the impulse to seize her and crush her in his arms. She turned to him, searching his face with bold eyes. What she saw there seemed to satisfy her, for she turned to Swift.

"And you?" she demanded. "What do you think?"

"I'm wondering," said Swift. "In a way I'm responsible for this. I remember that I told you—"

She went up close to him. "You won't tell on me, will you?" she asked.

"Suppose I did?" parried Swift.

"I know," said the girl, with a glance that made plain her meaning. "You want to be paid for being good. All right, then, be around here"—her voice was very low—"tonight when we close up." She stepped back. "I've got to go out in front now. Good-bye!"

The two young men sustained that disturbing glance, full of the blazing audacity of youth, and shot through with the allure of sex, for a moment, and then she was gone.

"Well," said Selden, "you've made a hit with her. I wish you a pleasant evening!"

"I'm going home," announced Swift, "and rewrite that chapter. I've just got an idea." And he started off.

So Jimmy Selden did not know what Murray Swift had done until two weeks later, when they met again, and Swift told him. Then he was aghast. "You fool!" he cried. "You Judas!"

For Murray Swift, sick at heart, had telegraphed Jessica's father. That night she slept in the police station. A few days later she was sent to an "institution" where girls are reformed by being made to work in a laundry for ten hours a day, together with religious instruction. Jessica's father had followed the expert advice of the police matron and the police magistrate, and hoped to see her emerge a "good girl."

"You betrayed her to them?" cried Selden. "You?"

"I tell you," Murray Swift sadly protested, "that she offered to go with me to a hotel—"

Jimmy Selden interrupted him. "Yes," he said, "of course she did. She wanted to be left alone, and all she had to offer was that. And, by God, you would have done better to take up her offer—than do what you did. I tell you it would have been better!"

THE PERIPATETIC PRINCE

John Reed

O N the barren Andean steppe, swept by the terrible winds that roar between worlds, a heroic granite statue of Peace—erected between revolutions—marks the meeting place of three republics: San Cristobal, Incana and Montemura. San Cristobal City lies a two-hour journey west, in a cleft of the mountains ten thousand feet above the sea; hanging to the steep banks of the Rio del Real, whose torrential thunder, as it plunges furiously down to the Pacific, makes a booming bass for the never-silent church bells of San Cristobal. Above it Santa Maria lifts its white, unscaled head into a sky always dazzling blue, shutting out the sun from the city in the afternoon. The right bank of the stream is the Indian town; and on the left squats the thick-walled Spanish city, with its narrow, steep streets, its plaza, its cathedral and monastery and twenty-eight churches, much as Pizarro built and left it.

"*Blitzen!*" said the Prince Friedrich Wilhelm Heinrich of Hohenzollem-Stüchau as he alighted from the Trans-Andean Railroad's train of honor. "It is beautiful scenery, yes. But livelier cities have I seen.... It is a good place to die in." His tired, dissolute face wore an expression of extreme ennui.

"The air is good here," answered the Baron Marshal von Loewenbrun deferentially, but with a note of satisfaction in his voice. "Your Highness can perhaps rest. The doctor—"

"The doctor!" sneered the Prince. "Didn't the idiot say that it would be dangerous for me to come to such a height? *Hein?* And am I not here in perfect health? *Gott*—the doctor had the impudence to tell me that drinking was bad for my heart! ... That is why I left him there." He jerked his thumb over his shoulder toward the coast. The Herr Baron merely shrugged his shoulders and said nothing. And the next moment they were confronted by a group of bowing little brown men, gilded and be-uniformed: el *Presidente*, Ramon Gonzalez; the Admiral of his Navy—which consisted of one tugboat; the Secretary of his Treasury—which was empty; and the Minister of his Foreign Affairs—which were badly balled up. It was, as a matter of fact, largely on account of these foreign affairs that the President and his cabinet were so obsequious and eager. The interminable, elaborate formalities of Spanish courtesy came sonorously from them; the President bowed; the Prince bowed; a brass band in the plaza played simultaneously "Die Wacht am Rhein" and "Viva Libertad," the national anthem of San Cristobal; cannons were fired and people cheered; an address of welcome was offered. Meanwhile the sun went behind Santa Maria, and the subtle chill of great altitudes crept into the air.

Said the President: "I cannot half convey to His Highness the pleasure he has done me in deigning to honor my poor capital with a visit. And since he has come against the advice of his physician, I and my republic are exalted to be able to charge ourselves with his safety and well-being...."

Prince Friedrich shivered and yawned. His manners were unconventional.

"Herr President," he replied, "your city is magnificent, and your welcome truly touches me. The friendship between two such great nations as the Republic of San Cristobal and the German Empire is a guarantee of the world's peace. Have you such a thing as a drink of Scotch whiskey?"

Locally, the principality of Hohen-zollern-Stüchau is known as "the Emperor's hip pocket." During the youth of Prince Friedrich, life in his father's capital city of Neustadt, as well as in Munich, Dresden and Berlin, was considerably accelerated by that young man. In fact, I may state authoritatively that the Prince had succeeded in doing away with much of the deadly ceremonial of Neustadt court life. Finally, after a stroke of epilepsy and an escapade with La Torella of the Folies, there came an underground hint from the general direction of Berlin that His Highness would be the better for a change of air. And shortly afterward Prince Friedrich was attached to the diplomatic service and ordered on a friendly mission. The sagacious eye of His Imperial Majesty had long dwelt on South America; colonists and consuls reported great unclaimed areas of arable land, boundless rubber forests and deserts underlaid with nitrate. Besides this, a revolution involving the destruction of German property had once made San Cristobal liable for an indemnity—which had never been paid. A show of friendship—a ceremonial visit by a German prince-ling—well, there was value in a foothold even in San Cristobal. The three republics were intensely jealous of each other. In the shadow of the statue of Peace, they watched each other like cats. Whichever republic secured a visit from the Prince would gain vastly in prestige, if not materially.

Thus the wherefore of Prince Friedrich's presence in San Cristobal against his doctor's orders, and the warmth of his welcome there.

"These papers having been signed," said the Prince dully, "I propose that the evening be given over to mirth and revelry. *Gesundheit!*"

"*Salud!*" responded the President politely, at the same time shudder-ing as the unaccustomed whiskey seared his throat.

Herr Baron Loewenbrun looked anxious. "If Your Highness would listen to me—"

"'You cannot, sir, take from me anything that I would more willingly part with,'" quoted Friedrich pointedly.

The Baron shrugged and rose. "Very well, Your Highness." He hesi-tated, cast a despairing glance at the whiskey bottle, at the feet of the Admiral appearing from under the edge of the table, and at the face of the President, seemed about to say something—and went out.

"A song! A song!" bellowed the Minister of Foreign Affairs.

"That old fool would put a damper on any party," said the Prince.

"Your Scotch, though not of the first water, so to speak, has sustain-ing qualities." He poured himself a four-finger tot. "The friendship of two such great nations—*Teufel!* Let us put by the formalities. You know and I know that if your little half-mark republic doesn't behave itself, the German Empire will send a torpedo boat down here and blow you off the map—"

"*Basta!* That is perfectly true," came the Admiral's voice from beneath the table.

"Señor! Your language is inexcusable!" Gonzalez had risen unsteadily to his feet.

"It is. It is," agreed the Prince affably. "Not more so, however, than your Scotch."

"*Carramba!*" cried the President. "Does Your Highness understand that you have insulted my glorious country?"

"It speaks!" The Prince made as if to examine a mechanical marvel." "*Blitzen!* The truth always insults someone. More Scotch!"

"Then, Señor," said Gonzalez, "you shall give me satisfaction in the *duello—*"

"No, no!" The Minister threw himself between. But too late.

President Gonzalez drew back and slapped the Prince smartly on the cheek with his open hand. Then an astonishing thing happened. His Royal Highness tried to rise, and sank back, staring-eyed. For a moment the red mark on his face stood sharply outlined. Then it faded suddenly, while a livid grayness spread over his countenance. The arms fell inertly by his side and swung there; and slowly, with convulsive jerks, the whole body stiffened and became rigid. In the awful silence came the voice of the Admiral gently from beneath the table: "Oo, la-la-la ... "

"*Madre de Dios!*" whispered Gonzalez. In one bound the Minister of Foreign Affairs had reached the Prince. He felt of the pulse, he put his ear to the heart, and raised a face as livid as Friedrich's.

"Dead!"

"A doctor! A doc—" But the Minister had clapped a hand over Gonzalez's mouth. "Fool! Cry out once more and we are lost!" he hissed. "We have charged ourselves with his safety. He is dead. Do you understand? The Prince of Hohenzollern-Stüchau is dead! If he dies in San Cristobal, that will mean the end of the republic!"

"*Basta!* But he is already—"

The Minister tiptoed to the door, which he carefully locked. For the moment he seemed possessed of demoniac energy. Both men were terribly sober. The sweat stood out on their foreheads. Beneath the table, the song of the Admiral was very faint. Gonzalez stirred him with his foot. "Sing!"

"Oo, la-la-la. ... "

"No man is dead until he is buried!" The words fairly seared.

The President threw out his arms miserably. "Ah, *zut!* I give myself up! My glorious country, for whose liberty so many patriots—"

The Minister gripped his arm until he almost cried out. "Drink! Drink, I tell you. We are weak—this will steady us. Now, let us consider. Prince Friedrich was left drinking with us in this room. It must not be believed that he died here. Think! For God's sake, think! San Cristobal was known to have a grievance against the Empire. The Prince is persuaded to visit this city. He dies here. Imagine what ugly rumors from Incana and Montemura will reach the ears of the Emperor!"

The President responded with a groan. He saw no light anywhere. "And when the Baron sees him—"

"The Baron will *not* see him!" hissed the other.

"You have a plan?" cried Gonzalez hoarsely.

"The Prince shall die in Incana!" The President looked at him as at one bereft of his wits.

"You are still intoxicated," he said severely.

"Can't you see?" exploded the Minister. "The Prince makes up his mind suddenly that he will travel to Incana. He is known to be extremely impulsive, and somewhat under the influence of liquor. We cannot be suspected. It is well known that we would do anything to persuade the Prince not to go to Incana—"

"Now?" queried the President in incredulous tones. "He shall travel now, at night?"

"Evidently if we wait for morning the Baron will travel also."

"*Carramba!* I believe it can be done!" Gonzalez got up from his seat and excitedly paced the room. "We will send a courier at once to Ventura, and the Prince shall start in one hour. ... Ah, *amigo*, this is a great service that you have done the republic!" He threw his arms around the Minister and kissed him. "We shall confound our enemies of Incana, and save ourselves for the glory which destiny holds in store. Quick! We will dispatch a messenger to Ventura! In the meantime, no one must know that all is not well!"

The Minister of Foreign Affairs stirred the Admiral with his foot.

"Oo, la-la-la-la-la ... "

Beyond San Cristobal the railroad does not go. Through that country of scorched and frozen desert, gigantic precipices and mountains that scrape the stars, a bowlder-strewn trail too rough for vehicles follows the ancient Indian and llama track upward to the high plateau where looms the statue of Peace at the meeting place of the three republics. A few wandering Indians, driving their llamas down through the starlight on the last stage of their long journey to San Cristobal, stared amazedly at the cavalcade which wound past them: an escort—ten nondescript cavalrymen, cursing the officer who had driven them from their warm beds—followed by two figures on horseback.

"Are you comfortable, Your Highness? ... Yes, indeed, you are right. It is indeed freezing at night in these altitudes." The Minister of Foreign Affairs shivered. "Really, are you sure you have no need of the extra *poncho*?" He removed it from the Prince's shoulders and placed it on his own. "Your Highness is most generous."

The Prince rode rather stiffly. His legs stuck out at each side, and his body did not give with the movements of his horse. In fact, a leather cinch thong knotted about each leg and the friendly arm of the Minister of Foreign Affairs were all that held him in the saddle.

"It is the German cavalry style of riding," said a trooper who had traveled.

Above them old Santa Maria glittered frostily on all its leagues and leagues of ice. The great stars, that seemed to hang near in the cold sky, shed a radiance surpassing moonshine. Jinglingly they wound upward, and the soldiers, looking back occasionally, noticed that the Minister was earnestly addressing the Prince, while the latter's gaze seemed intent upon the stars.

It must have been about two o'clock in the morning when the troop encountered the courier riding back. Almost simultaneously they came in sight of the statue of Peace and saw the escort of the Republic of Incana massed beneath it on the frontier. The Minister of Foreign Affairs opened his knife blade and cut the thongs about the Prince's knees.

He said: "What with the stiffness of the cold and Your Highness's natural rigidity, you will remain erect until the road slopes downhill. Then, I am afraid … "

The troopers of Incana were drawn up at attention to one side of the road. Those from San Cristobal stopped, according to etiquette, on their own side of the border, while the Minister rode forward with the Prince. *El Capitan* Miranda, being of rank too low to be introduced to His Highness, merely stood at rigid salute, while the two rode past.

"*Adios,* Your Highness!" said the Minister cheerfully, at the same time bowing low over his saddle. "I shall execute all your commissions." He gave the Prince's horse a sly cut with his whip. The animal bounded forward. Trumpets brayed. The two escorts saluted, and the Incanians wheeled and set out at a spanking trot on the trail of their illustrious visitor.

Ventura was in an uproar. Upon the arrival of the courier from San Cristobal, the astounding news had been immediately telegraphed to the capital. The President of Incana at once ordered that a suitable escort meet the Prince and bring him to the Ventura Palace. He himself would arrive by fast coach. It had somewhat astonished that executive that the Prince should travel without warning at midnight from one republic to another; but he decided to condone the habits of European royalty, and be humbly thankful for this unhoped-for blessing. A prince at Ventura! The old Spanish families of that ancient and aristocratic city prepared to sit up all night, if necessary, to welcome His Highness.

"*Carramba!*" said Señor Don Rogero del Segovia, who owned vast silver mine concessions. "If the Republic of Incana can secure the support of Germany, *por Dios* we can assault San Cristobal and secure a port upon the sea!"

It must have been about four o'clock in the morning when the four-horse mountain coach of the President strained galloping up the last rocky ascent and lumbered into Ventura. A great throng of silent people clustered in the plaza gave a few weak cheers. Disaster was in the air.

"*Basta!*" exclaimed the President in some annoyance. "A revolution now would be in the worst possible taste." Hardly had the oak palace courtyard gates clanged shut, when a maniac in disheveled uniform tore at the coach door.

"Señor Presidente! Señor Presidente!" cried Captain Miranda hoarsely. "A terrible thing has happened! The Prince—fell from his horse—dead!"

Morning came tranquilly in San Cristobal, with a peaceful clangor of church bells. Herr Baron Marshal von Loewenbrun lay on his back in his front room of the Hotel de la Paz, while a slatternly servitor, with a brown cigarette drooping from his mouth, arranged his breakfast of chocolate and stale rolls on the table. Through the window the Baron could see the plaza thronged with people awaiting the Prince's rising: a host of peasants and shopkeepers, each with his mantilla'd womenfolk, and behind them a few hundred Indians, dark, immobile, wrapped in the inevitable llama skins.

"Has His Highness risen?" asked the Baron. The man stared coolly at him, shrugging his shoulders. *"No entiendo,"* he answered surlily.

There came a rap at the door. Two frowzy soldiers, with impossibly ancient carbines, entered and stood at each side presenting arms.

"Ah, Señor Baron, I trust you have had an excellent night!" said the President. His face was pale, but cordial.

"Herr President!" said the Baron, rising in his pajamas and clicking his bare heels together. "Excellent! Few beds that I have ever slept in have made such an impression on me. The Prince—His Highness still sleeps?"

"Carramba!" said Gonzalez with an expression of great surprise. "You do not know? His Highness left word that you were to be notified as soon as you awoke. He did not wish to disturb you."

"Notified of what?" in a voice tinged with uneasiness born of a lengthy experience.

"Por Dios, that he has gone to Ventura!"

"Gone? When? And where is Ventura?"

"Ventura is a city in Incana, about twenty miles from here over the mountains. It was His Highness's fancy at midnight to go at once. He was my guest. All that is mine is His Highness's. ... High-spirited, you know. ... Youth ... " The President shrugged his shoulders and smiled deprecatingly, in a way which suggested the drinking bout of the night before. "Accordingly, I was obliged to yield to His Highness's demands. The Minister of Foreign Affairs accompanied him to the frontier and delivered His Highness over to the escort awaiting him."

"His Highness is a fool!" cried the Baron angrily, forgetting for the moment his tact. "The Emperor will be chagrined that I allowed him so to do without escorting—"

"Be not alarmed, Señor Baron," said the President with an effort. "The roads are safe. There is no danger. However, I may tell you that it grieved me greatly to see His Highness leave me. I used every means in my command to persuade His Highness—"

"Drunken young idiot!" muttered the Baron. Then aloud : "It is not that I fear for brigands, Your Excellency; it is that the Prince is subject to attacks of epilepsy—"

"Ah!" said the President blandly. "And what is that?"

"It is a dangerous illness," explained the Baron, knitting his brows in annoyance. "The body becomes rigid. The pulse almost stops beating. It is as if the invalid were dead. Since childhood—"

"Man—man!" gasped Gonzalez, gripping his arm. "What are you saying! The Prince—His Highness—is often so attacked?" Great beads of sweat stood out on his forehead. His eyes were like an insane man's.

"*Gott!* What is the matter, Your Excellency?"

"To horse! To horse! We must catch him!" Tearing himself away from the Baron's grip, Gonzalez plunged down the stairs. The two soldiers stumbled after, and the Baron, after a moment of stupefaction, hurried frantically into his clothes and did likewise. On the plaza a group of cavalry had hastily gathered, putting on coats, tightening cinches, obviously unprepared. The President, white as a sheet, leaned against the Minister of Foreign Affairs, who was in turn supported by the Admiral, still wobbly from the effects of the night before. Beyond them gathered a curious throng of spectators.

"For God's sake, Your Excellency!" said the Baron, who detested being hurried. "Has everybody gone crazy? Is anything the matter with His Highness? Did you not say there was no danger?"

Incapable of speech, Gonzalez waved weakly to the Baron's horse. It was, as usual, the Minister of Foreign Affairs who retained his presence of mind.

"His Highness looked rather—er—unwell," he stammered. "We are afraid. Not for anything would His Excellency have sickness overtake his guest—"

"But why—" insisted the Baron pettishly. Before the words were out of his mouth, the spurred horse of Gonzalez leaped savagely forward. With a shout, the troopers sprang to their saddles and followed in disorder. Someone lashed the Baron's mount.

"*El Principe!*" roared the people. "Where is *El Principe?*"

"*Carramba!*" groaned the Minister. "If we don't bring him back we'll have another revolution on our hands." And the cavalcade turned a corner and swept furiously up the dry *arroyo* which was the international road.

Early in the afternoon an Indian llama train about three miles from Ventura was scattered and stampeded by a band of horsemen led by a lunatic cruelly roweling his exhausted mount. Fifteen minutes later the horse of President Gonzalez dropped dead in the plaza before the palace, and Gonzalez himself was beating with bruised fists on the *patio* gates. Then came five troopers, galloping in a bunch; followed by the Minister of Foreign Affairs and a stout blond man who reeled in his saddle and said from time to time, "*Wasser! Wasser!*" Another detachment precipitated itself into the plaza, and from a distance rang numberless hoofs on the cobbled street.

"To arms! *Qui vive?* To arms! The enemy!" cried a sentry. A bugle shrilled, and out of the barracks poured the army of Incana.

"Treachery!" cried Captain Miranda to His Excellency the President. The latter mounted somewhat fearfully to the balcony of the palace. Still the horsemen of San Cristobal irrupted into the square; his own troops, in every stage of undress, loaded their rifles in great haste; beyond, Indians and townspeople, armed with axes or primitive rifles, flowed menacingly into the plaza from every side street. He discerned President Gonzalez beating at his gates, shouting, "Open!"

"Señor Presidente," called the chief executive of Incana sternly, "what does this invasion mean? *Carramba!* In a time of peace—"

"Where is my Prince?" shouted Gonzalez, shaking his fist at the balcony. "What have you done with my Prince?"

The President turned to Captain Miranda and grew excessively pale. "Withdraw your troops at once from this territory!" he cried, in trembling accents. "*Basta,* your Prince indeed! What manners are these,

Señor Presidente of San Cristobal, that demand at the point of the bayonet a guest who enjoys the hospitality of the Republic of Incana?"

Gonzalez breathed a sigh of relief. "Ah, then His Highness is here—and safe? I have come to escort him to San Cristobal. His Highness is in good health?" anxiously.

The other considered for a moment. Then: "His Highness was taken seriously ill upon his arrival this morning." Gonzalez groaned. *"Himmel!"* cried the Baron. "But he quickly recovered," continued the President, "and, in spite of all my persuasions, insisted upon continuing his journey—"

"What!" yelled Gonzalez, leaping into the air.

"At eight o'clock this morning His Highness set out for Bolivar in the Republic of Montemura."

Gonzalez stood quite still, swallowing two or three times. He was incapable of speech. Suddenly he burst into action. The nearest horse happened to be that of an Incanian trooper. Before the latter realized what had occurred, the President had climbed up one side and tumbled him off in the dust. "To Bolivar! To Bolivar!" he cried. The dispossessed cavalryman threw up his carbine and fired wildly into the air.

"Horse thief!" cried Captain Miranda.

"Carramba! Our President is called horse thief!" A quick burst of firing astounded the Incanians.

"Fire! Kill the insolents!" ordered Miranda. A scattered volley spent itself harmlessly, but the great throng in the plaza set up a cheer and pressed toward their hereditary enemies.

President Gonzalez turned in his saddle with a countenance mottled with rage.

"Scoundrel!" he cried to the President of Incana. "I will deal with you later! I will return with a German army and exterminate these vermin!" Hoofs drummed thunderingly, and they were gone.

Before dawn the President of Incana and Captain Miranda had descended the stairs of the palace, carrying between them the stiff and unresponsive person of Prince Friedrich Wilhelm Heinrich von Hohenzollern-Stüchau. They proceeded stealthily, but there was no need of caution. Everyone was asleep, even the two sentries. The coach that had brought the President still remained in the courtyard; and into this, with infinite difficulty, His Highness was forced. The blinds were then drawn. At sunrise a courier departed at high speed for Bolivar, and before the crowd had begun to gather in the plaza, the escorted coach rumbled out of Ventura. Between Incana and Montemura the road is practicable for wheeled vehicles. At the statue of Peace, Captain Miranda delivered over his charge to the waiting cavalry of Montemura.

"His Highness sleeps," he said. "You will not disturb him."

Five miles beyond the statue the road into Montemura cuts into the side of a hill of loose stones, which continually slip down in small landslides, making the highway a source of danger to travelers and expense to the nation. About halfway around this hill, a trooper suddenly heard a low rumble. "Look out!" he screamed. The lead horse of the coach sank back on his haunches; the driver strained at the lines, shouting. But too late. Slowly at first, but with increasing speed, the off wheels slid. The coach careened, toppled, and amid a yell of horror, crashed ponderously into the ravine.

"The Prince! The Prince! Where is His Highness?" demanded President Gonzalez, as he pulled his foaming steed to a halt ten miles farther on, in the dark of the evening. The troopers of Montemura were drawn up defensively across the road to face this horde of strange horsemen, pouring up from the south.

"What prince?" asked their captain elaborately.

"What prince! Idiot, were you not escorting Prince Friedrich to Bolivar? He is not here—"

"Ah, yes! The Prince, to be sure! He has decided to continue his journey to San Cristobal—"

"Liar!" Gonzalez raised his whip and cut the other across the cheek.

"*Carramba!* It is a deadly insult! And who are you, dog of a foreigner?"

"*Basta!*" cried the Minister of Foreign Affairs hotly. "He has insulted our President!" Swords flashed, and in two minutes a mass of fighting, snarling men swirled about them. Then suddenly the Montemurans broke and fled, outnumbered. "*Por Dios!*" shouted the officer from the turn of the road. "It is war to the death! Do you understand? San Cristobal shall pay!"

The expedition straggled up the road toward the statue of Peace, looming tremendous in the dark.

"If it be true," said Gonzalez, "and the Prince has indeed returned to San Cristobal—"

The Minister of Foreign Affairs shrugged. "It can very well be true. His Highness is of an impulsiveness extreme—"

"The young devil!" muttered Herr Baron von Loewenbrun. "*Ach, Gott*, what a chase he has led us!"

"Then we have done a good day's work in stirring up these pigs," said the President. "*Basta!* It constitutes a *casus belli*.... And with the friendship of His Imperial Majesty... *Carramba!* There is a territory of silver deposits that I would gladly annex from Incana—not to speak of a lake in Montemura."

The Minister shivered. "We approach the meeting place of the three republics," he said. "We had better be on our guard. One does not know what Incana may do. You will remember in the last war—"

As they passed beneath the statue Gonzalez breathed a sigh of relief. "At last we are within our own territory."

"It is well, nevertheless, to keep watch," said the Minister. "Do not forget the mouth of the *arroyo*."

Starlight bathed the road with ineffable light. Santa Maria towered magnificently above. The chill bit through them; but they felt that a brave day's work had been accomplished. The Minister lifted up his voice in song: "Oo, la-la-la-la," but stopped almost immediately. They jogged on contentedly, while President Gonzalez pictured in his mind's eye the Prince, seated at the Presidential buffet in the Hotel de la Paz, consuming Scotch whiskey and radiating benevolence toward San Cristobal.

And then, just at the mouth of the *arroyo*, his horse stopped so suddenly as almost to pitch him over his head.

"What is that?" said the President, chills running up his back.

A horse snorted—another plunged and reared. "An ambuscade!" cried one or two troopers, wheeling. But the President was not so easily daunted. He peered into the shadows, discerning there a man, motionless in the middle of the road, who seemed to be leaning against a rock, stiffly, with legs wide apart.

"Who goes there?" cried Gonzalez in a trembling voice. "Answer or I fire! Who goes there?"

"*Madre de Dios!*" said the Minister suddenly, clapping his hand to his head. "Hold—"

But too late. Gonzalez's revolver leaped from its saddle holster; then came a roar that echoed preternaturally among the great rocks. The figure slumped forward to the ground. The troopers stood with ready carbines, awaiting the assault that they were sure would come. With a low moaning sound the Minister had slipped from his saddle and was running toward the body.

"Look out!" cried the President. "It is a trap!"

But the Minister of Foreign Affairs knelt beside the dead man, scratching a match. The flame spurted—the match fell from his fingers; the Minister of Foreign Affairs crumpled up and fell on his face. An unreasoning panic seized Gonzalez. He got slowly off his horse, followed by the Baron. "Fainted!" said the Baron curiously. "I wonder—"

But the President had also lit a match at the dead man's face. He staggered back with a dreadful cry: "The Prince!"

"*Ach, Gott!*" barked the Baron. "You have killed him!"

THE GIRL WHO COULDN'T GO WRONG

Albert Payson Terhune

R AEGAN told it to me.

For a short, happy space in his mottled career, Raegan had been a settlement worker. But someone in charge was so base as to accuse him of a greater interest in the working than in the settlement. And he had departed—with a grievance and several more negotiable mementoes.

It was during the "Minimum Wage for Working Girls" legislation that I ran across Raegan. What or whom he was doing at the Capital I never clearly knew. I had a fine idea for an epigram which, if I could whittle it into scintillant, mordant keenness, I intended to embody somewhere in my wage story.

It was to the effect that the same low pay scale which keeps girls from being respectable keeps men from being anything else.

I rather fancied this statement of a double standard in the relation of poverty to goodness. And, in the first glow of inspiration, I repeated it to Raegan. Of course he did not grasp the idea. And when I put it in more and simpler words he flatly contradicted me. The fact that my pretty catch phrase could be proven untrue pleased me immensely. For it proved the thing an epigram.

I told Raegan so. But, perhaps thinking I was arguing the case, he undertook at some length to prove me wrong. Then, by way of illustration, he told me the following tale—gleaned during his brief, bright settlement experience. I do not vouch for it. Nor do I wholly know what it proves. But this I do know: it proves *something*. That is not an effort to be funny, but the statement of a solemn certainty. And wiser folk than I are at liberty to find the proof.

No (began Raegan), you're dead wrong when you spring that puzzle picture speech about girls finding it hard to live up to their Elsie books just because they're broke. Often as not, they find it harder to do anything different. Being broke is the very thing that keeps them in line. And Maudie Kirk's case cinches that.

There're two halves to Maudie's story. The first half reads like all the dreary, Heaven-Will-Protect-the-Woiking-Goil wheezes ever ground out. The second half isn't quite like anything else I've happened to run across.

Maudie came to New York from one of the "small time" towns that have names like a Roman general and populations like a road company Roman mob. I don't remember just what line of honest endeavor her father had chased. But there's no doubt he *was* honest. For he died, leaving a bedridden widow and Maudie and—after the M.D. and M.A. (why, Mortuary Assistant, of course) had taken theirs—about a hundred dollars.

That meant the bell had rung for Maudie to listen to the factory whistle. And, being a dutiful kid, she listened. There was no chance, up in her own bailiwick. So she hearkened to the call of the city. There were jobs to be had in New York. And a girl could live here on almost nothing, if she knew the right sort of food and clothes—and let them alone.

And she could send all her spare savings up-State to pay board for Mother, who was deposited at Uncle Barney's, on the Pompton road, at three fifty a week. Some money, in those parts, I'm told!

So Maudie came to New York. She was no fluff skulled Maid of Yaphank, to be lured or otherwise pleasurably excited by the hidden perils of the Big City. Not she. She knew what to steer clear of and why to steer clear of it. She was a good girl, clear down to her number six soles. And level-headed. And equipped with an 1840 New England conscience. Why, on form alone, you could have backed Maudie to go around the track six times without leaning over the rail once to crop any infield grass.

"I know what the city is," she told her mother, as she finished brailing the telescope bag and double-reefed the ancestral umbrella. "And I know the traps it holds for fools. I know, too, that a good, sensible, self-respecting girl can always make her way anywhere. So don't worry your precious old self about me."

Good talk, what?

So to New York came Maudie. And what's more, she got a job—after a while. It was in the basement (plus two) of a department store. The section that never is intruded on by Customers, Daylight or Real Air. And they paid her $5.50, as a starter. Just for pottering around pretty steadily from eight to six thirty, with very near twenty whole minutes off for lunch—sometimes.

Part of the while she was able to send home the three fifty a week for Mother's board. And part of the time she did it, anyway, by working overtime. You see, it was one of those generous stores that allow their girls overtime pay, except at the busy season.

Well, for a couple of months or so Maudie was pretty near as happy and carefree as a blind mule on a treadmill. Then there was a cut-down. And the bulk of the new girls were let out. Maudie was among the bulk. And by this time she'd trained off a whole lot of loose flesh that she didn't need.

But, bless you, even when her first landlady locked the door on her and lost the key, Maudie was as plucky as ever. And just as dead sure as ever that a good, self-respecting girl could win her way along the straight road—even if there were a few stray bumps therein, to keep the liver from getting torpid.

Next, after a kind of long stage wait, she got her chance in a steam laundry, at six per. No overtime. But she scalded her face and arms pretty badly one day in a steam escape. And by the time she got back from the hospital the laundry people had decided she was a hoodoo, and wouldn't take her on again.

Through the Y. W. C. A. (where she used to get weekly thrills by listening to those startling lectures on "Child Widows of India," and "How to Tell the Wild Flowers from the Birds") she annexed a nice general-housework job in a family of nine that kept boarders. The mistress was the grandniece, by marriage, of Simon Legree. She paid Maudie fourteen dollars a month and kept her from taking on fat. But Maudie fainted one day, when there was company. And she was fired. You see, they wanted a strong girl.

Did she lose her faith in that splendid Self-Respect wheeze? She did not. She still shut her eyes and her ears to the Easiest Way and stopped eating for a while; and then landed a fine position in a sweatshop.

She lasted for nearly five months. Then the girls "walked out," she at their head. One of the papers called her a Joan of Arc and printed a snapshot of her. The other girls got back. Maudie didn't.

Being a member of the Arc family isn't on the free list.

Then came a spell when there was no work. At least none for Maudie. The day that the last member of the Dollar Family quitted lodging with her a letter came from Uncle Barney. It said, among a lot of other demonstrative things, that Mother's board money must be paid up in full or the old lady must get out.

There was a poorhouse handy, went on Uncle Barney, with his inimitable dry wit, and he wouldn't grudge giving Mother a free drive there. He enclosed the doctor's bill for $98.60. And at the bottom the big-hearted old family physician had scrawled a line to the effect that he'd pay no more calls till a full settlement was forthcoming. Uncle Barney's love letter wound up by mentioning that Mother was some worse.

The letter got to Maudie Kirk on Christmas evening, early.

She read it all through a couple of times. Then she read again what the doctor had to say. After that, she crossed her room (one step did it) to the looking glass. The glass showed back about the sorriest-looking hallbedroom in the City of Hallrooms. The landlady had been soft-hearted, because Christmas was near, and she had told Maudie she needn't get out till New Year's.

Well, over to the glass went Maudie. It was a flawed glass at that. But it served her all right as an audience. She looked into it. And she began to speak, out loud, to the girl there.

"I've given it a fair trial," she said. "I came here strong in my faith that self-respect and willingness to work would carry a woman safe to success. I've slaved like a dog. And I've starved. I've given Decency all the chance it could want. I've lived as Mother would have wanted me to live. And I've suffered as she couldn't understand, if I told her. And what's come of it?

"I can't get work. I can't get food. I can't get the money that will keep Mother out of the poorhouse. I can't get any of those things honestly and decently. If I was the only one concerned, I wouldn't care. But Mother is going to have a home and a doctor's services.

"*She's going to have them.* And I'm going to get them for her. I've read a lot about a girl not needing to go crooked just because she's poor. And it's a lie. A silly lie. I've tried the heaven path. And it's bumped me into a stone wall. Here's where I go to hell!"

And just as carefully and as honestly as she had toiled heavenward, she set out to trip the Short-Cut, Down-Grade route. She planned it all out. But she overlooked one bet. She'd been too busy orating at herself in the glass to pay any sort of notice to what that same glass had to say in come-back. If she had, she might—or she mightn't—have noticed a few things:

First, that ten months of systematic starving had taken everything off her body but the bones; and had tried to square itself by making those twice as large. Second, that the eyes had gone hollow. Not with dark, fancy shadows, but with a burnt-hole-in-a-blanket effect.

Likewise her face was greasy and so was her hair. Hers was mouse-colored hair at best, and it had got thin and stringy and it was strained back. The only dress she had left was grease-spotted and shiny and darned. It had never been anything that Worth or Paquin would have thrown a fit over. And now it had lost whatever it had started with. Her shoes, too—well, never mind her shoes. And she had no gloves. Her hat, by the way, wasn't much the better for about forty rains that had landed on it since she had hocked the family umbrella.

Yes, sir, that was the general blue print front elevation of the damsel that had set out to go wrong. But off she started. She had pluck.

She sneaked out of her boarding house, and hit Broadway about eight o'clock. There's apt to be several people around at that hour of the evening. 'Specially Christmas night.

Maudie was resolved on her Hades trip, all right. But she didn't quite know the road. So up Broadway she started. She'd always scuttled along the streets like a scared little hen, with her eyes fixed, purely, on her feet, ever since she had struck New York. But tonight she acted up real brazen. She walked slow along the Big Blonde Path, eyes high, manner heroic and her heart hammering up in her poor thin throat.

From Thirtieth Street to Fiftieth she strolled. Then back again as far as Fortieth. Nothing happened. Just nothing at all. She couldn't understand. She'd heard about girls who walked Broadway. She'd just walked it. And she might as well have been stepping down to the store from Uncle Barney's house.

Something was wrong, somewhere. She couldn't guess what, till she saw a squab just in front of her drift dreamily alongside a fat man who looked as if his name belonged on a Rhine Wine List, and say something to him as she passed. Maudie could only catch the word "dear." It sounded rather free-and-easy for a total stranger. But it seemed to be the thing to do.

So up to a dapper little fur-coated man sidled Maudie. She tried to say "Dear," too. But the word stuck. The man looked at her, kind of cross. Then he grunted:

"This is Panhandleville all right. Fifth touch in six blocks. Oh, well, it's Christmas!"

And he flipped her a dime. Maudie gathered it up. Dimes had a market value, even if souls hadn't. Then she stood looking after him, all choked and white. He'd taken her for a beggar. Not for a Seductive Delilah at all. But just for a Christmas Night beggar.

Next time there was no chance for any mistake like that. She said "Dear," to the red-faced clubman who lurched toward her out of a side canyon. She said it right out loud. Pretty near hollered it. He stopped dead short with his mouth open. Maudie backed away a bit. She didn't know what was the next thing to say. Besides, he reeked of booze. But she got fresh hold of her courage and said "Dear" again. She said it the way McGraw coaches the runner on third.

The man let out a roar of laughter.

"Oh, if the boys could see!" he sniggered, hopeless-like. "And they'll never believe me! On Broadway, too!"

He hailed a taxi and rolled aboard it, still roaring. Maudie took a kind of bashful step toward the taxi. But he howled to the meter brigand to put on double speed, and slammed the door.

The next man told her to go get a new face. The next said the Scarecrows' Home ought to keep earlier closing hours. And so on, all the way down the line. It was raining, too. Once a cop saw her at work and he laughed himself sick. You see, the happy Christmas spirit was abroad.

The only job that is supposed to pay the amateur better than the professional followed the example of all the other jobs Maudie Kirk had looked for. Gee, but it must have been tough for a girl, with Maudie's conscience, to cut loose and turn her back on all she held holy—and then be refused the chance of profit by it. As if when old Faust offered to swap his soul, the red basso devil had carolled, "Nothing doing!"

A night's sleep gave her some new courage. And she made up her mind to try again. Women of That Kind wore ropes of gems and rode in limousines and had the sort of flat they call "Bijou"—whatever that means. Maudie had read so. Also, the wicked city was swarming with men who were eager to prey on defenseless womanhood. She'd read that, too. So she couldn't see where she'd failed.

She hadn't read—because nobody's yet had sense or nerve enough to write it—that the average plain working girl has about as many temptations in New York as she has on a desert island. And that at best—or worst—such a girl's unlawful earnings wouldn't keep her in carfare. But where's the living girl who doesn't snuggle to her heart the belief that she could rake in a fortune if only she chose to be wicked? And, after all, Glass is as precious as Diamonds—until one tries to sell it.

Maudie planned a new angle of attack. There is a famous "Red-Haired Siren" whose lures captivate Wall Street and who is by now richer than John D.

Poor Maudie had heard about her. Everybody has heard about her. Except perhaps Wall Street.

The Street was screaming next day over a story that nobody really believed. A story about a thin, ragged-looking wreck of a woman—most likely batty—who had managed to get past the sleepy door guard into old Cyrus Q. Spillaker's private office and had stammeringly hailed the old geezer as "Dear"—just before the whole working office staff had industriously run her out.

Well, it took Maudie Kirk just two days to learn—she was no fool—that she could no more go to hell than she could to Mars. Morally, she was a goner. For she'd said good-bye to Goodness and Decency and Conscience. Said goodbye to them, out loud, in front of her looking glass. But she'd never since had a chance to make that farewell anything but a solo. And she knew now that she never could.

That was about dusk, two days after Christmas.

A couple of hours later, a tug captain off East Twenty-sixth Street boathooked a bunch of sleazy clothes that had just hopped off the dock with a starved woman inside of them.

Maudie couldn't even score a success as a drowner. The captain lugged her to Bellevue, and pretty soon she came around and began to eat. She had a few months' arrears of food to make up. And she sure did her best at it.

You know young Galahad Templar? Sure you do. He runs the Settlement. He has all the cash that's fit to coin. And he spends it on the Uplift of his fellow man and woman. Fits up the Settlement gallery with pre-cubist pictures to elevate their souls, and has long-haired woplets from the Metropolitan and Carnegie Hall come down once a week to show them how Tschaikowsky really ought to be rendered. It's a big help to East Siders with rabbit families, I can tell you. Why, lots of them can tell a Corot from a Greuze and the "Largo" from Raff's "Spring Song."

Well, Templar happened to be on his monthly philanthropic butt-in at Bellevue when Maudie Kirk was brought there. He got interested in as much of her story as she could tell him between eats (we got the whole of it from her later at the Settlement), and he pulled wires to have her ambulanced over to his Settlement House.

Say, it was a miracle what a few weeks of rest and real food and warm clothes and a few dozen baths and shampoos did to that girl's appearance. And when she was all well again and plump and kind of pretty and winsome, Templar paid her mother's bills and found her a fine easy fifteen-a-week job in the office of one of his chums. She'd got a fair start at last, poor kid!

Did she hang onto *that* job? I'm sorry you had to ask such a question. And I'm pained, something terrible, to say she didn't. Templar was so proud of his work of reformation that he—well, last time I heard of them, he'd gotten her a nice comfortable little morganatic flat uptown, somewhere, near the park. The sort of flat they call "Bijou"—whatever that means.

MIRRORS

Robinson Jeffers

ABOUT Adair? It's a curious story—perhaps I can tell you more of it than anyone else. For it was to me that Adair came to unburden his soul, the night before he smashed all his mirrors and sailed for Africa.

Insane? Not at all. But he was excitable, you remember, and highly sensitive. Things irritated him—little things that you or I would barely notice. He had the vision of an artist, and the nerves of a decadent; but he had no art, no work—the artist's safety valve.

Adair used to visit me often in the evenings, and talle. He had strange theories, and a wonderful power of making them appear reasonable. There was a vividness in him ... I can see him now—his very expression—the whiteness of his long features. He used to sit in the big wicker chair, there by the hearth, and prove to me, step by step, that evolution is a progressive degeneracy, that man is less happy, less beautiful, less perfect, than an ichthyosaurus. Then he would light another cigarette—he smoked them interminably. He used to come in without knocking, silently, like a ghost, any time between nine and midnight. Often he would talk until dawn, and go home under the rising sun. Or he would sit silent until dawn.

But his last visit was different from the others. About eleven in the evening I heard a step before the door, and a knock, and Adair's voice calling me.

"Come in," I said.

But he wouldn't come in; I had to go to the door. Adair was standing in the passage, violently excited.

"You have a mirror," he whispered, 'on the wall, to the right of the bookcase."

"Yes?" I asked, wondering.

"Take it down," he said. "Take it down—out of the room. Then I'll come in." And, as a matter of fact, the mirror had *to* be removed before he would enter.

Then, "Shut the door," Adair said; and began to pace the floor with great strides. Three steps from that window to the opposite wall; three steps from the wall to the window; back and forth, back and forth, without speaking. And in each three steps his heel would strike twice on the rug, softly, and once, with a sharp tap, on the hardwood floor. Thud, thud, tap; tap, thud, thud—a queer rhythm which got on my nerves.

Then Adair spoke, and so abruptly that I was startled.

"Have you ever hated mirrors?"

"No," I gasped. "No. What—"

"Neither have I," he said, "till tonight. It never occurred to me. But why not? Why not? They're contemptible. Everything's contemptible."

Then suddenly, with a plunge and jerk, Adair was in the middle of his story. He talked so rapidly that my mind was outdistanced at once, and tagged along out of breath, always half a dozen words behind his meaning.

"You remember Millie Gaspard," he said. And before I could quite recall the blonde little actress, Adair was already speaking of Miss Converse, whom people regarded as his fiancée. Then Adair's talk veered back to the actress.

"You know that two years ago I was intimate with Millie Gaspard."

I nodded. That intimacy had been the root of a scandal which even Adair's inherited money was barely able to hush up.

"Millie had queer pet names to employ when she was feeling affectionate. She used to call me 'Baby of Love,' and 'Joy Child' "—Adair was speaking tragically, without a smile—"and she used to pat my hand, three little quick pats, holding it tightly in her own.

"My God!" he burst out incoherently. "I thought I was rid of her! I gave her ten thousand dollars, and thought I was rid of her

"But the memory sticks. We're like everybody we meet. Once I heard a coachman roar at his horse—filthy words. Ten months later I heard myself shou ing the same words at my terrier.

"And tonight, Alice—Miss Converse—caught my hand and patted it three little quick pats. And said, 'Baby of Love.' That was tonight, when I was leaving her."

Adair paused for breath, and I interrupted him. "But," I said, "Miss Converse—how did she—"

"She learned it from me," Adair answered. "Just as I had learned it from Millie Gaspard, who had learned it from God knows what brute when she was young.

"Alice learned it from me. I remember now that once I patted her hand—and was hot with shame, remembering from whom I had the trick. And once—perhaps twice—I called her—by the pet name."

"But why," I said—"what do you—"

"Idiot!" Adair whispered. "Do you think I can marry a woman who has learned the tricks of Millie Gaspard?

"Yet," he said, "that isn't the worst of it. The worst of it is that I know we are all mirrors—senseless mirrors—blank spaces which reflect. If I do a thing, or say a thing, it is only because someone else has done it, said it. Nothing but mirrors.

"And the sky and the earth and the water," Adair went on, "are mirrors. If I am happy, the sky is happy. If I am sorrowful, the world droops. Everywhere I look—my own face.

"And you, too," he said, raging at me with his dark eyes, "you are a mirror. You are bewildered because I am bewildered. You are exasperated because I am exasperated. If I should smile, you would smile. Bah!

"And," he whispered hopelessly, "God is a mirror. . . . My own face. My own face always. Or Millie's pet names."

With that, Adair tossed up one hand in a curiously final gesture and dropped into a chair—that wicker chair by the hearth.

But when I began to answer him—some foolish thoughts of remonstrance and consolation—Adair burst once more into speech, and raved like a mad prophet, tearing heaven and earth into shreds of similarity. "Everything is like everything else—everything reflects everything else—" So that it came to me to understand why Nero sought to destroy the world—because it looked like himself.

"There is nothing so terrible," I was thinking, "or so contemptible as one's own likeness. That is why monkeys seem unclean to us."

Then, through the cloud of my thought, I heard Adair bidding me good-bye.

"I shall sail tomorrow," he said, "for Europe, and get to Africa as quickly as possible. Perhaps in the desert, in the jungle, things won't look like myself. Good-bye."

So Adair went away the next afternoon, and has spent his life shooting big animals. Now and then he ships hunting trophies to his friends on this side, I hear that he has sent Miss Converse a rhinoceros head.

A SHEPHERDESS OF FAUNS

F. Tennyson Jesse

A RCHIE LETHBRIDGE arrived in Provence thoroughly satisfied with life in general and himself in particular. He had just sold a big picture; was contemplating, with every prospect of success, giving a "one-man show" in Boston of the work he would do in Provence—and the girl he loved had accepted the offer of his hand and heart.

Miss Gwendolen Gould was eminently eligible. Her income, though comfortable, was not large enough to brand her husband as a fortune hunter; she was pretty in a well-bred way that satisfied the eye without causing it to turn and gaze after her; and, above all, she could be relied upon never to do, say or think an unusual thing. Like all painters, when they are conventionally minded, Archie was the pink of propriety—he owned to enough wild oats of his own sowing to save him from inferiority in the society of his fellow men, and he held exceedingly rigid views on the subject of his womenkind. Gwendolen might—doubtless had, for she was one of the large army of young women brought up to no profession save that of sex—give this or that man a kiss at a dance, but she would never have saved all of passion and possibilities for one man, and lavished them on him, regardless of suitable circumstances. Archie's name (that he hoped one day to adorn with some coveted letters at which he now pretended to sneer) would be perfectly safe in Gwendolen's carefully manicured hands.

The only drawback to his complete content was that his fair, sleek person showed signs of getting a trifle too plump—for he was only young as a man who is nearly "arrived" counts youth. On the whole, however, it was with a feeling of settled attainment that Archie arrived at Nice and proceeded to strike up into the Alpes Maritimes, totally unprepared for any bizarre or inexplicable events—he would have laughed satirically at the bare idea.

To do him justice, he worked hard, and he had a tremendous facility and a certain charm that concealed his lack of true artistic sensitiveness. He painted here and there from Grasse to Le Broc, and then one day, feeling he had taken all he could from the soft-scented land of olives and flowers, he hired a motor to convey him up into the Back o' Beyond and drop him there.

After that he saw no living thing, neither bird nor beast nor human, for many miles: only rounded hills, opening out from each other in endless succession and covered with harsh yellow grass and strewn with gray bowlders; deep gullies that at one time had been set alight and now were scorched and brown like plague pits, with here and there a patch of pale stones showing up lividly from the charred thorns and blackened soil. Archie shivered, partly because of the keen wind blowing down from the great plateau beyond the hills, partly because something savage in the scene gripped at him.

The car throbbed on, higher and higher, till the road, winding acutely along the edge of precipices, developed a surface that caused his chauffeur to swear gently to himself. Valley after valley opened out, long and narrow, and Archie noticed signs of a long-past cultivation in the curved terraces into which the bed of each valley was cut, and forming an endless series of semicircles. There was no trace of any crops, and the whole effect was of some rude amphitheater where Neolithic man sat round and watched gladiatorial shows.

The car, sticking now and then in a rut, or jolting violently over stones, finally crested the last rise, and Archie found himself on a vast stretch of land ringed in by sharp-edged hills, like some dead, gigantic crater; to the right, far away on a slope of the mountain ring, lay a gray straggling town that seemed hacked out of the hardened lava. The only sign of life was in a patch of vividly green grass near at hand, where hundreds of crocuses had burned their way up through the earth and showed like a bed of thin blue flames.

Archie directed the contemptuous chauffeur toward the town, and they finally drew up at the inn—a little, green-shuttered affair, with a stone-flagged passage, and a tortoise shell cat drowsing beside the door. Outside a *buvette* opposite was a marble-topped table at which sat a couple of workmen drinking cider. An evanescent gleam of sun shone out, and the tawny liquid caught and held it, making each glass throw onto the table a bubble of gold fire enmeshed in the delicate shadow of the vessel itself. Archie stood transfixed for a moment with pleasure; then, as the gleam faded and died, he entered the inn.

Like most people with the creative temperament, Archie Lethbridge was the prey of environment. Draginoules took such a deep, sure grip on Archie that it did more than merely affect his work—it began to upset his neatly arranged values and to substitute fresh ones in their place. Draginoules, in short, behaved like a master of scenic effects, it allowed a couple of days for the background to permeate Archie's consciousness, and, when he was ripe for it, introduced the human element, which, to a man, must of necessity mean a woman.

It was one morning, when he was washing brushes in the dim inn kitchen, that he saw her first. She came out of the *buvette* to serve some workmen, and Archie stopped dead in the act of swirling a cobalt-laden brush round and round in the hollowed yellow soap he held. He always saw the whole scene in memory as clearly as he saw it then: the low-fronted *buvette*, the glass of the door refracting the light as it still quivered from her passage; the pools of blue shadow that lay under the table and chairs on the pavement; the blouse-clad figures of the workmen, particularly a young man with a deeply burnt back to his neck; and the girl herself, holding aloft a tray of liqueur glasses, that winked like little eyes. All this he saw framed by the darkness of the kitchen and cut sharply into squares by the black bars of the window; then, as he mechanically went on frothing blue-stained bubbles out of the soap, he said to himself: "I must paint that girl."

He found that she was the niece of the stout couple who kept the place, and her name was Désirée Prevost. As they mentioned her, most people shrugged their shoulders. Oh, no, there was nothing against the girl—and though it was true her eyebrows met in a thick bar across her nose, and old people had always said that was a sign of the *loup-garou* enlightened moderns did not really hold by that. The town was proud of her looks, for it considered her *"très bien,"* the highest expression of praise from a Provençal, who is a dour kind of person.

Archie approached the aunt of Désirée on the subject of sittings with some trepidation, but met with an agreeable pliancy from her, and a calm, though indifferent assent from Désirée herself. She had a high opinion of her own value, and no amount of appreciation surprised her.

Scanning her afresh as they stood on the pavement making final arrangements, Archie inwardly congratulated himself. From the heavy brass-colored hair massed with a sculptured effect round her well poised head to the firmly planted feet, admirably proportioned to the rest of her, she was entirely right for his purpose—she seemed the spirit of Draginoules incarnate. Owing to the opaque pallor of her skin, her level bar of fair eyebrow and heavily folded lids, big, finely modeled nose and faintly tinted mouth, all took on a sculptured quality that made for repose; the very shadows of her face were delicate in tone, mere breaths of shadows. Yet she was excessively vital, but it was a smoldering, restrained vitality suggestive of a quiescent crater. Her face was too individual to be perfect—the nose a trifle too big, the brow a shade too narrow for the full modeling across the cheekbones; but she had an egglike curve from turn of jaw to pointed chin. When she laughed her teeth showed large and strong, and her throat was the loveliest Archie had ever seen—magnificently big—and she had a trick of tilting her head back that made the smoothly knitted muscles of her neck swell a little under the white skin. As he painted her Archie used to find himself racking his brains for some speech that would make her head take that upward poise, so that he could watch the play of throat.

He chose his background well: a sheltered spot in a fold of hill just beyond the town, where a slim young oak sapling still retained its copperhued autumn leaves, that seemed almost fiery against the deep, soft blue of the sky. He had conceived of her as standing under the oak tree, so that, to him, working lower down on the slope, she, too, showed against the sky, seemingly caught in a network of delicate boughs. Being below her, he was also the richer by the soft, three-cornered shadow under her chin, and the whole of her became a tone of exquisite delicacy, as of shadowed ivory, in the setting of sky—that sky of Southern spring which seems literally drenched in light. The tawny note of the oak leaves was to be repeated in some sheep, which, though kept subservient to the figure of Désirée, were to supply the motive of the picture—or so Archie thought till the sudden freak that made him introduce the fauns.

Désirée was all for robing herself in her best—a black silk bodice with a high collar, and a betrained, jet-spangled skirt, but Archie coaxed her into wearing the dress he first saw her in : a mere wrapper of indefinite prune color, belted in at the waist to show the lines of her deep-chested, long-flanked figure, and cut so low as to leave her throat bare from the pit of it. Her sleeves were rolled back to the elbow and her arms showed milk white as far as the reddened wrists and the big work-roughened hands that held a hazel switch across her thighs.

Archie was Anglo-Saxon enough to feel a slight stiffness at the first sitting, but Désirée was a stranger to the sensation of tied tongue.

"I like the Americans," she announced. "Not many of them come here, but I have not spent my life in Draginoules, no, indeed! I was in a laundry once at La Madeleine. Do you know it? It is where they take in the washing of Nice. So I used to go much into Nice, and an English lady there painted me. She had a talent! She made me look beautiful. In Draginoules, do you know what they call me? They call me 'l'Americaine manguée.' "

"Because you like them so?" asked Archie.

"Because I have the nature, the habits of an American woman. Oh, I assure you! I like to live out of doors—to be out all day with one's bread and a bottle of wine, and sleep on the hillside—that is what I call living. I always open my window at night, though my aunt says it is a folly. I could go to England if I chose, as a maid. My English lady would have me. Ah, how I long to see England! One gets so tired of Draginoules."

"But your friends—you would be sorry to leave them?"

"Oh, for that, I do not care about the people of Draginoules. It was my mother's place, not mine. I was born in Lyons, where my father was a silk weaver. But he was a bad kind of man, so I came to my aunt to live. I do not think much of the people of Draginoules. They all like me, but I do not like them!"

"Why don't you go to England, then? Though I think you are far better here!" quoth Archie, on whom the glamour of the place was strong.

"My fiancé would kill himself," said Désirée serenely.

"Oh—you are *fiancée?*" murmured Archie, wondering why he felt that absurd mingling of relief and regret.

"To a mechanician in Nice. We are to marry when he gets a rise. *Hélas, je ne serai plus fille!*"

Her words, so simply and directly spoken, caught at Archie's imagination.

"What a *vierge farouche!*" he said to himself. "If I can get that feeling into my picture!" Aloud he said: "And your fiancé—he is very devoted, then?"

"He adores me. It is a perfect folly, see you, to feel for anyone what he does for me. He is mad about me."

Archie returned to the theme next time she posed for him.

"So you think a man can care too much for a woman?" he asked, and stopped for a moment with raised brush to watch her answer. She shrugged her shoulders.

"As to that, I think women are worth it. But it is foolish to care everything for one person."

"You could care for others, then—as well as M. Colombini?" asked Archie, with a sudden stir at his pulses.

"I? One can care a little—here and there. But commit a folly for a man, that is a thing I would never do. And I am very fond of Auguste. If I did not think we should be happy and faithful I should not marry him. I look round on all the married people I know, and see nothing but betrayal everywhere. Here a husband plays his wife false; there she in turn cheats him. Bah—it is not good, that!"

"How right you are," said Archie virtuously. "But you do not then think it necessary to care as much for Auguste as he cares for you?"

"*Dame,* no! How should I? He pleases me, and he is good—I can respect him. And I like him to kiss me. ... " The most charming look of self-consciousness mingled with reminiscence flitted over her face. "But for him—he is mad when he kisses me. Women do not care like that. It is a folly. And it is always happier, monsieur, when it is the husband who cares the most. That is how men are made."

Oh, yes, thought Archie, she was woman, after all, this *vierge farouche,* and more unashamedly woman, franker in her admissions of knowledge—for she admitted in her expressive face and gestures more than she actually said—than any woman of his world. He worked in sience for a while, then told her to rest.

She flung herself on the turf with an abandonment of limb and muscle usually only seen in young animals, and he came and lay a little below her, and lit a cigarette. Désirée lay serenely, her face upturned, and he studied her thoughtfully.

"Surely very few of your countrywomen are as blonde as you," he said. "Your eyes are blue, and your brows and lashes a faint brown, and your hair is—"

He paused, at a loss how to describe her hair. It was not golden—rather that strong brass color that, had he seen it on a sophisticated townswoman, he would have dubbed "peroxide." It was oddly metallic hair, not only in its color but in the carven ripples of it where she wore it pulled across her low brow and massed in heavy braids round her head. That way of wearing her hair right down to her brows, except for a narrow white triangle of forehead showing, boylike, at one side, gave her an oddly animal look—using the word in its best sense. A look as of some low-browed, heavy-tressed faun, fearless and unashamed—it was only in her eyes that mystery lay.

"My hair?" she exclaimed, showing her big white teeth in a laugh as frank as a boy's. "But that, you know, is not natural. It was an accident."

"An accident! How on earth—"

"Why, I was doing the *ménage* for a chemist and his wife over the border, at Vintimile. And she had her hair like this. One day she gave me a little bottle and said: 'Désirée, you're a good girl, but you don't know how to make the best of yourself. Put some of this on your head.' I rubbed some on one side only, just to see what would happen, and next day I found one-half of my head golden—golden like the sun. 'Mon Dieu,' I said, 'but what do I look like, one-half yellow and one-half brown?' So I poured it on all over. It is nothing now, because I have not put on the stuff for so long; but at one time it was beautiful. Such hair! Below my waist, and gold, oh, such a gold! Now, it wants doing again."

She ducked her head down for him to see the crown of it, and he perceived from the parting outward two inches of unabashed dark hair—almost blue it looked by contrast with the circling wrappings of yellow. Archie, immensely tickled at finding such a splendid young savage in the Back o' Beyond with dyed hair, could but shout with mirth. Désirée, totally unoffended, joining in; and when he went back that evening he felt he knew her far better than on the preceding day.

The next day he unconsciously took up their conversation of the day before. They were resting again, for he said it was too hot to work; and the sunset effect he wanted was growing later every day.

"So you could care a little for someone else before you marry Auguste?" he suggested, lightly enough, and looking away from her to the snow mountains that bared white fangs in the blue of the sky.

She laughed a little, stretched herself, drooped her lids, was in a flash and for a flash entirely woman—alluring, withdrawing, sure of herself. As she gained in poise Archie felt his own tenure of self-control slipping away from him.

"Could you?" he persisted, his eyes by now back on her changing face.

"How does one care? What is it?" she evaded. "I do not think *you* would be able to tell me. You are so cold, so English; you would care just as much as would be pleasant, and never enough to make you uncomfortable."

The penetration of this remark displeased Archie.

"But you are like that yourself," he objected. "You are the most cool, calculating girl I ever met—everything you say shows it."

She rolled over slightly on the grass, so that her head, the chin thrust forward on her cupped hands, was brought nearer to him but kept at the provocative three-quarter angle suggestive of withdrawal. Her thick, heavy lids were drooped, but suddenly they flickered, and half rose to show a gleam so wild, so unlike anything he had ever seen in her, that Archie caught his breath. It was as though some alien spirit, a pagan, woodland thing, was looking at him through the eyes of the self-possessed, level-headed young woman, who at times even seemed more bourgeoise than peasant.

"Désirée! How beautiful you are!" he cried.

"As beautiful as mademoiselle your fiancée?" asked Désirée.

With a run Archie descended into the commonplace, and Désirée became for him nothing but a pretty girl who went rather too far.

"Americans do not care to discuss the ladies of their choice," he said grandiloquently. "May I ask how you knew I was *fiancé?*"

"I have seen her picture in your room," said Désirée frankly; "the *patronne* told me there was one there. She is pretty—very pretty. Her hair is so beautifully done in all those little rolls, one would say it must be false. She is altogether *mignonne*—one would say the head of a doll!"

Désirée was absolutely sincere in thinking she was giving Miss Gwendolen Gould the highest praise possible. She would willingly have exchanged her splendid muscular body for the slim, correctly corseted form of Miss Gould, and have bartered her strongly modeled head for the small, regular features and Marcel-waved hair of the other girl. It was only his perception of this that kept Archie from anger, and as it was the truth of the praise hit him sharply. That night he sat down before the miniature and conscientiously tried to conjure up the emotions of a lover. The experiment was a failure.

When he came to go to bed he found a sprig of myrtle lying on his pillow.

"How did that get here, I wonder?" he asked himself, and then stooped, with an exclamation of disgust. A corner of the turned-back sheet that trailed on the floor was lightly powdered with earth as though a muddy shoe had stood on it. The footprint—if footprint it were—was oddly impossible in shape, short and rounded, more like the mark of a hoof.

"Can the *patronne's* goat have got up here? I saw it wandering in the passage today," thought Archie vexedly. "Beastly animal to drop half-chewed green food all over my pillow!"

The injured man thumped his pillow and turned it over, so that the despised myrtle sprig lay crushed beneath it. Then he went to bed and to sleep.

"I dreamt of you all night, Désirée," he told her next day, "and I feel as tired as though it had all been real."

"We are polite today!" laughed Désirée.

"Wait till you hear. I was pursuing you round rocks and over streams and through undergrowth all night long. You were you, and yet you weren't. Somehow I got the impression that it was you as you would have been hundreds and thousands of years ago. And I kept on losing you, and then little satyrs beckoned at me to show me the way you'd gone, and I stumbled on after hoofs that were always flashing up just ahead—just vanishing round corners."

"Satyrs? What are they?" asked Désirée.

Archie explained as picturesquely as possible, but was brought to a stop by a curious change in Désirée's eyes. They wore the strained, misty look of the person who is trying hard to catch at some long-lost memory. Again he was startled by that strange feeling that something else was looking from between those placid lids of hers.

"But I know!" she began. "Those creatures you are telling me—*what* is it I know about them?" She broke off and shook herself impatiently. "Bah! It is gone. And then what happened—did you find me at the end?"

"I can't quite remember," said Archie slowly. "Something happened, but what it was is all blurred. I believe you're a wood nymph, Désirée—a wood nymph whose father was a satyr—and he chased and caught your mother and took her down through his tangle of underbrush with his hands in her hair, never heeding her screams. You have very definite little points at the top of your ears, you know. We all have them a bit to remind us of our wild dog days, but yours are the most pronounced I've ever seen. Do you never take off all your clothes and go creeping and slipping through the woods at night, to bathe in one of the crater pools by the light of the moon?"

"How did you know?" She turned wide, startled eyes on him; her quickened breath fluttered her gown distressfully.

"What! You do it, then?" exclaimed Archie.

"No, no! What folly are you talking?" She sprang to her feet and slipped behind the oak sapling, as though it were a defence against some danger; across the boughs he saw her puzzled, fearful eyes. As he watched her, the expression of alarm faded—she put up her hand to her hair, gave it a quieting pat and tucked some stray strands into place, then she looked across at the easel.

"It must be time to work again!" she exclaimed. "Have we been resting long, m'sieu? I feel as though I'd been asleep and you'd just wakened me." She yawned as she spoke, stretching her strong arms in a slow, wide circle, the muscles of her shoulders rounding forward and making two little hollows appear above her collarbones. The sight aroused the artist in Archie, and he, too, scrambled up, and betook himself to work. The sheep, that he had bribed the shepherd to pasture there, happened to come as he wanted them that evening, and he began to work away in silence. One of the goats, a piebald, shaggy creature, reared itself up on its hind legs, with its forefeet against the tree trunk, and began to nibble at the foliage. Something about the pose of the creature sent a swift suggestion to Archie's mind, and he just had time to rough in the legs, with their slight outward tilt, the hoofs set firmly apart and the tail sticking out and up from the sharply curved-in rump, before the animal dropped on all fours and moved away. Archie, with the smile of the creator in his eyes, worked on, and the goat's legs merged into the beginnings of a slim human body with the hands leaning against the tree and the head, tilted on one side, peering round at the figure of Désirée. Suddenly he gave an exclamation of annoyance.

"What is the matter?" asked Désirée.

"There is someone watching us from those myrtle bushes. Confound the beggar—someone from the village, I suppose!"

Désirée turned sharply, just in time to see a brown face grinning through the leaves. It was a face compact of curiously slanting lines—upward-twitched tufts of brows, upward wrinkles at the corners of the narrow eyes, and a slanting mouth that laughed above a pointed, thrusting chin.

"That! That is only my little brother, m'sieu. It is one of God's innocents, and lame on both feet. Sylvestre! Come out and speak to m'sieu—no one will hurt you."

The bushes rustled and parted, and an odd little figure, apparently that of a boy of about ten, came scrambling out with a queer, lunging action from the hips. The child's legs were deformed, but he swung himself forward at a marvelous speed on a pair of clumsy crutches. Archie saw that when he was not laughing his brown eyes were wide and grave, with a look of innocence in them that contrasted oddly with the knowing gleam they showed a minute earlier.

"But he is exactly what I want for the picture!" cried Archie, running his hand through the boy's tangled curls and tilting his face gently backward. "He is exactly like the things I was telling you of. He must sit to me."

He deftly tugged the boy's shirt out of his belt and peeled it off him, exposing a thin little brown body with a skin as fine as a girl's. When he felt the sun on his bare flesh the child made guttural sounds of delight, flinging himself backward on the ground, and, supported by his hands, letting his head tip back till his curls touched the grass. As the shielding locks fell away, Archie saw with a thrill that was almost repulsion that dark brown hair grew thickly out of the boy's ears.

"Would he stay still, do you think?" he asked Désirée.

"He will, if I tell him," replied Désirée. "Come to me, Sylvestre," and drawing the child to her, she stroked his head and whispered to him.

After the addition of Sylvestre the picture made great strides, even if the intimacy between Archie and Désirée advanced less rapidly than before. And yet every now and again, in sudden flashes of wildness, in a half-uttered phrase totally at variance with her normal self—little things that she seemed to remember from some forgotten whole, Désirée would give him that impression of being two people at once; and always, on these occasions, she was as puzzled as he, and with an added touch of something that seemed almost shame. For the everyday Désirée, that calm, practical and comely young woman, Archie's friendliness was touched by nothing warmer than the inevitable element of sex; but the shy, bold thing that sometimes peeped from between her lids, that thing that seemed to take possession of her beautiful body, and mock and allure and chill him in a breath, that thing was waking an answering spirit in himself, and he knew it.

Miss Gould's portrait was unable to protect him from wakeful nights, when he turned his pillow again and again to find a cool surface for his cheek—nights when he would at last fling off the bedclothes and lean out of the window to watch the steel blue dawn turn to the light of everyday. He was living in a state of tension, and it seemed to him that some great event was holding its breath to spring, as though the very trees and rocks, the brooding sky and quiescent pools, were all in some conspiracy, hoodwinking yet preparing him for the moment of revelation.

It was onto the sensitive surface of this mood that a letter from Gwendolen, announcing her speedy arrival in Provence, dropped like a dart, tearing the delicate tissues and stinging the fibres to the necessity for haste. Gwendolen, aunt-dragoned, and Baedeker in hand, meant the return to the acceptance of the old values that had once filled him with complacency. And yet, with all the jarring sense of intrusion Gwendolen's advent instilled, mingled a feeling that was almost relief—as though he was being saved, against his will but with his judgment, from something too disturbing and beautiful to be quite comfortable.

Three or four days after receiving Gwendolen's letter, he put the last touches to the picture and informed Désirée he would need her no more. She received the news quite calmly, apparently without regret. Archie felt absurdly flat as he wrapped up his wet brushes in a week old sheet of the *Petit Niçois*. He also felt very virtuous, and told himself it was not many men who would have refrained from making love to the girl under the circumstances.

There was a little hut, used for stacking wood, close to where he worked, and here, thanks to the courtesy of the owner, he was wont to put his picture for the night. Désirée, as usual, helped him to carry it in and plant the legs of the easel firmly into the earthen floor. He had worked late, and the sun had just slipped behind the far ridge of the mountains: the tiny hut was filled with a deepening half-light; the stacked brushwood seemed wine-colored in the warm shadow; here and there a peeled twig stood out luminously. By the open door hoofmarks in the trampled earth showed that the *patronne's* mule had been carrying away wood that morning. That was as palpable as the fact that it must have been Sylvestre's deformed foot which had soiled Archie's sheet, yet those marks recreated the atmosphere of his dream, and seemed, in the sudden confusion mounting to his brain at the warmth and nearness of Désirée, to mix madly with Sylvestre, and rustled undergrowth and the glimmer of elusive hoofs round myrtle bushes—and the glimmer of something whiter and more elusive still.

He could hear Desiree's breathing beside him—not as even as usual, but deeper-drawn and uncertain; and turning, he met the sidelong glance of her eyes.

"Désirée—you said you sometimes slipped out at night and played in the woods—and the pools. Take me out with you tonight and show me where you go and what you do. I'll be awfully good—I swear I will; you're not a woman—you're a nymph, a strange, uncanny thing. I believe you meet your kinsfolk there and dance with them, Désirée!"

She looked at him for a moment in silence. In her eyes her normal and her unknown selves contended.

"It is true I often go out as you say; something drives me, but I do not know why myself. And I get very tired and can never remember clearly what it has been like. It is as though I did it almost in my sleep, or had dreamt it."

"It *is* a dream—everything's a dream, and I've got to wake up soon. Let's have this bit of dream together—Désirée!"

She yielded. They took bread and wine and apples for a midnight feast, and set off together over the lava fields to the woods that tufted the mountain slopes. Through the deep, soft light the pallor of her face and throat glimmered as through dark water. She held his hand to guide him over the fissures and round the piled bowlders; once he slipped on a hummock of hard grass, and felt her grow rigid on the instant to check his fall. They were silent, until, seated at the edge of the woods, they ate their supper, and then they laughed softly together like children, with fragmentary speech; and once Désirée sang a snatch of a Provençal song, Archie, who knew his Mistral, joining in.

Presently, when they fell on silence again, it seemed the wood was full of noises—stealthy footfalls, snapping of dry twigs, the rustling of parted shrubs. As the late moon, almost at the full, swam up the sky, making the distant snowpeaks gleam like white flames against the dusky blue, and shimmering on the pools cupped here and there over the hollowed expanse below, Archie could have sworn that the penetrating light showed quick-glancing faces and bright eyes from the thicket. Once a great white owl did sail out with a beating of wings, so close to them that they could see the stiff brows that bristled over his lambent orbs; and once a strong smell and a gleam of black and white told of a wildcat tracking her prey.

They buried the disfiguring remnants of their little feast, and then Archie solemnly poured out what was left of the red wine onto the slope below.

"For the gods!" he announced. "The liquor for us and the dregs for them!"

"Ah," cried Désirée, as though his action pricked sleeping memories to life, "now I remember it all again! I forget when I go home, but then the next time everything is clear again, and so it goes on."

She disappeared in a jutting spur of the wood, and Archie scrambled to his feet and followed her. As he broke through to the further edge, which hung over a wide pool, he caught his foot in something soft— Désirée's clothes that lay in a fairy circle, just as she had slipped out of them.

She stood at the pool's brim, her hands clasped at the back of her head, a thing to dream of. She was so lovely that all feeling died save a passionate appreciation, keen to the verge of pain; she was so lovely that of necessity she awoke an impersonal emotion. Slowly she stretched herself, and as the muscles rippled into curves and sank, the delicate shadows ebbed and breathed on the pearl white of her body. Archie's every nerve was strung not to lose one line or one breath of tone.

Putting out a foot, she touched the water, so that little tremors soft as feathers fled over the surface; then, as she waded in, deeper and deeper, the water parted from her in flakes of brightness that shook and mixed up and broke away. When she rose, dripping wet, the moonlight refracted off her was mirrored in the water, and thrown back again on her—a magic shuttle weaving an aura of whiteness. Long arrows of light fled back through the pool as she waded to shore, where she stood for a moment motionless; head slightly forward, arms hanging, and one hip thrown outward as she poised her weight. Myriads of tiny, crescent-shaped drops clung to her limbs like fish scales, so that she seemed more mermaiden than wood nymph; but Archie's eyes proclaimed her Artemis—she would have calmed a satyr as she stood. Thoughts of forest glades where chill, sweet sports were held, and the wildest hoof was tamed to the childlike kinship with nature that is pagan innocence, floated through his mind like visible things.

Suddenly she became conscious of his presence, and gave one glance in which invitation and a certain calm aloofness seemed to mingle.

"Désirée!" stammered Archie. "Désirée!"

Excitement tingled through him, blurring his ideas, just as chloroform sets the blood pricking with thousands of points and edges, while dizzying the brain. She stood still a second longer; then, either the fearful nymph swayed her utterly, or, as it seemed to Archie, a sudden rejection of him, the clumsy, civilized mortal, sprang into her eyes. She flung up her head, turned and was gone in the tangle of the woods. Without more than a second's hesitation he plunged in after her.

To Archie, whenever he looked back, that night seemed an orgy of chase-gone-mad, gathering in force as it went and sweeping into its resistless flow the most incongruous of elements.

He ran after her, stumbling, tripping, whipped across the face by brambles. Everything in life was crystallized into the desire to catch up, to track her to the enchanted green where, with her, he could become part of a remote free life he had never imagined before. All his own personality, except that in him which was hers, had ceased to exist; work, Gwendolen, the great world and the inn at Draginoules were wiped out of knowledge by the force of his concentration on one thing. The arbitrary line drawn between the actual and the unreal, the credible and the impossible, sanity and so-called madness, was swept away. She, the descendant of the gods, knew what strange race—a race that perhaps had lingered in these crater fastnesses and myrtled groves long after it had died off the rest of the earth—was fleeing before him through a wood alive with brightened eyes and quickened hoofs; and in her veins the slender strain of blood derived from some goat-legged, tall-eared thing—a strain asleep through the generations of her ancestors, had mastered all the rest of her heritage, and was as triumphant in her soul as in Sylvester's body. She ran on, swiftly and without effort, and Archie ran after her.

A large red motor car had been panting down through the Midi all day, hoping to arrive at Draginoules from the further side of the table-land. The chauffeur, who was a Gascon, would have died sooner than admit ignorance, and had taken whatever road seemed best to him; and the small hours of the morning found the red car, bereft of petrol, its acetylene at the last gasp and with a burst tire, stranded on a mountain pass high above the few faint lights of Draginoules. By the failing lamps the two ladies and the chauffeur tried to understand a road map with the result that they decided the lights must be those of Grasse, little knowing they proceeded from the electrically lit wash houses of Draginoules, where the women washed long before dawn.

The chauffeur addressed his passengers at length. He urged them to find their way down on foot; they had merely to follow the road, while he stayed with his sacred trust, the car. He did not add that he would sleep very comfortable inside it. The dawn would be breaking in an hour or so, and the saints would guard them, and Americans were always safe. Besides, what was there to fear? They would soon reach those lights and find a good bed, and, he added cunningly, a cup of tea. The elder lady was visibly allured by the prospect, but shudderingly declared, in French strongly tinged with a transatlantic accent, that they would be robbed and murdered.

"Nonsense, aunt," said the younger lady ruthlessly. "Who is there to rob and murder us? We'd far better go on now."

She thought to herself that if one must arrive at a hotel luggageless, disheveled and with one's fringe out of curl, it was better to do so at night than in the unsympathetic face of day and the eye of man. Her aunt wavered and gave in, after warning her dear Gwen against blaming her if they were killed; and the two ladies, grasping their little vanity-bags, set off down the mountain. And somewhere the gods that pull the wires were laughing as they drew toward each other, under incongruous conditions, four people whom those conditions made utterly incompatible.

Archie was shockingly out of condition. It was years since the running muscles of his legs had received any systematic encouragement, and his layer of superfluous flesh, though slight, shook with each stride, but he stumbled on. Each time he caught Désirée's low, mocking laugh it seemed a little further away, and now on one side and then the other, till he was running blindly, on and on; and, little as he knew it, toward the curve of the mountain track. Gwendolen and her aunt, tramping down it, heard the running feet and the breaking of bushes in the wooded slopes above them, and their hearts turned to water. They dived into that part of the woods which sloped below the road, and a moment later heard the footsteps crossing the stones of the track. ...

Dawn broke at last, reluctant, chill, showing the woods clear-edged and motionless as though cut out of steel; glimmering on the quiet pools and the ribbed lava slopes, though the hollow of the plain still held a great lake of shadow.

Désirée's clothes lay no longer by the pool where she had bathed; no trace of human presence remained; even the marshy edge showed only trampled footmarks, as though some goat-footed herd had watered there.

The human element was soon to be added, for, just as the cold blue light was bleaching to a pearly pallor, the strangest figure those woods had ever known came bursting and tumbling through them. Gwendolen's aunt did not look her best after a couple of hours' strenuous exercise through shrubs, with her motor bonnet on one side, her skirts torn, one shoe gone forever, and her once-elaborate gray locks hanging on her shoulders, the wire frame of her "pompadour" showing through the disordered hair in front. She sank down on a rock, with an expression of resignation on her heat-mottled face.

Archie, breaking through the trees a few moments later, with quivering legs, only spurred on by the expectation of at last finding Désirée, thought his brain must have given way under the emotions of the past night. The fact that he was gazing on the elder Miss Gould and had apparently been pursuing the elder Miss Gould—was in itself so impossible that it seemed equally natural to attribute it to hallucination or to a disordered universe, or even to wonder whether Désirée were, after all, a loup-garou who took on the form of others at will. Whether he or Miss Gould would have been the first to break the silence he never knew, for with a faint cry of "Aunt!" someone fell onto him from behind, only to recoil with a gasp of dismay. He was past surprise as he turned to support Gwendolen.

"Your aunt is here," he said, with the calm of utter indifference. "She is sitting on a stone."

"Archie! *Archie!* Then it was *you*—you who were chasing us?"

"Chasing you! I didn't know you were in France! I was chasing—" He stopped abruptly.

"Chasing whom?" put in the elder Miss Gould, turning to gaze at him from beneath the wry pompadour.

"Chasing no one, of course," said Archie hastily. "Whom did *you* think you were chasing, Gwendolen? I must say I am surprised to find you running after a young man like that. And in the woods at night, too! I think you owe me an explanation!"

"*I!* I lost aunt, and must have gone in a circle and got behind you, and then thought you were aunt. It seems to me the question is—who did you think aunt was?"

"I," broke in Miss Gould, "was pursuing someone whom I took for Gwendolen. Mr. Lethbridge—who was it?"

"I don't know," said Archie wearily; "I only wish someone could tell me, for I'm hanged if I know even *what* it was!"

They all three lay back in exhausted silence, looking at each other. The searching light of dawn revealed with pitiless impartiality not only their scratches and stains, but their suspicions and bitterness; the lack of harmony with their dignified and reticent surroundings. Nothing lovely or large found any kinship in them; they were conventional little souls in conventional little bodies, and they and their suspicions and explanations seemed of an awful insignificance—even to themselves.

The livid silver line edging the seaward mountains changed to fire, while the air grew vibrant with a warmer light. Far below the roofs of Draginoules caught the gleam as the sun swam up above the loftiest range, and the first skeins of smoke changed from blue to a dusty gold. Day, warm, human everyday, had come at last, and the cruel hour of searching was over. Archie's hand instinctively went to his tie, while the women straightened their bonnets and put back the wisps of hair.

They all chatted a little in a desultory manner as Archie led the way to the village, and they all avoided each other's eyes. The women felt that nature had tricked them in some incomprehensible way into emotion of which they were ashamed, and Archie was once more of their world; they owned him as strongly as though he had never broken away. Not as completely—for him there would always be a half-fearful but half-wonderful memory.

Once, several years later, he told an analytical friend the whole story, and received an explanation that should have satisfied him. His friend descanted on the way in which the glamour of the place had strung his nerves to receptiveness; analyzed with delight the pagan temperament of Désirée—doubtless a throwback—and the wildness of the peasant blood in her which, combined with the superstitious strain she probably drew from her Provençal mother, filled her with inherited cravings that seemed almost to assume the force of memories. He pointed out how Archie had described satyrs to her before she professed to remember anything about them, and dismissed the case of Sylvestre with a few remarks of a physiological nature. The apparently dual nature of the girl was a simple enough phenomenon, in the nature of a hysterical trance. When he came to the more subtle problem of the second self that had awakened in Archie at Désirée's ascent from the pool, the conviction of those chill, sweet revels and twilit paganism that had enveloped his consciousness, his theories took a psychological turn. Given Archie's state of unnatural receptiveness and the undoubted sincerity of Désirée's emotional trance, the effect of the latter upon the former would be quite sufficient to create an aura that would envelop them like a reality.

On that day itself Archie was far from wrestling with any theories, and he grasped at actualities to keep his poise. Toward evening, when clean beds and hot water had completed the regeneration of the ladies, he took Gwendolen to see the picture. She knew nothing of painting, but had enough tact not to make Archie shiver by saying that she "knew what she liked." Perhaps Archie's somewhat elaborately careless references to Désirée in his letters had made her a trifle uneasy—for under her smart shirtwaist she possessed, if not a womanly, still a feminine, heart—but the picture quite reassured her. The girl was not in the least pretty, merely a big, strong peasant; and how funny of Archie to have put little fauns among the sheep!

"I don't know why I did it myself," confessed Archie, "but it's given me a good title for it. I call it, 'A Shepherdess of Fauns.' "

"It ought to sell easily," remarked Gwendolen, as they turned to go back to the inn.

"I'm not sure I want to sell it," replied Archie. But he did sell it, for a very good price, and he was glad when it was gone. No one really likes to be reminded of the times when he dared approach nature unashamedly; and Archie, unlike Désirée the girl, who never remembered Désirée the nymph, had to cultivate his forgetfulness for himself.

They met Désirée outside the *buvette;* and Gwendolen, who had often been admired for her charming manners with the lower classes, spoke very kindly to her and asked about her marriage. Désirée, who looked pale and jaded, and not at all at her best, replied briefly, but with the true peasant dignity. It appeared she was going to be married very soon— Monsieur Colombini had had a rise that justified it.

"What would you have, mademoiselle?" concluded Désirée, with a shrug. "The men will not be kept waiting forever. And one must do something, after all!"

THE TEAR SQUEEZER

Barry Benefield

O NE of the late afternoon commuters streaming across West Street toward the Chambers Street ferry that April afternoon was a fattish, fuzzy, short-legged young man with a long, peculiarly fiat-tipped nose and a thin, brown beard trimmed affectedly to a Vandyke point. Abe Pittle was on his way from an insurance office on lower Broadway, where he was in the bookkeeping department, to Caldwell, N. J., where, with his wife Amelia and his daughter Alice, he occupied a stunted rented house, which he called his bungalow when speaking of it in the city. He was about to meet one of those tremendous trivialities that turn a life.

Abe was thirty-three years old, and his salary was eighteen dollars a week, to which he added six or seven by doing overtime. He had come originally from the country near Danbury, Conn., and his most abiding recollections of his home life were a paternal grandmother always harrying him for taking more butter than he needed, of his father threatening him for using too much sugar, of his mother weakly complaining that he wasted fully half of his meat by stripping out the lean and leaving the fat.

Inside the ferryhouse, Abe drew quickly away from the jostling crowd and began searching desperately through his pockets. For fear of extravagant impulses, he never brought to town more than thirty-five cents, for lunch and incidentals, unless there was something special to buy. He had meant to bring the money for a new commutation ticket that morning, but he had forgotten it. Though he knew perfectly well that there was not nearly enough money in his pockets to buy a single fare ticket to Caldwell, yet his hands went on searching, his big white eyes staring in suspense.

An amiable old gentleman, one of that somewhat large number who eagerly hunt for the not too costly inward glow to be got by helping other people solve small difficulties, stepped out of the crowd.

"I know what's the matter," he said, smiling triumphantly. "I've had it happen to me more than once. You've lost your commutation ticket and you're short of change. Where do you go? No matter; a dollar will take you there, won't it?"

"Yes, but—"

"Don't waste time talking," interrupted the happy old gentleman. "We commuters must waste no time talking until we're safely in the train. You'll see me here again some afternoon; pay me back then."

He hurried on, and Abe took his place at the end of the line at the ticket office, flushed with gratitude, resolved to stand on watch at the ferryhouse every day until he repaid the dollar and thanked its lender. He wished he had had presence of mind enough to ask the old gentleman for his business card; then he could have sent the money by mail that night.

"Pretty fine, that's what I say," he kept repeating to himself all the way home on the train. He told his wife of the incident, reviewing his impressions of his benefactor's appearance that he might the better remember him. But all the time, up to the last minute before dropping off to sleep, Abe was dimly conscious that in the back part of his mind was a thought—not quite a hope, yet—that possibly he would never see the old gentleman again; and so he would have gotten a dollar for nothing.

Something for nothing! It was a radiant thought that always flooded his soul with joy. To bear home some article bought with tobacco or some trade coupons pleased his heart for days. The restaurant where he lunched was run on the honor system; the rush of noonday patrons helped themselves from the tables and shelves, declaring and paying their indebtedness on the way out. Abe understated his bill five or ten cents every day. As often as he dared he enrolled for overtime in the office at night and then dawdled, doing nothing; that was cheering. And to find money was a rare happening, perfect in its exquisite quality.

The next day Abe went to town supplied with money to buy a commutation ticket, and a dollar besides. At the ferryhouse, in the late afternoon crowd ahead of him, his benefactor's gray head appeared before his eyes, but they turned away quickly. When they looked back the gray head was out of sight. Abe swore to his wife that night that he had not seen that fine old gentleman, as she called him; Abe swore even to himself that he had not seen him. After that he hurried through the ferryhouse, staring at the advertisements on the walls or scanning the headlines of his newspaper.

The idea of that dollar for nothing remained with him. It was banished to the back part of his mind, the darkest part; but even there he warmed it, and it was sprouting; he felt that every day it was becoming more fixed, spreading out, producing branches that frightened yet fascinated him.

One night early in May, having enrolled for overtime in the office, he stole an hour and went to the ferryhouse at nine o'clock. He sat down to wait for his boat. Suddenly standing up, he began searching frantically through his pockets until he attracted the attention of a man who sat near him, of whom he asked the loan of fifty cents.

Presently he was using this maneuver two or three times a week at the Chambers Street ferry. Then one of his victims called upon him for the return of a dollar, after which Abe spent five cents every day to ride up to the Twenty-third Street ferry, where he practised his new trick as often as he dared.

In July, the vacation period for the men in the insurance office having begun, Abe received the usual two weeks' pay in advance and was told to go and enjoy himself. It had been his custom to spend these vacations on the Jersey coast, where tents supplied with gas stoves and other housekeeping necessities could be rented by the week for a small amount.

At home that night Abe told his wife that his company had suffered some unusual losses and was giving only vacations without pay; he could not afford to take any at all; he would have to work straight through the season. Next year, though, they would have a rattling good vacation, he promised stoutly, whether the company paid for it or not. Alice cried all night with disappointment, for ten years sees little comfort at the tremendous distance marked by one-tenth of her whole past life. And at breakfast his large wife did not try to conceal her contempt for the inefficiency of a man who could not manage a two weeks' vacation once a year.

Though Abe had to get up every morning and return to New York to fulfill his falsehood, yet he could not go near the office. At night he worked the lost-ticket trick at the ferryhouses along the Hudson; the time between early morning and late afternoon he spent loafing in the parks. It was dull, but he was getting a little something for nothing, and that in addition to the thirty-six dollars of vacation money from the office.

After two or three days it occurred to him that he ought not to waste eight hours, and he went to the Grand Central Station to study how to adapt the lost-ticket trick for use there so as to fill in profitably the eight empty hours. It was easy.

In the daytime he oscillated between the Grand Central and the Pennsylvania stations; in the late afternoon he operated at all the ferries used by commuters. Sometimes the original theme of the lost ticket was varied, but the outline was always the same. There was ever a pressing necessity to get to another city and a lack of money, due to sickness or loss or some other sudden stroke of ill luck that might befall anybody.

On the Saturday before the Monday when he was to return to the insurance office Abe accomplished a feat that thrilled him. Up to that time he had never got more than two or three dollars from one person. Going to a telegraph booth in the Grand Central Station, he wrote out the following telegram to himself, dating it from Chicago: "Alice is dying and calling for papa. Come quick.—Amelia." Dropping it on the floor and stepping on it to make it appear much handled, he put it in his pocket folded and sank down despairingly on a seat by a man he shrewdly guessed to be a Westerner.

It was an inspiration on Abe's part to write his own daughter's name, for as he dwelt upon the idea of her dying and calling vainly for him his eyes moistened; and when he pulled out the telegram, opened it and began reading it he fell easily into tears, presently rising to the achievement of an audible sob.

"What's wrong, bud?" asked the Westerner.

Abe simply handed him the message, mumbling through his tears: "My baby. Lost my pocketbook in the subway on the way down here. Pickpocket, I guess."

Out of that he realized thirty dollars. In his two weeks he had gotten in a hundred and fifty dollars more money than he had ever made in his life within so short a time, and almost all for nothing. To soothe his sense of shame, which was aroused more by the size of his takings than by their nature, Abe told himself that his operations were in the nature of a vacation lark, and that on Monday he would go back to work.

On Monday, however, he did not go back to the office. He simply could not bring himself to desert a field whose products so nearly approximated the perfect principle of all for nothing. He continued to cultivate the field assiduously, coming to town early in the morning and often not returning home until late at night, when he explained to his wife that he had been doing overtime at the office. He was working harder, he said, in order to make sure that they could have a first class vacation the following summer whether the office paid for it or not. His wife was very proud of him, and was zealously tender in attending to all his wants at home.

In September a railroad detective in the Grand Central Station, who had been watching Abe for some time, arrested him for begging; and the police magistrate, being told that a bankbook showing deposits of over a thousand dollars had been found on him, sentenced him to a month in the workhouse under the assumed name of Samuel Gardiner.

Sam, alias Abe, saw his position not without comforting aspects. He would get a month's board free, for he would escape work somehow; and he wrote to his wife that he was about to lose his job, that he was discouraged, and that by the time the letter reached her he would be at the bottom of the East River. "Kiss little Alice good-bye for me," he concluded. He wept over that. And yet, when he should return from Blackwell's Island, there would be only himself to support. A turnkey mailed the letter for him.

The month in the workhouse took out what little poison there was left in the sting of the beggar's profession, and the new Sam came out with his mind made up to get all he could for nothing. It was necessary, however, to find new fields, the railroad stations and ferries having become too dangerous for constant cultivation.

Sam had studied that question in his leisure. Already he had learned that men, as a rule, are most generous after meals, because the physical exhilaration arising from the first flush of the filtering food brings with it an increase of amiability. He had learned, too, that an affected frankness and simplicity works powerfully on men. Three or four chophouses on and near Broadway constituted his new territory. His speech was always the same, and always accompanied by a plaintive, placating smile:

"One moment, sir, please. I won't tell *you* a lie; I see I couldn't fool you, sir, so I won't stall. I'm simply dying for a slug of plain old booze—that's all. I was—But you don't want to hear a hard luck story, and I don't blame you. God! I just want the booze!"

The chophouses paid well after dinner, but for breakfast and lunch they were almost barren. Then the men came out in a great hurry to go about their business; they were not often sufficiently relaxed to listen to even his cunningly abbreviated tale. To supplement his income he added the department stores to his field.

Returns there, however, were unexpectedly small; for though the women gave more frequently than the men, they gave such disproportionately small amounts; and that notwithstanding the fact that his labor with them was long and arduous. A simple affectation of frankness with them was futile; several times he tried the drink story on shoppers, and they were horrified and harsh. The husky throat, the brimming eye, the complicated lie, these were the tiresome tools he had to use upon their purses.

But even these two complementary fields could not contain the new Sam's ambition for long. Very few shoppers come to town before ten o'clock, so he waylaid clerks, stenographers and salesgirls coming out of the busy downtown subway stations in the early hours. Moreover, there was little to be got at the chophouses after the dinner period, so he cultivated the restaurants that do a heavy business after the theater. There was almost no work in his regular fields on Sunday, so he added the churches to his territory.

Most savings banks fix a limit beyond which they will not pay interest on deposits. The limit of Sam's bank was three thousand dollars, and before Christmas he had started an account in a second bank. Throughout the fall the fattish little father had been promising himself to sacrifice a day in a trip to Caldwell in the hope of seeing Alice, of hearing her laugh perhaps. He loved her tiny, gurgling laugh. But no day having come in the fall that he felt he could give up, he had postponed his hope until the winter holidays.

Starting the second bank account, however, seemed so to increase the value of the days to him, and Christmas brought so many additional people to town, and the holiday spirit so wrought upon their generosity, that the little seller of inward glows simply could not face his promise; he put off the trip until summer, and then didn't make it.

Now and then Sam worried somewhat about Alice's material comfort; not a great deal, however, for Amelia, he would say, was faithful, resourceful and a good worker. There was a satisfaction to him in the assurance that his daughter would never be in want while her mother was alive; and, heaven knows, the big blonde woman was strong and healthy enough, except for a little trouble of the heart, which was mostly in her head, though she fooled away a fearful lot of money on patent medicines for it. He guessed she had dropped that foolishness now.

A second and then a third year went by, and Sam's various fields, under more and more expert cultivation, yielded more heavily; and he was worth nearly ten thousand dollars. No longer content with the mere four per cent of the savings banks, and his work in the insurance office having taught him something about the best investments in New York, he now bought a twenty thousand dollar tenement on Avenue A, leaving a mortgage on the unpaid part of the price.

But he did not live there himself; it was too rich for him. Every room in it brought in more than the cost of his attic in a damp and moldy old private dwelling in Greenwich Village.

From time to time, particularly when the police were in one of their spasmodic clean-up campaigns, Sam was arrested, but he never again committed the beggar's solecism of being caught with his bankbooks on his person. Sometimes he went to the workhouse for a week or so; more often he was discharged by a fatigued magistrate.

Once, just after the appointment of a new police commissioner who was particularly hostile to beggars, the streets were made too uncomfortable for Sam. He knew from experience that this spasm of artificially stimulated zeal on the part of the police would wear off after a week or two; and, having nothing to lose, he yielded to the tender temptation of going to Caldwell to inquire about Alice. His mendicant clothes and generally changed appearance insured him against recognition.

An extremely sophisticated and hungrily talkative woman in a bakery near where he had lived said she could tell him something of the Pittle family. Mrs. Amelia Pittle had died, and the daughter Alice had been taken in by a neighbor; but after a year or so the girl had gone away, first to Newark to work in a store, it was said, then to New York. And now she was in the theatrical business there, some folks told her. The bakery woman shut her left eye in a long, hardly contracted wink, and turned to wait on a customer.

Well, he had done his best, Sam assured himself; no one could do more. If she was in New York, he might come across her some day if he kept his eyes open. He returned to the city as soon as he got a chance to hide himself in the lavatory of a passing train and thus save his fare. In a short while, the police zeal having abated, Sam took up once more the cultivation of his old fertile fields, always after that keeping a sharp eye on the crowds when he was working the theatrical districts. He sometimes wondered vaguely what that bakery woman had meant by her wink.

In the sixth year of his profession, after a short visit to the workhouse Sam made a radical change in the character of his operations. For some time he had been dissatisfied with his old methods. Though he did not definitely formulate his objections, yet he was painfully conscious that his operations fell too far without the perfect principle of all for nothing to gain him anything like artistic content. There was too much straining of the inventive faculty—in short, too much that approximated labor. He studied how to modify his methods and came to a decision.

He was now thirty-nine years old. Most of his face was hidden by a brindled bramble of gray-brown beard. The sandy hair on the back half of his partly bald head hung down upon his coat collar in gummy, grimy strings. Weakened by poor food and exposure, burned by the fires of bounding ambition, he saw with increasing satisfaction the fat drying out from under his fast wrinkling skin, and his cheeks sinking into pathetic hollows. His whitish eyes looked bigger than ever. It was his ability to give them the staring vacancy of the sightless, which had hitherto been of occasional use to him, that now decided his choice of methods.

At a secondhand clothing store on Seventh Avenue he bought a suit more ragged than the one he wore, deliberately choosing one much too large for him, and of a gay checked pattern of reds and blues. Because the suit swallowed up his figure, he seemed to be smaller and more fragile than he was; because its colors had been loud and brazenly boastful in its original high estate, it now commanded pity, so far and low had it fallen.

A pair of black goggles, a tin cup, a hand organ some twelve inches square from a junk shop, and a little tin sign to hang from around his neck down on his chest saying, "Sightless Sam," these completed his equipment. Removing one side of the organ, he stuck several holes in the bellows to still further weaken it, and so tampered with the rest of the machinery that it gave forth but two notes, one high and one low, which sounded like a ghostly scream and a ghastly groan from a bottomless pit.

The first day Sam went forth in his new part was filled with such tremendous adventure that he felt sick at the stomach and tremulous in the legs; for, besides the time he might lose, or almost lose, the equipment had cost over six dollars, more than half of which he must sacrifice if he resold it. And he was now worth only a little more than fifty thousand dollars.

But even the first day was a nerveracking success; and he settled down to meet the years as "Sightless Sam." It did not seem to him that his new system could possibly be improved upon in this grim world of merely approximate happinesses.

In the mornings he squatted on the pavement in the financial districts, desperately turning out of the tiny organ the ghostly scream and the ghastly groan. In the mature day hours he waylaid shoppers on Broadway and Sixth Avenue. In the night hours he moved uptown into the zone of diners and theatergoers.

Now there was no running about, no weeping, no standing in strained attitudes, no accosting of people in a hurry, no rebuffs to wound a tender heart. He simply sat, looking down, apparently in deep dejection, but really at his fascinating flat-tipped nose; or looking up in staring, mute appeal, turning the organ crank; frequently emptying the coins from the cup lest it become discouragingly full.

It is true he still had to turn a crank, and though it required little work to do that, yet it had the appearance of labor. This, however, did not at first occupy his mind enough to embitter him; in the beginning he largely waved it aside except when he was depressed.

And yet his artist soul could not be deceived and drugged into quietude by a partial success. There was no blinking the fact that he still had to turn the crank of the little organ. He studied hard year after year how to eliminate that last impediment in the way of the working of the perfect principle of all for nothing. After ten futile years he discovered what he sought, and that not through logic and psychology, but through an accident, as so many important discoveries have been made.

After theater hours uptown Sam usually walked down Sixth Avenue to his room in Greenwich Village to save carfare. Below Greeley Square, in a dingy side street, was then the Horseshoe, the largest, the most skillfully managed, the best protected and the most long-lived of New York's older dance halls; surrounded by obscure "hotels" in that and other unsavory side streets. The doors opened at eight P. M. and closed at three A. M., promptly.

One night after twelve o'clock Sam walked down Sixth Avenue, turned into the Horseshoe street and stood for some time on the sidewalk opposite the dance hall, watching the door. Men and women, individually, were constantly going into the place; men and women in couples were constantly coming out of it. Every time the inner door, beyond the vestibule, opened and closed, it cut off and left outside a quivering slice of tinkling music and babbling laughter.

Here, then, even after midnight, were many gay people and much liveliness. Sam put on his black goggles, pounded his way across the street with his stick, sat down on the sidewalk at the vestibule under the emblem that gave the place its felicitous name and began grinding out the ghostly scream and the ghostly groan.

At first he used this stand only after midnight, but it paid so well that he appeared at the Horseshoe ahead of the vanguard of regulars, and left only after the doorkeeper, the bouncer, the musicians and the waiters had gone home. At first, too, he generously ground out the organ's full two notes, but one night three quaint young revelers paid him twenty dollars for the organ and took it away in a hansom, which was otherwise heavily loaded.

Sam could not get his immediate consent to spend perhaps a dollar for another battered organ, and so the next night he sat under the horse-shoe with his cup on one knee and a bunch of lead pencils on the other. His receipts suffered no losses. Moreover, a week's average was quite up to a week with the organ. Sam was astounded. Here, then, it was not necessary to attract attention with a pathetic noise; his "sightless" eyes did the work with these abandoned women and their reckless companions.

Thinking afterward of his discovery, Sam could not help being sometimes in great pain when he considered the labor he had lost; but he was, for the most part, a cheery optimist, and he preferred to look gladly forward to the joyous future with the pencils, rather than sourly back at the dark past with the organ. The bunch of pencils became his only histrionic property. He never again turned a crank, nor heard the ghostly screams and ghastly groans struggling from the battered little black box and sinking unheeded through his ears.

After a year at the Horseshoe, Sam began to suspect what the fat bakery woman's wink had meant when she had said that Alice Pittle was in New York and in the theatrical business. One of the Horseshoe sisterhood, who had just begun to make that hall her nightly headquarters, possessed a thick, throaty, gurgling little laugh that awakened dim old associations in Sam when he first heard it. His mind played fearfully around the possibility, which was fast growing toward certainty, but he was afraid to talk to her openly about either himself or her; she was already a recklessly generous giver, and he was unwilling to disturb a status quo that included her rich tips.

Sam came to be an institution at the Horseshoe. After a while he brought a canvas-covered stool with him; and when it was wet or cold outside, the proprietor permitted him to sit inside the vestibule, thus purchasing for himself at little price from this convenient bank of magnanimity an unusual kind of glowing feeling for himself.

Sam developed several subsidiary sources of revenue. One of them was selling cocaine to the "sniffers" among the open-hearted sisterhood that walked under the horseshoe. Another was an ingenious trick of petty blackmail. Knowing them all by their "Christian" names, or by the names they had assumed, as well as the number of years they had been coming to the dance hall, he called them Tessie No. Three or Polly No. Five, advancing the numbers as time went by, unless they paid to hold time back. It was a great joke—but not a rare one—among the habitues who were in the secret to hear "Sightless Sam" address someone in his insinuating whine as Grace No. Ten, for instance.

They say that New Yorkers rarely see the sky; but by tilting his head back against the vestibule, and turning it slightly, Sam could raise his eyes above the elevated track out on Sixth Avenue; and out beyond that, beyond the Hudson River, above the State where he had once lived, he could see the stars through the black goggles. One night in April, as he sat thus staring, a plump, blonde little woman stopped by the stool and sat down on the edge of the vestibule floor that projected a few inches over the sidewalk.

"April is the swell month, ain't it, Sam?" she said. "Then you kind of breathe in the trees and flowers. But it sort of makes me blue."

"Does it, Edith No. Five?" asked Sam, emphasizing the numeral. For though he was still adrift among the goggle-dimmed stars, yet he was ready to attend to Edith's case at once. He remembered distinctly when she had come; she had been walking under the horseshoe two weeks over five years; and she had not paid up this year. He had already whispered the threatening "No. Five" at her several times without avail. He meant to have his customary generous gift from her upon the passing of a new year or know the reason why.

She paid no attention, apparently, to his threatening numeral; she sat silently staring out across the street, her chin in her hands. Assuming his most humble, most oily, most sympathetic tone—the tone he always employed when he wanted to trap a downhearted girl into giving him intimate confidences to be used later for petty blackmailing purposes—Sam spoke at the small plump blonde, not looking around:

"Well, Edith No. Five, summer will be here pretty soon. I suppose when it gets hot you'll go away for a while—and see your folks—the old folks at home, maybe."

"I haven't any folks, Sam."

"Dead?" The goggled little beggar smiled behind his hand.

"Yes, Sam, dead. It was kind of funny, too—my father and mother died the same day. He lost his job, got the blues and jumped into the river. He wrote my mother he was going to do it; and the shock killed her; her heart was weak, anyhow, though she did take a lot of patent medicines for it a long time."

Sam didn't say anything for a while. Then he asked:

"And how did you make out after that? Was that the reason you got into this business?"

"Partly, I guess, Sam. One of the neighbors out there in Caldwell— that's where we lived—took me in and made a sort of cheap servant out of me as long as I would stand for it, and then—aw, cut it out, Sam; don't try to make me tell you the sto-hory of me life. I wouldn't let you make any money off me on that, anyhow. If you knew all the sad sto-hory of me, Sam, I wouldn't pay you a nickel not to tell anybody you saw."

She laughed jokingly, poked him in the ribs, and he heard the rustle of her dress as she rose.

"Wait a minute, Alice Pittle," he called in a low, confidential, grieving voice, now turning on his stool to look at her through his goggles. "Wait just a minute, Alice; I want to tell you something."

"How the hell did you know my name was Alice? Aw, well, that don't make no difference. But I'm curious to know how you got it. How? Did some of my dear lady frien's squeal on me to you?"

"Bend your head down and I'll whisper to you, Alice." One of the cabdrivers standing nearby on the edge of the curb called over at her: "Stop that flirtin' with Sam, Edith. He's a dead one."

"I know your name," whispered Sam into the ear at his mouth, "because I named you. I am your father. Something got the matter with my eyes, I lost my job and had to take up this business. Yes, I'm your pore old father, Alice."

She had straightened up suddenly. He felt her looking him up and down. And then her scrutiny concentrated on his long, flat-tipped nose. Would she remember that? Except for his long schooling in maintaining a patiently gloomy countenance, he could not have helped smiling. She bent down to him again.

"Sam, you're a dirty old liar. A joke's a joke, but, believe me, you old faker, this is crowdin' it too far."

Laughing, she went on into the Horseshoe. But on her way home that night, she stopped by his stool and bent over him.

"How much to forget it, Sam?"

He knew that she knew, and he knew that she was ashamed of him. He hesitated to think a minute, to calculate how much she was ashamed.

"Ten dollars a week," he answered in his saddest, huskiest little voice.

She slipped it into his hand, and hurried away.

She continued paying him ten dollars a week as long as she lived, which was for four years, during which time he never mentioned his relationship again. After she was gone he did miss her thick, throaty, gurgling laughter floating in and out through the Horseshoe door, and he also missed the ten dollars a week.

One night a runaway cab horse dashed up on the sidewalk and trampled Sam to death. His body was saved from Potter's field by the charity of the Horseshoe sisters, who wept over him. It was later discovered that the Abe Pittle estate aggregated some half-million dollars. No will was found, nor any heir.

A FLOOD

George Moore

IT seemed to him that he was in very cold, muddy water full of little waves, and that by treading water and putting forth all his strength he was able to keep himself above them. But the wind blew them higher; they slapped him in the mouth, and he had much trouble in getting his breath between. All of a sudden it occurred to him that it would be much easier to abandon this painful striving and to lie back amid the waves. He took a long, deep breath, the water slipped down into his lungs, and he lay quite natural and comfortable until a dinning sound began over his head. He tried to sink deeper into the stream, but the noise grew louder, and he could not but think that he was rising to the surface. At last he opened his eyes.

"It's this infernal rain on the roof that makes me dream," he said.

A bed had been made up for him in the kitchen on three chairs, and when he awoke he found himself sitting bolt upright with his arms bent as if he were treading water, his legs stiff and numbed with cold. The hearth was full of ashes, with a last spark fading in the dawn light; and catching an end of his blanket, he rubbed his hands against it. His perceptions lengthened out and he went to the window, but seeing water everywhere, he fancied for a moment that he must be still dreaming. The pigs had broken out of their styes and were swimming amid various wreckage; the house dog was swimming alongside of his kennel; the hens rose in short flights—two were already drowned, the others were drowning—but the cock perched on his coop crowed defiantly. Tom looked to where the day was breaking; a thin, pale light soaked slowly through the clouds, and he could just distinguish the top of the willows above the water.

The staircase behind him creaked, and turning hurriedly, he saw old Daddy Lupton, awful in his nightshirt, like Death himself coming to bid him good morning.

"Well," said Daddy, "what do 'ee think about the jade now? She makes one feel young again. The biggest flood we've had these fifty years."

The old man's levity inspired hope in Tom that the river would not rise any higher, and that the house was not in danger. Tom asked him if this were so, but Daddy continued to babble of a great flood of sixty years ago in which he had nearly lost his life. A big flood it was, but nothing to the great flood of nearly eighty years ago. It had carried a village quite away, and the old man followed Tom to the window, telling him how the water had come down the valley faster than a horse could gallop.

"All my brothers and sisters were drowned, father and mother, too; but the cradle floated right away as far as Harebridge, where it was picked up by a party in a boat. There ha'n't been no flood to speak of since then. A fine jade she once was, and when it rained like this we used to lie quaking in our beds. Now we sleep sound enough."

"I must wake 'em," said Tom.

He rushed upstairs, called out, and in a few minutes the pointsman and his family were standing in the kitchen: John Lupton, a tall man with a long neck and thin, square shoulders, a red beard and small, queer eyes and hands freckled and hairy, and Margaret Lupton, his wife, a pleasant, portly woman of forty, with soft blue eyes and regular features. Her daughter, Liz, took after her father—a thin-shouldered, thin-featured girl with small, ardent eyes and dark reddish, crinkly hair. But Billy, Liz's brother, took after his mother. He was very like her, the same soft oval face with blue eyes and no distinctive feature; the same sweet, retiring nature, more of a girl than a boy; but the boy in him expressed a certain curiosity for Tom's boat.

"Shall we go in the boat, father?"

"What boat, sonny?"

"Tom's boat."

"Tom's boat wouldn't hold us all."

"We needn't all go together."

"My boat is far enough from 'ere by this time," said Tom, "or most like she's at the bottom of the river. I tied her last night to the old willow."

Tom was a fair-complexioned, broad-shouldered young fellow, an apple grower that lived on the other side of the river. He and Liz were to be married at the end of the week, and yesterday being Sunday, he had rowed himself across at sundown, and they had gone for their wonted walk. When they came home supper was on the table, and the hours after had gone by pleasantly, his arm being round Liz's waist, till the time came for him to bid her good night, but on seeing the swollen river she had turned her pretty freckled face to his and dissuaded him, and they had returned to the cottage.

"I never seed the river rise so quickly afore," said Lupton.

"I did. I did."

It was Daddy that had answered. He was still in his nightshirt, and his last tooth shook in his white beard.

"Go and dress 'eeself, father. And why, mother, don't 'ee light the fire? The morning is that rare cold we'll all be the better for a cup of tea."

"Yes, father, I won't be long now," and she began breaking sticks.

While the kettle was boiling Tom told them that the pigs had broken out of their styes; they lamented the loss of their winter food, and Billy burst into tears on hearing that Peter—his friend, Peter, the house dog—had gone away, swimming after his kennel.

"Come, let us sit down to breakfast," Lupton said.

But they had hardly tasted their tea when Billy cried out:

"Father, father, the water be coming in under the door yonder. Take me on 'ee knee, father. 'Ee did promise to take me to Harebridge. But if I drown I shall never see the circus."

Lupton took the little chap on his knee.

"There will be no danger of that. Grandfather will tell 'ee that this be nothing to the floods he knew when he was a little boy."

The water continued to come under the door, collecting where the asphalted floor had been worn, and they watched it rising out of these slight holes and coming toward the table. It came at first very slowly, and then suddenly it rose over their knees, and while Mrs. Lupton took the baby out of the cot the others searched for tea, sugar, bacon, eggs, coal and candles.

"We shall be wanting all these things," Lupton said, "for the water may keep us upstairs for hours to come."

And they were very wet when they assembled in Lupton's bedroom. Lupton emptied his big boots out of the window and called on Tom to do the same. Liz wrung out her petticoats, and standing round the table they supped their tea and ate some slices of bread and butter. The baby had been laid asleep on the bed, and Daddy sat by the baby, softening his bread in his mug of tea, mumbling to himself, his fading brain full of incoherent recollections.

"The folk in them fine houses will be surprised to see the water at the bottom of their parks," said Lupton, to break an oppressive silence.

"They be like to live so high up the water will never reach them," Mrs. Lupton answered.

"It hain't like them to think for to send us 'elp."

"They 'aven't no boats up yonder," said Tom. "They be a good mile up from the river."

"Tom, dear, it's a pity your boat be gone, for you might have row'd me right into Harebridge."

"Yes, Liz, if you'd set still I might have taken 'ee through them currents, or as likely we might have gotten sucked under by an eddy, or a hole be knocked in the boat by some floating baulk."

"I be lighter than Liz; would 'ee take me, Tom?" said Billy.

As the tops of the apple trees were still visible they judged the depth of the water to be about ten feet. Cattle passed the window, some swimming strong and well, others nearly exhausted. A dead horse whirled past, its poor neck stretched out lamentably, and they all laughed at the fox that floated so peacefully in the middle of a drowned hen roost. The apples came by in great numbers; Billy forgot his fears in his desire to clutch some, and a little later they saw two great trees rolling toward the pointsman's box.

"There she goes!" cried Lupton. "And how she do swim! She'd put me into the quay at Harebridge as well as a steam packet."

There was nothing to do but to watch and wonder if the flood were rising. Liz was certain it was sinking, and pointing to a post, she said there was no sign of it ten minutes before. Lupton was not so sure, and when the post disappeared, which it did a few minutes afterward, there could be no hope at all that the flood was not still rising, and then everyone began to wonder what the cause of the flood might be, and everyone, except Daddy, waited for Lupton to speak. But he was loth to tell them that he could only understand the great rush of water if the embankments up yonder at the factories had broken, and if that were so, "God help them!" As Lupton said these last words their faces grew paler, all except Billy, who returned innocently to his grandfather to ask if he didn't think the flood was as big now as the great flood of sixty years ago.

"It be a flood and a big one, but the biggest of all was eighty years ago, when my cradle was washed away down to Harebridge and stuck fast in the alder." And he began to tell a story of other children whose cradles had been carried just down to the sea, frightening everyone with his loquacity.

"Tom, 'as 'ee a bit of baccy to give to Daddy to stop his jaw with?" said John Lupton.

Tom fumbled in his pockets, and when their eyes met each read his own thoughts in the other's face.

"We must be doing something, that's certain," said Tom. "But what shall we be doing?"

"Yes, we must be a-stirring," Lupton answered. And without another word he began to look about the room. "Now, if we 'ad but a few bits of timber we could make a raft. It's a pity that bedstead is of iron."

Tom, who had gone back to the window, cried suddenly:

"Give a hand hore, John, for 'ee was talking about a raft, and blowed if I 'av'n't gotten one."

And looking over Tom's shoulder, Lupton saw that he had caught a few planks tied together—a slender raft that somebody up yonder had launched as a last hope.

"Very likely so," said Lupton; "anyhow it is ours. It might carry one of us."

"Yes, one of us might chance his life on it and bring back 'elp."

"That's right enough; it's an off chance, but one of us had better risk it. Get along, lad, get along, and come back in a boat."

"Don't leave me, Tom," cried Liz; "let us be drowned together."

"Be 'ee mazed, lass?" said Lupton. "For Tom will manage right well on them planks, and he'll come back in a boat."

"No, father, no; I'd sooner die with Tom than live without him."

"'Ee ain't the only one; 'ee'd better let him go or yonder church will see no wedding party next Monday. Tom, get astride of them planks at once."

"I think I'd better take this 'ere shutter with me," and while it was lifted from its hinges Lupton lashed two broom handles together.

"Not much of a punt hole, but the best I can give, and maybe it will get 'ee out of the current."

But Liz held Tom back.

"Yes, Liz, Tom loves 'ee and that is why he must go. Come, girl, hands off. I don't want to be rough with 'ee, but Tom must take the risk of them planks. Now, Tom."

And away he went in a swirl, trying his best to reach bottom with his broom handles, but the raft rolled in the current, and Liz's last sight of her lover was when he attempted to seize some willow branches. The raft slid from under his feet, and he fell into the flood.

"He's gone from 'ee now, and we shall soon follow after if we don't bestir ourselves."

"It matters naught to me now," said Liz.

"I ne'er seen one mazed like 'ee afore."

"But I seed many; sixty years ago all the sweethearts were parted, and by the score. The jade got them, here a girl and there a boy, all but Daddy Lupton, for a wise woman said she shouldn't get 'im, and her words came true. I ain't afeard of 'er. I've seen 'er in worse tantrums than today. It's the rheumatics that I'm afeard of. These 'ere walls will be that damp, will be that…" The old man's voice died away in the whiteness of his beard.

At that moment three tiles fell from the roof; a large hole appeared in one of the walls, and they all felt that the house was falling about them bit by bit. But the immediate danger was from the great baulks that the current swept down. If any one of these were to strike the house, Lupton said, it must topple over into the flood; and lest their luck shouldn't last, Lupton took a sheet from the bed and climbed onto the roof.

"See a boat coming, Liz?" her mother asked, for Liz sat looking toward some willows as if she saw something.

"No boat will come for me. I want no boat to come for me."

"Come, Liz, come, Liz, I wouldn't have 'ee talk like that," her mother answered. The baby began to cry for the breast, and while suckling Mrs. Lupton raised her head to her husband sitting on the broken wall, but he waved the sheet so despairingly that she did not dare to ask him if a boat were coming.

"I can't sit up 'ere any longer," he said at last. "Let us do something. I don't mind what, so long as it keeps me from thinking."

"I think we'd better say our prayers," said Mrs. Lupton.

"Prayers? No, I can say no prayers. I'm too bothered; I want something that will keep me from thinking. The babbling of that water will drive us mad if we don't do something. Let us tell stories. Liz, don't sit there looking through the room or what's left of it. You read stories in the papers—can't you tell us one of them?"

Liz shook her head. He asked for the paper; she answered that it was downstairs, and begged that she might take his place on the corner of the wall and wave the sheet on the chance that a boat might be passing within hail.

"She don't pay no attention to what we're saying," said Lupton. "Now that Tom's gone I think she'd just as lief make away with herself. And what may 'ee be smiling at so heartily, father? 'Ee and the baby are the only two that can smile this morning."

"What be I smiling at? I heard 'ee speak just now of stories. I can zay one, lots of 'em."

"Then tell us a story, father, and a good one. It'll keep our thoughts from that babbling water."

"Well, I was just a-thinking. It be now seventy years ago ... "

"Well, tell us about it."

"I've said it was nigh seventy years ago; I was a growing lad at the time. I remember it as if it were yesterday. Me and Bill Slater was pals. At that time Bill was going to be married; I can see her now, a fine, elegant lass, for all the world like our Liz. It had been raining for weeks and weeks—much the same kind of weather as we've had lately, only worse, and the river—"

"We don't want to hear about the river; we want to forget it. I suppose 'ee wants to tell us that Bill Slater and his lass was drowned? We don't want that sort of story; we wants a cheerful story with lots of happiness in it."

"I only knows stories about those that the river took—plenty of 'em, plenty of 'em. The jade didn't get me, for a wise woman said that she would never get me."

"Did she say, Daddy, that them that was with 'ee was safe, too?"

Daddy was sure only of his own safety; and waking suddenly he said: "I've 'eard John say that 'ee would banish thinking with something. Us better have some cards then. Cards will wake us up."

"The old chap's right," said Lupton. "Where be the cards? Be they downstairs too? Where's Liz?" Lupton climbed to her place, and after looking round he turned to those in the room and shook his head. "I'm afraid Liz has gone after her sweetheart."

"Very likely," said Daddy. "The jade always gets them in the end. Where be the cards?"

"Yes, where be the cards?" Lupton answered almost savagely. "Be they downstairs, mother?"

"No, John; they be in the drawer of the table."

"Then let's have them out. What shall we play? Halfpenny nap? Come, mother, and Billy, too, and Daddy. Come, pull your chairs round. I gave 'ee sixpence yesterday, father. Find them out; 'ee can't have spent them. And, mother, have 'ee any coppers?"

"I've near a shilling in coppers. That will do for Billy and myself."

As there were only three chairs, the table was pulled up to the bed where Daddy was sitting.

"Come, let us play, let us play," Lupton cried impatiently.

"I'm thinking of the baby," said Mrs. Lupton. "How unsuspecting he do sleep there!"

"Never mind the baby, mother; think of your cards."

After playing for some time Lupton found he had lost threepence.

"I never seed such luck," he exclaimed.

They played another round; again Lupton went nap and again he lost.

"Perhaps it will be them that loses that'll be saved," he said, shuffling the cards.

"Father, I can't play," said Billy.

"Why can't you play, my boy? Ain't mother a-teaching 'ee?"

"Yes, father, but I can't think of the cards; dead things be floating past the window. May I go and sit where I can't see them?"

"Yes, my boy, come and sit on my knee. Look over my cards; but 'ee mustn't tell them what I've gotten."

"Grandfather seems to be winning; he has gotten all the coppers, father."

"Yes, my boy, grandfather is winning."

"And what will he do with the winnings if he be drowned, father?"

"Grandfather don't think he will be drowned."

The old man chuckled, and turned over his coppers. His winnings meant a double allowance of tobacco and a glass of ale, and he thought of the second glass of ale he would have if he won again.

"Whose turn is it to play?" said Daddy.

"Mine," said Lupton, "and I'll go nap again."

"'Ee'll go nap again."

Lupton lost again, but this time, instead of cursing his luck, he remained silent, and at that moment the rush of water beneath their feet sounded more ominous than ever.

"I'll play no more," said Lupton. "I dunno what I be doing. There's naught in my poor head but the babbling of that water."

A tile slid down the roof. They sprang to their feet, and then they heard a splash. The old man played with his winnings and Billy began to cry.

"It's sure and certain enough now that no help will come for us," said Mrs. Lupton. "Let's put away the cards and say our prayers, and 'ee might tell us a verse out of the Bible, John."

"Very well, let's have a prayer. Father, give over counting your money."

"Then no one be coming to save us!" cried Billy. "I don't want to drown, father. I be too young to drown. Grandfather's too old and baby too young to think much about drowning. But if we drown today, father, I shall never see the circus."

"Kneel down, my boy; perhaps God might save us if we pray to Him."

"Oh, God, merciful Saviour, who has power over all things, save us! Oh, Lord, save us!"

"Go on praying, mother," Lupton said, as he rose from his knees; and taking another sheet from the bed, he climbed to the top of the broken wall; but he had hardly reached it when some bricks gave way and he fell backward and drowned. Mrs. Lupton prayed intermittently, and every now and then a tile splashed into the water.

"The way to manage 'er is to take 'er easy. She won't stand no bullying, and them giddy young folks will bully 'er, so she always goes for 'em."

Five or six tiles fell; the house rocked a little, and they could feel the water lifting the floor under their feet.

"Mother," said Billy; the child was so calm, so earnest in his manner, that he seemed suddenly to have grown older. "Mother dear, tell me the truth—be I going to drown? We have prayed together, but God don't seem like saving us. I'm afraid, mother; bain't you afraid? Father's gone and Liz's gone and Tom's gone, all except grandfather and us. Grandfather and the baby don't seem afraid. Mother, let me 'ave your 'and; 'ee won't lose hold of me."

Mrs. Lupton took the baby from the bed and looked at it, and when she looked up she saw the old man playing with the coppers he had won.

"Does drowning hurt very much, mother?"

The wall wavered about them; some bricks fell out of it. Billy was struck by one, struggled a little way, and fell through the floor. The floor broke again, and another piece of the roof came away, and Mrs. Lupton closed her eyes and waited for death. But death did not seem to come, and when she opened her eyes she saw that the floor had snapped at her feet and the old man was standing behind her.

"A darned narrow escape," he muttered. "As near as I have had yet."

"They're gone—they be all gone, all of them. Baby and all."

"'Ee must have let her slip when the roof came in."

"I let the baby slip!" And looking down she saw the child floating among broken things.

"Well, that was a narrow escape," chimed the quaking voice of the octogenarian. "I'm sore afraid the house is in a bad way. I seed many like…"

By some great beams the south wall still held firm, and with it the few feet of floor on which they were standing.

"They be bound to send a boat afore long, or else the wise woman … Everything's gone—table, cards and a shilling in coppers."

"They're all gone; everything is gone."

"Yes, the jade's got 'em. She 'as brought near everyone I knew at one time or the other."

Then the wild grief of the woman seemed to wake reason in Daddy's failing brain.

Her eyes were fixed on the bodies of her husband and child, dashed to and fro and sucked under by the current, appearing and disappearing among the wreckage.

"I can't grieve like that; I ken grieve no more. I'm too old, and all excepting me baccy and the rheumatics are the same to me now."

"Saved!" cried a voice. "Give way, my lads, give way!"

"Saved, and the others gone!" cried Mrs. Lupton, and as the boat approached from one side she flung herself into the flood from the other.

"Are you the only one left?" cried a man as the boat came alongside.

"Yes, the jade 'as got all the others. There they be down there; and my daughter-in-law has just gone after them, jumped right in after them. But it was told by a wise woman that the jade should never get me, and her words come true."

"Now then, old gent, let me get hold of you. Be careful where you step. Do nothing to risk your valuable life. There you are, safe, safe from everything but the rheumatics."

"They be very bad at times, and I must be careful of myself this winter."

WHITEMAIL

Joyce Kilmer

S PIKE RITCHIE and I worked together on the *Daily News* from 1904 to 1907, and I always liked him. He was bright, hard-working, companionable and—I thought—perfectly straight. The other day he told me about a pretty crooked deal he was mixed up in. In fact, he told me that he was an unrepentant blackmailer and traitor. And I like him more than I ever did before.

When I got back to New York last week I looked over the pictures I had bought in Turkey and decided that I had the material for some Sunday stories. So I went around to the *News* office. The elevator man didn't know me—he had been on the job only two years—but he knew Spike.

"Mr. Ritchie is assistant Sunday editor now," he said. "But I don't think you'll find him in his office. Today's Thursday, so I guess he's in the composing room."

I made him let me off at the composing room and went in. There was Spike, telling the foreman that Matty had a glass arm, and making up the fashion page. He had grown much balder, but otherwise he had changed very little since I saw him six years before. He was the same little stoopshouldered fellow, with the same rattail mustache and apparently the same cigar butt fixed in the corner of his mouth. Also, I discovered n a few minutes, he had the same alcoholic breath.

"Hello, John!" he said. "Wait till I fix this up and I'll go out with you."

Soon we were comfortably seated at a table in Jimmy's bar. Jimmy, I was absurdly pleased to notice, remembered me and put a few drops of syrup in my Irish as if I were still a daily visitor. Spike looked at my pictures and told me to go ahead with the stories. Then—of course—we both grew reminiscent, and after the third drink and a little lunch came his confession. That is, if you'd call it a confession ...

"You're not the only globe trotter," he said, lighting for the fourth time his amorphous cigar butt. "I went abroad two summers ago."

I expressed interest—without much enthusiasm, for I wanted to talk about Turkey.

"Yes," he said, "I had a little money saved up—I wasn't married then—and I was feeling pretty rotten, so I decided to knock off for a while. I traveled around the Continent for a few weeks and then I went to London. I wanted to see something of the country, so I bought a knapsack and made a leisurely walking tour of the Midland counties. And the result of that walking tour was a mighty queer experience—in fact, I may say a damn queer experience. And, in spite of the fact that you are bursting with the desire to tell me how you matched pennies with the Sultan and chucked the harem under its chin, I am now going to take up some minutes of the *News's* time in telling you about that experience. It has never been used as a news story, and it never will. But the villain—unless you call me the villain—is dead now, and I guess it wouldn't do any harm if you fixed it up with different names and made a fiction story out of it. Then if you sell it you can split with me fifty-fifty."

"Go ahead," I said.

Well (began Spike), I struck a little bit of a market town called Ashbourne that I liked pretty well. So I got a room at an inn entertainingly called "The Green Man and Black's Head" and settled down for a week's stay. There were very few other guests, so the proprietor and I got rather friendly. Of course, like all Englishmen, he was surprised that I didn't know his cousin who was on a ranch in Texas and his nephew who was manager of a grocery store in Milwaukee.

"There's one of your fellow countrymen I can't say that I care for," he said one evening. "There was a Mr. James Rodney who came here from New York City, and we all wish we'd never seen him, sir. Perhaps you know him—he's a tall, thin gentleman with a sort of a mole over his right eye. He told us that he owned a big flour mill, but I don't know as he told the truth. Do you know a man of that name?"

I told him that I had never before heard of James Rodney, and by asking a few questions I heard a story that was unpleasant though not particularly strange. Two summers before that an American calling himself James Rodney had come to Ashbourne and stopped with Mrs. Clarke, the widow of the old vicar. She had very little money, and made a living by taking lodgers. He was on his way up north, and he had a two hours' wait between trains in Ashbourne. He took a walk through the town, stopped to get a drink of water at Mrs. Clarke's house, found that they took lodgers and by that night he had given up all idea of going north. He said that he liked Ashbourne and the Clarke cottage but, said the innkeeper, "what really attracted him was Mary Clarke. She was an amazingly pretty girl in those days, sir; in fact, she is still, though she's had a hard time."

It did not take Rodney long to make Mrs. Clarke and Mary believe that he was a person of some importance in New York. He seemed to have plenty of money, his manners were those of a gentleman, and he became popular in local society. In fact, everyone was pleased when, after a tempestuous courtship, Mary and he were married in the beautiful old parish church.

Mary thought that her husband would take her to America at once, but he said that he would prefer to see a little more of Europe. So they went to Switzerland for a couple of weeks and then returned to Mrs. Clarke's cottage. Rodney had received a cable from New York, he said. He must go back to his mill for a little while. It was an urgent matter—he must get the boat sailing from Liverpool on the very next day. He would send a letter by every mail and within a month he would come back for his wife and her mother.

Of course you have guessed what happened. James Rodney, or whatever his real name was, never came back. He did not write and, what is more important, he did not send any money. Letters sent to James Rodney, the Rodney Flour and Grain Company, 13 West Ninety-eighth Street, New York City, U. S. A., were returned by the Dead Letter Office. His name did not appear on the passenger list of the steamer on which he said he intended to sail. For a while Mrs. Clarke and Mary thought that he had met with some fatal accident, but after a friend of theirs, visiting America, had found that no such concern as the Rodney Flour and Grain Company had ever existed and that there were no mills on Ninety-eighth Street, they knew that they had been cruelly deceived. In the course of time Mary had a baby, a very nice baby. It was a little boy, as pretty as Mary herself and resembling her strikingly. In only one respect he resembled his father—there was a small but unmistakable mole over his right eye.

This story interested me very much, and I took the liberty of calling on Mrs. Clarke the next day, on the pretense of looking for lodgings. Indeed, it became more than a pretext, for Mrs. Clarke was such a charming old gentlewoman and the cottage and Mary—it was hard for me to call her Mrs. Rodney—so attractive that I took a room and stayed for three weeks.

Of course I got from them all that they knew about the mysterious James Rodney, and that was little more than the innkeeper had told me. But just before I left Mrs. Rodney gave me a little kodak picture of her husband and herself, taken by her mother on the porch of the cottage.

I went back to America with a fixed determination to find this Rodney person, smash his face and make him send every cent that he possessed back to Ashbourne. You see, I knew the suffering that his little game had inflicted on Mary and her mother and I was pretty sore about it. I confess I didn't have much hope of finding the fellow, but I was going to make a good try at it, anyway. Well, I didn't have to try very hard. I never was much good at this suspense business, so I'll spring my sensation on you right away. James Rodney was Andrew Judd. Yes—don't spill your whiskey—Andrew Judd, president of the Judd Iron Works, philanthropist and reformer.

Two days after I got back, Boss Ridder sent me out to interview Judd for the Sunday edition. Judd had just invented a very fancy sort of model tenement with a gymnasium and swimming tank on every floor. In order to understand just what improvements were needed in the housing of the poor he had spent two days in a tenement house on the lower East Side, and was very eager to talk about it. As soon as I saw him I recognized him, and you can readily understand that my first desire was for a large encouraging draught of the beverage known as whiskey. And, by the way, ring that bell, will you, Jimmy? Two more, please, and a little lunch with it.

Well, of course I thought right away just what you thought—here is one hell of a big story! In spite of the fact that we were running this page interview in the Sunday, the *News* had no particular friendship for Judd. In fact, we were going to oppose him in the fall. He was going to run for Mayor on some crazy reform ticket, and we, of course, were organization Democrat.

I had all the facts and there was plenty of time to get the story in next morning's paper. All I had to do was to flash that little kodak picture (which I always carried with me) on Judd, tell him what I knew of his little European jaunt and let him throw me out of the office. Then back to the *News*, to grab all the space I wanted for the biggest sensation that the paper ever had. Think what a story like that would mean to me, an absolutely exclusive story with a picture to prove it! I saw myself getting a three-hundred-dollar bonus and a regular job at about eighty a week. Then, too, you know that I'm not talking sentiment when I say that I was—have always been—loyal to the *News*. You were long enough in the game to find out what a newspaperman's loyalty is—how his first idea when anything big happens is always to hammer it out on his machine and get it in before the first edition goes to press.

But I had sense enough to hold on to myself for a while. I shook hands with Judd—I guess I stared pretty hard at that mole over his right eye—and I went ahead with the interview as had been arranged. Judd was feeling expansive that day, and he really knew how to talk. He gave me a great little story, full of human interest, and with a lot of new stuff in it, but all the while I was listening to him I was thinking harder than I ever thought before. There were three different plans in my mind—I couldn't, to save my life, think just what I ought to do. After a while Judd felt that he'd given me all I needed and he stopped talking.

"Mr. Judd," I said, almost involuntarily, "when were you married?"

"Why, my dear boy, I don't see what that has to do with what we've been talking about; but I was married five years ago. In St. Marmaduke's Church, of which I am junior warden, if you wish the full particulars. My wife was Miss Emily Lindsay, and here is a picture of her."

He took from his desk a framed photograph of a very lovely woman with a little girl on her lap.

"I see," I said, vaguely. "And when was it that you went abroad?"

"Well, I really don't think that the public will be interested in matters like this," he said, "but I have been abroad several times. Two years ago I spent the summer in England, and then made a somewhat extensive tour of Germany. But I think that I must ask you to excuse me now. I've given you all you need, have I not? Oh, yes!" he added, "I suppose you will want a picture of me. I think I have some in my desk drawer. I'll look and see."

"No," I said, in a voice which seemed strange to me. "I've got a picture already."

His back was turned to me, and he was rummaging in his desk. "But I'm afraid that's been used before. I think I can find some new ones for you."

"This picture has never been used before," I said. "It was taken two years ago in Ashbourne."

At the word "Ashbourne" he turned suddenly and looked at the little square of gray cardboard in my hands. Then he grew very white and stood perfectly still.

For a minute neither of us spoke.

Then, with a self-control for which I could not help admiring him, he pushed his chair to the desk, sat down, turned his back to me and wrote.

I heard the rip of torn paper. He whirled his chair and stretched out his hands to me. In his left hand was an oblong of green paper with his name written in the lower right hand corner. His right hand was empty.

"Here is a blank cheque, which I have signed," he said. "Give me the photograph, please."

I admit I hesitated for a moment. I am not so devoted to my job that I would hate an independent fortune. But I didn't hesitate long.

It was a ridiculously theatrical thing to do, but I took the cheque, tore it into four pieces, and dropped them on the blotter on his desk.

"To hell with your cheque!" I said, in a quiet conversational tone of voice. "You'll need that money when you start defending yourself against the charge of bigamy."

Judd deliberately lit a cigar and sat looking at me.

"So you've got an interesting item for tomorrow's paper, have you?" he said. "But what's the idea? Just what do you gain by attacking me? That little picture is interesting, but it proves absolutely nothing."

I rose to go. "In the first place," I said, with my hand on the doorknob, "I know the girl whom you illegally married two years ago, and the *News* will bring her over here—with her child. We will gain two things—we will be purveyors of a very interesting story and we will bring punishment on a damned hypocrite."

He was perfectly calm. "I see your first point," he answered reflectively. "You can publish a very sensational story—there is no doubt of that. But I doubt very much your ability to substantiate your charge, and I fail to see why you are so bitterly enraged at me. There must be some motive. ... I think I see. Yes, I think I see. But what earthly good will it do the young woman to drag her name into this scandal? You cannot carry out your amiable design of ruining me without ruining also two women."

"All right," I said, "I'll tell you what I'll do. You've got to square yourself, and I'll keep quiet about this business. But you've got to square yourself."

"Just what do you mean by 'square myself'?" he said.

"James Rodney must die," I almost shouted.

"My God!" he exclaimed. "Do you want me to kill myself?"

"You must kill James Rodney," I said. "See here, Mary Clarke has never heard of Andrew Judd. What you've got to do is to write her a letter signing your own name, saying that James Rodney was Tom Smith, or John Jones, or anything you like. Anyway, you must say that he was a friend of yours and that he is dead. Say that he confessed to you on his deathbed that he had married and deserted a girl named Mary Clarke in Ashbourne, England, and that he asked you to notify her of his death and to send her all his money."

"I'll do it," he said. "I'll do it this afternoon. I'll send her ten thousand dollars—fifty thousand dollars—all the money you say."

"You certainly will do it today," I said, "for I'm going to stick around and watch you do it. You will write the letter at my dictation and I will mail it myself. But as to the money that you are sending, you've got the wrong idea. You will send Miss Clarke enough money to buy that little cottage so that they won't have to earn the rent by taking lodgers and enough to pay for a trip abroad for her and her mother. They need a little holiday after the trouble you got them into, you filthy cad. Then you must add enough to send your son through school and through the university. I guess we'll put it at twenty thousand dollars—that's letting you off pretty cheap, and I don't want to burden them with a lot of your dirty money. And you must send the money in English banknotes."

"I suppose you know," Mr. Judd said to me, as I left him late that afternoon, "that what you are doing is blackmail."

"Today," I answered, "I am, in suppressing this story, breaking the great commandment of the newspaper business—violating a code of ethics which you could not possibly understand. I am a traitor to the *News* and to my profession. And after that I don't mind a little blackmail."

Jimmy had taken away our empty glasses and was ostentatiously wiping the table with a gray napkin. Spike looked at his watch and got up to go. As we walked down the street I turned to him and said: "But didn't Mary What-you-may-call-her ever get wise? When Judd died last year she must have seen his picture in some English paper and known that he was the fellow that fooled her. I should think she'd sue his estate and get good money."

"Sure she got wise," said Spike. "But she wouldn't start anything now. She's perfectly comfortable, I guess."

"What is she doing?" I asked.

"Why," said Spike, lighting his cigar butt for the ninth time, "she's married to the assistant Sunday editor of the *Daily News*."

LITTLE GIRL

Lee Pape

IT was one of those spring evenings when the air is heavy with a name-less, unbottleable perfume, and even the smallest stars are allowed out. One of those evenings when only the soulless can study. ... Robins stood on a brightly lighted corner far from the dormitories and breathed deeply of it. His half-dreaming eyes viewed the countless strollers with friendly impartiality, his ears caught with intoxicating pleasantness the music from a dance hall across the way; athwart its high line of lighted windows couples zigzagged as though they were on skates. After a bit Robins raised his eyes to this endless procession of flitting silhouettes and held them there in a sort of fascination. He thought.

"That music's alive! I haven't been in one of those places since I was a freshman."

Slowly, without definite plan, he walked across the street and looked through the glass doors. Some girls grouped at the head of the long flight of stairs that led to the dance floor saw him down there and beckoned. Then, when he swung open the door and entered, the group broke up with shrill giggles, possibly of shyness, but Robins continued mounting the steps until he reached a square landing containing a stout woman smiling hospitably behind an oblong table, on which Robins laid a half dollar. The stout woman, still smiling, returned him fifteen cents and a blue checkroom ticket.

"Wardrobe to your left at the top of the stairs," she said through her smile.

Robins climbed the remaining thirty steps, found the "wardrobe"—a boy's face squinting through a hole in the wall, and turned his attention to the dance floor. It was big and square, and, though the orchestra was half way through a one-step, girls of any age up to twenty were still sitting along the walls waiting to be asked to join the throng that flashed past their impatient feet. A cluster of youths, the undue length of whose coats betrayed that few of them were leaders of fashion, hung nervously about the doorway, afraid either of their own dancing or that of the untried expectant maidens.

The first girl that Robins danced with had seemed of a practicable size until, when he had got half way through asking her, she rose (as far as she could) and showed her duplicity. She was one of those deceptive sitters-down who are in reality the tiniest girls imaginable. The initiated, who generally remember to look before they leap, can tell them by their toes, which are always pointed down to give their feet the appearance of reaching to the floor. No tall fellow can dance with them and half enjoy it.

The second girl that Robins danced with was tall and impossibly blonde and reasonably smooth, but every time Robins tried to interpolate a swagger step there would be a complication of feet, and, instead of being properly overcome with guilt, she would inquire haughtily, "What are you tryin' to do?"

The third girl (the first two really haven't anything to do with the story) attracted Robins' attention by the detached way she was blowing a wisp of hair off her forehead—as though it were somebody else's forehead she was blowing it off of, while her eyes gazed wide a million miles off into the future, or perhaps the past, which is also a million miles away. They were very light eyes, either gray or blue, depending on which was your favorite color, and the rest of her face was modeled with the most scrupulous attention to detail, from that wisp of hair on her forehead down to the little chin that made the turn of the oval. She was dressed in blue—dark blue, with a simplicity that can be made very expensive but which, with inborn expertness, may be approximately arrived at for, say, $6.48.

She had, seemingly, heard his voice rather than his words; her eyes flew back to the present, and him. She nodded, not too impersonally, as the tall blonde girl had nodded. The orchestra was playing *Cecile*.

She performed the miracle of making the "lame duck" as floaty as a waltz. A miracle of miracles.

"How many more may I have?" demanded Robins while, after the encore, he was still gratefully applauding the unresponsive orchestra.

She looked up at him—continued, rather, to look up at him, from under half-lowered lashes. Then, with a sudden little parenthetical puff at the disobedient wisp, she handed him her dance card. There were several initials on it.

"How many more do you want?"

"All of them!" replied Robins promptly. He shoved the card in his pocket; they were partners for the rest of the evening. She followed as though he were using her mind to guide his feet. Her name was Jessie.

Between dances they talked. Her grammar was not all it might have been, but her voice, shade for shade, startled Robins into memories of a voice that had rippled low and confidingly into his ear at the Junior Prom. He had been confident that he should never hear a voice like that again.

Her intimate friends, she let him know, called her Little Girl.

The owner of one set of initials managed to track them down in their secluded corner. He was a good-looking youth with very broad shoulders and an aggressive chin. She smiled pleasantly up into his glowering face.

"I'm sorry," she said, "but I've promised this dance."

"Yeh," he agreed grimly, "you promised it to me." And he stood planted there looking doggedly down. She smiled up at him even more pleasantly.

"No," she said gently, "I promised it to *this* gentleman."

He glared at that gentleman as though glaring was but a feeble substitute for what he really felt inclined to do to him. But, after opening his mouth to express himself further, he suddenly thought better of it and stalked away from Robins' bland counter stare.

"I've never did that before," she confessed. "It makes me feel—funny."

"It's done in the very best families," Robins assured her. "If you had red hair and freckles, now, or maybe a squint, it would never do for you to pull anything like that. But all good subjects know that the queen can do no wrong."

She gave him a demurely suspicious look.

"Are you trying to kid me?"

"Far be it. ... They're playing *The Geranium Rag.*"

After that, in a way, the place contained only themselves and the music. It was truly music that lived, riotously in the one-steps, tenderly in the hesitations; only five musicians, but they were young and their pulses beat to the same rhythm; the violin was king and the drumsticks knew their place. Perhaps it was the music that now and then, at the end of a waltz, surcharged Robins' arm so that it was only with a special effort that he could remove it from about his partner—an act of liberation that for a fraction of time seemed only to make the nestling Jessie a tighter prisoner.

There was a certain rare daintiness about her; a simple, artless tact that spoke in the shades of her voice, even, somehow, in her movements.

He asked if he might see her home.

Outside on the pavement the youth with the aggressive chin was standing in a group of other young fellows. He glared fixedly at Robins out of hostile black eyes. Robins returned the look just as fixedly, and the subject who did not seem to understand that the queen could do no wrong snorted and looked elsewhere. In her cocky little black hat and mannishly swagger "balmacaan" topcoat, Jessie again demonstrated that taste and a slim pocketbook can be the best of friends.

"Isn't that place," Robins ventured as they walked, "rather dangerous for a girl to see much of—alone? I heard several 'parties' being arranged, and some of the boys, while they were getting their hats and coats, were—well, talking pretty loud about their plans."

She declared solemnly, "I've never been inside a café in my life. You don't believe that, do you?"

"Of course I believe it. Why shouldn't I?"

"Why—I only meant that most of the fellows I've met up here don't believe nothing I tell them, hardly, and they don't seem to be surprised if I don't believe nothing they tell me, either. It's true, just the same. I been invited to join their 'parties' plenty of times, but I've always turned them down. I been afraid. Not that I haven't felt like going, sometimes. I've heard so much about cafés—the kind that have cabaret shows. They must be wonderful! But I knew I couldn't go without drinking. I've never took a drink in my life. You don't believe that, do you? I mean, it's true, I haven't."

" 'Cabaret show,' " said Robins after a pause, "is only the made-in-Paris name for the cheapest kind of singing and dancing—bum entertainment with French dressing. And if you don't drink, it won't seem 'wonderful.' It never gets wonderful till about the third round. It might be a good thing … Little Girl, do you think you could trust me to show you the inside of your first café?"

"Oh! You mean—without drinking?"

"With the lid on tight."

Yes, she thought she could trust him—she knew she could. And she took a little tighter hold on his arm, sending an electric thrill through him. They got on a car, and off, and then there were two blocks to walk. Two dark, slumbrously echoing blocks with lights winking down them from the far end. They walked the second one rather slowly, and in the middle of it he turned and faced her, just, apparently, as she was stopping to look up at him, the hand that had been on his arm now fluttering about one of the top buttons of his overcoat. He placed both his hands on her shoulders, and she made a little sound and drew away, only to return close, and closer. And then he had her in his arms and was kissing her. . . .

In the darkness her light eyes, so near, seemed mysteriously dusky, almost black. And once again he was reminded, somehow, of the girl at the Junior Prom. . . . A dim palm corner instead of a dark street. And the sensation of it had not been so different from this. Yet *she* had been a "first family" girl. . . .

Jessie readjusted her hat to its original tilt and silently took his arm again, and they walked on.

The café was rather crowded. In front of a rattling piano on a narrow platform built along the wall, a youth with plastered-back hair was singing in nasal tenor. Robins selected an inconspicuous little corner table. A waiter hovered. Jessie bent mysteriously a little way across the table, and Robins leaned towards her inquiringly.

"How would it be," she whispered, "how would it be if I just ordered a drink and let it stand in front of me, like as if—as if—"

"As if—I see. What would you prefer to have—stand in front of you?"

"A—a Martini highball."

"Ain't no such animal. You mean cocktail."

"Do I? What's the difference?"

"A cocktail is short and stout, but it has a longer reach. And now about eats?"

"Why," Jessie hesitated, "I don't know. I—I can't think of nothing but lobster à la Newburg. I don't know what it is, but it's all I can think of."

"It's not a bad thought for a beginner," consoled Robins, and sent the waiter off. Up on the platform a girl with bold eyes and a bolder gown was shouting off key, while behind her, at the piano, a mere boy with long yellow hair managed to extract an incredible number of sounds per second.

"If I couldn't sing better'n that!" shuddered Jessie. The waiter returned with two yellow drinks and the lobster.

"It's not really so bad," explained Robins. "It's only that you can't get the fine points while that cocktail remains in the glass—where it's going to remain. Art owes a great debt to alcohol. I've known a little colored gin to rouse a really passionate appreciation of music in fellows who couldn't whistle Yankee Doodle so you'd be sure of it. But, I say, how can I keep my mind on anything so mild as gin while you're blowing at your hair like that?"

"It's a habit," she explained hurriedly. "It don't mean I'm not paying attention. I always do that when I'm listening hardest."

"I am flattered. Still, it would require terrible concentration for a fellow to think straight while it's going on. If clothes make the man, it's 'habits' that make the woman."

"Woman?"

"Little Girl. Some bally little 'habit,' like a trick of the voice, or that blessed blowing stunt of yours, is liable to keep a chap awake nights, while the size of a girl's mind, or the dimension of her soul might not worry him any more than the name of her dressmaker."

She regarded him steadily.

"Who is it has a 'trick of the voice'?"

In his unpreparedness for this naïve uprearing of green eyes, he caught himself blushing.

"Oh, I don't know—nobody *I* know, especially. It was just an idea, merely—"

"That's all right. I just asked. *You* got a habit. You got a habit of twitching one corner of your mouth when you're going to say anything—funny like."

"Perhaps I just do it to let people know when they're expected to laugh."

"There—you did it then."

"Did I?"

And he did it again, while she laughed victoriously and sent upwards a joyous little puff that made the mutinous wisp sway triumphantly. And then they both laughed, and she said, "I like it, though. And I—I guess I know what you mean, because when I watch you doing it, it's—it's hard to keep my mind on what you're saying."

She suddenly dropped her eyes, and her face went a deeper pink than it owed to the shaded table lamp. Robins tingled all over and was silent because he was not sure that his voice would be steady. Oddly he felt almost as if, leaning to each other across the little table, they had kissed again. The high-pitched voice on the platform shrilled on, and stopped.

"Hear them clapping?" said Robins. Had she been deaf, she must have heard them. She raised her cocktail and for a still moment returned its wicked cat's eye stare.

"Do you mean," she said in a low voice, "that if I just drank only this one I'd really think that girl could sing?"

"I think one would do it. You see, cocktails are perfect mixers—it doesn't take 'em any time to get intimate with new acquaintances, though after you've known them a while they insist on introducing a few friends before they'll get really sociable. But that's the way the efficiency experts that run these places work it out—if they put lots of gin in the cocktails they can get a very expensive effect with very cheap singers."

Jessie put down her glass without taking her eyes from it.

"*Good* night!" she said.

"Then you're not so keen about your first dose of cabaret after all?"

"Are they all as bad as this?"

"Worse, some of them."

"Good *night!*"

"And you've no hankering after a second treatment?"

"With you?" She said it quickly, eagerly, and when, rather at a loss, he flushed and stammered a little, she added almost sullenly, "Oh, I know we won't never be seeing each other any more. You're a college boy. Ain't you?"

"College men, we'd rather hear it called. How did you know?"

"I can tell. To-morrow you'll go back to your books and the other rah, rah boys, and I'll go back to—to—"

"The store?"

"Yes, the store ... and that'll be the end of it."

He looked thoughtfully down into his own untouched glass, and then troubledly, wistfully, back at her. Passionately he wanted to give denial, but all her double negatives, subtly-armed symbols of bewildering injustices, seemed suddenly to line up between them, each an affirmative of her hopeless creed.

"I'm afraid that's about the philosophy of it, Little Girl. We won't lie to each other, will we? And it's a rotten, rotten shame."

She gave back his gaze steadily, and into her eyes crept the oddest look, longing, bewilderment, fateful submission, before she answered gently:

"Oh, well, I ain't blaming *you* for anything, you know. It's a case of has-to-be, I guess. It ain't your fault. It ain't nobody's fault."

"It's *somebody's* fault!" Robins, striking the table with his flat hand, said it almost loudly. Then, his voice dropping almost to a husky whisper: "Little Girl, it *must* be somebody's fault. Not yours. Not mine, and I might keep specializing on sociology and ethics and all that printed wind till I'm a hundred years old, and still not find out whose. And yet, in a way, you stand for all I like in a girl. ... "

Her hand, raised just a little, stopped him. She was trying to smile; her lips were parted slightly. Suddenly she reached over and patted his hand, though he felt how her own fluttered.

"Don't," she said. He could scarcely hear her. "It's all right. I know."

For a passionate moment, in the dusky rose of the shaded light, their eyes met in silence; their eyes for a brooding moment annihilated that figurative space. Then the wisp of hair stirred. as she sent it a determined little reminder that she was still Little Girl and no one else.

"Thank you for trying," she said, and her voice was suddenly back in control. "It was—very sweet of you, but I'm me and you're you and I know where I get off, I guess. And that's Markham's, to-morrow morning, at quarter to—"

"Markham's!" The word rang queerly. "Markham's! I might have known!" He laughed bitterly. "Oh, now, I say. That's rare! By all the laws of irony I ought to be John Markham's only son. Still, I'm his nephew— his adopted son, in a way; if it weren't for John Markham I'd probably be bucking the world for a living long ago. So the situation is as perfect as we have a right to hope for in this imperfect world, isn't it, Little Girl? Markham's! And you've been stifled so that...oh, come, let's get out. I must have some air with this!"

The yellow-haired boy was assaulting the piano apparently with intent to kill as they made their way out; its hysterical protests reached them, faintly, out on the street. Slowly they retraveled the two dim blocks to the trolleys.

"I'm sorry I began that about never meeting no more," she broke silence at length. "Everything's perfectly all right. Really. And I want you just to put me on my car without coming along. I'm not ashamed of the street or nothing, but I'm used to going home alone, and it would be more—more—"

"More perfect that way," he gravely finished for her. "Perhaps it would, Little Girl."

Far off a street car rumbled.

"And—you've showed me a most agreeable evening."

For the second time their lips found each other in the darkness of that sleeping street. The starlit silence enveloped them as in a protecting shield while he held her close, and she did not move until his arms loosened, and the rattle of her car was very near.

THE BOARDING-HOUSE

James Joyce

MRS. MOONEY was a butcher's daughter. She was a woman who was quite able to keep things to herself : a determined woman. She had married her father's foreman and opened a butcher's shop near Spring Gardens. But as soon as his father-in-law was dead Mr. Mooney began to go to the devil. He drank, plundered the till, ran headlong into debt. It was no use making him take the pledge: he was sure to break out again a few days after. By fighting his wife in the presence of customers and by buying bad meat he ruined his business. One night he went for his wife with the cleaver and she had to sleep in a neighbor's house.

After that they lived apart. She went to the priest and got a separation from him with care of the children. She would give him neither money nor food nor house-room; and so he was obliged to enlist himself as a sheriff's man. He was a shabby, stooped little drunkard with a white face and a white moustache and white eyebrows, pencilled above his little eyes, which were pink-veined and raw; and all day long he sat in the bailiff's room, waiting to be put on a job. Mrs. Mooney, who had taken what remained of her money out of the butcher business and set up a boarding-house in Hardwicke Street, was a big, imposing woman. Her house had a floating population made up of tourists from Liverpool and the Isle of Man and, occasionally, *artistes* from the music halls. Its resident population was made up of clerks from the city. She governed the house cunningly and firmly, knew when to give credit, when to be stern and when to let things pass. All the resident young men spoke of her as *The Madam.*

Mrs. Mooney's young men paid fifteen shillings a week for board and lodgings (beer or stout at dinner excluded). They shared in common tastes and occupations and for this reason they were very chummy with one another. They discussed with one another the chances of favorites and outsiders. Jack Mooney, the Madam's son, who was clerk to a commission agent in Fleet Street, had the reputation of being a hard case. He was fond of using soldiers' obscenities : usually he came home in the small hours. When he met his friends he had always a good one to tell them and he was always sure to be onto a good thing—that is to say, a likely horse or a likely *artiste*. He was also handy with the mitts and sang comic songs. On Sunday nights there would often be a reunion in Mrs. Mooney's front drawing-room. The music-hall *artistes* would oblige; and Sheridan played waltzes and polkas and vamped accompaniments. Polly Mooney, the Madam's daughter, would also sing. She sang:

> *"I'm a … naughty girl.*
> *You needn't sham:*
> *You know I am."*

Polly was a slim girl of nineteen; she had light, soft hair and a small, full mouth. Her eyes, which were gray with a shade of green through them, had a habit of glancing upwards when she spoke with anyone, which made her look like a little perverse Madonna. Mrs. Mooney had first sent her daughter to be a typist in a corn-factor's office but, as a disreputable sheriff's man used to come every other day to the office, asking to be allowed to say a word to his daughter, she had taken her daughter home again and set her to do housework. As Polly was very lively the intention was to give her the run of the young men. Besides, young men like to feel that there is a young woman not very far away. Polly, of course, flirted with the young men, but Mrs. Mooney, who was a shrewd judge, knew that the young men were only passing the time away : none of them meant business. Things went on so for a long time and Mrs. Mooney began to think of sending Polly back to typewriting, when she noticed that something was going on between Polly and one of the young men. She watched the pair and kept her own counsel.

Polly knew that she was being watched, but still her mother's persistent silence could not be misunderstood. There had been no open complicity between mother and daughter, no open understanding but, though people in the house began to talk of the affair, still Mrs. Mooney did not intervene. Polly began to grow a little strange in her manner and the young man was evidently perturbed. At last, when she judged it to be the right moment, Mrs. Mooney intervened. She dealt with moral problems as a cleaver deals with meats, and in this case she had made up her mind.

It was a bright Sunday morning of early summer, promising heat, but with a fresh breeze blowing. All the windows of the boarding-house were open and the lace curtains ballooned gently towards the street beneath the raised sashes. The belfry of George's Church sent out constant peals and worshipers, singly or in groups, traversed the little circus before the church, revealing their purpose by their self-contained demeanor no less than by the little volumes in their gloved hands. Breakfast was over in the boarding-house and the table of the breakfast-room was covered with plates on which lay yellow streaks of eggs with morsels of bacon-fat and bacon-rind. Mrs. Mooney sat in the straw armchair and watched the servant, Mary, remove the breakfast things. She made Mary collect the crusts and pieces of broken bread to help to make Tuesday's bread-pudding. When the table was cleared, the broken bread collected, the sugar and butter safe under lock and key, she began to reconstruct the interview which she had had the night before with Polly. Things were as she had suspected : she had been frank in her questions and Polly had been frank in her answers. Both had been somewhat awkward, of course. She had been made awkward by her not wishing to receive the news in too cavalier a fashion or to seem to have connived, and Polly had been made awkward not merely because allusions of that kind always made her awkward but also because she did not wish it to be thought that in her wise innocence she had divined the intention behind her mother's tolerance.

Mrs. Mooney glanced instinctively at the little gilt clock on the mantelpiece as soon as she had become aware through her revery that the bells of George's Church had stopped ringing. It was seventeen minutes past eleven: she would have lots of time to have the matter out with Mr. Doran and then catch short twelve at Marlborough Street. She was sure she would win. To begin with she had all the weight of social opinion on her side: she was an outraged mother. She had allowed him to live beneath her roof, assuming that he was a man of honor, and he had simply abused her hospitality. He was thirty-four or thirty-five years of age, so that youth could not be pleaded as his excuse; nor could ignorance be his excuse since he was a man who had seen something of the world. He had simply taken advantage of Polly's youth and inexperience : that was evident. The question was : What reparation would he make?

There must be reparation made in such case. It is all very well for the man: he can go his ways as if nothing had happened, having had his moment of pleasure, but the girl has to bear the brunt. Some mothers would be content to patch up such an affair for a sum of money; she had known cases of it. But she would not do so. For her only one reparation could make up for the loss of her daughter's honor : marriage.

She counted all her cards again before sending Mary up to Mr. Doran's room to say that she wished to speak with him. She felt sure she would win. He was a serious young man, not rakish or loud-voiced like the others. If it had been Mr. Sheridan or Mr. Meade or Bantam Lyons her task would have been much harder. She did not think he would face publicity. All the lodgers in the house knew something of the affair; details had been invented by some. Besides, he had been employed for thirteen years in a great Catholic wine-merchant's office and publicity would mean for him, perhaps, the loss of his job. Whereas if he agreed all might be well. She knew he had a good screw for one thing and she suspected he had a bit of stuff put by.

Nearly the half hour! She stood up and surveyed herself in the pier-glass. The decisive expression of her great florid face satisfied her and she thought of some mothers she knew who could not get their daughters off their hands.

Mr. Doran was very anxious indeed this Sunday morning. He had made two attempts to shave, but his hand had been so unsteady that he had been obliged to desist. Three days' reddish beard fringed his jaws and every two or three minutes a mist gathered on his glasses so that he had to take them off and polish them with his pocket handkerchief. The recollection of his confession of the night before was a cause of acute pain to him; the priest had drawn out every ridiculous detail of the affair and in the end had so magnified his sin that he was almost thankful at being afforded a loophole of reparation. The harm was done. What could he do now but marry her or run away? He could not brazen it out. The affair would be sure to be talked of and his employer would be certain to hear of it. Dublin is such a small city: everyone knows everyone else's business. He felt his heart leap warmly in his throat as he heard in his excited imagination old Mr. Leonard calling out in his rasping voice: "Send Mr. Doran here, please."

All his long years of service gone for nothing! All his industry and diligence thrown away! As a young man he had sown his wild oats, of course; he had boasted of his free-thinking and denied the existence of God to his companions in public houses. But that was all passed and done with ... nearly. He still bought a copy of *Reynolds's Newspaper* every week, but he attended to his religious duties and for nine-tenths of the year lived a regular life. He had money enough to settle down on; it was not that. But the family would look down on her. First of all there was her disreputable father, and then her mother's boarding-house was beginning to get a certain fame. He had a notion that he was being had. He could imagine his friends talking of the affair and laughing. She *was* a little vulgar; sometimes she said "I seen" and "If I had've known." But what would grammar matter if he really loved her? He could not make up his mind whether to like her or despise her for what she had done. Of course, he had done it, too. His instinct urged him to remain free, not to marry. Once you are married you are done for, it said.

While he was sitting helplessly on the side of the bed in shirt and trousers she tapped lightly at his door and entered. She told him all, that she had made a clean breast of it to her mother and that her mother would speak with him that morning. She cried and threw her arms round his neck, saying:

"Oh, Bob! Bob! What am I to do? What am I to do at all?"

She would put an end to herself, she said.

He comforted her feebly, telling her not to cry, that it would be all right, never fear. He felt against his shirt the agitation of her bosom.

It was not altogether his fault that it had happened. He remembered well, with the curious patient memory of the celibate, the first casual caresses, her dress, her breath, her fingers had given him. Then late one night as he was undressing for bed she had tapped at his door, timidly. She wanted to relight her candle at his for hers had been blown out by a gust. It was her bath night. She wore a loose, open combing-jacket of printed flannel. Her white instep shone in the opening of her furry slippers and the blood glowed warmly behind her perfumed skin. From her hands and wrists, too, as she lit and steadied her candle, a faint perfume arose.

On nights when he came in very late it was she who warmed up his dinner. He scarcely knew what he was eating, feeling her beside him alone, at night, in the sleeping house. And her thoughtfulness! If the night was anyway cold or wet or windy there was sure to be a little tumbler of punch ready for him. Perhaps they could be happy together....

They used to go upstairs together on tiptoe, each with a candle, and on the third landing exchange reluctant good nights. They used to kiss. He remembered well her eyes, the touch of her hand and his delirium....

But delirium passes. He echoed her phrase, applying it to himself: *"What am I to do?"* The instinct of the celibate warned him to hold back. But the sin was there; even his sense of honor told him that reparation must be made for such a sin.

While he was sitting with her on the side of the bed Mary came to the door and said that the missus wanted to see him in the parlor. He stood up to put on his coat and waistcoat, more helpless than ever. When he was dressed he went over to her to comfort her. It would be all right, never fear. He left her crying on the bed and moaning softly: *"O my God!"*

Going down the stairs his glasses became so dimmed with moisture that he had to take them off and polish them. He longed to ascend through the roof and fly away to another country where he would never hear again of his trouble, and yet a force pushed him downstairs step by step. The implacable faces of his employer and of the Madam stared upon his discomfiture. On the last flight of stairs he passed Jack Mooney, who was coming up from the pantry nursing two bottles of *Bass*. They saluted coldly; and the lover's eyes rested for a second or two on a thick bulldog face and a pair of thick, short arms. When he reached the foot of the staircase he glanced up and saw Jack regarding him from the door of the return-room.

Suddenly he remembered the night when one of the music-hall *artistes,* a little blonde Londoner, had made a rather free allusion to Polly. The reunion had been almost broken up on account of Jack's violence. Everyone tried to quiet him. The music-hall *artiste,* a little paler than usual, kept smiling and saying that there was no harm meant: but Jack kept shouting at him that if any fellow tried that sort of a game on with *his* sister he'd bloody well put his teeth down his throat, so he would.

***

Polly sat for a little time on the side of the bed, crying. Then she dried her eyes and went over to the looking-glass. She dipped the end of the towel in the water-jug and refreshed her eyes with the cool water. She looked at herself in profile and readjusted a hairpin above her ear. Then she went back to the bed again and sat at the foot. She regarded the pillows for a long time and the sight of them awakened in her mind secret amiable memories. She rested the nape of her neck against the cool iron bed-rail and fell into a revery. There was no longer any perturbation visible on her face.

She waited on patiently, almost cheerfully, without alarm, her memories gradually giving place to hopes and visions of the future. Her hopes and visions were so intricate that she no longer saw the white pillows on which her gaze was fixed or remembered that she was waiting for anything.

At last she heard her mother calling. She started to her feet and ran to the banisters.

"Polly! Polly!"

"Yes, mamma?"

"Come down, dear. Mr. Doran wants to speak to you."

Then she remembered what she had been waiting for.

THE FRUIT OF MISADVENTURE

Waldo Frank

" … and they entered the Palace and golden fruit was served unto them on platters of amethyst. But the fruit satisfied them not, so that they went empty to their couches."

—Caspar de Maîstre-Joie.

IT was not the cold of the fresh room that made it difficult for Thomas Braceby to arise from bed in the morning; it was the weariness in his heart. But for all his forty-five years, Mr. Braceby was not wise enough to see this clearly, nor honest enough to avow it. So one night, after he had tucked himself under his luxurious blue quilt and between the linen sheets that seemed hard to him and unfriendly, he said to his valet:

"Jones, from now on open the windows in the library and throw aside the portières. That'll give me enough air. With the windows in this room open also, there's too much chill in the morning and too much draught for my catarrh."

And Jones told Cook, as they sat over their midnight beer, that the master was getting old.

"Why, he's been old for five years," said Cook, pouring a glass and munching a slice.

"How's that?" asked Jones, who had been only five months in the service.

"The sign of a bachelor's getting old is when he puts a stop to women— not when he sleeps in a room with the windows shut. Mr. Braceby ain't had a love affair since he was forty."

"That's gettin' old awful young," observed Jones. "Perhaps he had an unhappy turn-down and that's what stopped him."

"Perhaps," said Cook with a superior air, "but it's not true, just the same. Mr. Braceby never cared for no woman yet that didn't care for him. He never had a turn-down. He just got disgusted—that's all,—tired. And what's gettin' old, if it ain't that?"

"He's a handsome gentleman." Jones thought of his waistcoats.

"A fine one." Cook thought of his Christmas gifts.

"Well," Jones slapped the bottle on the kitchen table with the philosophical emphasis consequent on thinking of waistcoats. "Such is life!"

"Even the most gifted and the most blessed of us has to bear bitter fruit." Cook could mix metaphors as well as sauces.

"Wha' d'ye mean?" Jones was startled by a statement so obviously above him.

"What do I mean, young man? What I say. Mr. Braceby's been a gay and mighty man these twenty years."

"Well?"

"Well," said Cook, "sooner or later, the tree has to bear fruit!"

With all the contempt of a baffled Philistine, Jones looked at this new Deborah. "Annie, you're talkin' like a rabbit. I'm going to bed."

II

THE following morning Mr. Braceby rose early—at nine—and ate his breakfast in quickened tempo. With his last cup of coffee he instructed Jones to call Mrs. Martin Linck on the wire. Up to now there had been a heavy scowl upon his usually gentle face. But after he had made a luncheon engagement on the telephone his expression softened and his cheeks wreathed with a benign smile. All of this, however, was beyond the comprehension of Jones, for he knew Mrs. Linck, and she was fifty if she was a day. But Jones did not speak of his puzzlement to Cook, for Cook might have understood what he could not—and that would have touched his masculine pride.

Five years before all this, Thomas Braceby had undergone a revolution. He had been sitting in his library one winter night, too weary to undress and too apathetic to ignite his gas-logs. It was in the same apartment where he lived now, a rather colorless, yet elegant and completely comfortable suite of rooms in the club district of New York. While by no means ideal, it had always seemed to him the most convenient setting for his cultivated vagabondage. Braceby had never become attached to a home, and the conception of aught more than a purely physical roost did not enter his mind. What he needed was a cozy living-room for those brief hours when he should choose to live there; a dining-room fitted for the exigencies of a capacious dinner; a bed-chamber in which he could sleep, and a pair of additional rooms in which he could house chance masculine and feminine guests. What he demanded in particular was freedom to live as he wished and a retinue of servants, in his apartment and in the entrance-hall below, who were eager and efficient in carrying out his wishes. All this he had. And everything else that he required he found in his near vicinity; to the east of him in the stately homes where he was always welcome, and to the west of him in café and theater, where he had long been known.

Upon the evening in question, Braceby did not return shivering from his hollow club, stand disconsolate in the mocking light of a Tiffany lamp and yearn for a little cottage with a wife. He had had an interesting time at the club, hearing the tale of a chum who had walked five hundred miles unescorted up the Yalu River. And whereas the subject of cottages did not engross him, Braceby was convinced that he knew more of certain wives than their husbands. What irritated him was that there was no one within earshot to kindle those artificial gas-logs. And what frightened him was not the gray, cavernous vision of a deserted old age with two rheumatic knees unadorned by grandchildren, but the perverse impulse within him to go to bed with his clothes on, out of sheer dislike for taking them off. Needless to say, Braceby drove the impulse from him like a leprous thing, and resolved upon the instant to discharge his valet in the morning. True, he had granted him leave of absence. But a valet not clairvoyant enough to feel that his master was coming home that evening, soured and frozen and tired out, was no valet for Thomas Braceby. Body-servants and priests must be possessed of a workable, mystical sixth sense.

The elaborate gilt clock, shaped like a globe and supported by two rather distorted angels, ticked away. The shadows were thick on the mahogany bookcase, within whose glass doors, ribbed in satin rose, Braceby stored his spirits, his cordials and his poker-chips. On the thus prostituted piece of furniture stood a handsome silver frame, from out of which came the eerie eyes of a famous actress. And on the silk-muffled walls between the brocade drawn windows, the head of a moose loomed ominous and imposing. The light emanating from the lamp (a huge bronze structure upon three carved legs, which blossomed six feet from the floor into a heavy replica of gnarled oak-leaves) served merely to emphasize the gloom. And Thomas Braceby sat in his armchair (it was a family relic and its two arms represented the necks and heads of very elongated lions) and impotently shivered.

Then the bell of the house-telephone gave a sharp ring and subsided. Braceby's orders downstairs were of long standing—that he was not deaf and that a fifty-second clamor was no more convincing than the notice of a moment.

"Damn. Who's that?" muttered Braceby, and wondered whether it might not perhaps be someone who would oblige him by turning on his heat.

"There's a lady down here, sir," said the well-trained Cerberus, who, according to Braceby, was distinguished from most of his variety by the fact that he actually had one solid head on his shoulders.

"Is she short and rather thin?" asked the bachelor.

"No, sir. She's tall. She's dark. She's veiled."

"Let her up."

Braceby moved laboriously to the hall, loosed the door-latch so it could be opened from without, and returning with a meditative step, sank back into his mid-Victorian armchair. The precise picture of the hall-boy had prepared him for an untoward occurrence. A moment later the woman stepped into the light. Braceby rose from his chair. Instead of coming forward he turned toward the fireplace.

"You shouldn't have come here, Florence," he said calmly, "but now that you're here—" he bent over and placed a match to the gas-logs, "sit down."

"Is that the way you greet me on my first visit?"

The tall, slender woman stood before the door, which she had shut behind her. An opaque veil, glistening with her frozen breath, was still over her face.

The gas took fire with a sharp explosion, and the clumsy man jumped back in momentary fright. Mrs. Narvin, without a tremor, threw a seal coat upon a chair and placed her hat on the bookcase. She then drew off her gloves, tossed them before the silver frame upon whose occupant she found time to bestow a candid glance, and came forward toward the man. The entire score of her actions had been executed with a despatch of which a *comédienne* in a Protean rôle might well have boasted and with a power of deliberate suggestion whence Balzac could have gleaned her history.

Braceby, upon whom such evidence of feminine prowess was not wasted, stood expectant, well aware. that she had more to say.

"Why do you receive me like this? Is it the way you feel?"

Braceby drew up a chair and sat beside her in the heat of the gas-logs.

"It is precisely the way I feel, my dear friend."

Mrs. Narvin measured the man before her with restrained bewilderment. There was in her careful scrutiny the interest of a calm yet worried combatant who realizes that to win one must first have understood, and that to understand one must first convey the impression that one already does. Braceby looked exactly his age. His sleek, black hair was faintly, regularly greying. His eyes twinkled with a constant inner observation, even as they gleamed somewhat coldly with that lack of real good-will which accrues from too much looking-on and too little taking part. His face, withal, was as kindly as it was strong, and the lines about his large, thin mouth were the tracings of a wholesome sensuality and a great readiness to smile and to respond. In contrast to the soft chiseling of his chin and to the slight bagginess of his cheeks that were gently wreathed, his forehead appeared serenely aloof, and his heavy, protrusive brows that offset the sunken grey of his eyes seemed almost dangerous and certainly austere.

With an easy grace, indicative of experience and assurance, Braceby stretched out his hands and held hers, tenderly poised between his upturned palms. His fingers tapered and were thin.

"You have come to see me, Florence," he said, "because, presumably, you wanted me."

"Yes. Because I wanted you."

"And you shall have me. But in a far sincerer manner than you suppose. This shall not be the usual love affair. Instead of taking you in my arms and giving you *that*—and for all the lovely alchemy of women, that is still a coarse, masterful, faulty thing—I shall keep you near me, as you are now, my friend, and I shall give you myself." He paused. Mrs. Narvin was thirty. The thought struck him that he was an impudent fraud to treat her as if she knew less than he did. "I am going to make a confession," he added, hesitantly.

"The confession that, now I have come, your love is frightened and has disappeared?"

"Just that—" said Braceby, "Now that you have come, my love is frightened at such a splendid, heedless sacrifice. And, in the realization of how small, compared to it, is that which I have offered to you and which you have at last come to take—I no longer dare, I no longer want to offer it. In fact, I withdraw it; it is too petty."

There was a silence. Mrs. Narvin withdrew her hands from his and then returned them. The room still froze.

"Do not judge yet," Braceby went on, heartened. "You do not understand. Listen and perhaps you may."

Like a heroine in a Pinero play, Mrs. Narvin dropped into a chair and prepared to give ear. This man before her, alas, was no romantic lover; what he had to offer was vastly more vocal than passionate, but such as it was, she felt a yearning to receive it, and so she sat in silence while he rumbled on. A woman wants all. If that all is less than one per cent., she still wants that less than one per cent.

"Florence," he began, "what I am saying now would sound truer, doubtless, in the mouth of a sentimental youth addressing his first flame. The point is that such a youth and I have a point in common. We have never loved. But the lad who could speak so has never loved because he has never had a chance. And I have never loved because I have had too many chances. So it is that while the words of the boy would be comical, my confession is nearer tragedy. You are going to leave this room, in half an hour, far cleaner than you came into it. For there is a part of me that has the power of chastening, despite that other part that has so often defiled. And that part alone you shall have. The other part, that other women knew, I shall tell you of. For I want you to take that away with you also—to bury it; it will not stain your life. And I crave to be rid of it. Oh, you do not dream how I crave to be rid of it!"

Mrs. Narvin coughed sympathetically and Braceby plowed on.

"Can you imagine, Florence, what it is like not to be able to respond, with one's whole heart, to the life-bestowing embraces of a woman? Well, when I have felt anything at all—which has not been often—that is what I have felt. I have felt emptiness, disgust; I have felt unworthiness and anger. But the most fearful of feelings is that of silence, of inner silence against the bestowal of a woman; it is the fear that this and this alone, might arise from what you offer which must keep me, for once, from running such a risk. For that inability to forget and to be equal to a woman's gift is killing me. I love you so dearly now that it would kill me to feel this with you. And yet, so often have I felt it when I seemed most certain not to, that I am afraid—I am a coward. I will not risk the joy I have now, of being your equal in love and in devotion. I will not put my feeling to the test; for I am afraid I might fail. And that is the reason, Florence, why you must go back to your house."

Mrs. Narvin pressed her lips to his cold hands. And Braceby, pausing a moment, went on with a diminished ease.

"Let me tell you, Florence, of one event in my life which will help illumine this. I never knew the woman's name. But there were a thousand ways of being sure she was a gentlewoman. She looked something like you. Perhaps that is why I was reminded of her. For any other of my miserable misadventures would have served as well. Perhaps because she also was tall and dark and silent and because her eyes, like yours, seemed simply to be the splendid symbols of a woman's tears, I am the stronger to prevent this ending as that did; and the more fearful lest it might.

"She came to me, as I say, nameless. I never sought to learn her name. But I wanted to marry her. I proposed, if she had a husband, that she should divorce him and let me legitimize her gift. She said she had no husband; but that she would not marry me. And I understood why. There was no continuity in my love. It was a passion, a tenderness, built upon no deep giving of myself. And this she felt; and the fact that she felt it and that I did not prove her wrong was torture to me. That was more than ten years ago. I pleaded with her: 'Tell me who you are and this deeper thing will come.' She shook her head."

Braceby buried his face in his hands. The scene was going very well. Then, once more, he sought those of Mrs. Narvin.

" 'Bear me a child,' I pleaded, 'and all this will change!' My friend shivered as if I had suggested an unnatural thing; and a horror came into her eyes that I would die rather than see again in yours. 'No,' she said, 'I could not bear *you* a child. It would not be your child. Only your mind— not your heart—would know that it was your child.' I never saw her again after that time. Months after, I received word telling me that a child had been bom. Her word framed her indictment: I must never try to find that child; even as I had sworn never to try to find her."

"But you must have prayed God to find them for you!"

"No," answered Braceby, "I did not have the heart to pray for that. The woman was right. She had felt the truth about me, but only in the act which was to make that truth so tragically present. I do not want you to feel that truth. Rather than have you come upon it in the flaying of your own ecstasy as did she, I would flay myself as I am doing. I was condemned by the one Justice that is never wrong—the instinct of a mother about a father. I have no doubt it was for their good. It was a bitter good."

"All good is bitter good," mused Mrs. Narvin.

"You do not think I am feigning this to be free of you?"

"I know you love me as you are able, Tom."

"Listen then—" Braceby resumed her hands and the meretricious logs pelted little yellow gleams upon his quiet face. "Once, I think, I loved a woman in the way that that silent woman knew I had not loved her. It was the splendid period of my life. I was twenty-five then—fifteen years ago. She did not love me. And that love died."

"Perhaps it really didn't die."

"It amounts to the same thing."

And Florence rose and went home. They parted friends.

III

BRACEBY returned to the room and turned out the gas. Thank God, he was rid of another woman! And not only of another woman, but in a larger sense, of woman. In all his play-acting, indeed, there had been a strong element of honesty and sincerity; if the face that he had turned to Mrs. Narvin had not been wholly his real face, it had at least been the face that he wanted to present to women, to the world, to life itself. Old memories thronged in his mind, beguiling him and torturing him. He saw the dead years as vain and hollow things; he felt all the bitterness of cold emotions and wasted days. Until the blue grey of morning oozed through the dark green of the window shades and cast a clammy, sepulchral light through the room, he sat there in his chair, mulling over forgotten and poignant things. Then he went to bed—in his clothes.

When he awoke he was cold and stiff, but somehow the feeling of futility, of emptiness, of tragic vanity was gone. It had driven him out of his club; it had caused him to turn away from the proffered kisses of Florence Narvin; it had given him the worst evening of his whole life. But now that feeling was gone, and in its place was the thrill of a new purpose. The idea came to him that the pale day outside, raw and anemic as it was at its birth, would see great changes for him, and perhaps go down into his history as a great turning point. A notion flitted around the edges of his consciousness; he reached out for it, trying to pin it down to coherence; it finally showed itself as a determination to make a call upon an old friend, Mrs. Linck. He was done with women; he would now try humanity. A vast sentimentality surged through him. He ceased to pity himself and began vaguely to admire himself.

Mrs. Linck received him in her working library. She was one of those wealthy women of New York in whom charity has become as great a passion as, in others, bridge or dancing or adultery. In all cases, the passion has a common ground. It is regarded, in the given light, as the thing to do. If the woman be temperamentally fitted for her chosen field, as was Mrs. Linck, there may even come of it some measure of accomplishment. A great city produces some charity-workers who actually do good, even as it possesses some bad wives who actually bestow love. Mrs. Linck was the president of a great orphan asylum and trustee in a dozen allied philanthropies. She had a private telephone in her private library and her private secretary was a great gleaner of publicity. She was a well-rounded automaton.

As the much-affaired woman and the denaturized Don Juan sat together over their doilies and their mushrooms, Mrs. Linck pushed the talk to a quick conclusion.

"So you've decided, Thomas, that you want the girl?"

"Yes, I've decided. If she's all you say she is and that she seems to be—I am ready. I have made a failure of my life as a companion of women. I've never been so much as a bad husband, I'm eager to see if Nature singled me out, perhaps, to be a father."

Next day club New York, social Manhattan and bibulous Broadway had a common interrogation point about which to huddle heads, chatter queries and produce preposterous explanations. Why was Tom Braceby giving up his staid, time-proved apartment? Why was he moving into a country house surrounded by forty green acres, in the vague wilds of Westchester County, where he would have no neighbor more exciting than John D. Rockefeller? And who, on earth, was this beautiful, shy, fifteen-year-old wisp of a girl with whom he was determined to brave such solitude?

Sophia Linck disseminated through the more casual channels of her well-trained publicity that Mr. Braceby, at the express bidding of her orphan asylum, was adopting a daughter. Broadway, craving ever her enormities, whispered that this daughter he was adopting had probably an old, biological right to her new legal title. And in the Fifth Avenue clubs which had refused complacently and patronizingly to accept Braceby's sudden and amazing virtue as other than a concealed viciousness, the smoky fumes of the Scotch highballs had it that the girl was neither daughter nor adopted daughter, but prospective wife, and perhaps even wife *de facto*.

"It is very possible," mused Braceby, when the ideas of these three great schools of conjecture were detailed to him, "it is more than possible that all these theorists may be wrong. It is impossible that more than one of them be right."

In the meantime, he thought he was profoundly happy. Only Cook, in her less sporadic duties, regretted the Egypt in which she had been accustomed so long to prepare flesh-pots. Diet was a point in the new father's careful preparation.

"This plain food will be good for my gout," he apologized one day when he had made a visit to the kitchen, "and besides, Annie, you're getting altogether too fat."

IV

HE called her Cherette. Her hair was indeed a crown and a halo to her face. It waved like an amber-tinted cloud over her forehead; it went in exquisite offsetting to the transparent texture of her cheeks. Far below her ears it fell, terminant in a delicate, pale down that accentuated the soft fulness of her neck, whose nape curved out. What one noticed first about Cherette was her hair. What one pitted against that first delight was her eyes. From their large, half-shut casements looked forth a different creature from that suggested by the rest of her.

Her hair was that of a child—exquisite, innocent, untrammeled in her youth's poesy, ignorant of any ugliness against which to struggle. Of such a flowering was also the lithe lightness of her body, its instinctive grace, the swift response of mouth and hand to the airy pulse of girlhood. Such was the sum of her every action: the craning of her neck, the unconscious bend of her waist, the curious habit of placing her long, nerveless hands upon her boyish hips, the sudden kicking-out and crossing of her little slippered feet as she sat in her rocking-chair and laughed and sparkled. But to all these fair tokens her eyes were a discountenancing denial. Braceby, when he had first met her at the asylum, had noticed her hair and her laughter before he was struck with her eyes. Else he had never adopted her. His first impressions seemed to brand as ridiculous the vague feeling which came later that the child knew more than he did and that she was more likely to be his master than his pliant charge.

Perhaps it was a sub-conscious impulse of self-concealment that caused Cherette forever to hold her eyes half-shut and to let her girlish tresses fall on her forehead in such a manner as to shield her eyes from a too unhampered scrutiny. Her pupils were a light, piercing blue, curiously near in nuance to the blueish white about them. And they peered forth from long, dark lashes with the wisdom of a second life. They gave the suggestion of disillusioned, compelling womanhood. However gayly they seemed to laugh, however bitterly to weep (although that was strangely seldom), the soul behind them seemed eternally aloof from these natural effusions, and too worldly wise in any way to be a part of them.

In the actions of Cherette, however, there was no slightest reinforcement to the canny look of her eyes. She was a child in every word of her mouth, in every creation of her mind, even as in every movement of her body. The crass, seasoned creature that peered forth from this gentle frame seemed inarticulate and independent of the actual, living girl. So Braceby forgot promptly that he had ever been impressed by its existence. Indeed, it would have required a mystic to remain aware of it, longer than a moment, in the face of her confuting presence. And Braceby was only a repentant bachelor, blindly adoring before the mystery of girlhood, bathed in a flush of Spring after too long consorting in a hot-house.

Braceby's chief joy in his new duties lay in the feeling that this seductive child was beyond comprehension. His stubborn optimism impelled him to apply all virtues to this Unknown because of the sharp lessons of his life, which had taught him to apply all vices to what he understood. Five hundred years ago Braceby might have burned his instinctive incense to the Unknown. As it was, a luxurious estate became his monk's-cell, and Cherette became his goddess. Each age has its own technique for the expression of the music of all the ages. Braceby would not have appreciated his analogy with Saint Simeon Stylites. But then, the ascetic who worshiped God on a pillar would not have liked the imputation that he, too, was a mere human animal, feeding his senses a sharp ration of the Unknown because they were not content with more obvious fodder. Simeon, in his sensual disgust, became a saint. Braceby, in his, became a father. Both conditions, in man, are secondary states. One can attain to neither without having been first a lover.

It was not long before Cherette had become attached to her protector. The situation between the pair took on the fresh, airy nature of its setting. Braceby was guilty of no far-fetched trope when he said that his heart was as new and as green as the lawn about his country-house. What time the slender, tall girl was not busied with her various masters, who came daily from town to teach her the amplified "three R's" of culture, she spent with

Braceby. They took long walks, reaching far out from his estate. They went on smashing gallops after a few lessons had made of Cherette an efficient Amazon and Braceby had become relimbered of muscle. And evenings, they would sit on the porch and she would chatter, or in the glow of the living-room's real log-fire, and he would read aloud.

They read "The Idylls of the King," and Cherette was in love with Guinevere and bored by Arthur. They read an expurgated "Gulliver's Travels," and when the girl learned that the tale she had read was but a part of the tale Swift had written, she was disconsolate and her favorite book became the object of her anger. Braceby tried Scott, but the child buried her head in the rug and fell asleep while the blaze of the logs turned her hair to liquid bronze. Then, he resorted to "Paul and Virginia," but Cherette was disgusted and refused to listen. The Indian romances of Chateaubriand fared no better.

"I don't like stories," she said, one day. "They're so slow. I could make 'em up much faster. Besides, so many words one right after another sound ugly."

Musically, the child was exceptionally promising. She had already had five years' instruction on the piano when Braceby adopted her. And to a swift facility in technic, she soon added a joyousness of interpretation which made her an adept in the lighter, more brilliant manner. Her teacher, eager for quick results, realized her penchant and versed her in the modern French and Italian schools to the neglect of the nobler Germans. At this, Braceby was, if anything, rejoiced; Brahms and Schumann and Beethoven had always seemed to him the mere necessary *impedimenta* of boring musical afternoons. The only really great composer for whom Cherette had active sympathy was Bach—the most cruel, the most unsentimental, perhaps the most eternal of them all. By the same token, she despised Mozart, even as she thought "silly" the Madonna of Raphael that had hung over her bed and which she had caused to be removed. She might have become attached to Wagner if her instructor had given her more than "Lohengrin" and "Tannhäuser" to know him by. But the unerring instinct of the girl caught the cloying effusiveness, the blatant Teutonism of these operas and unstintingly condemned them. Sentimental music of a sort she liked—the sort that was really cold and heartless underneath. Mendelssohn and Massenet, whose sweetness is that of a deep, feminine, uncritical nature, she did not love. But the false surface-sentiment of Puccini, with its basis of bitter cynicism, attracted her; the delicate, metallic coldness of Debussy she portrayed with an exquisite although of course unconscious sympathy. And Grieg, that sensual pessimist with the soul of a stage necromancer and the hand of a dandy, was for a long time her favorite.

To a musician, these tastes would have served to bare her soul—and annotate her eyes. To Braceby, they were mere tastes, signifying nothing. For to Braceby, music was the mere pleasurable pelting of sound on ears. To how many professional musicians, in good sooth, is it anything more? If folk knew better the meaning of the music they instinctively prefer they would be more chary of confession. But, then, if folk knew the meaning of the features on their faces, we should all wear masks. Life and Ignorance-of-Life were created at the same instant. Had the birth of the latter been delayed one moment, it would have sufficed for Knowledge to snuff out the former.

And so, in this gentle haze of illusion, a blissful year passed for Thomas Braceby. In both, there was the gleam of a newly discovered youth—in the young girl as in the man. And against the lying texture of their so different, yet so pathetically like illusions, glowed the deepest of truths—the resurgent impulse of life to feed rather on dreams than upon facts; to spin webs of fancy rather than unravel knots of actuality. Life knows, in its workings, how to transcend the tawdry confines to which Reason would hold it. Cherette, in her childish conviction that the world was a joyous theater fashioned and centered for her dalliance, might be mistaken; Braceby in his belief that Cherette was all that his suppressed and atrophied idealism conjured up, might be mistaken. In the essence both were right—both lived truly. And the stuff of their dreamings was more eternal than all those paltry marks of mind and body which men call truths and scientists set up as their exclusive idols. Unfortunately, these diaphanous webs were not to preserve.

V

CHERETTE was now seventeen. And Braceby had become "Daddie." Indeed, they were chums, and the guardian was the docile member of the fraternity. He went even so far as to take lessons with her. He crammed his recalcitrant mind with dry pages of history and abstruse algebraic formulae in order to sustain himself at her level. Even such of his acts as had no immediate bearing on her own were colored and tempered by her presence. Thus, he tightened his friendship with all the matrons that he knew in the city and dropped totally from heterodox companionship, even as he had ceased entertaining thoughts and theories at variance with the salubrious bringing-up of his charge.

For two years, he had gone to no theaters, save at matinées. Cherette loved the theater—indiscriminately. The sheer joy of performance and illusion sufficed her. She sat ecstasied before the garish carpentries of a musical comedy; and she sat ecstasied at a great actor's rendition of Hamlet. For opera, however, she did not care. The music she loved, per-haps—in musical form. But to such spectacles as those of pot-bellied tenors amorous before obese sopranos, who rent the air with their lung power while in the last throes of consumption, she could not bring her suffrage. Her sense of the ludicrous was too poignant. And her instinc-tive demand for simplicity—in dress, in speech, in art—prevailed against this bastard commodity under cover of which so much divine music is palmed off upon a jaded public. Since moreover, Braceby was not in advance with a command that she should love this and disdain that, her judgments came honestly and with a reason.

Save for such expeditions to the city in search of plays and concerts, the pair kept strictly to themselves on the Westchester estate. Their summer trips were curtailed to a single month. Cherette preferred her home to the hotels and her Daddie to the slightly ironic kindness of the persons she met in them. She had no longing, whatsoever, for the companionship of girls of her own age. She felt herself older and wiser than these daintily garnished dolls. And the callow, slack-chinned youths who dawdled in the wake of them and were only too eager to transfer their rudimentary dandyism from the dolls to herself, inspired her with a withering contempt. They were silly; the little girls were silly; their severe mothers were silly; the hotels were silly. Cherette preferred her Daddie. And Braceby preferred Cherette.

It was a ruddy morning of new Autumn. The eager pair were off early for a ramble in those flushed hills whose depths have been scarce discovered by New Yorkers. There was one spot to which they had frequently gone in the past year—a spot thickly garlanded in aspen, where generations of foliage had spread a gentle carpet of moss and underbrush. It was away from the by-path, and so tightly tucked in from the more open woods that a faithful people would have deemed it the retreat of some seclusive god. The materialistic Cherette called it her Bird-cage.

Braceby seated himself carefully on a rock and Cherette flung herself flat upon the ground, burying her sharp, fine nose in the soil, and tossing her heels. The love-song came down to her from a dozen nests. The Bird-cage seemed to be as thick with birds as it was with trees. In the back of her head, she felt the powerful caress of the cold, clear heaven as it shone through the lacing of green and brown. She did not see it, but it was as real a part of her mental picture as the little red ant before her, struggling over its infinitesimal hills and dales and carrying a wisp of straw three times as large as itself. The sibilant brush of leaves against the air, the musical give of slender trees and the suffused minor murmur of all the feverish, innumerable world that buzzed and chirped and breathed in the wind-driven grass, conjoined into one subtle harmony and drenched the girl with a strange, delicious pain. Her heels ceased their tossing, as if wearied by some invisible resistance; her head sank to one side upon the moss and her eyes closed.

Through her thin dress, Cherette felt the sharp embrace of the earth upon her little, eager breasts and instinctively she huddled closer. A languor crept through her limbs and she stretched them out, aware that they too were hard—almost brutally hard—against that mysterious earth. Two slight twinges went out from her temples and met in a warm, seductive agony that quickened breath and benumbed thought. And so she lay, her hands clasped before her, her body tense and prone, her eyes burning against her lids. The blue of the sky shot through and merged with the warm, vital harmony of the birds and the Autumn-painted verdure. And to melt it rose a warm perfume—the soul of the earth—stinging her flesh to a new consciousness and quickening her senses until they lay quivering and receptive within the alluring notes of the woodland.

At first, it all seemed strange and Cherette was but half helpless before its ecstasy. But gradually, the myriad chants of the forest took on a more accustomed guise and became distinct; the girl's senses grew used to the sharp delights that were possessing them. Her mind bathed in the flood of feeling and became drenched, at one with it. The vital potency of Nature—ever most resurgent in Autumn when it is about to die—now merged her totally, soaking this young life with its eternal liquors until she became a vivid part. And when that moment came, Cherette was asleep—asleep in the world-rhythm which the leaves might whisper and the birds might chant, but which she was still too young to swing to, waking.

On the rock sat Thomas Braceby—and looked at the still, lithe figure and wondered and looked again. He was no longer a young man. There was grey in his hair and two thin creases forked out from beside his nose, tokens of long years of pressing his lips in resolution and shutting his eyes in pain or meditation. But of a sudden, all the weighing consciousness of age went from him, like a mist against the sun. And there came out, unveiled, a gleam of landscape which was new in his sight and glistening as if with dawn. Braceby had never had a youth. His life had been one endless missing it—all save the last two years whose color had been that of resignation. And now, blindingly alive for its unnatural long wait, and the more blindingly so for the drab mental field upon which it burst—a field of regret without an object and of submission without past pride—came this pent-up Spring with the Autumn chill and made the man possessed.

Braceby rose and stepped lightly—it was the tread of a boy—to the side of the sleeping girl. Gently, he touched her hair. Gently, he held his breath to consonance with hers; gently, he gazed at the sun-kissed down on her neck, at the curve of her back that withdrew within the wide-sashed, supple waistline. And as he pastured, the gentleness was swept up—not lost—in a new flood of fever that resembled the scarlet splashing in the trees, even as the softer impulse seemed mothered by the croon of branches and the slow slant of the sky above him.

Braceby clutched himself and regained his seat. In all ways, his passion was that of youth—even to the extent that he was unaware of it. Nature had caught him up in her interminable whirlwind, wrenched him from the flat strand of misadventure in which twenty years had stationed him and blown him to the tropic stronghold of her dominion; yet he sat serenely ignorant, as heedless of where he had been rocked as was Cherette, in her dreamless sleep, of the rhythm which had mastered her.

Braceby's love had devoured every fibre of his personality before Braceby became conscious that he was in love at all. Storm clouds become saturate before they burst. And to render this driving tempest, with its years of repression and its years of preparation, still more formidable, there came the need in its bursting to catch it up and hide it, lest one drop or flash of it fall upon the sunny object over which it was foregathered. Braceby tasted the essence of struggle in his need—once he was conscious—of keeping this new truth from the playful, heedless child he had made his daughter. Can you imagine a black cloud, bristling with lightning, bulging with thunder, bursting with rain, swung by a naughty god over a sun-bathed hamlet and there rent asunder? And can you imagine what Titanic force it would require to muffle up that thunder, to drown that fire, and to snatch away that deluge ere it had reached the hamlet in its terrific downward charge? As such a gentle, budding life, the sentimental Braceby looked upon Cherette; and as such a devastating cloudburst, Braceby looked upon his love for her. He had not grown aware of it until the moment of its breaking-out. And now his passionate need was to catch up this blight, to swerve it, to hide it, to annihilate it. Cherette must not only never hear; she must not even guess. The rift of a single fibre in her mind away from him would lose her altogether. And at the thought of such an end, the poor old fellow's temples beat like hammers.

Meantime, life went on. Cherette grew blithely toward womanhood and Braceby assumed his martyrdom with an ironic smile and a calm tendency to moralize that his high-spirited ward took as the concomitant of a completed life and as a text for her own sharp-aimed cajoleries. What made most unbearable Braceby's passion to kiss her mouth was the freedom he had to kiss her cheeks. This point was symbolic of his torture. Three years of comradeship had endeared him to Cherette. She loved him; it was her only love. And in a thousand pretty ways she showed it; it was her one field of nonmusical demonstrativeness. She did not weary, even at eighteen, of her Daddie's knee and of the fond teasings which she knew how to direct against his composure while she was seated on his lap, her bare arms about his neck. And while she played and fondled, incarnate gaiety, poor Braceby was forever warding off his autumnal passion; constrained to sit still and act the father while every nerve in his body cried for crushing her in his arms and burning her against his lips.

The usage of romantic writers notwithstanding, all things have two sides—even emotions and even the emotion of love. Braceby adored Cherette, but he also hated her. His hate was the respite and the revenge of his starved passion. And it made his life still more insufferable. A mute, blind resentment surged, at times, against the innocent subject of his agony and the innocent object of his love. Tortured nature, its own victim, gave sinister voice to the right of hunger and the need of escape. If Braceby lay burning in his bed, battling the need to pour out his heart and to overwhelm with a life's tenderness the young, delicious creature who lay in the adjoining room, he had also to repress the will to be rid of his cross and to crush out what his tenderness dared not absorb.

VI

THEY went walking one day.

"Daddie," said Cherette, close to him and looking directly up into his eyes, "why don't you want to go to the Birdcage any more? We've not been there since last year."

Braceby pushed forward the blue bonnet which had fallen over her back. His fingers caressed her hair and his lips smiled. For the first time the girl caught a tinge of pathos beneath his gentleness.

"Why, Daddie!" she said and stopped.

Braceby took her upturned face in his hands and bent down for a kiss. He felt that he was not going to kiss her cheek—or her forehead. It was so easy; her lips were so near. And a youthful smile played so protectingly upon them. It would be safe—a quick kiss. That smile of childhood would ward off his passion and her response. He might even find solace in her cool taking of his embrace—a cure, indeed. Had he not perhaps whipped his craving with this too Quixotic denial? A sip sometimes quenches thirst which in parched abstinence seems insatiate. After all, what poison could be gleaned from this chaste fount? Was she not his daughter? Bah! His passion was the fever of starvation. With the taste he had all claims to, it would fade to a mere righteous fondness. On, then—to spite this gnawing, fearful hunger with a nibble. He put forth his lips. And then, their eyes met, really.

If there is a Heaven for heroic deeds—if Braceby's life up to that moment had been composed of whinings and betrayals—for that moment, that Heaven would have been assured him.

"Let's visit the Bird-cage."

They trudged on. His lips had touched her forehead and from her, somehow, managed to glean a smile. That it was a passable smile, Cherette proved amply by her prompt forgetting that she had, a moment before, been vaguely conscious of its faintness. The last lap toward their embowered goal they traversed running—Cherette in the fore, singing and leaping and laughing, and Braceby after, puffing and grim—a sad, autumnal man!

But there was sure to be an end—the most natural of all ends. Braceby, in mortal conflict for all these harsh years, with this fresh birth of Spring in his sclerotic arteries, was to fall finally into the master delusion that he was still as young as his passion—that the folly of youth was identical with youth itself. The persuasion of the blood had been accomplished so gradually and so insidiously that he was scarcely aware of its stages. At forty he had dismissed his youth; at forty-five he had said good-bye to women; now, at the brink of fifty, he was suddenly consumed by a boundless love for this girl of nineteen. The period of mocking struggle which had preceded was gone from his consciousness as the *Sturm und Drang* fades in a young man's mind before the vision of his inamorata. He remembered the reasons which had plunged him into war against love, but he saw them now as dead and empty, and he forgot their force and appositeness in the fever of his new passion.

But until such time as he should tell all, Braceby decided to continue in the fatherly rôle of the past four years. And having put a term to the part which had caused him such unutterable suffering, the pain of keeping it went out and so pleasurable did it become in the anticipation of being free of it that he almost swerved in his resolve. He learned quickly, however, in that vague wavering, that the old state was dependent for its pleasantness upon his knowledge that it was a doomed state. So his decision to speak returned to stay.

The day he had long set for his hazardous proposal was that of his fiftieth anniversary. A desire to clinch his youth at the half-century mark was behind this choice, although Braceby was unaware of it. In his mind the resolution had been a sentimental one—the bestowal upon himself of a gift worthy of what he deemed his real advent into life. The dramatic relevance of the date attracted him, although he did not realize of what deep stuff the drama was. To him, it seemed a point in romantic comedy—an apposite first act. To the gods, it may have appeared otherwise. But Braceby was thoughtless of any otherwise. And his heedlessness was the strongest triumph of his will. He had fixed a date for his proposal because he knew that he would never rise to the climax unless he thus compelled it with a dogmatic impulse. And if he had thus chosen a day of conventional rejoicing in which to cast his die, it was to preclude any sneaking hint that there might perhaps be no cause for rejoicing after all. Braceby refused admittance to the thought of a refusal. And in his need for encouragement and for conviction, he did as men have always done— he buttressed up his resolution with a ritual, and he knocked down his doubtings with starvation.

Excitement on that climacteric morning had kept him wide-eyed in bed for several hours. And then had come a heavy, violent slumber, that seemed to grapple and possess him, and which, after appeasement of its passion, flung him to consciousness with the late morning sun hot upon his face. Braceby woke with the blood surging in his body and his head cool and clear. All the time of that pulsing sleep he had been preparing and enacting a dream. And when, at last, he was hurled back into consciousness, it was upon no middle station—no yawning, limb-stretching compromise between the trance of night and the labor of day. Nor was it with his mind bathed in the misgivings, half timid, half febrile, of the foregone evening. The brewings of that deep slumber had been both mental and physical. They had restored the steely quickness of youth to his body and engendered a defeat-ignoring confidence in his mind. Braceby jumped exultant from his covers. He stood long in the open window and allowed the May sun to pour its liquors of optimism upon his body. And then, he plunged into his icy bath. There had been a long and salutary way since that false surrender to old-age when Braceby had ordered his valet to leave closed the windows in his bedroom. A not too fastidious preparation followed, and now—he was on the stairs.

VII

CHERETTE was practicing in the living-room. The sun, glowing through the cretonne curtains of three French windows, advanced over the low-raftered chamber and touched her shoulders. She was clad in a light-blue jumper, caught in over her still boyish hips with a broad sash of a darker tint. The dress fell loosely from about her neck; and the sun beamed its last breath upon the slight disclosure of her back, whose curve it transformed into a gentle harmony of rose lights and blue shadings. The girl's fingers went over the keys with a faint suggestion of lingering longer than the *tempo* warranted. Her head was forward to one side and her eyes tilted up. In their distant gaze shone a sensuous satisfaction for the sun's caress, of which she was aware—subtly, amorously—as if it had been the worshipful glance of a lover. It is through such fair delusions as this—the dreaming of the sun's rays to be a wooer's eyes, the reading of a declaration into the low song of an evening glade—that girls prepare for their first love encounters and learn to take them with the canny knowledge that to men seems mystical.

Braceby stood on the landing and watched. Cherette looked up to him and smiled. "Good morning, Daddie." She stopped to rise.

"Finish your piece," said Braceby.

Cherette went on, tossing her head with the sustained *Andante*. It was a different playing, now: the vivid playing before an audience. And as Braceby stood there, listening, he understood the luxurious completeness of this girl in her own life, the ease with which, in four years' space, she had absorbed all of his thoughts and all of his surroundings, and, with youth's direct assurance, made them singly and ineradicably hers. In her acts and in her air there seemed no memory of a time prior to her being here. The house and all that was within it, he and all that surged within him, had accepted her and become stamped with her. With what tacit grace she had moulded his world and attuned it to herself. How insidiously it had become a whole of which she was the heart; how perfectly her spirit had shot him through, in his present and in his past. Verily, it was as if she had been there, all of his days; and as if days had not been her measure. And now, at length, this harmony was to reach consummation. The last reserve, the last holding-off, was to be effaced. The deluded man swam in ecstasy. All of his soul had grown contiguous to this little, playing stranger. The very chairs gave forth the incense of her presence; and the trees that stooped over the wide piazza were murmurous, through the open casements, of the sweet, troubled years of their communion. It was a compelling rhythm.

The breakfast table was cleared; Cook and the man-servant had caught a train upon Braceby's gift of a day off. The couple sat by the fireplace and Braceby gleaned comfort from the silent room. He had managed with no difficulty to keep the date of his birthday a secret. They were going to lunch in the city. And now Cherette sat ensconced in her high-backed chair, kicking the cushion below her feet, toying with her necklace of tiny pearls.

Braceby invited her to a quiet talk. Nor was Cherette loth. Such talks, however serious at their outset, were always jolly. She had a way of swerving them to express and to attain what new fancy happened to possess her fancy-ridden heart. At the end of the hour the girl had coaxed the promise that they were to lunch at a particularly fashionable restaurant for which Cherette had an evil predilection and which Braceby sought to avoid, like all his former haunts. And that was all. No word of the proposal. And a third of the appointed day was over.

They sat in the open car and watched the monotonous landscape whip past them. Braceby reasoned that the task was not a morning's one. Something in the crisp, Spring-suffused air seemed to hint a rebuke to his resolution. There was an advantage in star-drenched darkness. The sun seemed ironical, that day: a stubborn ally to the old order against the new.

It was a sumptuous luncheon—since Braceby ordered it. And it was followed by a visit to the Bronx Zoo. Cherette loved wild animals, even as she had a contempt for domestic ones. She welled a secret strain of sentiment from the sight of caged lions and space-tortured elephants. And

Braceby followed, mournfully hugging his endeavor, watching the sun sink under a bank of violet-green trees and welcoming the long shadows on the sylvan walks. And so another third was gone of the appointed day. Braceby asserted his authority in order to avoid dining in town and they had a cozy late feast in their home.

And now, they were on their porch and the night was in league with Braceby, even as had been the day against him. Throughout the entire wracking trip the man had sensed a conflict. Despite himself and his convictions, he could not but feel that if the serene light of the May sun was against him—and the strained conventionalism of the restaurant, and the subtle crowd-instinct of the park—they had been in favor of Cherette. And still, what he was about to do was not against his charge. Whence came this seeming antagonism, this pitting of interests against each other? Braceby could not grasp the source, so he dismissed the fact. There was no such conflict. What he was about to ask was for Cherette as well as for himself....

"Cherette, I wonder if you know how I love you," he said, his voice atremble.

The girl's smile came to him, suffused with the night.

"Of course I do, Daddie."

"Do you love to call me Daddie?"

"Why, what else could I call you?"

He took her hand and kissed it—a moment too long. For Cherette withdrew it. It was the pinch of resistance necessary to compound his passion and send it plunging toward its goal, with the power of a pent-up life load, seeking its level. Braceby was to his feet and the shoulders of the girl he loved were between his hands.

"Look here," he cried, "there is something else you could call me. ... Oh, don't you understand, Cherette? Dear little, adored Cherette. I love you—I love you."

There was a pause. A dry branch cracked from a distant tree and fell dead to the brush. The rustle of its fall was caught up in a myriad symphony of forest-life—a minute veil of sound shot through with the glowing pall of the receding woodland. And above it, rose the hot breathing of Thomas Braceby. He pressed her thin shoulders as in a vice. He refused to look down at the bewildered, canny eyes that were prepared to pierce him with their infernal irony; he wet his lips and he dashed on. And as he talked, the slowness and the measure of his words amazed the passion of his heart.

"Cherette, my darling. It hurts me—for years, it has hurt me to hear you call me *that*. It has been torture. At first it was well. That was how I loved you then. But when I came to know you, it all changed suddenly, Cherette. And for long, I have loved you in a far deeper, far greater way. And now I can stand it no longer. I am not an old man, little girl. Never have I loved before—really, wholeheartedly—as I love you. Doesn't that make me young? What else is youth but that? See: we both stand at the same threshold—the first love. I have known women of all sorts—girls and those who were as if they never had been girls. But what have they given me? Bitterness! What have they taught me? Merely to appreciate you, to know how rare and how sublime this love is that I have for you. All else—it has but gone to prove how real, how enduring, how unbearably deep is my need of you."

He loosed her shoulders and his fists clenched in a moment's agony. And now, he bent more closely. "Is what I ask not natural? You will find me young; you will find me a real lover. For what else could you find me, since that is All—All I have become? Everything in my life that is not you has died away. I am re-awakened; no—for the first time, I am awake. I stand on a threshold. Let me in, Cherette. Say that you love me. Say that you understand."

But again there was silence. A bird carolled in the gloom and a motor went slashing through the stillness on the distant Post-road. Braceby sank down before her. His knees were not stiff and he was reckless of a damp floor. Above all, he feared this silence. It seemed to scathe and cut and there was a smile within it, as if it had been a human face. He feared to look up, lest he should find that it was the face of Cherette that had a smile. He went on, more measured of voice, more quaking of soul.

"Cherette, don't give me your answer now, if you don't care to. Above all, don't say No. If you could only feel what your Yes would mean to me! And I can make you happy—happier, beloved. Otherwise, you would have to leave me, some day. You would find that you were not completely happy; that there was something lacking—another sort of love. Give me that! Let me give you that. Oh, if you knew what it was like, after so long a wait, to find one's desire so near and not to dare to grasp it. You are so perfect, so beautiful! And all I have—beside the grosser things—is this love, strong for a lifetime of preparation. It will transform all, Cherette, even as it has transfigured me. Give me a chance. Become my wife!"

He held her knees in his palsied hands. His tears stained her dress. His mouth begged her hands. He loved her. And the bird ceased its gossip. And the sibilant live things of the forest were murmurously still.

Cherette jumped from her chair; violently so that her knee struck Braceby's lip and made it bleed.

"You old fool!" she said, standing over him.

He saw her eyes. They were laughing. They were very old and very sharp. They seemed to curl up within themselves and from their immemorial retreat to dart forth a biting harmony of frost and flame. They had nothing to do with Cherette. It seemed they, rather than she, that spoke.

"Why—you're old enough to be my father. For all I know, and for all you know—" Braceby felt what was coming—felt it in the pervasive cut of pain that went through his body. And he trembled to avert it. He was helpless. The words were uttered. "—for all you know, and for all I know, you may *be* my father."

VIII

CHERETTE was gone. All that was left was a certain light, world-withering laugh that never had been uttered. Yet, that was all that was to stay. And that was never to be gone.

Braceby raved in his mind and writhed in his body. He wanted to protest; he wanted to cry out; he wanted to be taken back as a father. He caressed the name of "Daddie." He spat out at his fatal burst of madness which, surging over the flood-dykes, had in the moment of its ecstatic triumph sunk to nothingness on the farther side of the world. A thousand pleas and a thousand resolutions played havoc in his heart. And no sign came forth from all the bitter, inner seething.

An hour later, he found himself still kneeling on the lone verandah. His knees were stiff with aching; and the floor was soaked with the damp gall of the night.

He rose and crawled into his bed.

And the windows in his room stayed shut.

THE TREASURE

C. Y. Harrison

GLANCING about him, but still running rapidly he rounded the corner at full speed. He paused for a moment and then ran to the outskirts of the town. He stopped and took stock of himself. Terror was outlined on every feature of his face. Night had fallen and the trees cast hideous and fearsome shadows.

"I must get there before anyone discovers it," he thought. Looking around again, he fancied that he saw something dart behind that big black rock. Who could it be? Someone was following him! His heart beat more rapidly at every passing moment. His body quivered. Inwardly he wished he had not acted so rashly in burying it in a spot where anybody might discover it by accident.

Yes, he would walk on very slowly, so that no one might suspect him. One must use discretion in a matter of this nature!

He walked until he reached the border of a clump of trees and bushes. He took a final glance about him and entered the woods.

Ah! now for the end of this confounded affair. Yes! there is the spot over there by that big moss-covered tree.

He fell to digging feverishly, and at last he struck it. At last, with a joyful bark, he seized the bone, and ran off with his tail wagging.

THE SENTIMENTALIST

Sara Teasdale

S HE had taught for seven years in a boarding-school for girls, and though she was not always patient, half of the pupils adored her. She watched their worship with an amused reserve that baffled them; and in spite of her sense of humor they thought her romantic—perhaps because her parents were dead and because she wrote short stories. The back numbers of the magazines that held her work were soiled with much treasuring. They had passed from generation to generation of school girls, but the delicate intensity of the tales looked to an older audience for appreciation.

One morning while she was dressing, she noticed three white hairs. She felt that they had come too soon—she was twenty-eight—and they made her a little bitter. After that, she saw them every time she arranged her hair.

It was some months later that she learned of a small fortune, her inheritance from a great-uncle. The news was as a sudden coming of spring to her. In the girls' eyes she was beautiful that day; life was waiting for her. She handed in her resignation for the fall term, and at night, when she met one of the girls in the dark corridor, she kissed her. It was a wonderful kiss—the girl never forgot it.

By autumn she had arranged her affairs and was settled in a small apartment in New York. Her short stories brought her friends, and both the men and the women liked her. She liked them equally, though she felt more at her ease with the women—she had known very few men in her life.

It was at the house of one of her new friends that she met a poet whose work she had always disliked, though it had a certain fascination for her. His poems were cold and hard, with sudden touches of an almost cruel sensuality that made her think of a glowing coal cast into a bowl of ice. She saw him talking with the hostess before he entered the room. Neither his face nor his manner pleased her, and it seemed to her that in an unusual degree the man and his work were one. She was watching him intently when he turned, and across the intervening space, filled with men and women and the sound of voices, their eyes met. A feeling of resentment that he should have divined her glance made her join hastily in the conversation of those near her. But she was deeply conscious of his presence, which seemed to pervade the room, and to call to her almost audibly. When he was presented to her at last, she felt that love was in her eyes, and she blushed. He enjoyed the blush and sat beside her. They talked of his poetry, and moment by moment she asked herself why she loved him. It was characteristic of her that she immediately acknowledged this love to herself, and characteristic of him that he knew of her love as soon as she felt it. She wanted to like his voice, but she found it monotonous and unsympathetic—the voice of a man who has given little to life, and who has ceased to expect much in return.

Intense women pleased him, and he asked if he might take her home. The hostess whispered, as she helped her on with her cloak, that he had never done such a thing before and that he seldom went any place. She blushed again, and the hostess kissed her. He had already made her like a child, yet she realized that he took her home because she loved him—not because he loved her.

That night she read his latest book of poems through before she went to bed. She did not like them any better than before. They should have been bound in black and scarlet, she thought, When she finished them she looked into the mirror for a long time, trying to see herself with his eyes. She was sorry that her hair was not "red gold." He must like that color since he had used it so much in his poems.

After that he came to see her once a week with chilling regularity, and sometimes took her to dinner or to the theater. The week revolved around the day when he came. Everything in her life existed for the few hours when she was with him. Sometimes he sent her a note or two between his visits. They came often enough to make her always impatient for the postman.

One day in late March they took a long walk together in the park. The branches under the cold sky were feathery with the promise of new leaves. It was dusk and the lights were lit. Standing on the Belvedere overlooking the reservoir, they could trace the walks and roadways by their lamps like bordering chains of amber. He was less somber than usual, for the first warm day had brought back the ghost of his youth and made him gently sentimental. He told her that he was forty-one. He thought that she would be surprised, and was piqued when she said simply, "You are twelve years older than I am." She had thought him as old as that. Nothing that he had ever told her about himself surprised her. He had an uncomfortable feeling that she knew all of his weak points. She was too honest to flatter him, and he never had from her the boundless admiration that he craved. He was silent for a while, but the contrast of her fair skin and dark hair pleased him, as they always did, and he took her hand. Before she could draw it away, he felt a shiver run through her.

She had planned to go to Europe in the summer, but she let the weeks go by without engaging her passage, and ended by leaving the city for only a fortnight at the seashore. The fall and winter that followed were so much like the ones before that she sometimes wondered if the year had not slipped back. She tried to become interested in charity, and he listened with a bored politeness to her talk of Christmas trees and Christmas dinners.

In the spring, just as in the year before, a little wave of sentiment swept over him. He wrote verses to her, and even took the trouble to evolve a sonnet or two. But they never rang true, and the occasional touch of sensuality was so false a note that it hurt her. She knew that there was no passion in him. The battle between them was pitifully unequal, and when the little wave ebbed away again, his visits became evenly spaced as before.

In June she bought a small cottage at Ardeen in the Catskills. She wanted to be away from him—but not so far away as Europe. The voyage was postponed for still another year. With a methodical regularity he wrote to her twice a week, and when the letters came a tremulous happiness made her long to be friends with every living thing that she saw. The rest of the week existed only to bring the letter-days nearer. In spite of his lack of humor, he could talk well, if he were in a good mood, but his letters were uniformly brief and commonplace. They were like his stiff, regular handwriting.

When she came back to the city in September, he was at the station to meet her. She had not expected him, and when she saw him coming toward her in the crowd, a thrill of pain shot through her to the tips of her fingers. He took her hand and felt that it was cold through the thin summer glove. She found him looking at her critically. He was relieved to see that she loved him as much as ever. Her letters had been so light and whimsical that he had wondered if she might not have changed. He put her into a cab to drive home alone. She waited impatiently for her trunk, and when it came she took from it the package of love-letters that she had written to him during the summer. She had never meant to have him read them. It was a little device to make the other letters easier for her. His look when he met her made her want to destroy them, and she put them on the ashes in the grate, and watched them smoke and blacken. It was the first autumn fire.

The monotonous weeks began revolving again around his visits. It was two years since she had met him, and she asked herself if this was the life that had waited for her. He came sometimes wet with rain and sometimes powdered with snow, and when three hours had passed he went out into the rain or into the snow, without a regret at leaving her. At Christmas the usual package of books came. Each one bore the greeting that he had written in his gifts of the years before. His way of repeating the same action week after week and year after year was maddening to her. She wondered what he had been fifteen years before. Had passion always been for him only a subject for art, a thing of his brain?

They walked together in the park when the days grew warmer at last. She would have been glad to escape the spring, but the seasons are piti-less and full of memories. One of their walks in the silvery May twilight brought them again to the Belvedere. In the great buildings that loomed far away over the trees, windows were lighted here and there. She saw them—the buildings were full of homes. He was absently watching the park lights change from amber to white as it grew darker. Neither of them spoke. When he turned toward her from the long chain of lights, he saw that she was crying without making a sound. A little wave of tenderness made him take her in his arms. He kissed her and his face was wet with her tears. Her mouth was convulsed with weeping. He half regretted that, and yet it made the sensation more novel. He kissed her again and again. She grew quiet, and he took off her glove and kissed the palm of her hand. It was damp against his lips. Suddenly she drew away from him and ran into the twilight. He hurried after her and took her arm, trying to speak to her as a lover would speak. But he saw that he failed. She seemed scarcely able to stand, but she walked on, looking straight before her and never speaking—not even when he left her at the door.

When she found herself in her room, she sat down on the bed to draw off her glove. She looked for a second at the palm of her hand, and then she laid it against her lips. It was a long time that she sat there. After several hours had passed, the tumult of her thoughts receded, leaving one voice that had the insistence of a cry. She felt that life was possible to her only on one condition. At last she got up, turned on the light and found pencil and paper. She did not know what she was going to write, but after the first sentence there was no hesitation, and she wrote rapidly: "You know that I love you. Tomorrow morning I am going to my cottage at Ardeen on the early train. Come to me there. You need not stay long— only come to me. You will not have this letter until after I have gone, but you can take the second train. You will come—for a little while." She put the paper into the envelope, stamped it, sealed it, and directed it to him. Then she looked for her hat and jacket to take the letter to the post box. They were still on. She had not taken them off since she left him.

✳✳✳

A boy carried her suit-case from the station at Ardeen to the cottage, and when they reached it, the cold, dead air of the closed house made her feel faint. She tried to open the window while the boy laid a fire, but she had to ask him to help her. At her order he went to get some provisions, and left her alone. She sat down in the chair before the fire. When he came back, she tried to eat a piece of bread from the loaf that he brought, but though she had eaten nothing since noon the day before, she could not swallow a morsel. Everything in the house was exactly as she had left it except for a delicate coating of dust. In a vase were sprays of withered wild asters that she had forgotten in the fall. She looked up at the shelf where the clock had stood idly during all the winter. It had stopped at a ridiculous hour. She wound and set it, and it began to tick. She sat down again. The light fire had gone out. She watched the clock so closely that she could see the minute-hand move with little jerks. She was shivering, and she remembered a shawl that she had left in the cottage. It was in the bedroom. She went to the door and opened it a little way—then suddenly she turned as though she could not enter it, and came back to the black hearth.

***

Like the swinging of a sword in the air, she heard the whistle of the train that had left the city at ten o'clock. She went to the window, though she knew it would take him twenty minutes to walk from the station. A feeling of terror took her. She could scarcely stand, and she went back to the chair. She put her hands over her eyes so that she would not look towards the window. Her heart was beating madly—the throbs were like blows. She counted the ticks of the clock. They grew louder and louder until she felt that they were deafening her. By their terrible insistence they seemed to be measuring eternity. She felt that she had been counting them forever.

There was a step on the veranda—the heavy, hurried step of a man. She reached the door and opened it. An overgrown boy stood there with a telegram. It read:

"Sorry cannot accept your invitation. Sailing for Europe next week."

I'M A STRANGER HERE MYSELF

Sinclair Lewis

TRAVEL broadens the mind. It also quickens the sympathies and bestows on one a ready fund of knowledge. And it is useful to talk about when you get back home.

The Johnsons have now been broadened and quickened. The signature "J. Johnson & Wife," followed by Northernapolis, G. C.," appears in hotel registers from Florida to Maine. "G. C.," of course, stands for their state, the state with the highest bank-deposits and moral standards of any in the Union—the grand old state of God's Country. Let me tell *you*, sir, whenever you meet a man from God's country, he's willing to tell you so. And does.

J. Johnson & Wife had raised their children and their mortgage, and had bought a small car and a large fireless cooker, when the catastrophe happened. Mrs. Johnson was defeated for the presidency of the Wednesday and Chautauqua Reading Circle by a designing woman who had talked herself into office on the strength of having spent a winter at Pasadena, California, observing the West. Mrs. Johnson went home with her hat-brim low and her lips tight together, and announced to Mr. Johnson that they would travel, and be broadened and quickened.

Mr. Johnson meekly observed that it would be nice to explore the Florida Everglades, and to study business conditions in New York. So, in December, they left their eldest son in charge of the business, and started on an eight-months' tour of the Picturesque Resorts of Our Own Land. In fact, they were going to have an itinerary. Mrs. Johnson's second cousin, Bessie, had suggested the itinerary. Cousin Bessie had spent two weeks in Florida. She said it was all nonsense to go to places like Palm Beach and St. Augustine—just because rich snobs from New York went there was no reason why independent folks from God's Country, that did their own thinking, should waste their good money. So, with Cousin Bessie's help, Mrs. Johnson made out the following schedule of the beauty-spots of Florida:

Jacksonville, East. Palatka, South Daytona, North Tampa, West Miami, Sulphur Water, Jigger Mounds, Diamond Back Ridge, Flatwoods, New Iowa, New Dublin, New Cincinnati, and New New York.

It takes a lot of high-minded heroism to stick faithfully to an itinerary, what with having to catch trains at midnight and all, but with the negligible assistance of Mr. Johnson, Mrs. Johnson stuck to it, though they often had to do two towns in one day. And oh! the rewards in culture! It is true they didn't have time to stop and look for orange-groves or Seminoles or millionaires, but they often felt as though they could smell the odor of oranges wafted to them on the gay breezes, though that may perhaps have been due to fellow-tourists eating oranges and peanuts. Certainly they saw plenty of palms, and at Jacksonville, in the Boston Museum of Curiosities, Including the Biggest Fish Ever Killed, in Fierce Marine Battle, by Capt. Pedro O'Toole, the Johnsons beheld a real live alligator.

After the trials and weariness of their explorations, Mrs. Johnson permitted them to settle down for a six-weeks' rest at the Pennsylvania House, in New Chicago, the City Beautiful of the Southland.

New Chicago may not be as old as St. Augustine and these towns that make such claims about antiquity, and heaven only knows if Ponce de Leon really did find any Fountain of Youth at all, and New Chicago may not be filled with a lot of millionaires chasing around in these wheel-chairs and drinking brandy and horse's necks, but New Chicago is neighborly, that's what it is, neighborly. And homey. It was founded by Northern capital, just for tourists. If a gentleman wishes to wear comfy old clothes, he doesn't find some snob in white pants looking askance at him. And New Chicago is so beautiful, and all modern conveniences— none of these rattletrap houses that you find in some Southern cities. It has forty miles of pavement, and nineteen churches, and is in general as spick and span as Detroit or Minneapolis. Why, when you go along the streets, with the cozy boardinghouses, and the well-built private houses of frame, or of ornamental brick with fancy porches and bay-windows and colored glass over the front door, and these nice new two-story concrete bungalows, you can scarcely tell you aren't in a suburb of New York or Chicago, it's all so wide-awake and nicely fixed up and full of Northern hustle. And there's very little danger of being thrown into contact with these lazy, shiftless, native Florida crackers, just fishermen and farmers and common, uninteresting people that have never heard about economics or osteopathy or New Thought or any modern movements. Not but what New Chicago is very Southern and resorty, you understand, with its palms and poinsettias and all sorts of exotic plants and beauty in general.

There isn't any liquor or dancing to tempt the men-folks, and there is an educational Chautauqua every January, with the very best entertainers, and finally New Chicago has, by actual measurement, more lineal miles of rocking chairs and nice women gossiping and knitting than Ormond and Daytona put together.

At first Mr. Johnson made signs of objecting to the fact that nobody at New Chicago seemed to go fishing. But the hotel and Board of Trade literature convinced him that there was the best fishing in the South within easy reach, and so he settled down and got a good deal of pleasure out of planning to go fishing some day; in fact, went so far as to buy some hooks at the drug-store. He found some men from God's Country who were in the same line of business as himself, and they used to gather in the park and pitch quoits and talk about business conditions back home and have a perfectly hilarious time swapping jokes about Ford cars, and Mike and Pat, and Jakey and Ikey.

Mrs. Johnson also made many acquaintances, such nice, chatty, comfy people, who just took her in and told her about their grandchildren, and made her feel welcome right away.

You see, the minute you arrive at New Chicago, you go and register your name and address at the Board of Trade Building, and all the people from your state look you up immediately, and you have Wisconsin picnics, or Ohio card-parties, or New Hampshire parades, or Middle-West I. O. O. F. suppers. Almost every evening there is some jolly little state gathering in the parlor of one of the hotels, with recitations and songs—Gospel and humorous—and speeches about the state, if there are any lawyers present. Everybody has to do a stunt. Mrs. Johnson made such an impression at the God's Country Rustic Skule Party, when she got up and blushed and said, "I didn't know I was going to be called on for a piece, and I hadn't thought of anything to say, and after hearing all the nice speeches I guess I'll just say 'ditto'!" Mr. Johnson told her afterward that her stunt made the hit of the evening.

New Chicago was no less desirable from a standpoint of economy. For thirty-two dollars a week the Johnsons had three meals a day, nice, wholesome homey meals, with no French sauces and fancy fixin's, and a dainty room such as would, to quote the hotel prospectus, "appeal to the finest lady of the land, or most hardened tourist, with handsome Michigan Chippendale bureau, two chairs in each room, and bed to lull you to happy dreams, after day spent in the jolly sports of New Chicago, strictly under new management, new linen of fine quality to appeal to heart of most fastidious, bathroom on each floor, ice water cheerfully brought by neat and obliging attendants."

If you were one of these nervous, strenuous folks who felt that you had to have a lot of young people, why, there were several nice young people in town, though it is true that there was quite a large proportion of older people who had reached the point where they were able to get away from business in the winter-time. Still there were some girls who played the piano, and knew pencil and paper games, and they were the life of the knitting circle with their gay young chatter, especially Miss Nellie Slavens, the well-known Iowa professional reader, who scarcely looked a day over thirty, and was a college graduate, the South Dakota Dairy College. Then there was the clerk of Ocean Villa, right next door, such a sociable young man from Trenton, always in demand for parties, and looked so well in his West Palm Beach suit.

And if you wanted sports there were athletic exercises a-plenty, though there wasn't this crowd that show off their silk bathing-suits on the beach, and pay twenty-five dollars for an aeroplane ride, as they do at Palm Beach. Any bright day you could see eight or ten people in bathing at Rocky Shore. Almost every boarding house had a croquet ground, and three of them had tennis courts. The Mayberry sisters, Kittie and Jane, nice sensible girls of thirty or so, were often to be seen playing. And you could always get up a crowd and charter Dominick Segui's launch, when the engine was in repair, and have a trip down to the shell mound. So, you see, there was any amount of rational sport, and no need for anyone to go to these sporty places.

In short, the Johnsons found every day at New Chicago just one round of innocent pleasures. After a good, wholesome, hearty breakfast of oatmeal, steak, eggs, buckwheats, sausage, and coffee—none of these grits and corn-bread that they have the nerve to offer you for breakfast some places in the South—the Johnsons read the *Northernapolis Herald,* which they got from a live, hustling newsdealer from Minneapolis, and had so much enjoyment out of learning about the deaths and sicknesses and all back home, though it did hurt Mrs. Johnson to see how the new president of the Wednesday Reading Circle was letting it run down. Then they went over to the drug-store, run by a live, hustling Toledo man, and Mr. Johnson bought three Flor de Wheeling cigars, while Mrs. Johnson had a chocolate ice-cream soda and some souvenir post-cards. Then for the rest of the day they were free to walk, or talk, or just sit and be comfy on the porch of their hotel. And there was always such an interesting group of broad-gauged, conservative, liberal, wide-awake, homey, well-traveled folks on the porch to talk to.

For you who may not have been broadened and quickened, or had opportunities for elevating and informative talk, I will give an example of such a conversation as might have been heard on the porch of the Pennsylvania House at any time between seven-thirty A. M. and nine-thirty P. M., and I assure you it isn't a bit above the average run in New Chicago:

"Well, I see there's some new God's Country people come to town, Mr. Johnson—Willis M. Beaver and wife, from Monroe County. Staying at the Chateau Nebraska."

"Well, well! Why, I've met his brother at the state convention of the Order of Peaweevils. Funny, him being here, way off in the Sunny South, and me knowing his brother. World's pretty small, after all. But still, it certainly is a liberal education to travel."

"Oh, Mrs. Johnson, don't you want to come to our basket-weaving club? We make baskets out of these long pine needles, with rafia—"

Before Mrs. Johnson can answer her husband says, quick as a flash, with that ready wit of his, "Say, uh, Mrs. Bezuzus, I'm glad those pine needles are good for something anyway!"

"Ha, ha!" asserts Mr. Smith. "You said something there! Why, I'd rather have a West Virginia oak in my yard than all the pines and palms in Florida. Same with these early strawberries they talk so much about, not but what it's nice to write home to the folks that you're having strawberries this time of year, but I swear, we wouldn't feed 'em to hogs, up where I come from."

"You hit it right, Brother Smith." It is Dr. Bjones of Kansas speaking, and after Mrs. Bezuzus has suitably commented on the manners, garments, and social standing of some passing newlyweds, Dr. Bjones goes on in his forcible scientific manner : "Same with these Southern fish, not but what I like fresh sea-food and crabs, but I tell you these bass and whitings can't hold a candle to the fresh-water pickerel you get up North. Then these Floridians talk so much about how poisonous their darned old rattlesnakes are. Why, we got rattlers in Kansas that are just as bad any day!"

"But what gets me is the natives, Doc. Shiftless. What this country needs is some Northern hustle."

"That's so, Brother Snuck. Shiftless. And besides that—"

"Oh, Mrs. Smith, I want to show you the sweater I'm knitting."

"—besides being shiftless, look at how they sting us. Simply make all the money they can out of us tourists. Oranges two for a nickel! Why, I can buy jus' good oranges at home for that!"

"And the land! They can talk all they want to about rocky hill soil, but I wouldn't give one of my Berkshire Hill holdings for all the land south of Baltimore. I can sell you—"

"Pretty warm to-day."

"Yes, I was writing to Jessie, guess she wished she was down here. She wrote me it was snowing and ten below—"

Mrs. Johnson was always afire for accurate botanical information, and of the scientific Dr. Bjones she inquired, "What are these palmettoes good for?"

"Well, you know, I'm kind of a stranger in Florida, too, but I believe the natives eat the nuts from them."

"Oh, can anybody tell me what connections I make for Ciudad Dinero?"

"Why, you take the 9:16, Mrs. Bezuzus, and change at Lemon Grove—"

"No, you change at Avocado and take the jitney—"

"Is there a good hotel at Ciudad?"

"Well, I've heard the Blubb House is a first-class place; three-dollar-a-day house. Oh, how did you like the Royal Miasma at—"

"Oh, I suppose it's awful famous, and it's very dressy, everybody changed their clothes for supper, but I prefer Cape Cod Court, not an expensive place, you understand, but so homey—"

"Yes, but for table give me. Dr Gunk's Health Cottage, and the beds there—"

"Well, we started in on the West Coast and went to St. Petersburg and Tampa and Fort Myers, and then back to Ocala and Silver Springs, and took the Ocklawaha trip and all, and we stopped a day at Palatka—"

"Oh, Mrs. Bjones, how do you do that stitch?"

Often the crowd on the porch ceased these lighter divertissements and spoke seriously of real highbrow topics, like Bryan and Villa and defense and T. R. and self-starters and Billy Sunday and Harold Bell Wright. The Johnsons certainly had come to the right shop for being broadened and quickened, and Mrs. Johnson often told her husband that she would take back to the Wednesday Reading Circle such a fund of ready information and ideas as a Certain Person couldn't have gotten in California if she'd stayed there a hundred years!

So went the Johnsons' hours of gaieties many-colored and tropical, and when the long, happy day was over, New Chicago afforded them a succulent supper or a dainty repast, and then ho! for the movies, and no city has better movies than New Chicago, scenes from the whole wide world spread before you there on the screen, scenes from Paris and Pekin and Peoria, made by the best Los Angeles companies. At least once a week the Johnsons were able to see their favorite film hero, Effingham Fish, in a convulsing comedy.

How wondrous 'tis to travel in unfamiliar climes!

151

Spring was on its way, and at last the Johnsons were ready to bid farewell to New Chicago, the land of mystery and languor, adventure and dolce far niente.

Their trunk was packed. Mr. Johnson's slippers had been run to earth, or at least to dust, under their bed, and his razor-strop had been recovered from behind the bureau, when Mrs. Johnson suddenly exclaimed, "Oh! Why, we haven't studied the flora and fauna of Florida yet, and I don't know but what we ought to, for club-papers."

"Well, you haven't got all the time in the world left for it," said Mr. Johnson, who had a pretty wit.

"Well, we're all packed, and we have three hours before the train goes."

She dragged him out and they hired a surrey driven by a bright, hustling Northern negro—not one of these ignorant Southern darkies—and they galloped out to Dr. Bible's orange-grove, admission ten cents, one of the show-places in the suburbs of New Chicago.

There it was, trees and fruit and—and everything; a sight to broaden and quicken one.

The Johnsons solemnly gazed at it. "Yes," said Mrs. Johnson, "that's an orange-grove! Just think! And grapefruit. . . . It's very pretty. . . . I wonder if they sell post-card views of it."

"Yes," said Mr. Johnson, "that's an orange-grove. Well, well! . . . Well, I guess we better drive on."

They next studied the shell mound. There's something very elevating about the sight of such a relic of long-past ages—shows how past ages lived, you know—gives you a broader sympathy with history and all that. There she was, all in layers, millions of shells, just where the Indians had thrown them. Ages and ages ago. The Johnsons must have gazed at the mound for five or ten minutes. Mr. Johnson was so interested that he asked the driver, "Do they ever find tommyhawks in these mounds?"

"Don't know, sir," said the driver thoughtfully. "I'm a stranger in New Chicago."

"Yes," said Mr. Johnson, "I shouldn't wonder if they found relics there. Very, very ancient, I should say. When you think of how filling just one oyster-fry is, and then all these shells—Well, mama, I guess that's about all we wanted to see, isn't it?"

"Well, we might drive back by Mr. Capo's estate; they tell me he has some fine Florida shrubbery there."

They passed the Capo estate, but there wasn't much to see—just trees with kind of white berries, and tall shrubs with stalks curiously like the bamboo fish-poles that boys use, back home. Mrs. Johnson's eagle glance darted to the one object of interest, and she wanted to know something:

"Stop, driver. John, I wonder what that plant is there, like a little palm, with that thing like a cabbage in the center. I wonder if it isn't a pineapple plant."

We, having the unfair position of author, know that it was really a sago palm—not that we wish to boast of our knowledge of floras, and so, if you will pardon our interruption :

"Well," said Mr. Johnson helpfully.

"I understand they grow farther south. But even so this might be an erotic pineapple, just grown here in gardens."

"Well, maybe. There's a couple of people coming. Why don't you ask them?"

They let the first of the two approaching men pass them—he was only a common, ignorant native. But the second was a fine, keen, hustling fellow on a bicycle, and Mrs. Johnson hailed him: "Can you tell me what that plant is?"

"That, madam—"

The Johnsons listened attentively, alert as ever in acquiring knowledge.

"—that plant? Well, I don't just exactly know. I'm a stranger here myself."

The Johnsons had to hurry back for their train, but they interestedly discussed all the flora and fauna on the way, including pines, buzzards, and pickaninnies. "Isn't it nice," said Mrs. Johnson, "to plunge right out and explore like this! I just bet that cat, with her winter in California, never stirred out of her own dooryard. Well, Florida certainly has been a novel experience, and improved our minds so much. Driver, is that a mocking-bird, on that skinny dead tree?"

"Yassum, that's a mocking-bird ... Or maybe it's a robin."

II

ADDING experiences in Georgia and Virginia and the Carolinas to their knowledge of Florida, the Johnsons saw and drank deep of Savannah, Charleston, Asheville, Richmond, and Newport News. They were able to do all five cities in six days, while the Bezuzuses had taken eight for them. In Charleston they saw Calhoun's grave and learned all about the aristocratic society. They were so pleasantly entertained there, by a very prominent and successful business acquaintance of Mr. Johnson's, a Mr. Max Rosenfleisch of New York, who had bought a fine old Southern mansion in Charleston and thus, of course, was right in with all the old families socially. Mr. Rosenfleisch said he liked the aristocrats, but was going to change a lot of their old-fashioned social ways, and show them how to have a real swell time, with cabarets and theater parties, instead of these slow dances, and teach them to dine at seven instead of three or four. The Johnsons were quite thrilled at witnessing the start of this social revolution—I tell you, it's when you travel that you have such unusual adventures. They themselves would actually have met some of the inner social set of Charleston, but Mr. Rosenfleisch was having the den redecorated before giving any more of his smart, exclusive parties, and meantime the Johnsons had to be getting on—to a tourist, time is valuable.

At the beginning of spring, when the narcissi and the excursionists are out, the Johnsons arrived at Washington, where every good citizen should go, to show the lawmakers that we uphold their hands, and to give them our ideas about enlarging the army. The Johnsons found the nicest sightseeing car, with such a bright young man from Denver for barker, and he told how high the Washington Monument was, how much the Patent Office had cost to build, how long it had taken to decorate the Congressional Library in the Spanish Omelet style, how far the guns in the Navy Yard would shoot, where Joe Cannon lived, and numerous other broadening and quickening facts which filled them with pride in being citizens of the greatest country in the world.

The Johnsons' congressman received them with flattering attentions which would have turned heads less level than theirs; he rushed over and shook hands with them the minute they came into his private office, and while just for the moment he couldn't remember their name, he had it right on the tip of his tongue, and said, "Why, of course, of course," when Mr. Johnson refreshed his memory. He recalled perfectly having shaken hands with them once at Northernapolis. He was so sorry that he was expecting the Ways and Means Committee to meet in his office, right away, for he did so want to have them stay there and chat with him about the folks back home. As an indication of his pleasure in seeing them, he honored them with a special card which enabled them to hear the epoch-making debates in Congress, from a gallery reserved just for distinguished visitors and friends of congressmen. As they listened to a vigorous oration on the duty on terrapin, Mrs. Johnson said triumphantly: "John, I guess that cat never heard anything like that in her Pasadena that she's always talking about at the Reading Circle!"

Travelers have to be of heroic mold to endure the dangers and disasters of exploration; and the Johnsons showed the quiet dignity of *noblesse oblige* during a most disagreeable incident at Washington...Mrs. Johnson wished to find the house in which Commodore Decatur had lived, as an ancestor of hers had been a very near and dear friend of one of the Commodore's gun-swabbers. She asked quite a number of apparently well-informed tourists, but, with a pathetic lack of sound information, they all murmured that they didn't know, being themselves strangers in Washington. Then she had the original idea of asking the clerk at their hotel.

"Decatur House?" he said. "I know where the Ebbitt House is, and the White House, and Colonel House, but I pass up the Decatur House. Sorry...Here, boy, shoot this package up to 427."

"Why, I mean the historic old mansion of Commodore Decatur."

"Madam, I can tell you where to get your kodak films developed, and where to find the largest oysters in town, and where to pay your bill, and what time the 5:43 train goes, but that's all I know. I come from Chicago, and if God is good to me, I'm going back there, where there's no congressmen, and they keep the tourists inside the Loop."

"Well, can't you tell us where we can find out?"

"Madam, you will find a guide-book at the news-stand."

From the news-stand they overheard the clerk saying to a fellow menial:

"—yes, I know, I oughtn't to be a grouch, but she wouldn't take 'no' for an answer. And ten minutes ago some other female wanted to know where Lincoln was buried, and just before that an old boy was sore because I couldn't tell him what is the sum total of all the pensions the Government is paying, and before that somebody wanted to know how much the dome of the Capitol weighs. These tin-can paper-bag tourists drive me wild. I ain't just an information bureau—I'm a whole bedroom suite, instalment plan."

Mr. Johnson said to his wife with that quiet force which all his associates in Northernapolis know and admire, "If he means us by 'tin-can paper-bag tourists,' I'm going to chastise him, I am, no matter what it costs! In fact, I'll speak to the manager!"

"Now, John," his wife urged, "he simply is beneath your contempt."

"Well, perhaps that's right."

The Johnsons decided not to waste a quarter on a guide-book, and strolled out to ask a policeman where the Decatur House was.

Although they found that Washington was like Florida in needing Western hustle, what with the service so slow that they didn't finish dinner before twelve-thirty, some noons, yet the Johnsons discovered a news-stand where they could buy the *Northernapolis Herald,* and there was the nicest big drug-store run by a live, hustling Milwaukee man, where Mr. Johnson could get his favorite Flor de Wheeling cigars, while Mrs. Johnson had a chocolate ice-cream soda and some post-cards. And a movie-theater featuring Effingham Fish in comedies. So, altogether, in their Washington sojourn they had much homey pleasure as well as broadening insight into how public affairs are conducted. And the nicest souvenirs.

Again they took their staves and wardrobe-scrip and continued their pilgrimage to the ancient and historic spots of our own land. They were able to do Baltimore and Philadelphia thoroughly in two days, and would have finished up Atlantic City in another day, except that they found it was so much cheaper to get rates by the week. Then off for New York.

Mrs. Johnson was willing to sacrifice, to wear herself to the bone, studying the deeper esthetic, psychological and economic problems of New York, that she might bring home new ideas to the Wednesday Reading Circle. But New York wouldn't let itself be studied. It was perfectly crazy. Everybody in New York, they found, spent all his time in cafés, tea-rooms, cabarets, or Bohemian restaurants where women smoke. The only homey, comfortable place they found was a nice quiet drug-store where Mr. Johnson got his Flor de Wheeling cigars. And the prices—! They were glad to pass on to New Haven, to Hartford, the Berkshires, and Boston—where they saw several headquarters of Washington, and the most interesting graves, Emerson and Hawthorne and all sorts of people, and such nice artistic postcards. Then to Maine, and, in midsummer, down to Cape Cod, and Provincetown.

The Johnsons didn't plan to spend more than one day at Provincetown. They felt that Northernapolis was beginning to need them, and they had really seen everything there was to see in the East and South. But at Provincetown they had such a pleasant surprise that they stayed two whole weeks—they ran into Dr. and Mrs. Bjones of Wichita, with whom they had had the jolly times at New Chicago. With the Bjoneses the Johnsons picnicked on the dunes, and even went swimming once, and sat on the porch of Mrs. Ebenezer's boarding house, discussing various hotels and the Bjoneses' interesting itinerary. They didn't want to be mean, but they couldn't help crowing a little when they found that they had seen six graves of famous men which the Bjoneses had missed entirely!

The Johnsons didn't really like Provincetown. Of course the Bjoneses were interesting, and after a time they met some nice comfy people from Indianapolis and Omaha, and Mr. Johnson was able to get his Flor de Wheeling cigars. But Provincetown was filled with fishermen, acting as though they owned the place, and smelling it all up with their dories and schooners and nets and heaven knows what all, dirty, common Portuguese and Yankee fishermen, slopping along the street in nasty old oilskins covered with fish-scales, and not caring if they brushed right up against you. And the old wharves, all smelly. Mr. and Mrs. Johnson were the first to be interested in any new phenomenon, and once they went right out on a wharf and asked all about the fishing industry and whaling. But still—as Mr. Johnson said with that ready satire which made him so popular a speaker at the dinners of the Northernapolis Chamber of Commerce—they didn't care to associate with dead fish all their lives, even if they did like Effingham Fish in the movies!

When the Bjoneses left there was nothing more to study, nothing to observe.

Said Mrs. Johnson, "We've seen every inch of the South and East, now, and no one can say we haven't been unprejudiced and open-minded—the way we've gone into the flora and fauna, and among industries and all— but I must say we haven't seen a single place that begins to come up to Northernapolis."

"You never said a better thing in your life, mama, and what's more, we'll start for Northernapolis to-morrow!"

They were due to arrive in Northernapolis at two P. M. Mrs. Johnson was making notes for Wednesday Reading Circle papers about the Fruit of the Tropics, the Negro Problem, Fishing on Cape Cod, and How the Government Is Conducted at Washington.

"Guess that hen won't talk so much about Pasadena after this," Mr. Johnson chuckled. "Say, we'll have time to say 'howdy' to the folks and go to the movies to-night, to celebrate our return. And I'll be able to get a decent cigar again—can't buy a Flor de Wheeling on a single one of these trains. Well, mama, it'll be pretty good to get back where we know every inch, and won't have to ask questions and feel like outsiders, eh?"

Such a surprise as it would be for the children! The Johnsons hadn't wired them they were coming.

Northernapolis! The fine, big, dirty factories—evidences of Northernapolis's hustling spirit! The good old-fashioned homey station! The Central House 'bus!

They stood out on Main Street, excitedly hailing a street car. Then—

You see, as a matter of fact this isn't a satire, but a rather tragic story about two pathetic, good-hearted, friendly yearners, as you should already have perceived—

Then Mr. Johnson dropped his suitcase and stood amazed. A block down from the station was a whole new row of two-story brick stores.

"Why," he exclaimed, "I never read about that row going up!" He was bewildered, lost. He turned to a man who was also waiting for the car and inquired, "What's those new buildings?"

"Dunno," said the man. "I'm a stranger here myself."

THE END OF ILSA MENTEITH

Lucia Bronder

O N the outskirts of large cities almost invariably they are found—the long rows of commonplace little dwellings, generally two stories high, and with two flats to a story, all exactly alike, all erected under the astute eye of the real-estate magnate, who, catering to the middle classes, with the bait of middle-class appurtenances of luxury, draws his patronage from those who are called the brawn and sinew of great nations. They are highly genteel abodes, these rows of little houses resting just between the city boundaries and the suburbs. Clerks and tradesmen inhabit them with their families—people honest and unimpeachable, people of innumerable progeny, people who go to church, who celebrate on New Year's Eve, who dine in restaurants regularly each Saturday night, write letters upon public affairs to the newspapers, say "How well you're looking," over the telephone; women of cotton stockings and double chins, men of stern standards and dirty finger-nails—thrifty, humdrum, well-balanced folk.

In just such an orderly little abode, located on the outskirts of New York, one night at precisely ten minutes after ten, a revolver shot rang out. A woman had committed suicide. ...

There followed a sudden flurry. The lady in question had been a divorcee of somewhat questionable repute, who, sprung of humble origin, had within ten years acquired four successive husbands, all of them wealthy, and all, it was rumored, made to turn over to her very substantial settlements in place of alimony, when the four successive divorce cases came up. The newspapers made of her demise a nine-day sensation. The women in the neighborhood whispered; the men winked. The real-estate agents were worried, but strove successfully to hush the scandal. Within a short time tongues ceased wagging, and Ilsa Menteith, who invaded the domain of salubrious respectability to make her effective getaway, was speedily forgotten.

I

THE flat on the lower right of the house was occupied by a family of unlimited offspring and exemplary conduct, named McCabe.

A young doctor, blond and pink-cheeked, rang the McCabe bell on the day after the suicide and smiled with more than a touch of deference in his eyes upon the neat, gray-haired woman in curl-papers and gingham house-dress who opened the door. She was decidedly unattractive, the traces of erstwhile prettiness on her face only enhancing an effect as of damp, unpleasant decay, like that which emanates from flowers left in water to die—an effect which not even the spick-and-spanness of her attire, not even the cleanliness of her well-kept rooms, could quite efface. Nevertheless, the doctor contemplated her with genuine respect as together they entered the room where the patient lay.

It was the fledgling physician's first big case. One of Mrs. McCabe's children had undergone a dangerous operation, and during the long weeks when things hung in the balance, and the most painstaking nursing was required to meet the complications that arose, the doctor had found in this frail, aging woman a devotion so devoid of hysteria, a patience so unswerving, a judiciousness and self-control so adequate to the exigencies, as to astound him.

This morning, however, he was disquieted by a slight tension in her manner, a flush, as of delight, on her face. At the convalescent's bedside she was simply the efficient nurse he had come to know, but once in the hallway, as she touched his arm and led him into her bedroom, he quivered and blushed. The young doctor was keenly susceptible to external impressions, and acutely affected by them. He had been in practice only a year, but had learnt already to recognize the signs of approaching confidence from middle-aged women, to gauge at its value the look of anticipatory gusto on their faces, and he was as yet unable sympathetically to comment upon the gynecological details so rapturously disclosed without the color rising on his fair, young face.

Unquiet, he awaited a tale of symptoms and sufferings. But she surprised him by pointing upward:

"You've heard about that woman, doctor? That Ilsa Menteith?"

He nodded. And seating herself in a straight-backed chair, eyes glistening with the gluttony of gossip, she took a breath deep enough to last through a long discourse, and launched into a torrent of words :

"Fine goings-on for a respectable neighborhood! To think of a woman like that right here in a house where there's nobody that's not decent! Right here among our sons and husbands! A woman of ill fame, for that's what she was, and the worst kind of a one, inveiglin' men into marriage to get their money, and then divorcin' them one after the other. None of us here suspected who she was. You couldn't have told it to look at her—she wasn't even pretty, and dressed quiet, too. Always with her red head in the air, and smiling like she was some queen! I knew why she done it—it was remorse, that's all. She saw decent people and little children around here, and it made her repent and make off with herself. Divine justice, that's what it was! She got her deserts all right, but"—a look of foiled vengeance shot from the faded eyes—"she didn't get enough of 'em! She got off too easy, the jade. Her kind makes my blood boil—the kind that covers up their sinful doings by marriage, and thinks they're so much grander than honest, decent folks. An out-and-out fast woman we can find out, and show up, and make 'em suffer and reform, and turn respectable. ... But to think that one got off so easy. It—it isn't fair."

Mrs. McCabe broke off abruptly, and looked up into the doctor's vague, troubled face. Something there arrested her. She appeared for a moment to ponder, and presently he saw the wrath of thwarted vengeance fade from her face, to be replaced by the composed look he had met always at his patient's bedside.

"Maybe you don't understand, doctor," she went on slowly, and in softer tones, "I guess only a woman, and a respectable woman, can understand. We respectable women can't tolerate jades like that, with their heads in the air, and their smiles. Our heads ain't in the air, we don't smile any too much. ... I've had nine children, and it's a lot of trouble and pain and time, havin' children—she had none, and she never kept house, or worked, or done any of the things a wife ought to do to earn her keep.

And I've cooked for my family all these years; I've scrubbed and done the washing when we couldn't afford a washwoman, and I seen that my children went to church and dancing school. Gave 'em a good education, too, and kept cultured myself. I belong right now to a literary club connected with the Sunday school. Culture—that's the most important thing of all! Well, I been a good wife and mother, and there's many another like me, and it's not fair for women like her upstairs to have had all she's had, and then slip off so easy with 'er head in the air! I was good-looking myself once, but work kills all that, although—well, Mr. McCabe still says"... She simpered a little, and stopped.

The doctor had learnt how to hide a look of amusement under an interested smile. Noting it, immediately she became eased and expatiatory, ready to reveal secrets not at all germane to medicine, the secrets bosom friends and husbands never hear, which women pour into their physician's ears.

"I saw him, doctor, through the keyhole—that night," she whispered dramatically, "I made it my business to see him, for I was just beginning to suspect her with her fine airs! I made it a point to know who comes to see all the tenants. He was the first visitor she had here. Doctor, I'm sure of it"—she rose, approached him, and breathed her conviction into his ear—"that night she brought sin right into this respectable house! And after she done it, she was sorry. She killed herself in remorse. I know it, because I saw him—a wicked looking man, he was. The kind you don't want your daughters to go out with. The kind that waylays young girls. I just got a peek at him, but his sin was in his eyes. And he looked ready for more prey. I—I was scared, even behind the locked door."

She faced him, indignant virtue battling with pleasurable excitement in her eyes. The doctor endeavored to smile even more sympathetically, and at the same time to back out of the room. But his smile was his destruction. It invited to confidence, and the woman's eyes lit.

"Sin and love's not the same thing. Now in my case, doctor"—In dread expectancy he shuffled his feet—

—And broke out into a sweat of agony, as, after a tremendous anticipatory inhalation, she launched forth without niggardliness into gynecological mysteries, occult obstetrics, esoterics of the connubial state, expounded in such detail and so dramatically evoked as to smite the man of medicine as with a sense of vicarious guilt. ...

Even after a year of practice he remained a romantic, and in anguish, his eyes roved, as with alert ears he awaited the first indication of waning breath control. When for only an instant she paused, he broke out into a feeble shout:

"Yes, yes, Mrs. McCabe. Maternity's a beautiful thing!" Discreetly, determinedly, he edged door-wise.

"I'm glad you're one man thinks so. Most of 'em's got hankering for Jezebels like her upstairs. Children and culture—they're the most important things. Now just before I had my eldest"—

"Maternity—a beautiful" ... In exultant despair his voice drowned hers, and, backing through the doorway, with a vague, uneasy wave of his arm, he pointed by chance to a print of the Sistine Madonna hanging over the bed.

"Isn't it, doctor?" Her voice softened; the glutted look went out of her eyes; with something of awe in her face she contemplated the picture. "Nice painting, isn't it? I'm very fond of high art, and make it a point to study it, and always keep cultivated. That's the Raphael Madonna, you know."

II

WHILE they were bearing the remains of the *felo de se* from the house, two young women, one with a fat, healthy baby gurgling in her arms, stood at a window of the flat at the upper right, and watched the grim procession. Both appeared under twenty; both were wide-eyed, pink-cheeked, and innocent looking. The little room they stood in was tastefully furnished in an inexpensive, instalment-plan fashion. A fresh wholesomeness entirely devoid of viscosity pervaded the place, a wholesomeness suggestive of young life, young love, young ignorance untrammeled by the onerousness of ideas.

"Oh, dear," the little mother chirruped, as she shifted her baby from one arm to the other. "Oh, dear, but it's funny watching 'em carry her out that way, for all the world like they used to carry you, Irene, after a shindy, at five in the morning, when you couldn't navigate any more."

The other tossed her pretty head: "Well, anyhow, if I can't stand my grog, at least I always keep my sense. Now you, Lily, if you hadn't had me to take care of you, many's the time you'd have given your last cent, and the last ring off your fingers, to any cabaret singer or professional dancer you happened to be sticky about. Remember the time"—

"Never mind that," the first interrupted, tossing the infant high into the air to hear its laughter, "I believe he's cutting another tooth, Irene. Look here."

But the other, her eyes a little wistful, shook her head.

"You've been married over a year now, Lily. Tell me, don't you ever want to get back at the game?"

"I should say not."

"Then why do you always want me to come to see you, and tell you what the crowd's doing, when you know your husband don't like to have me here?"

"I don't know," the first laughed, rattling a toy to amuse the child. "It's just kind of like reading a story, or seeing an exciting play, now—to have you tell me what they're all doing. But I'm as happy as I can be. I'm tickled to death with marriage, and my husband, and my baby. And do you know what, Irene? I'm particularly tickled to death right this minute, now I've seen 'em carry, the Menteith woman out that way."

"Why?" While she reached for her hat, the other meditatively rouged her lips at the mantel mirror.

"Oh, because"—the little mother's mouth hardened—"it's not the wives and the families, it's her kind that makes life hard for the rest of us. Holding her head up, and thinking herself so awful respectable and above everybody! Walking like some empress, when she was no better than any of us. Grabbing the kale, and the husbands, and off on yachts when we were washing our own stockings in hall bedrooms! I didn't know who she was, but I saw her pass two or three times. ... She thought she was so almighty grand and clever. It makes me sick to think of it! Well, she got hers at the end like any other Jane. And it tickles me to death to think that here I am with a husband, and a baby, and a nice home, and nobody suspecting anything,—and I'll see that they never suspect,—while she with her haughty ways cashed in at the finish like any other third-class rounder. ... And all because of a John who threw her down!"

"What do you mean, threw her down?" Interested, the other turned from the mirror.

"I'll tell you.... The night it happened, Freddie called me up at ten o'clock. He was delayed late at work. I had to go downstairs to the 'phone. That's the only thing I don't like about this house, there's no private 'phones. I had on my pink kimono, and if I do say it, I look good in kimonos. Well, I saw the man. He was just coming out,—the only man she ever had to see her here. Take it from me, he was there some. You know the kind,—the kind you'd sneak away from a wine racket to drink nickel beers at Danny Clancy's with. And the way he looked at me—sort of bored but interested! Say, I tell you I know he'd just given her a good, proper squelch of a throw-down. And it makes me feel fine, Irene. It makes up for the hall bedrooms. She thought she was such a wonder, but the night she quit I got a ve-ry much taken look from the John who threw her down.... Say, Irene, you'd better hurry. Freddie'll be home soon, and you know he don't like me to have you here."

"I'm going." With a sigh the other took up her handbag. "But, you know, I think you're hard on that Menteith woman just because you're happy, Lily. I feel sorry for the poor thing. It's awful the way all the nice chaps throw a girl down. I guess she was tired of those rich husbands, and wanted to marry somebody she liked. I guess she asked him, and they always balk at that, the nice ones,—not meaning anything against your Freddie, only.... Remember Gus? I've been running around with him off and on for three years. He had a birthday last month, and I spent twelve of my last eighteen-fifty for a present. Pajamas it was,—all pink silk stripes. I guess he thought I had intentions. I guess he thought I was hinting at the honeymoon, and the old fourteen karat band,—and I guess I was, at that. Haven't seen him since.... I'd like to marry someone I liked, and settle down. I suppose that poor dead thing did, too."

She sighed again, and kissed the baby. "Well, good-bye, Lily, call me up some time."

III

IN the flat on the lower left dwelt one Matthew Sylvester Jennings, a mild little man of excessive corpulence, a resigned, henpecked little old man, too oscitant ever to protest against anything. A shop in which he dealt in tame household pets, a wife yclept Lucretia with a cast in her eye, and no waistline, a black Siamese cat he called Aspasia, and a shelf of books, four of which, "Hamlet," a General Anthropology, a Complete Zoology, and a collection of William Blake's illustrations to the Book of Job, lay always at his side when, night after night, he sat in ponderous immobility, smoking his pipe,—these Matthew Sylvester Jennings possessed. All other worldly goods the invitiate Lucretia had appropriated,—bank account, insurance policy, the very state of his soul.

Upon the heavy layers of fat which, save where the lines of a good chin defiantly proclaimed themselves, and where, among rolls of adipose tissue, two vivid blue eyes peered through slits, seemed to enwrap his whole personality as in the folds of a Persian yashmak, Lucretia looked approvingly. But with grimness she would contemplate both the cat Aspasia, an animal abominated, but tolerated withal, and a massive patriarch, her husband's boon companion, a creature likewise tolerated with abomination. For, with a sort of inanimate, milk-and-water stubbornness, Matthew Sylvester Jennings clung to his cat, and his friend. All the disapprobation of Lucretia could not remove Aspasia from his knee; all her acid expostulations availed not a whit when it came to the subject of the patriarch's biweekly visits.

On the evenings when he was expected, always at the stroke of eight, an additional tinge of sourness overspread her crabbed features. But invariably she fetched a jug of claret, the only beverage she permitted, and a tobacco jar, set them on the table with a ferocious bang, and, as at precisely five minues after eight the door-bell rang, retired into the kitchen for an hour, when, with her reappearance, the two old men stirred, rose heavily, and shook hands in silence.

Massive and tall, the great, white beard which fell to his waist gave the patriarch an effect of infinite magnanimity. He sat always in the same attitude, chin sunken, eyes raised, one elbow on the arm of his chair, with the hand extended and unconsciously assuming the position of blessing used by priests of the Latin church. As he sipped his claret, he seemed to invest it with the augustness of consecrated wine. As he puffed at his pipe, Matthew Sylvester Jennings was reminded of the illustrations to the Book of Job,—Blake's pictures of a dispassionate deity blowing hurricanes over a sin-ridden world. He suggested omnipotence, omniscience. He looked at once benignant and all-terrible. ... And when he spoke it was in the squeaking falsetto of senile disintegration.

Three days after the suicide the old men met. For some time they sat smoking in the silence wontedly maintained. Both were men of few words. The patriarch, moreover, was afflicted with extreme deafness, which precluded facile confabulation, since it was only with difficulty that his host could force a voice much above a wheezy whisper, while audibility to the sharp ears in the kitchen neither desired. Nor was it often that their eyes met. Matthew Sylvester Jennings' were habitually lowered meditatively, his friend's lifted as in rapt contemplation. Ordinarily they spent their hour of communion, sipping their wine, smoking their pipes, with scarce a word exchanged.

This evening, however, there was a tension in the air. The nature of the suicide, the prominence the newspapers had given it, caused even these two to feel a stir. Presently they looked at one another. It was in the flat above that Ilsa Menteith had died. Significantly the patriarch rolled his dark eyes to the ceiling, and, in a sort of vehement squeak:

"Why?" he queried.

Matthew Sylvester Jennings at first made no reply. His eyes fell slowly, and as if with great difficulty, he laid his pipe on the able, and folded his hands. Each one of his gestures, every movement, the very play of his lips when speaking, seemed to accomplish themselves only after infinite care and deliberation. It was as if his unwieldy ponderosity were an alien substance folded about him, a something as incongruous to his real personality as to his vivid blue eyes and good chin,—a something obtrusive and distressing which impeded his movements, checked smooth utterance, interfered with the workings of his brain.

Very slowly now the puffy lips parted. Very slowly he leaned toward his friend. And then suddenly, with astonishing rapidity, one word piled pell-mell upon the other.

"She had big green eyes," he panted, in a sibilant monotone, "and red hair. She was beautiful. She had a sunny smile,—this Ilsa Menteith. The very day she did it—in the vestibule—I saw her. She was beautiful. ... She should be denied decent burial,—she should be drawn, and quartered, and fed to wild beasts. She did a terribly immoral thing. She committed the one unpardonable sin. Anybody is an unspeakable criminal who deprives the world of a lovely woman in her prime,—so long as ugly-tempered women with casts in their eyes exist."

Confused and fatigued at the unprecedentedly long speech, he passed a hand across his forehead, and sank back into his customary lethargy, the mobile eyes alone betraying an inner unrest. His friend still stared ecstatically into the ceiling. The cat Aspasia leaped upon his knee. And, passing a cumbersome hand over her sleek coat, very gradually his lips parted again.

"I am a man of imagination,"—scarcely above a whisper he spoke now, with a certain weighty deliberation, and tardiness, as if his utterance were behindhand, were but an echo of a mind working always far in advance of his words,—"Imagination is a bane; it galls and wounds when one is fat and lazy and easily imposed upon. Activity? Impossible. Achievement? Absurd. Love? Ridiculous. Speech? Difficult,—only this strange event upstairs spurs me to it to-night. ... But nevertheless I am a man of imagination. I have my God, my books, and my animals, and love them as my William Blake loved his God, his books, and his animals. And then, too, I have my women ... "

Guardedly he glanced, first at the patriarch whose fixed gaze never altered, then toward the kitchen, and presently, laying his hand affectionately on the General Anthropology, droned on :

"I have my women,—here ... here,"—he tapped the volume significantly,—"most men have their mistresses in the flesh and turn to the poets to have them in the spirit, too. I have them in the spirit, and turn to my Anthropology to have them in the flesh.

"This Ilsa Menteith was beautiful," he went on, his voice sinking even lower, "civilization coarsens women. Only among a few savage races do you find the refined, feline types. There are pictures of them,—in here. ... What's uglier than a civilized woman's leg? Great, clumsy, conical thing, humpy at the top, ending in knock-knees. The masculine thigh is columnar, and so, for instance, the Javanese girl's; narrow hips, too,—fine shoulders, long legs, long arms, long hands, long feet, long, slim fingers ... litheness ... slenderness,—fine points, fine points! These doughy, civilized women,—faugh! But Ilsa Menteith was beautiful,—she was like a savage, like a cat. ...

"Woman is very seldom feline," he went on after a pause. "Why do people continually cast aspersions upon the loveliest animals in existence by comparing them to women? A well-rounded woman continually writhing and twisting, half-closing her eyes, and trying to look inscrutable,—is she like a cat? Some tabby with many a litter to her credit, perhaps ... but bovine, rather—bovine,—a cow with the blind staggers! The fine specimen of feline, like my Aspasia here, is a gourmet, an æsthete, a masculine beast, the most masculine of animals. The fine specimens suggest long, lean men, decadent aristocrats, high-bred indolents, subtle, bored, indifferent, dispassionate souls. ... But this Ilsa Menteith, I saw her only once or twice, but she was beautiful like a cat. ... Why did she do it, you ask?"

The patriarch continued to stare up into the overhead unattainable. And now the voice of Matthew Sylvester Jennings grew even fainter, fell into a stifled whisper, seemed to come from an immense distance, as if the essence of his personality were struggling once to express itself against awful, and hitherto victorious odds.

"Why did she do it? I am a man of imagination,—I know, I know. I saw the man, you know, as he went out at the door a few minutes before it happened. I saw a great sadness,—and weariness, and aloofness. He was hurrying, and absent-minded. He almost knocked me down. He had a sensitive mouth and fine eyes,—small, grey, keen. It was the face of an extraordinary man. And it was the face of a man who loves, because it was the face of a man brooding upon things bigger than love, a book he was writing, perhaps, or some great enterprise,—or, who knows, perhaps even an animal store. It was the face of a man who had been profoundly moved, and I know he had been moved by her,—not to pity, not to desire, but to things bigger than she, bigger than love itself."

Faintly in his chair, Matthew Sylvester Jennings stirred. Very slowly his eyes opened so that the big, blue irises completely revealed themselves, giving, as it seemed, a passing glimpse of the real man. His voice sank now to a well-nigh inaudible whisper, but with a suggestion of energy and power behind it.

"I who have never seen it know the face of the man who loves. Through my animals I know it. What are the animal sounds dear to lovers? The buzzing of bees in midsummer, the crooning of frogs, the cooing of doves. And why?—Because to them all there is an unchanging, never-ceasing note, a something lulling, soothing, indefinite, unending,—a something with an eternal quality. And that's what love means to an extraordinary man. Something eternal in its very evanescence, something gentle and not disturbing to bigger things. He loved her, and that's why she did it!

"Do you see, do you understand, my friend? He loved her, and with his love, this woman of husbands and sordid affairs attained her apex. She reached the empyreal zenith, and so,—"

"Why?"

In his quavering treble, the patriarch, seated massive and still, as if planning the destinies of countless generations, broke in.

"A sad case, that, upstairs," he continued. "What do you make of it, Matthew?"

The venerable man finally lowered his eyes from the ceiling, blinked stupidly, looked blank, and put his hand to his ear the more readily to catch a reply.... Throughout his discourse, Matthew Sylvester Jennings had failed sufficiently to reckon with his friend's excessive deafness.

His pudgy face reddened slowly as he realized he had been addressing unhearing ears. In complete exhaustion he fell back into his chair. Now his voice was inaudible. His lips scarce moved.

"My Blake's Deity in the flesh afflicted with deafness! My Mad William's Jehovah incarnate squeaking in the tones of octogenarian decrepitude! A god who listens as if attentively, and hears not a word.... Perhaps,—why not ... I am a man of imagination ... "

Grim, determined, just then his wife came into the room. The two old men stirred, rose ponderously, and in silence shook hands.

IV

"Hullo, Ilsa."

"Hello there, master musician. Awfully nice of you to've come."

Throughout her meteoric career Ilsa Menteith had been the topic of club-room confabulation entered upon in an attempt exactly to define her attraction, and ending invariably in puzzled shrugs. There are women made for laughter, or for languor, for speech, eye-play, lithe movement, anodynous repose,—lovely women who, realizing the potency of their most salient asset, propel it unerringly in the grace of a gesture, the dart of a lambent orb. None of her attributes could be designated the Menteith's most living charm, neither the timbre of her carolling laugh, the poise of her carriage, nor her green eyes' chatoyant allure. Many another damsel possessing charms, of equiponderant value exhaled in composite with far more finesse, many another wittier, tenderer, more beautiful, more adequately equipped to outdazzle, outpassion, outmaneuver, had lost in emulative joust to this fiery-haired woman of little guile.

Her most obvious attractions she seemed deliberately to belittle, intentionally to expunge. A supple body, slender to a fault, was never permitted the sinuosity it suggested. No one had ever extolled her green eyes as mystic; for all their undulant luminosity, her wide-open gaze was direct and ingenuous as the glance of an unsophisticated boy. Without a tinge of color there was yet no deadness to her nacreous skin,—it irradiated life, and joy, while, rather than a wound, the curled scarlet lips suggested something artless, something candid and engaging. Accoutred by nature for the rôle of an inscrutable enchantress, she chose to play another part, and, without entirely obliterating the maternal and infantile, emphasized the good-fellow note so successfully that with her entrance into a room crowded with more beautiful women, even the man propense to diminutive daintiness with his desire's embodiment seated beside him, even the man who sought languishing opulence, and was looking into its eyes, turned to her with more than interest on their faces.

Oddly enough, too, despite her manifold attractions, the many who had sought in vain for her favor never developed any of the chagrin of disgruntled suitors, while, as for her quondam spouses, none of the four had been known ever to speak disparagingly of her either before or after the rupture. Hers was a charm light, volatile and excessively engaging, in no wise suggestive of profundities and violent amours. And she herself had once declared that it was her pride never in her life to have inspired a profound and lasting passion. At the time that her fourth divorce was being made the chief topic of club-room gossip, her first husband discussed her among a circle of friends in a fashion all present adjudged conclusive and eminently fair.

"She's untrammeled with soul," he declared, "and that's her chief charm. She has red hair and green eyes, but she's not temperamental. Her name is Ilsa, but she's not temperamental. There's something feline about her, and yet she's not temperamental. No sooner you see her come in at a door with her wide-open smile and blithe eyes, but you think, 'Here's a ripping good sportsman.' She wouldn't look at any but an affluent suitor, but what difference does that make? I know perfectly well that she wouldn't have considered me for a moment if the coffers hadn't been brim full, and I like her none the less for that. She made an excellent wife for the time being, and knew when the game was up. She's not the sort to pursue you when you're finished, or throw you over before you are, not the sort to exact adherence after things begin to pall, nor yet the sort that affects heart agony, and depths, and other tiresome things. She's simply the kind one plays around with for a few stimulating years, and then quits in mutual good-will. And she knows it, is content with her part, and plays the game well, like a clever business woman. Never negotiates a bargain sale, on the one hand, and never goes in for fleecing, on the other. Extraordinarily refreshing, that woman. Would there were more Ilsas!"

In the fluttering candle-light she was standing now, erect as always, eyes flashing their laughter at the man who faced her. That she was not strictly beautiful never struck any but women in her presence, and in no wise troubled her. The jaws and chin were a little too heavy, but successfully counterbalanced by the insouciance of a slightly tip-tilted nose. The eyes a trifle too large, the lips a trifle too full, every defect of feature was completely annihilated by the impression she gave of dazzling, joyous luminosity. This evening a trailing gown of old-gold chiffon enswathed her entirely, so high at the throat as to touch her chin and ears, and with sleeves falling well below the wrists.

"Oh, Chris," she carolled, "it's droll seeing you so awfully well-dressed, and suave looking, and everything. Who'd think that five years ago you went in for Byron collars, and Italian tabled'hôtes, and life missions, and such things? I admit I've missed my guess,—never dreamt the youth who wanted to steer me from worldly standards would ever escape from his pseudo-æsthetic rut. And here you are, America's first and only master composer, serving us Debussy virilized à la Strauss, austered à la Brahms, gayed up à la Ravel, and,—well made awfully novel and winning à la Christopher Ritchie whom I once threw down. ... Splendid!"

She had a habit of topping her speeches with a "Splendid!" At the word her voice throbbed and rang out, while her eyes sparkled with more brilliance. It was as if the sense of enjoyment she imparted to her every utterance, her every look, were epitomized in the way she caressed the word.

The man smiled. Prematurely grey, and with a slight stoop to his shoulders, he was distinguished looking in an unobtrusive way suggestive at once of softness and underlying adamant. Lips somewhat full and indefinite proclaimed an indolence at odds with the trenchancy that shot from penetrant grey eyes.

"Want to grog it up a bit?" She pointed to the table where whiskey and soda bottles stood. He nodded, and indicating that he should play host, she sat watching him, her lips parted, her chin pillowed in her hands.

"Do you know, it's most awfully nice and like you, Chris, to have done what I asked in my note. It's an unholy journey up here to the city limits, but I wanted so badly to see you. Tell me, were you surprised to hear from me? Pleased? Annoyed? And why have you come as I asked you,—I, whom you haven't seen for five years, and who threw you down?"

He passed her glass and lit a cigarette before answering :

"I came because I'd do anything in the world for you, Ilsa, which didn't interfere with something I'd rather do. Because quite the kindest deed ever done me was your abrupt dismissal five years ago."

"And I asked you to call, because tonight I wanted to see the only potential life-mate I've ever rejected. Tell me, Chris,—I'm curious. How long did you feel crushed after I turned you down in favor of spouse number three? How long did the rancour last?"

"One day of anguish," he answered after a moment, "another of unhappiness, three full of schemes for vengeance, five of vague unrest. Ten days, Ilsa."

"And then what,—another girl?"

"Not immediately. Then I discarded the Byron collar and had a haircut. Went to work, too,—on a symphonic poem, if I remember rightly.

Miserable, immature mess it was, but nevertheless the first significant thing I'd ever—"

"Chris," she broke in laughing, "you don't mean to tell me I was your inspiration?" Leaning across the table, she laid her fingers lightly on his hand.

"*A chaque saint so chandelle,*" he replied, contemplating her perfectly manicured nails. "I was twenty-five,—high time to be done with mooning adolescence, and get down to work. You taught me the incidental charm of women, and instead of letting me grow gradually tired, you were kind enough to refuse me, and left behind, after the first few days, a pleasant memory. Thanks awfully."

"That's just what I, too, have to say," she commented. "Thanks awfully, Chris. I've never been really in love, but I came closest to it with you. Thanks for having been long-haired and unkempt looking. Thanks for having disparaged my mundane aims. Thanks even for those dreadful jade earrings you gave me,—you remember? As if my hair and eyes weren't enough to contend with, without having exotic, erotic jade earrings thrust upon me! If you hadn't done these ridiculous things I should have fallen in love with you, for you're the kind my sort falls in love with. There's a bit of the fascinating cad about you for all your gentle mouth. And you saved me from falling for *amants de coeur,*—they're as fatal as woman confidantes. Thanks!"

For a moment there was silence.

"How old are you?" he queried finally.

"Thirty-one."

"And you're telling me that in all these years I was your nearest approach to a genuine *amant de coeur,* that the four moneyed maintainers were the only favored ones?"

"Absolutely."

"H'm." He eyed her reflectively, the furrows of a slight frown indicating themselves on his forehead. "I believe you and dislike believing you. At any rate, why vaunt any such prudery? I'd imagine it a dubious asset; I'd imagine that even the open-eyed purchaser of costly wares would hesitate at such unswerving allegiance to Mammon. ... Smacks a bit of the third-rate."

She withdrew her hand. "You're silly. What do I want with lovers? All my inclinations and capacities were for the marriage game played, with changing. partners, on a big scale. And I've stuck to my craft. ... Come, Chris, don't look so disapproving."

He checked his frown and smiled. "I suppose there's your side to consider as well. *Au bon chat bon rat.* But don't you ever grow tired of the steady diet of roast beef and potatoes, and—"

"Pine for sugar and cream? Emphatically I do not. And give me credit at least for consistency. You know you quoted before this evening. *A chaque saint so chandelle.*"

"And I'll quote again. *Caveat emptor.*"

"Meaning?"

"Let the buyer be careful."

Even while her smile flashed, it lost a little of its sunniness, and her eyes narrowed slightly.

"Take care, Ilsa," he cautioned, "at this moment your expression tends to the sphinx-like you despise."

At his words she sprang to her feet and, leaning over the table toward him, laughed softly, mockingly.

"I was almost angry,—and it's very, very seldom that I get angry. Come, come, Chris, your remark was cheap. The buyers haven't been cautious, didn't need to be, and never regretted not having been. ... There's a streak of the prude in you still. Nothing is more puzzling to me than the way men, notably without moral scruples, grow crotchety over what they call legalized courtezanship. You get away from commonplace standards only to adopt them in another form. You make yourself a censor of immorals! Because I've always been quite respectably married, because I'm not sentimental, because it's been altogether pleasant, and I've had no heartaches and sufferings and *grandes passions,* then,—let the buyer be careful. I'm crafty and nasty and liable to trick him!

"I'd been brought up in penury," she went on, lightly, "had no taste for it, and determined very early to put a lot of zest and care into the pursuit of avoiding it I admit freely that I've been out for the money from the start. I got me my husbands, all of them likable and excessively affluent chaps who enjoyed a few placid, respectable years with me as greatly as

I did, and were complimentary enough to think it was worth the expenditures involved.... And let me tell you, you censor of immorals,—I've never ruined a man, never broken a man's heart, never uprooted a family, nor fleeced inordinately, never reproached, nor annoyed, nor clung when I was no longer wanted, never played the Tartuffe. There's a record for you! And on the other hand, I've never been hungry, nor ill-clad, nor unhappy. I've never played around with an out-and-out boob no matter what he was worth; never had anything but a very enjoyable time, and parted from each successive liege lord with a whacking good settlement, and not a trace of ill-will on either side! How's that for a record? Life's just been one *entente cordiale* after another.... Splendid! ... And what have you to say to that, you censor of immorals?"

Her underlids were quivering. Her smile grew even more expansive and inviting. She walked around the table, and stood before him.

"Only that indignation suits you. You look very lovely to-night, Ilsa."

"Bother that!" With a toss of her head she backed away, and paced the floor, her eyes always on him, over her shoulder when her back was turned, full in his face, and glittering, as she approached. She walked very lightly, noiselessly, rapidly, her chin always high over the slender neck, lips always parted, big, even, milky teeth shining. The flickering candle-light cast an iridescence over her face, and the man who sat watching her, immobile and composed, followed with his sharp, grey eyes her every movement.

"I must try to convince you," she halted abruptly, and poised herself on the arm of his chair. "You look so sneerily disapproving as if I were some poor fool who had missed the vim of life. I've had my thrills, Chris—no nightingales, and roses, and Swiss chalet episodes, but I've had my thrills. Husband hunting is a tremendously exciting pursuit. When the victim's a bit wary.... To break down little by little the wall of only half-assumed indifference, to get him to talk, to argue, to look at you, to be interested. And then to watch for the next stage: the stupid ones tell you you're the only woman who understands them, the nice ones impress upon you how completely they understand and see through you. And there,—then ... the crucial moment! It's stupendously stirring finally to hear the little break in the voice you've been waiting for, to touch the hands, and find them warm with just the finger-tips icy. Nothing nasty about it,—I don't particularly fancy troglodytic ardor,—but something a little tender, and reverent, and gentle. ... And to know you've inspired it! It's tremendous,—as stimulating as listening to '*Ein Heldenleben*' or some such thing must be to you. ... And what have you to say to that, censor of immorals?"

"Only that old-gold chiffon makes for seductiveness, and you're bewitching by candle-light. But why the enswathement, Ilsa? All evening I've been wondering what made you seem a bit different, and it just struck me. Where are the dazzling neck and shoulders I remember of old? In altruism, why conceal the ornamental arms?"

For the first time her smile faded entirely. She darted a searching glance at him, and shifted her eyes.

"But I look as nice as ever? The unwonted,—er,—suppression of facts detracts, perhaps?"

"Not a whit."

"Good! Splendid!" From her face the fleeting shadow passed. She caught his hand in hers and suddenly laughed.

"He extols my allure, and seems a bit taken, but his hands are as cool and non-committal as a nice, crisp lettuce leaf. Turned ascetic, Chris?"

"No, but I'm broke and sad." Her hand still in his, he looked her over appraisingly. "You're certainly in form, Ilsa. But why the expended energy when you know symphonies aren't lucrative. Surely you don't consider me a potential fifth?"

She moved as if to lay her head on his shoulder, but quickly checked herself.

"Poor old Chris! Horrid thing, indigence, isn't it? I'm having a taste of it myself now."

He turned away, and glanced questioningly about the little room. Despite such impedimenta as ugly wall paper, and a built-in mantel of cheap wood, an agreeable, if by no means extraordinary effect had been produced. A buhl table aired its graces. On the wall he recognized a good Toulouse-Lautrec, under his feet an excellent if usual, Kermanshah. There were soft colored draperies hung about,—a couch covered with gay cushions, a pair of Barye bronzes. No bulbs were lit under the hideous colored-glass dome, and the two tall candles in wrought-iron sticks enhanced the room's good points.

"And why the sudden penury, Ilsa? Why—this?" He waved his hands to indicate the surroundings.

"Because I'm poor now. Because the place is cheap, and moreover, clean, which the cheap places with,—you know, atmosphere and fireplaces and things, never are. Because for the last year I've been flinging away the rewards of thrift as lavishly as ever I could."

"Why?"

"Oh, just because!" she retorted quickly. "Let's not talk about it. Let's return to our discussion. I don't fancy your condemnation of all my theories of life. I want to convince—"

"And I insist upon knowing," he cut in. "You've aroused my curiosity. Why the cessation of activities and the flat in the Bronx? Why—"

"And I refuse to go on with the subject." Bending over him from the arm of the chair, she laid her fingers on his lips. ...

Just then one of the candles sputtered, and went out ...

And, in a flash, the atmosphere changed. The street noises ceased abruptly, as if intermitted by the subtle influence, which as they looked into one another's faces, she as animated, he as collected as before, brought to her smile a quality of hesitant timidity, eradicated the softness about his lips, supplemented, with a mellifluent glow, the mordancy of his eyes. It was a trivial incident,—the extinction of a candle, but, with the dimmed light, an impalpable tenseness stole over them. Her face was in shadow; he saw only the glints in her russet hair, only the pellucid whiteness of the hand she withdrew slowly from his lips. After some minutes of absolute stillness, a little uneasily she stirred, and started to rise.

And as she stirred, the tension broke. With a quick movement he made to take her in his arms.

"Don't!" Her voice was a half gasp. With almost ferocious sinuosity, she eluded him, and sprang to her feet. He, too, rose.

"You're full of surprises, Ilsa. Why the virtuous indignation? Going in for grubbing and coyness as well as poverty these days?"

"Don't, Chris." She made the mistake of lifting her head a trifle too high, of rendering her voice the decisive trifle too imperious.

"Rot!" In perfect equanimity, collected, tranquil, he faced her. She appeared to take courage at his composure, laughed uncertainly, started to cross the room. And at her first step with a quick, rough gesture he caught her to him.

"Don't, I tell you."

Piercingly her voice rang out this time, and, lifting her hands to his shoulders with a sudden outburst of unexpected energy which took him by surprise, landed him back into the armchair, an undignified, ridiculous figure.

"Don't!" she reiterated in a whisper.

A flush of anger flooded his face. "Very good, casta diva, I won't, never fear. Far be it from me to curtail even the most sporadic attack of the virtues. But I don't find them particularly amusing. One more guzzle,—" he filled a whiskey glass, and emptied it in a swallow,—"and I'll leave you in vestal security."

"But I don't want you to go just yet, Chris." Full of inveighing self-confidence, she half blocked his way. But with a courteous "Sorry," he slipt past, and, as she followed him out of the room, reached for his hat.

"But I don't want you to go. Don't be childish. You don't understand...."

Persuasively she brought her smiling face close to his. "It's not disinclination or coquetry, dear. It's just—" suddenly her trilling laughter rang out,—"just bones, Chris!"

She ran her fingers along neck and shoulders. "Here,—and here,—and here,—all bones, and hollows, and ridges, and ugliness! I couldn't bear to have you touch them. That's why the high collar and the long sleeves. That's why the termination of activities. Oh, Chris, isn't it droll?" she carolled gleefully, "the damphool doctors,—they say I'm to mimi-camille!"

For an instant incredulity, and then blank astonishment inundated his face, as he stared at her standing before him, irradiate of life and joy.

"What's—what's this?" he stammered at last.

"Phthisis and tuberoses, nothing less, dear fellow." Motioning him to follow, she re-entered the room, and as he seated himself perplexedly, perched again on the arm of his chair.

"Don't look dumbfounded and appalled," she pleaded, laughing, "and above all else, don't wax compassionate. I'd always planned to quit about this time. Thirty's a good age to make one's getaway. I couldn't go on much longer acquiring husbands, it's against my principles pertinaciously to adhere after a year or two, and as for living on the spoils of my activities, could anything be duller than eventless middle age? I'm altogether ready, and willing, and content. Only... tuberculosis! Fate's always been nice and tractable and I rather fancied something unusual for a dénouement, an acute stomachache of some sort, for instance. ... To sublimate the stomachache! There'd be something worthy of my steel. But can you imagine me the star of a 'Traviata' finish? Can you imagine me going in for pathos, and wan woe, and deathbed scenes? Can you imagine the women gloating their sympathy, and the men all uneasiness and white flowers? Do you realize I've powder on my face to hide the hectic flush, that I'm all doped up to keep from coughing, that very, very soon my eyes are due to 'shine with febrile intensity'?" She grimaced at the quotation.

"Chris, will you please smile. It's not the least bit tragic. You don't really imagine I'd stand for any such foolery, do you? No! I've enjoyed the world so immensely that I don't at all mind leaving it. But in my own way! I've always had things my own way, and I'll have them my own way to the finish."

He looked up at her quickly. Hair, eyes, gown, skin, teeth, all shimmered. She seemed lustrous with the joy of existence. And watching her, even as his face paled slightly, he broke out into laughter.

"It's—it's simply impossible to feel sorry for you, Ilsa, while you sit beaming there. What's it to be, chloral or a jewelled poinard?"

"Poniard nothing! Daggers imply remorse, poison despair. It's to be a solid serviceable forty-four—and kindly omit flowers."

"*Coup de théâtre*, eh? Sublimate the revolver shot?"

"*Coup de théâtre*? Never in my life have I striven for effects. *Coup d'état*, rather. I'll purge the revolver shot of sentimentality, disconnect it from the idea of melodrama villainesses' sad ends...I'm not a bit unhappy, not a bit repentant, or dissatisfied, or unwilling. In fact I rather fancy just such a stimulating exit, and happy ending to the tale."

She leaned her head against his shoulder, and for a long time neither spoke. The candle flickered as if merrily; her smile was as bright as ever. Finally, slipping from the chair, she went over to the couch, and threw herself full length upon it, her hands clasped at the back of her neck. A translucent quality to her loveliness gave her an effect almost of other-worldliness, drew him to her, impelled him to rise, approach and with a frown of perplexity rather than censure, look steadily into the eyes that laughed up into his. At length she spoke:

"You still look a bit disapproving...I'm not such a much, eh, Chris?"

"Not such an any too much, bu—but splendid, old girl."

As she noted the break in his voice her eyes gleamed, and she caught his hand.

"Hot, and with icy finger tips," she whispered, "and you look gentle, tender, and a little awed, Chris, dear."

He bent over, kissed her quietly, and turned away.

Stretching her arms in lazy ecstasy, "Splendid!" she breathed. "The culminant thrill! Tenderness without desire, tenderness volatile, and therefore of lasting value—the one thing I've always wanted from men. ... And despite the bones! And from my one almost *amant de coeur!* Now I know I'm going in my prime ... now I know I've reached the apogée!

"Oh, Chris dear," she went on, shaking her head, "why do you still look a little discontented—as if things weren't quite as they should be? Come here—sit beside me—here, on the edge of the couch, and listen. ... I'll make you understand. ... "

Slowly she raised herself a little; leaned on her elbow; propped her chin in her hand.

"You've not been at your best tonight, Chris. You've sneered a little, and sentimentalized a little, and been a bit childish and—troglodytic as well. But you're a big man, a great man. I've heard your music. I know. And I think I know a little, a very, very little, about the great man's soul. Life's a sorry business to you, isn't it? A jumble and a joke? Just a long series of meaningless oscillations between the gutter and the stars? And you can't conceive, can you, of people absolutely honest with themselves finding it all delightful? I have, and therefore in a measure, unwillingly you condemn me, find me cheap and shallow... Oh, but Chris, I confess to cheapness and shallowness—I glory in it... Listen well...."

She slipt her arms about his neck, and proceeded, with her cheek against his :

"You know music. You know women. And, above all, you, the musician, must know sentimental women. What's music to them? A stimulant to the emotions, nothing more. They wax weepy over a Chopin nocturne, sentimental over Puccini, amorous over Tschaikowsky, sleepy over Brahms—and then say how they love the art, subscribe to symphony concerts, lionize the virtuosi, meddle with what should inspire awe. I've seen 'em; I know. And that's how they are in every way, inquisitive, meddlesome creatures always trying to mould a man's destiny, to ruin him, to reform him, to overturn no matter what, in no matter what way. I've watched the harpies many a time. ...

"Well, I don't pretend to understand music, nor to love it particularly. I hear Beethoven's Fifth—know that it's something stupendous and super-earthly, but don't feel, and don't pretend to feel, that it's so. I know it's something too big for me to understand, and don't meddle. And I've never in any way meddled. The only destiny I chose to mould was my own, and I've moulded it—according to my cheapness and shallowness, if you will, but according to a cheapness and shallowness which I never sought to hide, which never hurt a soul, and never made me ashamed. My stars—they're close to your gutter, Chris, but at any rate I've grasped them, and they please me!

"And do you know"—sitting bolt upright, she continued in whispered transport—"there's just where my significance, Ilsa Menteith's significance, will lie. Unceasing conflict, discontent, vacillation, striving, attainment without fulfilment—I've seen so much of that, and many a time lately I've lain here all day puzzling it out. They're the things that you, that all big beings contend with. I'm not big, I'm not even as much as a high-bred rounder—I'm just... middle-class! But praiseworthy, never -before -quite -attained -middle-class! I've had material, middle-class aims and ends, but I've achieved them, and they've made me happy. ... And I've never, never meddled with the big things that didn't concern me. I spent my early years among the middle classes, I belong to them, and I'm making my hejira here, in the Bronx, among my middle-class brothers and sisters. There's a little old man in this very house, a fat, slothful old man, a sanctimonious-looking little man with lewd lips—typical of them all, typical of the worst of them, of their crassness, and sluggishness, and meddlesomeness. Well, to-morrow there'll be a big sensation, and I tell you, they all—not only the distinct types who live here, but middle-class plutocrats, middle-class rowdy girls, middle-class whatnots as well—all of them, I tell you, will realize that I was one of them, and the first one absolutely to justify them. My life—Ilsa Menteith's life, will have had a real meaning! They'll pause, and ponder, and understand, if only dimly. ... And I'll be a symbol, a prophecy, a lesson, a watchword, a rallying cry! You'll see!"

She fell back among the pillows, panting in ardent exhaustion. With a touch of sadness, the man smiled into her enthusiastic eyes:

"Better not do it, Ilsa. You'll be an overnight sensation, that's all—copy for the sob-sisters, another opportunity for the pachyderms to sentimentalize, and flay the transgressor, and——"

"Sentimentalize? Flay the transgressor?" she broke in, "You're quite mad to think it, for why in heaven's name should they, Chris, dear? Prudishness and hypocrisy—there're the great middle-class attributes. Well, I've been a prude. I've insisted upon legitimatized alliances. And I've been a hypocrite in this very insistence, for no-one realized more keenly than I that material advantages were what I was after, that I'd have gotten them in the usual way if this one hadn't been successful, and that my game was merely a version of the jaded, old game. ... But I haven't meddled, and I haven't sentimentalized, and they'll all see. ... "

"You poor darling," he interrupted gently. "You're nothing but a wildly romantic, misguided darling for all your brave words. Not a one of them will understand."

Her lips drooped for an instant.

"You mean, Chris—my life—just a muddle, just a jumble—like everyone else's?"

"Just a hopeless muddle, dear."

"And they'll have a garbled version of it?"

"They'll be as sure they've penetrated its meaning as you are—as I am. And they'll be as wrong as you and I probably are. Sometimes, Ilsa … sometimes I think of a deity all of whose majesty, all of whose augustness and omniscience lies behind the fact that he doesn't pretend ever to understand his own creation."

Very tenderly he pressed her unresisting head to his shoulder, and stroked the silken hair, as he whispered :

"Don't do it, Ilsa. Not because it will be a futile thing, but because you'll be in for a few excessively nasty hours before the—the culmination. Stick to the deathbed finish fate's ordained. You can do it gracefully. You've done everything gracefully. You——"

But springing to her feet, "I'll not have it so!" she broke in, "You're the only one that's hopelessly muddled. I see it all so clearly. And they—if only dimly, if only each in his own, vague way, they'll understand, too, and they won't forget me! It's going to be exactly as I say. … Splendid!"

Just then the other candle sputtered, and went out In the darkness he could discern only the glint of her teeth as she smiled.

A church bell in the vicinity tolled ten times. In silence she waited for the last stroke, and then stretched out her hand.

"Good-night, Chris. Good luck with the oboes, and bassoons and things. … I'm going game?"

"Don't do——"

At her blithe smile he stopped short, and shrugged his shoulders. "One can't remonstrate." And after another pause:

"You're going game, Ilsa. … All luck in limbo, dear."

As he opened the door, a light from the hall gave him his final view of her. Vague, indistinct in the dimness, she seemed not so much a being as an impression—of a dauntlessness, a vim, a joy, of a smile—she seemed a wraith abrim with the verve of existence. …

At the landing he passed a pretty young woman in a pink kimono. In the lower hall he experienced an unpleasant feeling as of being peered upon through closed doors. And, going out into the street, in his abstraction he almost knocked over a little, fat old man.

A HUMORESQUE IN HAM

Ben Hecht

I

THE name of Jim Sloan was powerful in Chicago. There was a certain familiar magic to the ring of it. Just as the name of De Maupassant evoked for the people of Chicago visions of lacy bedrooms, and the name of Caesar visions of Ed. Pinaud's hair tonic, and the name of Pere Marquette visions of a bad railroad, so was the name of Jim Sloan also potent in the evoking of visions. People spoke his name and thought not of him but of a ham, a large ham, shaped like a lopsided, inverted mandolin and labelled *"Sloan's Premium Ham—The Best."*

This ham was Jim Sloan. To a few intimates there was a man who bore the name, who exercised himself in human activities, but to the people of Chicago there was no such person. There was only the ham. Outlined in electric lights this ham blazed above the night-hidden roofs of State Street. It gestured in the crowded cars. It grimaced in the newspapers. Magazines were full of its potent contours. It hung in the windows of butcher shops.

For sixty-two years the name of Sloan had meant the lithograph of a ham. That many years ago Mike Sloan had started killing pigs out around Thirty-ninth and Halsted streets. At first Mike Sloan had managed to kill only some ten or twelve pigs a day. But being a man of genius he had, in the course of time, risen to the height of killing 857 pigs a day. And thus, at the zenith of his career, he had died and been buried with all the pomp befitting the killer of 857 pigs every twenty-four hours. But the death of Mike Sloan had meant no respite for the pigs. To the contrary, Jim Sloan, his only son and inheritor of his wealth and genius, had leaped into the breach and upheld the family honor by taking the lives of 903 pigs every day of each year following Mike Sloan's interment.

Already the name of Sloan had become a ham. Now, after fifteen years, the ham had engraved itself on the consciousness of every nation of the earth. Certain modern minds knew that Jim Sloan also killed cows and sheep and owned a large section of South Water Street wherein butter, eggs and vegetables were sold. They were aware of him as a series of huge, ramshackle buildings surrounded by pens full of animals and reeking with blood, hides and fats. But in a world given to superficial perceptions, such rare discernment was for the minority.

"Sloan's Premium Ham—The Best" remained Jim Sloan and Jim Sloan remained a being worshiped and admired by the proletariat as a succulent, juicy ham shaped like the map of Africa and purchasable in all corners of the earth.

In his office on the second floor of the James Sloan & Company plant, Jim Sloan sat at a flat-topped mahogany desk and stared out of a carefully washed window. It was early afternoon of a gloomy Spring day. A gray-mustached man appeared in the door of the office and said in a precise and respectful voice:

"Mr. Archer wants to see you, Mr. Sloan."

"Can't see him," said Jim Sloan.

The man in the door looked for an instant perplexed.

"I beg your pardon, Mr. Sloan. "It's the Archer from the Brimstone Ranch. I think he's finally come around. He's had a break with Armour's, and I think…"

"Can't see him, Wilson," said Jim Sloan, without removing his eyes from the window. "Tell him to come tomorrow. I've important things to attend to."

Wilson hesitated and then, with a faithful sigh, removed himself from the door.

Jim Sloan remained staring out of the window. He was a man of forty, groomed and barbered into a creature becoming the poise and affluence of his estate. There was about his solid features and his portly figure, likewise, the decisiveness and power which the consciousness of "Sloan's

Premium Ham—The Best" had brought in fifteen years. Men who had known Mike Sloan proclaimed the son somewhat softer, somewhat less pugnacious than the father. Nevertheless they perceived in him the same sterling genius which had enabled the father to begin killing ten hogs a day and die with a record of 857.

Encasing himself in a gray, light overcoat, Jim Sloan moved from his office. His passage down the long corridor, nodding here and there to grayhaired employés who sat among the two hundred and eighty-four desks within the main office enclosure, created, as always, a stir among the men and women bending over files, ledgers and letters. Although they saw him daily, Jim Sloan remained to them as aloof and unknown a creature as he was to the multitude which respected him in the name of a ham. They became conscious of themselves as a smear of atoms combining to complete the organism known as James Sloan & Company.

The odor of salt, freshly stripped hides, vats of blood and fats, enveloped Jim Sloan as he progressed down the broad steps of the red brick office building. In front of the door stood a clean and luxurious automobile. In this automobile Jim Sloan rode home.

For the first ten minutes the automobile bumped along over roads wet with the drippings from the carcass wagons. The sounds of a vast and orderly activity came to his ears. About him stretched a zigzagging world of wooden enclosures alive with silent, restless animals. Men in dirty white aprons and smeared overalls emerged suddenly from scores of gloomy doorways. Wagons piled high with the steaming semblance of cows, sheep and pigs crisscrossed in all directions. Overhead ran a network of wooden walks and the automobile was continually passing under puzzling and enormous scaffoldings.

But to Jim Sloan the scene was a curious blur, a familiar thing seen out of focus. His eyes took no account of the slaughter-houses and the pens, of the curving, trampled road. His nose apparently registered none of the flat, pungent and salty odors which hung, steam like, over the huge areas about him. His ears remained undisturbed by the clatter and shriek of the marvelous places in which 903 pigs were being put to the knife and 605 beef cattle adroitly tapped on the skull between each sunrise and each sunset. There was curious thought in Jim Sloan's brain and he remained lost in the elaboration of it as the automobile sped out of the rickety cross-streets on to the boulevard and spun leisurely northward towards Lake Shore Drive.

The sightseers, when they rode down Lake Shore Drive in the $1 round trip carryalls, were always bidden by the enterprising assistant charioteer to "gaze, ladies and gentlemen, on your left. The mansion we are now passing is the home of James Sloan, the man who makes The Ham. In that wonderful house lives James Sloan himself, his wife and daughter, Elizabeth." As the carryall rumbled on, the sightseers turned their necks and allowed their eyes to linger with casual fascination upon the place. Visions of large and tempting hams drifted before them and a sense of the curious incongruity of life abided with them as they bestowed their itinerant attention upon succeeding objects. The thought of "Sloan's Premium Ham—The Best" having a home, moving about within four walls and sleeping in a bed, offered this incongruity.

II

JIM SLOAN entered his home on this gloomy spring day with an eager step. The stern and placid composure of his face gave way suddenly to a certain brightness of his eyes, a certain movement of his lips which made him appear younger and less important than the Jim Sloan who had walked down the corridor from his office. A servant materialized in the spacious, tapestry-hung hall of the Sloan home and assumed charge of Sloan's gray light overcoat and hat. Rubbing his hands together and delivering himself of a cheerful cough, Jim Sloan walked hurriedly toward an open door.

The room which he entered was spacious and gray-walled. It had the air of being a chamber devoted to utter rarity and exclusiveness. It was the music-room of the Sloan home. It was a cheerless and magnificent *salle*, furnitured with forbidding chairs and cabinets, and distinguished by the presence of a grand piano, five massively framed oil paintings of famous composers, a glass-covered case in which reposed an assortment of curious instruments, and a short, wiry-faced man who resembled a monk because of a peculiarly located bald spot, and whose name was Professor Enrico Sansone. Godowsky had played in this room. Grainger had sat before this grand piano. Paderewski and Josef Hofmann had looked out these long, shining windows at the stretch of lawn. Zimbalist and Kreisler, Ysaye and Heifetz had likewise trod these ivory-tinted and golden-gleaming carpets. And yet it was a room to make a musician like Enrico Sansone uncomfortable. Despite the massively framed portraits of Mozart, Beethoven, Schumann, Liszt and Wagner, there was no music in the room. Despite the ebony spread of the piano there was no hint of melody about the precincts.

Thus Professor Enrico Sansone turned with a fretful air. He spoke like one privileged to say things. He said:

"Ah, Mr. Slowan, you come late."

Jim Sloan nodded his head and smiled.

"It's all right, Professor," he answered. "I'll make it up by surprising you this time in another respect."

"Ver' well," said the professor. "To work!"

With another rub of his hands and a spontaneous clearing of his throat, Jim Sloan walked to a corner of the room and from one of the cabinets extracted a black leather violin case. From the case he brought forth a violin, after removing a brocaded velvet covering. It was a Cremona, low-chinned, full of garnet and russet shadings.

Professor Sansone, his hands thrust in his coat pockets, his legs apart, watched enigmatically the operations attending the tuning of the violin. As Sloan placed it under his chin and tucked his head to one side, the professor cried :

"No, no. The exercises first."

The look of an aggrieved boy passed over Jim Sloan's face.

"I would like to show you the *Legende*," he murmured.

"The exercises first," repeated Professor Sansone, "and then you can show me, Mr. Slowan."

With a grim air, the little Italian walked into a corner of the room, removed from the shadows an elaborately carved wooden music stand, placed it beside the piano and dressed it with a large green folio labeled "David's Violin Studies." Jim Sloan faced the stand and began the execution of a page arranged for the bewilderment of all violinists. For ten minutes the endless arpeggios continued, interrupted only by sudden exclamations of the professor. At their conclusion the little Italian became full of fury.

"What have you studied?" he cried. "It ees worse, ver' much worse. Your left hand is like a cow."

Jim Sloan winced at the word.

"But, professor," he remonstrated weakly.

"No, no, no. I tell you you must practise scales, exercises. The *Legende* ees nothing. Thees ees ever' thing. Play heem once more."

A glutton for punishment, Professor Sansone threw himself into one of the forbidding chairs and sat stoically silent as Jim Sloan went through the jarring double stops, the intricate and unharmonious passages of the two pages before him.

When he had finished the second time, the little Italian again arose, walked the length of the chamber, frowned upon the portrait of Wagner, and exclaimed:

"Your fingers are like a child. They have no power. Your wrist ees stiff. Your right arm ees cramp all the time."

Jim Sloan, holding the Cremona by its neck, looked appealingly at the little Italian.

"I've put in an hour a day," he explained.

"And what ees that?" cried Sansone. "One hour! Oh, God, one hour! How many hours you spend keeling pigs? If you wish to be violinist you cannot spend twelve hours keeling pigs and one hour keeling music. Oh, God! One hour!"

A look of poignant shame came into Sloan's face. He shifted uneasily on his feet and seemed at a loss for answer.

"I guess you're right," he finally said. "But I promise to make it two hours."

A grin spread the lips of the little Italian.

"The *Legende*," he commanded.

Professor Enrico Sansone sat staring out of the window of the Sloan mansion, his back turned upon Jim Sloan, the packer. The slow, melodious gusto of Wieniawski's little piece filled the gray room.

"It is not bad," Professor Sansone murmured to himself, "like an earnest boy. Too stiff, too slippery."

He continued listening with a frown as the music progressed.

Jim Sloan, standing beside the piano, let his soul run out of his fingers. It was not the soul of Jim Sloan, the meat packer, that came thus to the strings. It was rather a nebulous and awkward thing, which threw itself feverishly, if impotently, into the doublestop trio, which whinnied dolorously on the high E, which gurgled languorously on the low B. It was a soul which had never known the power of "Sloan's Premium Ham—The Best." It was a strange, frostbitten, crippled, spavined soul, airing itself in the unfamiliar luxury of song.

There was a Jim Sloan who bartered in South Water Street, who swung deals involving one million eggs, who sat smoking, swearing and spitting at directors' meetings, who fought and intrigued over pigs grunting obliviously in far places of the earth, who excited himself over shipping marines and international contracts, who, in short, was "Sloan's Premium Ham—The Best," vitalized. But a curious thing had happened to that Jim Sloan.

Unrest had fought its way through the labyrinth of pig pens and office corridors into his heart. Mike Sloan had found no time for unrest. Mike had exhausted his genius enthroning himself behind 857 dead pigs a day. Not so Jim, his son. The slaughter-house was no longer the battleground for undiluted energies in the Sloan & Company plant. Efficiency had removed Jim Sloan further and further from the stress of actual conflict. It was as if 903 pigs came into his life daily and committed suicide. He signed documents for their disposal. He negotiated sterile though impressive contracts. He became bustlingly idle, pompously abstract. He began to feel ennuied at thirty-five. His wife and daughter, moving in state from capital to capital, graced his vision two months out of the year. For two months he buried himself in distracting leisure among men who danced and gambled, and women who maintained a mysterious excitement in their lives.

It was at a concert five years ago at one of his summer homes that Jim Sloan had discovered his soul. From some hidden and incongruous depths of his being had been suddenly liberated a desire to make music. Since that day he had, like a man conducting an awkward liaison, given himself to a secret dream. Daily Jim Sloan, the meat packer, had become more and more of a husk, and Jim Sloan who sat enraptured at concerts, who sawed on his Cremona in his empty house, who aspired to things he dared not even name to himself, became the reality.

Standing now playing the *Legende,* he was conscious of a curious warmth in his body. Lost in the sweet intensity that music making brought to him, he remained unaware of the flatted tremolos that issued into the room, of the slurred cadenza that deepened the frown on Professor Sansone's face. With an amorousness which rendered him almost grotesque, he gave himself over to the production of sound. He finished and stood flushed and silent, regarding the back of the little Italian.

Professor Sansone, turning, hesitated a moment. In the eyes of his pupil he saw a light which confused him.

"That ees ver' fine," he whispered.

Jim Sloan laughed softly.

"I thought you'd like it," he said. Both men became silent. At last Sloan resumed.

"Tell me candidly, Professor, what are my chances?"

"Chances?" murmured Sansone. "There ees no such thing as chances. Practise, Mr. Slowan. That ees all which make perfec'."

"I mean," said Sloan slowly, "have I got it in me? Is there any hope of my becoming... becoming a..."

Jim Sloan paused and drew a deep breath.

"Becoming... becoming," cried the professor abruptly. "What ees it you wish to become? If you practise you become able to play the violin. Ees that not enough?"

As his pupil remained silent, Professor Sansone bethought himself suddenly of the $40 he received for each hour spent in the Sloan mansion, and a kindly smile lighted his wiry face.

"Ah, Mr. Slowan," he added, "if you started to play as a boy you would now be one great violinist. But you start late and who knows? Perhaps in five more years, perhaps in seven, you will be an artist. You have it in you, Mr. Slowan."

III

NONE of the people who saw and knew Jim Sloan had ever suspected his devotion to violin playing, had ever imagined for an instant that he was other than a quietly domineering force in the finances of the western world. Through this world which knew him as the shrewd and compelling dealer in cattle, grain and produce, Jim Sloan moved, thinking intently of passages from serenades and concertos, going over in his mind the fingering of curiously contrived exercises. His dream seemed in no way to impair his efficiency as head of Sloan & Company. With a cunning almost automatic, he indited letters, oversaw reports, made suggestions, attended conferences.

Jim Sloan's ambition to play the violin was in the beginning devoid of any desire to achieve public recognition as an artist. It was at the outset no more than a dogged and mechanical longing to master an unknown field, just as Mike, his revered parent, and founder of the Premium Ham, had mastered the then chartless field of wholesale slaughter. But as the years progressed, Jim Sloan's preoccupation with his new and intriguing craft became confused with disturbing fancies. At night he lay awake in his soft bed visioning himself upon a stage, he and his violin. He saw himself as an arresting figure of genius, as a virtuoso whose name inspired awe in the minds of men. True to his promise to Sansone, he increased his daily practise to two hours. The little Italian, calling twice a week at the Sloan mansion, saw developing under his tutelage one of those tragedies of misplaced effort which to a great teacher is like unto crowns of thorns.

It was at the close of one of his lessons late that spring that Jim Sloan first heard the curious name of Slovel Selzow. The little Italian, after much frowning, spoke it.

"There ees a boy who work in your company," he said, "by name Slovel Selzow, a Lithuanian. Have you heard of heem?"

Jim Sloan smiled, bethinking himself suddenly of some two thousand creatures who might or might not bear the name of Slovel Selzow.

"No," he said.

"Too bad," Sansone exclaimed. "He ees one great violin player."

"Is that so?" inquired Jim Sloan carelessly.

"It ees," snapped the little Italian. "And because he have no money to learn, this great artist must keel pigs."

A frown passed over Sloan's face. There was in the Italian's voice something which penetrated the placid indifference he had always held toward the toilers who brought into the world "Sloan's Premium Ham— The Best."

"I give heem one lesson now and then," Sansone went on, "but I cannot afford ver' often. And he can come only on Sunday when he ees not at work, keeling pigs."

"A Lithuanian butcher who plays the violin," mused Jim Sloan, "would be interesting."

Five years ago Jim Sloan might have, with certain magnificent gestures, scribbled a check which would have insured the future of Slovel Selzow, killer of pigs. This afternoon he remained staring with narrowed eyes out of the window of the music-room. After a pause he spoke slowly:

"I know what you expect, Professor. But I am not a philanthropist. If this pig killer is a genius let him be one. We're both in the same boat, he and I. He hasn't any more to contend with, killing pigs, than I have running the plant. I'm asking help from no one."

"You," began Enrico Sansone and stopped. Jim Sloan caught the word and the tone of it.

"How old is this violinist?" he asked brusquely.

"Twenty year old," said Sansone, recovering his calm.

"Twenty years old, eh? And a genius? Well, Professor, if he shows himself a good killer of pigs I'll promote him to a dresser. I'm not employing violinists."

This somewhat slight conversation marked a strange turning point in Jim Sloan's life. The name Slovel Selzow somehow stuck in his imaginings. With it the tone of the professor remained. As he passed down the lumpy, worn road of Packingtown to the office of the Sloan plant the next day, he eyed the ramshackle and monstrous buildings in which animals were suffering death and dismemberment with an odd sensation of interest. Within one of them worked this Slovel Selzow. Several young men emerged from the doorways and hurried in their overalls and aprons across the road. Any of them might be Selzow, he thought, watching them as the automobile in which he was riding bore him serenely forward.

There was something about the idea of a young Lithuanian pig killer aspiring to be an artist of the violin that exercised a fascination over Jim

Sloan's thought, as he moved through the routine of his work that day. For a number of succeeding days the idea abided with him.

At first he thought only of Slovel Selzow with an impersonal speculation. He pictured him standing on the blood-soaked platform, knife in hand. He pictured the huge wheel revolving like some monstrous rack with four pigs always dangling by their hind feet from as many projections. It was the duty of the killer of pigs to slash their throats as they revolved slowly. He pictured Slovel Selzow doing this mechanically callous thing. And when he had done with his impersonal picturings, the words of Professor Sansone would come to his thought.

" ... this great artist must keel pigs!"

In the course of two weeks Slovel Selzow became an inspiration to Jim Sloan. No longer was there anything impersonal about the Lithuanian pig killer. Logical in the presence of his friends, always shrewd and controlled in the society of his fellow men, Jim Sloan reserved for his secret and dream world the caprice of an infant. Things which came into this world, little things of utter unimportance, uncentered him more than the most strategic difficulties which came before him at his desk in the Sloan plant. Thus Slovel Selzow, whom he had never seen, suddenly acquired for Jim Sloan the depressing characteristics of some violent rival.

Inspired by this notion, he telegraphed his wife that he would not have time to spend two months this year at their summer home. He would show Slovel Selzow who was the greater genius. He would reveal this matter to Sansone. He would, above all, make certain of it to himself. There could be no half measures. He thought with elation of the eight-hour day which all faithful killers of pigs were forced to put in at the Sloan plant. The work was tiring. Slovel Selzow could not survive it. Yet it was no more demanding than his own work.

These were the almost grotesque cogitations which darkened Jim Sloan's brow during the early days of summer and which kindled in his eye exultant lights. Professor Sansone was the first to notice the change which had overtaken the famous packer. Instead of an enthusiastic dilettante, the good professor found suddenly on his hands a creature consecrated heart and soul to some strangely pathetic ideal. The half-hearted technique, which his pupil had been wont to exhibit in the rendition of the finger exercises, was replaced now by a desperate attention to detail, an arresting fidelity to bowing and the sliding of the wrist. A certain improvement was achieved. But, sitting one day late in summer in the familiar music-room, listening to his pupil execute a Viotti concerto, Sansone mused sadly upon the oddities of life.

"He is impossible," he murmured to himself. "He has no soul. No fire. Why does a man without soul or fire seek to play the violin? He is like a fat baby. He is no good. God, what a waste of time, what a waste of money! What a waste of ambition! And Slovel must kill pigs six days a week. Yet Slovel is a genius. I must make the boy an artist. Six. months and he will be ready. This fat baby could play sixty years and not create a note."

Aloud, when Jim Sloan had finished, he said:

"Ah, Mr. Slowan, you are working hard. There is improvement. It ees fine."

Jim Sloan smiled with grimness. He understood, in some crevice of his brain, the antagonism which Sansone cherished toward him. To the professor he, Jim Sloan, was a brash and insolent interloper, a pork butcher de luxe invading with dripping boots the fields of art. Sansone was necessary, however. He was the best teacher in the country. And he, Jim Sloan, needed no further inspiration than the peculiar hate which had sprung up in his heart.

For Jim Sloan had reached the final altitude of hate. He had achieved an enemy with whom he had hourly to contend. The enemy was Slovel Selzow. By a series of distorted and bizarre imaginings Slovel Selzow had grown to Sloan to embody the mockery of fate—a phrase which he left unexplained. He reasoned only that he would not permit a Lithuanian butcher to surpass him playing the violin. Hour after hour he harassed the echoes with page upon page of Kreutzer and David, De Beriot and Viotti. For the two months of his usual vacation, Jim Sloan absented himself from his huge business and, closeted five hours a day in the music-room, pursued his monomania, his driving ambition, his determination to become now a great and overwhelming master of the violin.

IV

PROFESSOR ENRICO SANSONE had never mentioned the name of Slovel Selzow to Jim Sloan after their first talk of him. It was thus through the medium of an artistic lithograph inserted within one of the glass cases in the lobby of Orchestra Hall that Jim Sloan first learned of the great event. The lithograph eyed by Sloan as he was emerging one evening from a symphony concert, accompanied by two friends, revealed the face of a young man with a shock of uncombed hair and the pronounced features of a Slav. Above and beneath the face was printed :

Prof. Enrico Sansone
Presents
SLOVEL SELZOW
in a Violin Recital
September 23.

When he had quitted his friends, who chanced to be social acquaintances of his wife, Jim Sloan walked bewilderedly past his home. He had dismissed his chauffeur. He walked now along the lake front, a sharp, gloomy wind sweeping him from the water. As he walked a furious emotion confused him. He had failed. Sansone had not bidden him to give a recital, to make a début. Sansone had played with him for the few dollars there was in it. Slovel Selzow, the enemy, the creature who killed pigs and stood covered with blood on a platform eight hours a day, was to come into his own as an artist. He, Jim Sloan, was to remain as a butcher de luxe.

As always, the situation presented itself to him with neither lucidity of thought nor analysis. His pride now, as he walked, choked him. The night was a tempestuous, wounded thing to him. The gloom of it on the water was like the gloom in his soul. The wind sweeping him was like the aimless wildness of his thought. Gradually Slovel Selzow outlined himself before him as a man who had stolen from him his dreams, robbed him of something fearsomely precious.

That night as he lay in his bed Jim Sloan wept, "Sloan's Premium Ham—The Best" wept because it could not play the violin as well as a

Lithuanian butcher boy. During the month that preceded the concert Sloan never touched the Cremona. It lay gathering dust and uncovered on the piano where he had thrust it one evening. The 23d of September became for him a day of dark forebodings. He thought of it as of some hideous climax to his life.

At his desk Jim Sloan was the silent, imperturbable chief he had always been. As by some last mockery of fate, the business of the Sloan plant expanded during the month. A meeting of directors yielded a dividend more luscious than any in the history of the institution. Jim Sloan, glowering and domineering, recalling in this exaggerated guise of his the contours and manners of his parent, Mike, presided at this meeting, made a brief address concerning his satisfaction in the matter, and returned to his empty home that night thinking blackly of a Lithuanian named Slovel Selzow. A letter from his wife, awaiting him, served only to increase the darkness in his heart. In the letter were ridiculous sentences concerning tardy trains and unsatisfactory hotels and banal personages encountered in London. He tore it up and shoved the pieces in his pocket. The 23d of September was a week off.

The people in Chicago who attended concerts had cultivated a faith in Enrico Sansone. He had in the past revealed to them notable performers. Like Campanini, he was one of the rallying points of dinner conversation and one of the boasts of the élite. Thus on the night of the 23d Orchestra Hall was well filled. Professor Sansone had announced in an interview published in all the music columns that he would stake his reputation on the genius of this, his latest find.

A flutter of applause greeted Slovel Selzow as he walked stiffly out of the wings and took his position to the left of the piano. He was a tall, stocky youth with a large head. He played a Beethoven concerto.

Through the spaces of the hall which had stirred to the echoes of Thomas and Bull, of Joachim and Ysaye, of Wieniawski and Wilhelmj, throbbed the music of a new master. Clear and resonant, possessed of a strange urge and a stranger repression, tone poured from Slovel Selzow's violin. For moments it was the sound of seraphim singing shrilly at the feet of God, for moments it was the *passionata* of abandoned souls. But always, clear and possessed, the music reared and plunged against the hearts of the silent listeners. There were groups of violinists in the audience. These sat with heads lowered, listening to their dreams embodied in sound, perceiving their ambitions issuing from the strings of the violin on the stage.

When it was over a demonstration occurred seldom witnessed in the famous hall. Men and women leaped to their feet and cheered. Others cried :

"Selzow ... Selzow! Encore!"

On the wave of this tumult which filled the auditorium, the name of Slovel Selzow swept triumphantly into the world. The boy who had stood on the platform in the slaughter-house sticking four pigs in the throat every ten minutes became an idol at whose feet the world rushed to lay its love and worship.

The door of the hall opened and a single man emerged. The tumult was still at its height. The cries of "Encore! Encore!" were still rising. Jim Sloan walked through the lighted and deserted lobby and into the avenue. People who did not know Slovel Selzow was playing the violin that night were passing in the avenue. Jim Sloan joined them. He had left his light overcoat behind. He walked with his hat in his hand for a space and then automatically placed it on his head.

A curious fever burned in Jim Sloan's blood. He had heard Slovel Selzow play. He raised his eyes to the night. He had walked out of the avenue into the narrow parkway which skirted the lake on the Drive in which he lived. Standing above the water, the wind pressed against him and toppled his hat from his head. His emotions were unaccountable. A pain throbbed in his heart and the sound of Slovel Selzow's playing uncoiled in his brain like threads of fire. From his eyes came tears. For moments he stood facing the night-hidden water. Then he turned and with eyes raised still, gazed at the sky blurred with yellow, which covered the streets behind him. High against the night, outlined in a brilliant necklace of electric bulbs, he saw, blazing above the roof tops, the effulgent and triumphant sign,

Sloan's Premium Ham—The Best Buy It Now!

A block away a street-organ was playing "The Justine Johnstone Glide." Jim Sloan looked into the water. For several minutes he was immovable. Then, shrugging his shoulders, he turned upon his heel and started slowly home. ...

CRÊPE DE CHINE

James Stephens

Author of "Here Are Ladies," "The Crock of Gold," "Mary, Mary," etc.

THE thing came on her like a thunderbolt, and indeed while she was submitting to destiny the phrase "like a bolt from the blue" did detach itself for an instant in her consciousness, but it was fallen upon and buried by the avalanche of emotions and angers and plannings which her mind was trying so vainly to deal with.

She had gone, it was a custom of hers on sunny afternoons, into the Saint Stephen's Green Park and had walked a little, and sat a little, and looked for a while at the flowers and at the ducks swimming each with a tiny brood bobbing lightly in its wake; and at a seagull that swooped and slanted to touch the water with the tip of its bill, and then, without a pause, slid widely sideways, and up easily again, and away on adventures never to be recorded.

Her purpose was to go down Grafton Street to a shop in the window of which, too late for action on the previous evening, she had seen a blouse marked at a price which she believed must be a mistake or a shop trick. She foresaw there would be trouble in the shop when she asked for it at the price marked on the ticket, and that the salespeople would say the blouse was too small for her, and would try to make her take another of the same kind at three times the price. But she meant to give battle and was determined not to leave the shop without the identical blouse whether it fitted her or whether it did not.

She was in the Green to prepare herself for this battle, for by gazing on tranquil water we gain something of its tranquillity, and the untroubled serenity of flowers and blue skies would give her the serenity of mind which could break even the will of a drapery salesman.

If, she thought, they send me a saleswoman I shall have a hard fight, but if they send me a man I may win without much trouble, for men get tired easily. Also, she thought, men cannot fight well when they know they are in the wrong, but women fight as well for the wrong as for the right. The man will know that the figure marked on the blouse is an advertising trick designed to entice people into the shop, and when I accuse him of that he will give in where a woman would not.

The influence of the peaceful, sunny place had done its work and feeling braced and tranquil she arose from the iron seat and turned up the alley by the lake towards the Grafton Street exit. When she stood she looked across the pond and noticed that two friends of hers were seated in the shade of a small tree, and the thought came to her that she would tell them of her errand. She might even ask them to accompany her, for in a shop all discussion closes when several voices are raised in protest.

She went across the steep little bridge and bore down on her friends. They did riot notice her approach, and she thought smilingly: "When women so lose themselves in talk they are either talking scandal or dress." And she halted a moment so that she might not come on them too abruptly. The short, bushy tree was between them, and on this side of the tree also there was a seat.

The instant she halted she heard her own name mentioned, and knew that she was the subject of the scandal if scandal it was. She smiled shyly, slipped into the seat on her side of the tree, and listened to the talk of her friends.

In a few seconds she was no longer smiling, and where she had been listening carelessly she now listened with her whole being.

"How did he come to marry her?" said one voice.

"He didn't marry her, my dear," the other voice replied, "she married him."

"She must be at least ten years older than he is."

"Yes, at least, and I'm sure he knows it by this."

"Do they get on together, do you think?"

"One never knows, but I would say they do not. They snap a good deal at each other, and even when he does not snap he seems always impatient when she is speaking."

"Well, she has a strident voice."

"She never talks, she yells, and he is one of those strung-up people who get shivers when—Do you know what I think?"

"What do you think?"

"I think that some day or other he will run away from her."

"I don't think he will do that. I don't think he is the kind … of man—"

"I do. I think he is exactly the kind of man. If they had children he is the kind of man who would never leave his children: but they have none, and that is the only thing which could hold him to her. Think of the way she yells in a room or in a restaurant, and how quiet he is. Every movement of hers must seem to him like the worst kind of vulgarity. And she is vulgar, look at the day she dresses. She is always a fright. If she has the right skirt she has the wrong boots, and when her blouse is right, her hat is wrong. She hasn't got a particle of taste, the poor thing."

"She has no taste in dress, that is true, but—"

"She has no taste in anything, and she draws attention to herself always, always. He must hate to be with her."

"Men don't see these things."

"Don't they, my dear! Don't they! That type of man notices everything. I've seen him looking at her when he didn't know anyone was looking at him. Oh! I'm no fool, and I tell you this, that I'll bet you anything he'll run away from her."

"Oh, now, she is not so bad as you say."

"Not for us, but for him she is worse than anything we could say. He hates her, and if he doesn't run away from her before the year is out I—I'll never believe in my own judgment again."

"If only she had a child, the poor thing!"

"She hasn't one and she'll never have one, you and I know that."

Listening to them, she grew livid with rage. She rose to her feet, stepped carefully to the grass and walked away.

These were her friends!

These gabby monsters who kissed her every time they met and kissed her every time they parted! And they were always meeting. She went to tea in their houses : they came to tea in hers. Oh! They would not take tea together again. Never again would either of these women put a foot inside her door. That was one thing gained from it all. She knew her enemies now. She was warned at least. Ah, but she would meet them. She would meet them once more and she would cut them to the bone. Now she knew the run of their tongues, but they did not know hers yet. Her husband did, and they would, too. Her husband! He was to run away from her! Well, she would see about that, too. That man! Man! He was more like a snail than a man. And he was to run away from her! She would like to see him run. Indeed, if there was a run in him she would make him run. And he wasn't pleased with her ways. He looked at her, it seemed, when he thought no one observed him, and looked at her as if he hated her. One of these days he might have cause to hate her. A stuck-up prig that thought no one was to open their lips except himself. And he had to have two clean collars every day. And no one but himself was under any circumstances to go into his study. And no one was to open their mouths while his mouth was open. And he wanted a bedroom all to himself. And he wanted his meals at regular hours. And he wanted to go out whenever he liked and come in at all hours. And he wanted his clothes properly brushed. Well! All those things would be seen to, and he would learn that he wasn't a gay bachelor any longer. She would teach him that he had a wife, and that she had her rights, and that she would have her rights.

As she walked her brain was reeling with rage and spite. She would joyfully have learned that her two friends were dead : that they had been crushed by a tram or that a roof had fallen in on them. Less than that they did not deserve, but for her husband no catastrophe could be enormous enough, no torment sufficiently harrowing : no death or disaster of which she could think would be adequate to that man's perfidy. Man! and away her mind went again denouncing and sneering and threatening.

She forgot all about the blouse which was marked vastly below its proper price in the Grafton Street window; she forgot about her two friends and what they had said of her under the tree in the Park: she forgot about the street and the people in the street whom she jostled and pushed aside without raising an eye to them : she remembered only that there was someone whom she could make pay for all this : someone whom she would make pay and she was hastening towards him to make him pay.

The evening was advanced and although the sun was still shining it was shining with a difference. That limpid clarity of the morning was gone: the strong white glare of afternoon had changed : here was now a dust of gold, the first veil of those innumerable veilings which the evening does not cease to spread until her obscurity is complete, and life is hushed, and all the eyes that were open close in quietness.

Under this tender radiance she walked home and untouched by it, touched only by the lowest passions of her being she reached home.

The maid who opened the door said, in reply to her question, that the master was not in yet; and she remembered that at that hour he always went for a walk. "He has been out a long time today," said the maid.

She went upstairs and took off her hat.

Reminders of her husband were visible everywhere through the house. Here was one of his waistcoats; there was a cigar case; yonder a pair of his slippers, and the sight of them set her off again. ... "And he must have a separate bedroom, and he must have this, and he must have that, and no one else is to have anything. And no one is to say a word until he has finished speaking. And no one is to go into his study. ... "

She arose and marched resolutely downstairs and into his study. She sat down, looking about the room with a feeling of dislike that was almost hatred even for the room. A sheet of paper was lying on the table and she drew it idly towards her. It was written upon. She read it. It was a short note saying he could no longer live with her and giving the address of his solicitors, who would regulate their affairs and make all the necessary arrangements. It said that under no circumstances would he ever return to her.

As she read the blood ebbed at one stroke from her cheeks, and at a stroke rushed blindingly back again, and her hand that held the paper began to tremble violently.

SOME LADIES AND JURGEN

James Branch Cabell

I

IN the old days lived a poet named Jurgen; but what his wife called him was very often much worse than that. She was a high-spirited woman, with no especial gift for silence. Well, in the old days Jurgen was passing the Cistercian Abbey, and one of the monks had tripped over a stone in the roadway. He was cursing the devil who had placed it there.

"Fie, brother!" says Jurgen, "and have not the devils enough to bear as it is?"

"I never held with Origen," replied the monk; "and, besides, it hurt my great toe confoundedly."

"None the less," observes Jurgen, "it does not behoove God-fearing persons to speak with disrespect of the divinely appointed Prince of Darkness. Then, to your further confusion, consider this monarch's industry! Day and night you may detect him toiling at the task Heaven set him. That is a thing can be said of few communicants and of no monks. Think, too, of his fine artistry, as evinced in all the perilous and lovely snares of this world, which it is your business to combat, and mine to make verses about! Why, but for him we would both be vocationless. Then, moreover, consider his philanthropy! and deliberate how insufferable would be our case if you and I, and all of us, were today hobnobbing with all other beasts in the Garden which we pretend to desiderate on Sundays! To arise with swine and lie down with the hyena?—oh, intolerable!" So he ran on, devising reasons for not thinking too harshly of the devil. Most of it was an abridgement of his own verses.

"I consider that to be stuff and nonsense," was the monk's glose.

"No doubt your notion is sensible," observed the poet; "but mine is the prettier. ..."

Well, and then Jurgen met a black gentleman, who saluted him and said:

"Thanks, Jurgen, for your good word."

"Who are you, and why do you thank me?" asks Jurgen.

"My name is no great matter. But you have a kind heart, Jurgen. May your life be free from care!"

"Glory be to God, friend, but I am already married."

"Eh, sirs, and a fine, clever poet like you! No matter, the morning is brighter than the evening. How I will reward you, to be sure."

So Jurgen thanked him politely. And when Jurgen reached home his wife was nowhere to be seen. He looked on all sides and questioned everyone, but to no avail. So he crossed himself, prepared his own supper, went to bed, and slept soundly.

"I have implicit confidence," says he, "in Lisa. I have particular confidence in her ability to take care of herself, in any surroundings."

That was all very well: but time passed, and presently it began to be rumored that Lisa walked on Morven. Her brother, who was a grocer and a member of the town council, went thither to see about this report. And sure enough, there was Jurgen's wife walking in the twilight and muttering incessantly.

"Fie, sister!" says the town counsellor, "this is very unseemly conduct for a married woman, and a thing likely to be talked about."

"Follow me!" replied Dame Lisa. And the town counsellor followed her a little way, in the dusk, but when she came to Amneran Heath and still went onward, he knew better than to follow.

Next evening the elder sister of Dame Lisa went to Morven. This sister had married a notary, and was a shrewd woman. In consequence she took with her this evening a long wand of peeled willow-wood. And there was Jurgen's wife walking in the twilight and muttering incessantly.

"Fie, sister!" says the notary's wife, who was a shrewd woman, "and do you not know that all this while Jurgen does his own sewing, and is once more making eyes at the Countess Varvara?"

Dame Lisa shuddered; but she only said, "Follow me!"

So the notary's wife followed her to Amneran Heath, and across Amneran Heath to where a cave was. This was a place of abominable repute.... A lean hound came to them there in the twilight, lolling his tongue : but the notary's wife struck twice with her wand, and the silent beast left them. And Lisa went silently into the cave, and her sister turned and went home to her children, weeping.

So the next evening Jurgen himself came to Morven, because all his wife's family assured him this was the manly thing to do. He followed his wife across Amneran Heath until they reached the cave. The poet would willingly have been elsewhere. For the hound squatted upon his haunches, and seemed to grin at Jurgen: and there were other creatures abroad that flew low in the twilight, keeping close to the ground like owls; but they were larger than owls, and were more discomforting.

Jurgen said, a little peevishly:

"Lisa, my dear, if you go into the cave I will have to follow you, because it is the manly thing to do. And you know how easily I take cold."

The voice of Lisa was as the rustle of dead leaves.

"There is a cross about your neck. You must throw that away."

And indeed, Jurgen was wearing such a cross, through motives of sentiment, because it had once belonged to his dead mother.

But now, to pleasure his wife—"I am embarking upon an apologue," was his appraisal—he removed the trinket, and hung it on a barberry bush; and with the reflection that this was likely to prove a deplorable business, he followed Lisa into the cave.

Well, all was dark there, and Jurgen could see no one. But the cave stretched straight forward, and downward, and at the far end was a glow of light.

So Jurgen went on and on, and, after divers happenings which do not here concern us, he came to a notable place where seven cresset lights were burning. These lights were the power of Assyria, and Babylon, and Nineveh, and Egypt, and Rome, and Athens, and Byzantium: and six other cressets stood ready there, but fire had not yet been laid to these. And here was the black gentleman, in a black dressing-gown that was embroidered with all the signs of the Zodiac. He sat at a table, the top of which was curiously inlaid with thirty pieces of silver : and he was copying entries from one big book into another.

"You find me busy with my accounts," says he, "which augment daily—But what more can I do for you, Jurgen?"

"I have been thinking, Prince—" begins the poet.

"And why do you call me a prince, Jurgen?"

"I do not know, sir. But I suspect you are Koschei the Deathless."

The black gentleman nodded. "Something of the sort. Koschei, or Norka, or Chudo-Yudo—it is all one what I may be called hereabouts. My real name you never heard: no man has ever heard my name. So that matter we need hardly go into."

"Precisely, Prince. And I have been thinking that my wife's society is perhaps becoming a trifle burdensome to you."

"Eh, sirs, I cannot report that I enjoy it. But I am not unaccustomed to women. I may truthfully say that as I find them, so do I take them. And I was willing to oblige a fellow rebel."

"But I do not know, Prince, that I have ever rebelled—"

"You make verses, Jurgen. And all poetry is man's rebellion against being what the creature unluckily is."

"Well, be that as it may, Prince! But I do not know that you have obliged me."

"Why, Jurgen," says the black gentleman, in high astonishment, "do you mean to tell me that you want the plague of your life back again?"

"I do not know about that, either, sir. She was certainly very hard to live with. On the other hand, I had become used to having her about. I rather miss her."

Now the black gentleman meditated. "Come, friend," he says, at last, "you are a poet of some merit. You display a promising talent which might be cleverly developed, in any suitable environment. The trouble is"—and he lowered his voice to a whisper that was truly diabolical—"the trouble is that your wife does not understand you. She is hindering your art. Yes, that precisely sums it up : she is interfering with your soul-development, and your instinctive need of self-expression, and all that sort of thing. You are very well rid of her. To the other side, as is with point observed somewhere or other, it is not good for man to live alone. But, friend, I have just the wife for you—"

Then Koschei waved his hand; and there, quick as winking, was the loveliest lady that Jurgen had ever imagined. Fair was she to look upon, with her shining gray eyes and small, smiling lips, a fairer woman might no man boast of having seen. And she regarded Jurgen graciously, with her cheeks red and white, very lovely to observe. She was clothed in a robe of flame-colored silk, and about her neck was a collar of red gold. When she spoke her voice was music. And she told him that she was Queen Guenevere.

"But Launcelot is turned monk, at Glastonbury; and Arthur is gone into Avalon," says she : "and I will be your wife if you will have me, Messire Jurgen."

The poet was troubled.

"For you make me think myself a god," says Jurgen. "Madame Guenevere, when man recognized himself to be Heaven's vicar upon earth, it was to serve and to glorify and to protect you and your radiant sisterhood that man consecrated his existence. You were beautiful, and you were frail; you were half goddess and half bric-à-brac. Ohimé, I recognize the call of chivalry, and my heart-strings resound : yet, for innumerable reasons, I hesitate to take you for my wife, and to concede myself your appointed protector, responsible as such to Heaven. For one matter, I am not altogether sure that I am Pleaven's vicar here upon earth. I cannot but suspect that Omniscience would have selected some more competent representative."

"It is so written, Messire Jurgen."

Jurgen shrugged. "I, too, have written much that is beautiful. Very often my verses were so beautiful that I would have given anything in the world in exchange for somewhat less sure information as to the author's veracity. Ah, no, madame, desire and knowledge are pressing me so sorely that, between them, I dare not love you, and still I cannot help it."

Then Jurgen gave a little wringing gesture with his hands. His smile was not merry.

"Madame and queen," says he, "there was once a man who worshipped all women. To him they Were one and all of sacred, sweet, intimidating beauty. He shaped sonorous rhymes of this, in praise of the mystery and sanctity of women. Then several ladies made much of him, because, good lack, 'he understood women.' That was very unfortunate : for more reasons than one, all poets should be kept away from petticoats. So a little by a little he began to suspect that women, also, are akin to their parents; and are no wiser, and no more subtle, and no more immaculate, than the father who begot them. Madame and queen, it is not good for any man to suspect this."

"It is certainly not the conduct of a chivalrous person, nor of an authentic poet," says Queen Guenevere. "And yet your eyes are big with tears."

"Hah, madame," he replied, "but it amuses me to weep for a dead man with eyes that once were his."

Now said Queen Guenevere :

"Farewell to you, then, Jurgen, for it is I that am leaving you forever. I was the lovely and excellent masterwork of God : in Caerleon and Northgalis and at Joyeuse Garde might men behold me with delight, because to view me was to comprehend the power and kindliness of their Creator. Very beautiful was Iseult, and the face of Luned sparkled like a moving gem; Morgaine and Viviane and shrewd Nimuë were lovely, too; and the comeliness of Ettarre exalted the beholder like proud music : these, going about Arthur's hall, seemed Heaven's finest craftsmanship until the Queen came to her dais, as the moon among glowing stars : men then affirmed that God in making Guenevere had used both hands. My beauty was no human white and red, said they, but a proud sign of Heaven's might. In approaching me, men thought of God, because in me, they said, His splendor was incarnate. That which I willed was neither right nor wrong: it was divine. This thing it was that the knights saw in me; this surety, as to the power and generosity of their great Father, it was of which the chevaliers of yesterday were conscious in beholding me, and of men's need to be worthy of such parentage: and it is I that am leaving you forever."

Said Jurgen:

"It is a sorrowful thing that is happening to me. I am become as a rudderless boat that goes from wave to wave: I am turned to unfertile dust that a windwhirl makes coherent and presently lets fall. And so fare-well to you, Queen Guenevere, for it is a sorrowful thing that is happening to me."

Thus he cried farewell to the daughter of Gogyran. And instantly she vanished like the flame of a blown-out altar-candle. . . .

II

THEN came to Jurgen that Queen Anaïtis who very long ago was the bright bane of nations. Words may not describe her loveliness. And she talked of marvelous things. Of the lore of Thaïs she spoke, and of the schooling of Sappho, and of the secrets of Rhodopê, and of the mourning for Adonis.

"For we have but a little while to live, and thereafter none knows his fate. A man possesses nothing certainly save a brief loan of his own body: and yet the body of man is capable of much curious pleasure. As thus and thus," says she.

And the bright-colored woman spoke with antique directness of matters that Jurgen found rather embarrassing.

"Come, come!" thinks he, "but it will never do to seem provincial. I believe that I am actually blushing."

Aloud he said:

"Sweetheart, there was once a youth who sought quite zealously for the overmastering frenzies you prattle about. But, candidly, he could not find the flesh whose touch would rouse insanity. The lad had opportunities, too, let me tell you! Hah, I recall with tenderness the glitter of eyes and hair, and the gay garments, and the soft voices of those fond, foolish women, even now! But he went from one pair of lips to another, with an ardor that was always half-feigned, and with protestations that were conscious echoes of some romance or other. Such escapades were pleasant enough; but they were not very serious, after all. For these things concerned his body alone: and I am more than an edifice of viands reared by my teeth. To pretend that what my body does or endures is of importance, seems rather silly nowadays. I prefer to regard it as a necessary beast of burden which I maintain, at considerable expense and trouble. So I shall make no more pother over it."

But then again Queen Anaïtis spoke of marvelous things; and he listened, fair-mindedly, for the queen spoke of that which was hers to share with him.

"In Babylon I have a temple where many women sit with cords about them and burn bran for perfume, while they await that thing which is to befall them. In Armenia I have a temple surrounded by vast gardens, where only strangers have the right to enter : they there receive a hospitality that is more than gallant. In Paphos I have a temple wherein is a little pyramid of white stones, very curious to see: but still more curious is the statue in my temple at Amathus, of a bearded woman, which displays other features that women do not possess. And in Alexandria I have a temple that is tended by thirty-six exceedingly wise and sacred persons, and wherein it is always night: and there men seek for monstrous pleasures, even at the price of instant death, and win to both of these swiftly. Everywhere my temples stand upon high places near the sea: so they are beheld from afar by those whom I hold dearest, my beautiful broadchested, hairy mariners, who do not fear even me, but know that in my temples they will find notable employment. For I must tell you of what is to be encountered within these places that are mine, and of how pleasantly we pass our time there."

So she told him. . . .

Now he listened more attentively than before, and his eyes were narrowed, and his lips were lax and motionless and foolish-looking.

To Jurgen this queen's voice was all a horrible and strange and lovely magic.

Then Jurgen growled and shook himself, half-angrily; and he tweaked the ear of Queen Anaïtis.

"Sweetheart," says he, "you paint a glowing picture; but you are shrewd enough to borrow your pigments from the daydreams of inexperience. What you prattle about is not at all as you describe it. Also, you forget you are talking to a married man of some years' standing. Moreover, I shudder to think of what might happen if Lisa were to walk in unexpectedly. And for the rest, you come a deal too late, my lass, so that all this to-do over nameless sins and unspeakable caresses and other anonymous antics seems rather naïve. My ears are beset by eloquent gray hairs which plead at closer quarters than does that fibbing little tongue of yours. And so be off with you."

With that Queen Anaïtis smiled very cruelly and said:

"Farewell to you, then, Jurgen, for it is I that am leaving you forever. Henceforward you must fret away much sunlight by interminably shunning discomfort and by indulging tepid preferences. For I, and none but I, can waken that desire which uses all of a man, and so wastes nothing, even though it leave that favored man forever after like wan ashes in the sunlight. And with you I have no more to do. Join with your graying fellows, then! and help them to affront the clean, sane sunlight by making guilds and laws and solemn phrases wherewith to rid the world of me! I, Anaïtis, laugh, and my heart is a wave in the sunlight. For there is no power like my power, and no living thing which can withstand my power: and those who deride me, as I well know, are but the emptied dead, dry husks that a wind moves, with hissing noises, while I harvest in open sunlight. For I am the desire that uses all of a man; and it is I that am leaving you forever."

Said Jurgen:

"Again it is a sorrowful thing that is happening to me. I am become as a puzzled ghost that furtively observes the doings of loud-voiced, ruddy persons; and I am compact of weariness and apprehension, for I no longer discern what thing is I, nor what is my desire, and I fear that I am already dead. So farewell to you, Queen Anaïtis, for this, too, is a sorrowful thing that is happening to me."

Thus he cried farewell to the Sun's daughter. And all the colors of her loveliness flickered and merged into the likeness of a tall, thin flame, that aspired; and then this flame was extinguished. ...

III

Now silently came Queen Helen. She said nothing at all, because there was no need. But, beholding her, Jurgen kneeled. He hid his face in her white robe, and stayed thus, without speaking, for a long while.

"Lady of my vision," he said, and his voice broke, "assuredly I believe that your father was that ardent bird which nestled very long ago in Leda's bosom. And now Troy's sons are all in Hades' keeping, in the world below; fire has consumed the walls of Troy, and the years have forgotten her proud conquerors': but still you are bringing woe on woe on hapless sufferers." And again his voice broke. For the world seemed cheerless, and like a house that none has lived in for many years.

Then, with queer pride, he raised his time-lined countenance, much as a man condemned might turn to the executioner.

"Lady, if you indeed be the Swan's daughter, very long ago there was a child that was ill. And his illness turned to a fever, and in his fever he arose from his bed one night, saying that he must set out for Troy, because of his love for Queen Helen. I was once that child. I remember how strange it seemed to me that I should be talking such nonsense; I remember how the warm room smelt of drugs; and I remember how I pitied the trouble in my nurse's face, drawn and old in the yellow lamplight. For she loved me, and she did not understand; and she pleaded with me to be a good boy and not to worry my sleeping parents. But I perceive now that I was not talking nonsense. Yours is the beauty which all poets know to exist, somewhere, and which life, as men have contrived it thus far, does not anywhere afford. For that beauty I have hungered always. Toward that beauty I have struggled always, but not quite whole-heartedly. That night forecast my life. I have hungered for you; and"—he laughed here—"and I have always stayed a passably good boy, lest I should beyond reason disturb my family."

And Queen Helen, the delight of gods and men, said nothing at all, because there was no need. For the man who has once glimpsed her loveliness is beyond saving, and beyond the desire of being saved.

"Tonight," says Jurgen, "through the shrewd art of Koshchei, it appears that you stand within arm's reach. Hah, lady, were that possible—and I know very well it is not possible, whatever my senses may report—I am not fit to mate with your perfection. At the bottom of my heart I no longer desire perfection. For we that are taxpayers as well as immortal souls must live by politic evasions and formulæ and catchwords that fret away our lives as moths waste a garment: we fall insensibly to common sense as to a drug; and it dulls and kills that which in us is fine and rebellious and unreasonable: so that you will find no man of my years with whom living is not a mechanism that gnaws away time unprompted. I am become the creature of use and wont; I am the lackey of prudence and half-measures; and I have put my dreams upon an allowance. Yet even now I love you more than I love costly foods and indolence and flattery. What more can an old poet say? For that reason, lady, I pray you begone, because your loveliness is a taunt that I find unendurable."

But his voice yearned, because this was Queen Helen, the delight of gods and men, who regarded him with grave, kind eyes. She seemed to view, as one appraises the pattern of an unrolled carpet, every action of Jurgen's life: and she seemed, too, to wonder, without reproach or trouble, how men could be so foolish and of their own accord become so miry.

"Oh, I have failed my vision!" cries Jurgen. "I have failed, and I know very well that every man must fail; and yet my shame is no less bitter. For I am transmuted by time's handling! I shudder at the thought of living day in and day out with my vision! And so I will have none of you for my wife."

Then, trembling, Jurgen raised toward his lips the hand of her who was the world's darling.

"And so farewell to you, Queen Helen! Oh, very often in a woman's face I have found this or that feature wherein she resembled you, and for the sake of it have served that woman blindly. And all my verses, as I know now, were vain enchantments striving to evoke that hidden loveliness of which I knew by dim report alone until tonight. Oh, all my life was a foiled quest of you, Queen Helen, who came too late. Yes, certainly, it should be graved upon my tomb, *Queen Helen ruled this earth while it stayed worthy. . . .* But that was very long ago. Today I ride no more a-questing anything : instead, I potter after hearthside comforts, and play the physician with myself, and strive painstakingly to make old bones. And no man's notion anywhere seems worth a cup of mulled wine; and for the sake of no notion would I endanger the routine which so hideously bores me. For I am transmuted by time's handling; I have become the lackey of prudence and half-measures : and so, farewell to you, Queen Helen, for I have failed in the service of my vision, and I deny you utterly!"

Thus he cried farewell to the. Swan's daughter : and Queen Helen vanished as a bright mist passes, not departing swiftly as had done the other two; and Jurgen was alone with the black gentleman. . . .

IV

"COME, come!" observed Koshchei the Deathless, "but you are certainly hard to please."

Well, Jurgen was already intent to shrug off his displayal of emotion.

"In selecting a wife, sir," submitted Jurgen, "there are all sorts of matters to be considered. Whatever the first impulse of the moment, it was apparent to any reflective person that in the past of each of these ladies there was much to suggest inborn inaptitude for domestic life. And I am a peace-loving fellow, sir; nor do I hold with moral laxity, except, of course, in talk when it promotes sociability, and in verse-making, wherein it is esteemed as a conventional ornament. Still, Prince, the chance I lost! I do not refer to matrimony, you conceive. But in the presence of these famous fair ones with what glowing words I ought to have spoken! upon a wondrous ladder of strophes, metaphors and recondite allusions, to what stylistic heights of Asiatic prose I ought to have ascended! And instead, I twaddled like a schoolmaster. Decidedly, Lisa is right, and I am good-for-nothing. However," he added hopefully, "it appeared to me that this evening Lisa was. somewhat less outspoken than usual."

"Eh, sirs, but she was under a very potent spell. I found that necessary, in the interest of law and order hereabouts. We are not accustomed to the excesses of practical persons who are ruthlessly bent upon reforming their associates. Indeed, it is one of the advantages of my situation that such folk rarely come my way." And the black gentleman in turn shrugged. "You will pardon me, but I am positively committed to help out an archbishop with some of his churchwork this evening, and there is a rather important assassination to be instigated at Vienna. So time presses. Meanwhile, you have inspected the flower of womanhood; and I cannot soberly believe that you prefer your termagant of a wife."

"Frankly, Prince, I also am, as usual, undecided. Could you let me see her, for just a moment?"

This was no sooner asked than done : for there, sure enough, was Dame Lisa. She was no longer restricted to quiet speech by any stupendous necromancy, and seemed peevish: and uncommonly plain she looked, after the passing of those lovely ladies.

"Well, you rascal!" begins Dame Lisa, addressing Jurgen, "and so you thought to be rid of me! Oh, a precious lot you are! and a deal of thanks I get for my scrimping and slaving!" And she began scolding away. She said he was even worse than the Countess Varvara.

But rather unaccountably Jurgen fell to thinking of the years they had shared together; of the fine and merry girl that Lisa had been before she married him; and of how well she knew his tastes in cookery and all his other little preferences; and of how cleverly she humored them on those rare days when nothing had occurred to vex her: and of how much more unpleasant—everything considered—life was without her than with her. And his big, foolish heart was half yearning and half penitence.

"I think I will take her back, Prince," says he, very quietly. "For I do not know but that it is as hard on her as on me."

"My friend, do you forget the poet that you might be, even yet? No rational person would dispute that the society and amiable chat of Dame Lisa is a desideratum—"

But Dame Lisa was always resentful of long words. "Be silent, you black scoffer! and do not allude to such disgraceful things in the presence of respectable people! For I am a decent Christian woman, I would have you understand. But everybody knows your reputation! and a very fit companion you are for that scamp yonder. Jurgen, I always told you you would come to this, and now I hope you are satisfied. Jurgen, do not stand there with your mouth open, like a scared fish, when I ask you a civil question! but answer when you are spoken to! and do not say a single word to me, Jurgen, because I am disgusted with you. For, Jurgen, you heard perfectly well what your very suitable friend just said about me. No, do not ask me what he said, Jurgen! I leave that to your conscience. So, if my own husband has not the feelings of a man, and cannot protect me from insults and low company, I had best be going home and getting supper ready. I daresay the house is like a pigsty. And to think of your going about in public, even among such associates, with a button off your shirt! You are enough to drive a person mad: and I warn you that I am done with you forever."

And Dame Lisa walked with dignity toward the mouth of the cave. "So you can come with me, or not, precisely as you elect. It is all one to me, I can assure you, after the cruel things you have said. But I shall stop by for a word with that high-and-mighty Varvara on the way home. You two need never think to hoodwink me about your goings-on."

And with that Dame Lisa went away, still talking.

V

"Phew!" said Koshchei, in the ensuing silence; "you had better stay overnight, in any event. I really think, friend, you will be more comfortable, just now at least, with me."

But Jurgen had taken up his caftan. "No, I daresay I had better be going too," says Jurgen. "I thank you very heartily for your intended kindness, sir, still I do not know but it is better as it is. And is there anything"—he coughed delicately—"and is there anything to pay, sir?"

"Well, not, of course, for the freedom of Dame Lisa. We very rarely molest the wives of poets. -It is not considered sportsmanlike. But I must tell you it is not permitted any person to leave my presence unmaimed. One must have rules, you know."

"You would chop off an arm? or a hand? or a whole finger? Come now, Prince, you must be joking!"

Koshchei the Deathless was very grave as he sat there, in meditation, drumming with his long fingers upon the table-top that was curiously inlaid with thirty pieces of silver. In the lamplight his sharp nails glittered like flame-points. "Eh, sir, the toll which I exact you have already paid, though not to me. You have retained nothing that I esteem worth taking. So you, friend, may depart unhindered whenever you will."

Jurgen meditated this clemency, and with a sick heart he understood. "Yes, that is true. For I have not retained the faith nor the desire nor the vision. Yes, that is very true, worse luck. ... Meanwhile I can assure you I admired each of the ladies very unfeignedly, and was greatly flattered by their kind offers. More than generous, I thought them. But it really would not do for me to take up with any one of them now. For Lisa is my wife, you see. A great deal has passed between us—and I have been a great disappointment to her, in many ways—and I am used to her—" Then Jurgen considered, and regarded the black gentleman with mingled envy and commiseration. "Why, no, you probably would not understand, sir, because I suppose there is no marrying or giving in marriage here, either. But I can assure you it is always pretty much like that."

"I lack grounds to dispute your aphorism," observed Koshchei, "inasmuch as matrimony was not included in my doom. None the less, to a bystander, the conduct of both of you appears remarkable."

"The truth of it, sir, is a great symbol," said Jurgen, with a splurge of confidence, "in that my wife is rather foolishly fond of me. Oh, I grant you, it is the fashion of women to discard civility toward those for whom they suffer most willingly: and whom a woman loveth she chasteneth, after a good precedent. ... For, Prince, they are all poets; but the medium they work in is not always ink. So the moment that Lisa is set free from what, in a manner of speaking, sir, inconsiderate persons might, in their unthinking way, refer to as the terrors of a place that I do not for an instant doubt to be conducted after a system which furthers the true interests of everybody, and so reflects vast credit upon its officials, if you will pardon my frankness, sir"—and Jurgen smiled ingratiatingly—"why, at that moment Lisa's thoughts take form in very much the high denunciatory vein of Jeremiah and Amos, who were remarkably fine poets: and her next essay in creative composition is my supper. Tomorrow she will darn and sew me an epic. Such, sir, are Lisa's poems, all addressed to me, who came so near to gallivanting with mere queens! Oh, Prince, when I consider steadfastly the depth and the intensity of that devotion which, for so many years, has tended me, and has endured the society of that person whom I peculiarly know to be the most tedious and irritating of companions, I stand aghast, before a miracle. And I cry, *Oh, certainly a goddess!* Hah, all we poets write a deal about love : but none of us may grasp the word's full meaning until he reflects that this is a passion mighty enough to induce a woman to put up with him. And the crowning touch is that Lisa is jealous. Think upon that, now!" And Jurgen chuckled. "Yet still you probably would not understand, sir, because I suppose there is no marrying or giving in marriage, here either. No less, the truth of it is a great symbol."

Then Jurgen sighed, and shook hands with Koshchei, very circumspectly, and went home to his wife. And he found her quite unaltered. Thus it was in the old days.

THE EDUCATION OF PAUL GANT

Howard Mumford Jones

I

PAUL GANT, Ph.D., instructor in English, closed his rickety desk in the dingy office in Main Hall, took from its top a faded green bag stuffed with Freshman themes for correction, put on his shabby overcoat, and went out of the building into the chilly November rain. The office he shared with four other harassed instructors in English; and if the light was so bad they had to burn electricity most of the day, they were lucky to have office room at all, since Main Hall, old, stately and inconvenient, was overcrowded with the departments it was supposed to house. The five of them, one after the other, had visited the oculist, but the university wants classes taught, it is not interested in oculists.

It can not be said that Gant was extremely cheerful as he pushed home through the rain with his coat collar turned up.

In the first place, his overcoat had already outlasted more November rains than its makers ever intended; and in the second place, the bag, with its stuffing of badly scrawled, carelessly phrased compositions which he was vainly trying to keep dry, was a burden alike to his arm, his brain and his heart. And in the third place, there was the undeniable fact that he and Susan could not live on his salary of $1,200.

Something must be done, or—or—he was not quite sure of the alternative. Finally, he was tired—epically, immorally tired.

Education is a great thing. Especially higher education. The republic is founded on education. Moreover, we believe in lots of education, the higher the better. Every boy and girl is encouraged to go to college and so make the world safe for democracy. This being true, let us consider the case of Paul Gant, Ph.D.

Paul Gant, not yet even B.A., graduated from high school in your town at the head of his class. He was thin, lank, anemic, passionately fond of books. You will recall that you never had much to do with him, but he was always on the debating team, and you told him jocosely "he had swallowed the dictionary." Everybody said it would be a shame if he did not go to college. So he went to college—any college—-your college. He spent four years there and was graduated with a B.A. degree. If you will get out your dusty diploma you will see that is the kind of degree you hold. You may remember his name on the Commencement program: "Paul Gant—major subject, English—Honors." You don't remember? Very well. It sounds like bridge but it is not. English is the subject the girls always take because they expect to teach and get married. Paul elected it because he liked to read books.

Now, among the English faculty the professor whom Paul especially admired, became interested in him. That was unfortunate. They talked about books. They would have done better had they talked about plumbing or aviation. The professor, who was a kindly soul, but impractical, told Paul he ought to "continue his studies." And Paul did.

He went to a university noted for the profundity of its scholarship and the size of its library, and enrolled as a candidate for the degree of Master of Arts in English. He borrowed four hundred dollars at four per cent interest to do it. And for a year, in an atmosphere of terrific intellectual pressure, he ground away. He grubbed up the date of Mrs. Browning's birth and discovered it was wrong in most of the text-books, and the relation of Chaucer's final *e's* to their Anglo-Saxon originals, and the indebtedness of *Selimus* (which is a play and not a patent medicine) to the tragedy of *Locrine*. Also he learned an Old English grammar by heart. Here is a sample : "Before *h* plus a consonant, *r* plus a consonant, *l* plus a consonant, and *h* final, *ae* breaks into *ea*, *ei* breaks into *ie*, and long *i*—"

I have forgotten what happens to long *i*. Also I have probably got it wrong. Let us return to Paul Gant.

When he had any time to spare, he did two things. Most of the time he worked on his master's thesis which bore the fascinating title: "The

Indebtedness of the Anglo-Saxon Poem of the *Phoenix* to the Latin Poem of Lactantius on the Same Subject." Maybe that wasn't it, but never mind.

And in the rest of his spare time Paul wondered vaguely what all this had to do with reading H. G. Wells and Robert Herrick.

By and by his thesis was "accepted" and he was "examined" by a committee of the graduate faculty. Let us pass over this. Then he stood in line with a herd of other candidates and a grayhaired man in a black gown pronounced a Latin incantation over them, and presto! Paul Gant, B.A., became Paul Gant, M.A. Susan, who had scrimped and saved out of her salary as a high school teacher of French in order to be there, nearly wept when the dean gave Paul his diploma, because she thought that now they could be married. They had been engaged two years. You will have to forgive Susan's unmaidenly boldness. Have you ever taught French in high school?

Paul and Susan were not married that summer. In the first place, there was that four hundred dollars with interest, and in the second place, Paul hadn't his doctor's degree. You have to have a doctor's degree before you can teach about Shelley properly. Paul got him a job in a small college that graciously overlooked his undoctored state in consideration of Paul's receiving $1,000 a year for teaching seventy-five Freshmen how to write their mother tongue. Susan returned to her French classes in high school.

II

AT the end of two years Paul had accomplished a miracle. Do not ask me how he did it. Probably it was education. He not only paid off the four hundred dollars with interest, but he had accumulated four hundred and fifty dollars besides. Also he had given his sister (whom he was partially supporting) two Christmas presents; he had given Susan the silk for a waist and the money for a hat; and, on her birthday, he had presented her with a pair of kid gloves.

Then he went to Susan's town. This was extravagance, but then, he had not seen her for a year and a half.

They concluded not to indulge in the riotous luxury of wedded bliss, but to go after the doctor's degree instead. Then Paul's salary would increase and they could be married. So Paul hied him to an older and even more erudite university and Susan sighed and looked into the mirror twice each morning before going to school. The reason was that Paul was now twenty-six and Susan twenty-five. No, that wasn't the reason. Have you ever taught French in a small town high school in the middle west?

Of course I realize that Paul should have waited on table or sold aluminum ware to the farmers' wives. All the successful men do that to go through college. But the doctor wouldn't let him wait on table and the time was too precious to peddle aluminum ware. Likewise, I realize that Paul should have hunted up another profession. But, unfortunately, he thought he could teach. Also, he was right.

When you are in Paul's position, it takes two years—sometimes three, four or five years—to obtain a doctor's degree. They give it to you when they judge you are ready for it, not before. Among other things you have to prepare a suitable thesis—"an original contribution to knowledge" in your "field." You must hunt up somebody sufficiently dead and prove something about him, and the older and deader and more difficult your subject is, the higher your thesis ranks as a contribution to knowledge. Paul liked to write little, graceful essays (he did them rather well), but an original contribution to literature won't do. He gave up reading Arnold Bennett and Galsworthy and other unprofitable authors— what he wanted was a job—and made a study of the prepositions in Anglo-Saxon.

At the end of a year he had done very well. He had a drawer and a half full of Anglo-Saxon prepositions and their Middle English equivalents, all arranged on cards, and he had accumulated a fund of information about authors and books and dates and editions and sources that would have dazzled his audience, if he had had one. Also he had a cough.

At the end of three months spent in the summer session, he found one day in the university library a newly received pamphlet by a German student in a university Paul had never heard of, setting forth the doctrine of the Anglo-Saxon preposition completely and exhaustively. Four days later Susan received a letter from the Belle-view Hospital, in consequence of which she drew her savings from the bank and travelled night and day to reach Paul before he died. But he didn't die.

III

PERHAPS, however, you are losing interest in this sort of thing. Let us skip a year.

Paul was now twenty-eight and Susan was twenty-seven. In the interval Paul had more or less recovered his health—less rather than more—and he had conceived a brand-new subject for his thesis: A New Theory Concerning the Latin Works of Walter Mapes. You are still losing interest? So was Paul.

At the end of another eighteen months, Paul sat in a somber recitation hall, looking like a tired and timid victim of the Inquisition facing his judges. Around him and above him, in the tiers of seats, sat the members of the faculty of arts, or such numbers of them as cared to attend the torture. And they asked him questions. They asked him about Milton's theory of church government and about Gottfried von Strassburg and the plays of Hrothswita and Swinburne's religion and the inner meaning of Blake and Orm's *Ormulum* and the probable dates of Marie de France and Byron's relations to three different women and Shakespeare's grammar. And when Paul could, he answered them in a tired, spiritless voice (he had been preparing himself three weeks for the ordeal, using the *Cambridge History of English Literature* in fourteen volumes and quarts of black coffee by way of stimulants); and when he could not answer, he looked at them vaguely and murmured apologetically. Also he wondered whether they were ever going to stop and whether the room was really circular or was it Browning's dates that made it go round.

At length the chief inquisitor relented and the rest said they were satisfied, and Paul promptly fainted. Three weeks later, Paul Gant, M.A., became Paul Gant, Ph.D. And then he and Susan were married.

It is not our business to inquire into the next three weeks. At the end of that time Paul permitted himself an inventory of the situation. He had a debt of $635 with interest at five per cent to pay off; he was required to publish his thesis—it would cost him $150 or $200; and he had discovered that Susan was a dear and wonderful wife, but that two could not live as inexpensively as one.

To offset this side of the ledger, however, he had a position as instructor in English at a university. Let us call it your university. No? Then we will call it a State University. This position paid him $1,200 a year; and as you will see, this was $200 a year more than he had received from his teaching some years before. The difference was, no doubt, attributable to his doctor's degre. The faculty in English numbered sixteen; and in the course of twenty years, if enough older members died or quit or went elsewhere, Paul might hope to become a full professor at the opulent salary of $3,000 a year. This is about the wages of a master plumber.

The Allies were hanging on at Ypres and other unpronounceable names that year. Paul remembered vaguely something about an Austrian archduke, but as he had been reading mediaeval Latin all year, you will have to forgive his lack of interest. He did not put the Allies in his inventory at all. That was a mistake.

Susan mothered him a good deal that: summer. Paul's nerves were raspy, but he rather liked being fed egg-nogs and hearing Susan read from the works of Mr. Robert W. Chambers. If he had looked at himself with Susan's eyes, he would have seen a pallid, emaciated, "gangly" man with weak eyes and constantly twitching muscles. Or, no—he would not have seen that with Susan's eyes. But if he had looked at Susan with your eyes, dear reader, he would have seen that, though she was only twenty-nine, she looked thirty-five. Fortunately, he did not have your eyes.

IV

PAUL was not thinking about his past as he plodded home; he was wondering, instead, about his future. He went over and over what the president of the university, a kindly, brusque, successful man of fifty, had told him in yesterday's interview, when, with the permission of the head of his department, Paul had requested an increase in salary. Gant had been awkward and embarrassed, and the president felt sorry for him.

"It's no use, Dr. Gant," he had said. "This is a war year. You can't get money out of the legislature for anything that does not directly and obviously pertain to the war."

"I've been here two years," timidly expostulated Paul.

"We're very well satisfied," hurriedly returned the president. "And your salary ought to be raised. But, Gant, the appropriations for the college of liberal arts have been cut down $24,000. I'm sorry for you. I'm sorry for anybody who has to struggle along on an income that was already meager in 1914. But I'm helpless—absolutely helpless."

The door of the office had opened at this point and the president's secretary put in his head.

"Major Dennis is here," he said, "about the training corps."

It was evident even to Paul that the president was much more interested in the training corps than he was in Gant's salary. Don't blame the president. The training corps would bring an additional 400 students to the university. Paul picked up his hat, he remembered, and the president had made a vague noise in his throat intended to indicate sympathy. Then Gant had left—awkwardly, of course. He had not told Susan about his interview yet; perhaps that was why he kept reviewing the scene as he went home, trying to find some loophole, some unturned stone. But he could not. He would tell Susan tonight. Together, maybe, they could figure out something.

Paul was now near home. It was the same apartment house in which Dr. and Mrs. Paul Gant had been at home after September first, some months before. Before he reaches the doorway, let us indulge in a little figuring.

For the sum of $30 a month the Gants were permitted to occupy a large room with a bed that slid under the china-closet; a bath room containing a tub in which no one but an infant could bathe; a kitchenette intended for persons with Lilliputian appetites; a dressing room six feet by eight; and two closets. Paul paid the electric light and the gas bills, but the heat, hot and cold water, and a gas range were miraculously furnished.

Paul likewise rented one-thirtieth of a janitor—when he could be found. You will readily see that this arrangement left them $65 a month to squander, but as Paul insisted on putting aside $10 a month to accumulate against his debts, the Gants were left $55 a month with which to buy furniture, dishes, clothes, food, light, books, entertainment, and vacations. Paul had reduced his debt to about $360, but his thesis—alas!—had not yet been printed. He would have made a brilliant financier.

Paul looked up through the rain at the window on the top floor where Susan usually sat waiting. Tonight Susan was not there. Perhaps she had not returned from the Red Cross rooms. Paul felt illogically resentful—he wanted Susan. When he had fitted his key to the lock, he paused and looked absently around him. It was not a nice neighborhood, but Paul had got used to that—except when some club woman asked Susan why they lived way off *there*. Then Paul was willing to murder almost anybody.

He stumbled toward the electric-light button when he had entered his apartment. Something was wrong with the room. Was it—oh, the bed had been pulled out into the center of the floor. What was the matter? When Paul had turned the switch, he dropped his bag of themes on the floor where they fell with a dull, mushy sound. Susan was lying, fully dressed, on the bed.

She sat up. She looked at Paul. Paul had never seen or like that before. It was not that she had been crying, it was the hunted look in her eyes. He sat down on the bed beside her. She snuggled up to his wet overcoat.

"It's so co-old and dreary," she moaned.

"I'll telephone for some heat," said Paul courageously, starting to get up.

"You can't," said Susan without interest. "The janitor got drunk and Mr. Whelpley discharged him, and he's still looking for somebody."

In summoning up his courage, Paul forgot about his interview with the president.

"You're tired, sweetheart," he said. "I'll start supper."

Susan let him get up. When she heard him clattering away in the kitchen, she tidied the bed and pushed it back into the gaping recess in the wall. That made it possible to reach the china closet. Then she brought forward the dining-room table and spread a cloth on it—one of three. She then proceeded slowly to set the table. When she had denuded a shelf in the china-closet, she paused and, leaning against the table, drew her hand, palm outward, across her forehead. She was a slender, palely attractive woman, still bearing the marks of her former occupation in the form of two deep lines between her eyebrows, a habit of nervously tapping the floor with her foot, and permanently impaired eyesight.

"Paul," she said in a low voice. She was not tapping her foot now.

At the sound Gant hastily dropped a pan on the kitchen stove and entered the room. What was the matter? Susan stood with both hands flat on the table, her body slightly inclined toward him so that the electric light clung to her brown hair. Her face looked tired, and in her eyes was still that dumb look of suffering.

"What is it, Sue?" he cried sharply.

"I—I didn't go to the Red Cross this afternoon," began his wife, hiding her face. "I went to the doctor's."

Paul took a step toward her. Into his eyes came a look of stupefaction! That was replaced by troubled understanding.

"Not—?" he queried elliptically.

"Yes, Paul."

The Gants, husband and wife, stared at each other across the cheap table. The light made little pools of yellow on the dishes and shone dully from the buttons on Paul's vest.

Of course I know that the proper thing for Mrs. Gant to have done was to hold up for Paul's beatified admiration a dear, little garment. That is how they do it in the movies. People in the movies, however, do not have to live on $55 a month.

V

A LONG moment went over them. Something was burning on the gas range, but neither was conscious of it. Susan still kept her head down, but now she was playing aimlessly with a knife and a fork. Paul stared at her as if he was never going to see her again. He could hear his watch ticking in his pocket.

"Now, what are we going to do?" he asked dully.

"I don't know, Paul," said Susan, raising her eyes. Then she added irrelevantly. "Bread has gone up to fifteen cents a loaf."

The Allies, being determined to figure in Paul's ledger, had chosen this underhanded method.

"I—I saw the president today," ventured Paul, still staring at his wife with fascinated eyes. "The appropriation for liberal arts has been cut down. And the faculty is going to be reduced. I'm safe, I guess."

"Oh Paul, dear!" cried Susan.

She looked at him. Then she shuddered a little.

"I'm cold," she whimpered, groping her way around the table.

Paul put his arms around her and kissed her.

"There, there, sweetheart," he said, and tried to comfort her. It was not a very convincing job. Then he put a shabby coat around her, hauled out the bed half way, made her lie down, and went to do salvage work in the kitchen. On the way he stumbled over his bag of themes. It can not be said that these products of education received the consideration recommended by the books of pedagogy. The fact is, Paul kicked them vigorously against the side of the room. Susan giggled hysterically.

The fried potatoes were a hopeless mess, and the stewed com no longer recognizable. This did not add to Dr. Gant's optimism. As he cleaned up the stove and began ruefully to prepare another supper, he reflected on his situation, bitterly and without illusion.

His mind went back, for one thing, to the classes he had taught that day; two sections of hopelessly mediocre Freshmen into whose uninterested perceptions he was supposed to pound the fear of comma blunders and respect for the England language. It was incredible that the human intellect could so withstand instruction. A month and a half had gone by, and yet his students, despite the incessant repetitions of the class room, despite patient and continued individual "conferences," despite the simple instructions of the manual of compositions each one possessed, doggedly continued writing sentences without verbs, coupling plural subjects and singular predicates, mistaking adjectives for adverbs, and generally failing to indicate that any progress had been made in them since they left the eighth grade.

Do not be unfair to Paul. His classes were quite as good as the average, and the high schools say they are not to blame. Only, he was grinding out the best years of his life in a wearying battle against stupidity, and even the gods. But the proverb was made in Germany.

Paul reflected on the situation. In fact, his mind went into a committee of the whole on the state of this particular union. And the more he thought, the madder he got. His training and his inclinations were more or less literary: he could write a little; and yet he was set to work, day in and day out, to explain that a verb is conjugated and should never be declined.

He thought about Susan and the long wait to be married; he thought about his studies in the graduate schools; he thought about the way Susan had scrimped and saved; he thought how they had wanted children and had denied themselves for the sake of publishing Paul's thesis; he thought how they could not support the one that was now coming. In fact, he thought so much that he was in danger of burning the potatoes a second time, when Susan's voice recalled him to his surroundings.

"I'm so cold," she whimpered, "I'm freezing."

Paul turned off the gas under the frying pan.

"Where are you going?" asked Susan in alarm.

"I am going," said Paul distinctly from the hall door, "to the furnace room. And I am going to build a fire and get some heat into this damned apartment."

As swearing it was not much, but then, instructors do not have much practice in profanity.

Paul did not build the fire. When he reached the basement, he found Mr. Whelpley, fat, red and perspiring, his head thrust into the maw of the furnace, his voice booming in a series of smothered explosions that should have successfully heated his tenants. But they did not, for on the wall behind him hung the shattered house telephone. He emerged from the furnace and glared at Paul.

"Where's the kindling?" he roared.

"Right over here," said Paul promptly. "And the fine coal is over there."

"Do you know anything about this furnace?" demanded Dr. Gant's landlord, smearing his wet face with black as he brushed back his abundant hair.

"I do," said Paul.

Ordinarily he was timid, but he was still thinking about Freshman composition. "You pull out this damper first."

Together they built the fire. Once the telephone jarred faintly, but Mr. Whelpley might have the scriptural idol for all that his ears could hear.

When the furnace had commenced a comfortable purring, Paul turned. It was one of the great moments of his life.

"The janitor is discharged?" he asked crisply. The president of the university would not have known him.

"He is," responded Mr. Whelpley, "good and discharged."

"How much did you pay him?" asked Paul.

"I paid him," said Mr. Whelpley with growing heat, "one hundred and fifty dollars a month. And I gave him an apartment to live in. I paid him that much because I wanted to keep him. All he had to do was to keep this place clean and warm, and now—"

"Are you thinking of hiring another janitor?" interrupted Paul.

"I am," answered Mr. Whelpley, "if I can find one. Otherwise—"

"Would you hire me?" said Paul.

Let us not dwell on the astonishment of Mr. Whelpley. Also the ensuing conversation between Dr. Gant and his landlord is lost to history.

A half an hour later Dr. Paul Gant stood rummaging through his desk, one foot unconsciously planted on the bag of Freshman themes.

"What have you got?" asked Susan, drowsily comfortable with a good supper and plenty of heat.

"I have here," said Paul in his best class-room manner, coming toward her with a handful of papers, "a diploma certifying that I am a Bachelor of Arts. Here is another certifying that I am a Master of Arts. Don't try to read it—it's Latin. And I have here a third document stating that I am a Doctor of Philosophy and may enjoy all the rights and perquisites of that degree. This," he continued, holding forth a smaller paper, "is my appointment as an instructor in English at $100 a month. This," he said triumphantly, drawing a fifth document from his pocket, "is my contract as the janitor of this apartment house at $165 a month. I am now going down cellar to start the fire under the water-heater which has not been in operation all day."

"But—" ejaculated the wide-eyed Susan.

"These?" said Paul, following and interpreting her gaze. "These are to start the fire with, under the water-heater."

And he went out with his diplomas in his hand and shut the door.

THE STORY ASHLAND TOLD AT DINNER

Ludwig Lewisohn

N O, the Ashlands haven't entertained formally for years. And they've given up their lodge at Dobbs' Ferry. I saw it the other day; it looked like a blind, deserted thing. They stick to their old house down-town—five stories, you know, stone-front, dwarfed all around by sky-scrapers.

Every now and then I see them in a casual way. She's taken to powdering her hair; you know how easily those brilliant dark women turn grey. But she's still the same—like a japonica in moonlight, I used to say, shining among the dark leaves. He's the same, too—good-looking, golf-playing lawyer, apparently quite impassive and without much subtlety. But that's a mistaken impression produced by his wife's attitude to him. ...

I can prove that by telling you about a certain dinner—the last they gave at Dobbs' Ferry. You've heard foolish stories, the lurid kind people tell. I happen to have been there. ...

It was late October and when I think of that afternoon and evening it seems to me that nature's gone off in looks like the rest of us. Leaves! They were bronze and scarlet and gold and a foot deep and in the immense silence you heard nothing but the wind rustling in them. The river curves there and looks like a lake—deep and still and solemn—olive, it seems to me, with bronze flecks and golden pools at sunset. The dining room was in old mahogany (they've left all that fine stuff to moulder out there, too) with the candle flames making amber splotches in it and festoons of Autumn foliage all around.

There were just eight of us, including Bill and Margaret Ashland, and we could all see the river and the still trees through the French windows. It wasn't too cool, but the air had a fine, stringent tang. Everybody felt braced and a little exhilarated, don't you know.

The talk was good at the start. Only there were queer little halts in it—sudden general pauses. And I can tell you why:

We all wanted to ask Ashland, who had been Frye's college chum and later his lawyer and had wound up the estate, why the deuce Tom Frye had put a bullet through his fool head.

There wasn't anybody there who hadn't been glad of the invitation in the hope of light on that subject. It was amusing to see how everybody edged up to the question and then edged away again till finally Stimson— who had also been at college with Frye and Ashland—Stimson, fat, blond, rosy and blatant as ever—called out to Ashland :

"Look here, Bill, you knew all about Tom Frye; he'd hardly talked to *me;* why don't you tell us something?"

I was sitting next to Margaret and she said, "Oh," in a quick, deprecatory sort of way. I nodded my agreement with her. It was coarse and I thought Ashland would turn Stimson down. But he didn't. He seemed to feel that he had shown great perspicacity in this matter, and I think he wanted to convince Margaret of that publicly. You remember how she used to twit him: "Lawyers have no instinct for truth!"

"All right," Ashland said, laying his hands flat on the table before him, "it's really a very curious story. I meant to tell it sometime. I didn't know so very much more than the rest of you when Frye died three months ago. But I've gotten a lot of insight into the situation since—oh, a lot!"

Margaret lifted her fine profile with an incredulous, almost bitter little smile. All her weariness at what she thought his lack of understanding was in that expression.

"How did you?" she asked.

He looked down at his hands.

"Wait and see," he said slowly.

"He's never told you?" I whispered to Margaret.

She merely shook her head gravely and let her husband continue.

"When his wife left him and went to Europe two years and a half ago—"

"We thought the separation did it!" Stimson's fat voice broke in.

"No," Ashland said, "when she left he felt relieved. She's a fascinating creature, as you know, in her slim, golden-blonde way. But she had led him an awful chase. She's the restless, temperamental kind—one scheme today, another tomorrow and at each scheme with a sort of hectic intensity. Always, too, and this is the point, blindly self-centered. She'd either drag everybody along with her or—or die in her tracks. One week she'd keep him out every night till three; next week she'd shut herself up with her writing—she did poetry of a kind—and scream at any interruption. But that was no relief to him. Because when she came out she'd torment him to the quick with her jealousy and make him account for every minute of the time.

"Finally she came to the conclusion—just like a woman, isn't it?—that *he* stifled *her* individuality—and off she went! Frye always was the sensitive, delicately balanced sort, even at college, and her goings on had pretty nearly wrecked his nerves. So when she went he had a chance to recuperate. You've, got to remember, of course, that she planned to stay in Paris just six months. He had no anxiety and they corresponded and when she wasn't there to torment him he loved her as much as ever. But the life , she'd led him had sunk into him so deeply—had upset him so thoroughly—that he couldn't, just couldn't bring himself to ask her to come back. And, although she was the one who had left, she wouldn't come back without being asked. Again—just like a woman!"

"Quite natural, though," I ventured to put in and again Margaret nodded gravely.

"Maybe so," Ashland went on, "and Frye's morbid conscience made him consider her point of view closely. But he couldn't do it. That's all. His nervous system was to constituted that the very thought of the old life made him tremble—actually tremble and shake. He would test himself and just to imagine his wife at him again made him turn pale."

"He didn't love her!" one of the women threw in sentimentally.

"Yes, he did," Ashland insisted. "He finally, at the end of the first year, stated his case to her rather frankly."

"Did you see his letters?" Margaret asked quickly.

He shook his head.

"No, but her answers. They were in his desk. Immediately after his death I read a good many of them on an impulse. Of course, this needn't go farther." There was a murmur of assent. "The facts are as I have stated them. At that time he dropped hints to me of his situation and the letters confirmed them. A little later he stopped telling me anything, seemed, in fact, rather to avoid me."

He took a sip of wine. No one spoke. We all felt that he was but now coming to the momentous part of his story. When he spoke again we knew that we were right.

"At the beginning of the second year he drew closer to another woman. It's clearly marked in Mrs. Frye's innuendoes and his evident attempts to evade but not deny. At that time, too, he began to jot down notes—you couldn't call it a diary—in a year book."

He paused for a minute. A hush was in the room. The dusk had now floated in and seemed to isolate the yellow points of the candles and the pale faces and shoulders of the women which rose out of the soft gloom.

"I'm not supposed to be a sentimental person," Ashland said slowly, "and it's true, no doubt. But I think I have hold of the situation that developed in Frye's life. Remember the hectic sort of a chase his wife had led him—clawed at his life and soul continually (that's his own expression) like a bird of prey; kept him in excitement, suspense, terror. ... The other woman was the kind that gave and—and—sustained, did everything Gertrude Frye could never do. He said the other woman was like a Spring evening—serene and cool and sweet! Evidently she helped him get a grip on himself again and made him happier, because more at one with himself, than he had ever been before. And they didn't have much of a chance, either.

"Everybody, of course, knew Frye to be a married man and expected Gertrude back and, for all we know, the other woman was bound, too. Anyhow he complains that they never had more than two or three hours of each other, that they had to sneak around and hide. What consoled him deeply—especially by contrast—was her punctuality. He made quite a long note on that. Gertrude had always kept him waiting, hanging around, wearing his nerves thin. This woman, with so much more reason and excuse, never did. So their meetings, pitifully few and brief as they seem to have been, never began with a jar. Whenever they met they stepped out of the misery and jangle and ugliness of life into a purer and a finer world."

He paused again and I thought I saw a gleam of moisture in Margaret's eyes. But she couldn't take anything he said at its full value.

"You're getting poetical," she threw out lightly though with a little catch in her voice.

"I'm only reporting, you know," he said with just a touch of irritation.

Then he spoke in a more matter of fact way.

"It's clear enough that he wanted her to go away with him openly and let Gertrude divorce him. But she wouldn't do it. I'm not sure that she had any moral scruples. But, whether from experience or not—maybe just from his—she hadn't any very high opinion of married life. He has a long note on an afternoon they spent walking by the Hudson—an Autumn afternoon too, curiously enough—and he plead with her passionately and even taxed her with not caring for him. But she refused, according to his account, just because she cared so much. She told him that, somehow, marriage developed an evil sense of possession in most women and that then, illogically to be sure, they despised the man for letting himself be possessed and run so completely. She became quite intense and even epigrammatic, according to him, and ended the discussion by saying: 'All marriages are ruined and vulgarized by home-life!' "

II

ASHLAND looked around and a little hubbub of protest arose and Stimson rather amused us by saying naively he hadn't ever noticed it, and Mrs. Stimson said petulantly it was another example of women always slandering their own sex. But Margaret remarked quickly :

"No, it was just saying what everybody knows but is too polite to express."

A discussion threatened to arise, but I urged Ashland to go on.

"You've got to motivate a suicide, you know," I told him. "All this sounds rather—"

He waved his hand. "I'm trying my best to make you see it all as I've come to see it. In spite of the reluctance of the woman to go farther than she had gone, and that was a very little way—those two were happy. Frye wrote it down deliberately, over and over again. He had never, in fact, been happy before. He had lost his mother early and married young. He had been hustled about and dominated and battered spiritually—as he put it—all his life. This woman, even when they were together, especially when they were together, knew how to put his soul at ease, how to let his own mind expand and his own impulses have free play at last and unchidden. She understood him, she knew what he needed; she never troubled him with her own cares and difficulties but curbed the insistence of her own personality in the service of his. Even more than most American men he hadn't believed such things possible. Oh, our women are devoted nurses in sickness and will stick to you if your troubles are melodramatic. But did you ever see one who, after marriage, subdued herself, didn't, in however high-class a way, nag—but try to give her husband a chance to live his own life? No, let's not discuss it! At all events, Gertrude Frye wasn't that kind and the other woman was. When they separated Frye went home and thought about her and once in a while he would grow quite mystical and call her an Angel with healing on her wings."

A gust of the autumnal air came in and made the candles flicker. No one spoke and we heard the rustle of the leaves outside. The story had gripped us at last and Margaret shaded her eyes with her hand.

"The trouble was, of course," Ashland went on, "that Frye had to correspond with Gertrude. Her letters—I've seen them, as I told you—were like nasty little explosions. She wouldn't come back and she wouldn't leave him alone either. Sometimes she described herself as lonesome and tried to wring him with compassion; sometimes as in a whirl of people and attentions and then she wanted to make him jealous. In every note there was some jar, some stab, some hidden threat, something disturbing and rasping. She kept her note-paper in sachet so long that even from Europe her letters troubled him with the perfume that reminded his senses of her most intimately.

"I don't say she did that intentionally. But the trick was characteristic of all her instincts. However, he got to the point where he could live down each letter in a day or two. Then, as he said, he went back to his Paradise. Both he and the other woman, by the way, deluded themselves more and more as to the precariousness of their situation. In the intervals between letters they forgot about Gertrude—agreed to forget about her. That was the size of it. Of course, he tried to make his angel come to him openly. But on that point the lady's decision seems to have been final.

"Then the crash came suddenly—from their point of view—as it might, of course, have come at any moment. Gertrude got into trouble about money and about a man. She had flirted too outrageously and the man demanded what he had been made to expect. She cabled for funds and then announced her departure for America.

"Frye was shaken by a cold terror: he was wretched in proportion to the happiness he had enjoyed. He saw the old nerve-racking life ahead of him. He committed his first flagrant indiscretion, it seems, by going to the house of the other woman and begging her, piteously, to flee with him. She couldn't bring herself to yield but she half-promised that, if Gertrude could be persuaded to release him, she would try, as she told him, not to desert him."

III

ASHLAND stopped rather suddenly and looked up as though he were aware of something uncanny. Other candles had flickered out and we were almost in darkness. He half rose but I said to him: "Go on!" because I thought that the mood and the scene suited the story.

"Frye went to the pier to meet Gertrude," he continued, "she had half a dozen boxes in addition to her trunks, tried to smuggle through all sorts of stuff, half-fainted in the taxi, recovered suddenly and insisted on luncheon at the Ritz, became every moment more radiant and domineering and, before they got home, filled Frye with a prostrating sense of the old terrorized whirl. She didn't reproach or question him this time, but acted as if nothing had happened—nothing! Only she kept him busy, attending to her, waiting for her, making love to her, leaving not the loophole of a moment for escape or communication with anyone. He tried to formulate that in his diary and she pounced on that and tried to destroy it. She failed—he caught her just in time—and then it was she who acted the part of supremely injured innocence over the glimpses she had had and immediately grasped the magnificent weapon of what she called his 'outrageous infidelities!' "

"Good Lord," the honest Stimson burst out, "why didn't he rum—just run?"

"Because," Ashland said slowly, "he found his condition worse than all his fears. Not only did Gertrude absorb him, but he found the memory of the other woman—that memory which was his dearest possession—slipping irretrievably from his heart and mind: because he discovered that, torment him as Gertrude would, yet—in spite of his irritation and wretchedness and, at moments, flaring hatred—he loved her ... loved her in the weakness of his subjection and despair and so was doomed to that subjection and despair forever."

Ashland sprang up by some irresistible impulse and I saw Margaret stagger to her feet just as, with a swift gesture, he switched on the electric light. In the full glare they faced each other across the table and he saw the unrestrained tears of an immitigable sorrow in her eyes. I caught at her hot hand in a warning grasp, but already the words were out:

"He didn't love her ... you don't understand ... " And her voice had a mournfulness that I shall never forget.

Ashland went white to the very ears, but he played the game. He sat down and I drew Margaret gently back to her seat. Then he swallowed a few times as if he had something furry and bitter in his throat and said:

"You see how the man was tied down. He couldn't get away, he felt degraded and crazy. So he—stepped out." He gulped down a glass of wine and we all began to jabber—yes, that's the word—just to make a noise, don't you know. And I can't tell you how we ever—it's like the grisliest nightmare-managed to say good-bye to our host and hostess and get out of the house and walk to the station—(we swore we wanted to walk) over all those solemn Autumn leaves. ...

IV

OH yes, the Ashlands have lived together right along. Of course, no one knows on just what terms. He hadn't anything vulgar to reproach her with and he's very punctilious by nature. Margaret has never betrayed anything except that, just once, a long while ago, in a discussion that came up she looked at me hard and said that cowardice in the face of life and love was an awful crime, that it killed souls.

And Gertrude—she's now Mrs. McFarland, you know, very rich and fashionable—has been known to complain that, especially in the Autumn season, some impudent person persists in decorating the grave of the late Mr. Frye.

A CYCLE OF MANHATTAN

Thyra Samter Winslow

I

THE Rosenheimers arrived in New York on a day in April. New York, flushed with the first touch of Spring, moved on inscrutably, almost suavely unawares. It was the greatest thing that had ever happened to the Rosenheimers, and even in the light of the profound experiences that were to follow it kept its vast grandeur and separateness, its mysterious and benumbing superiority. Viewed later, in half-fearful retrospect, it took on the character of something unearthly, unmatchable and never quite clear—a violent gallimaufry of strange tongues, humiliating questionings, freezing uncertainties, sudden and paralyzing activities.

The Rosenheimers came by way of the Atlantic Ocean, and if anything remained unclouded in their minds it was a sense of that dour and implacable highway's unfriendliness. They thought of it ever after as an intolerable motion, a penetrating and suffocating smell. They saw it through drenched skylights—now and then as a glimpse of blinding blue on brisk, heaving mornings. They remembered the harsh, unintelligible exactions of officials in curious little blue coats. They dreamed for years of endless nights in damp, smothering bunks. They carried off the taste of strange foods, barbarously served. The Rosenheimers came in the steerage.

There were, at that time, seven of them, if you count Mrs. Feinberg. As Mrs. Feinberg had, for a period of eight years—the age of the oldest Rosenheimer child—been called nothing but Grandma by the family and occasionally Grandma Rosenheimer by outsiders, she was practically a Rosenheimer, too. Grandma was Mrs. Rosenheimer's mother, a decent, simple, round-shouldered "sheideled," little old woman, to whom life was a ceaseless washing of dishes, making of beds, caring for children and cooking of meals. She ruled them all, unknowing.

The head of the house of Rosenheimer was, fittingly, named Abraham. This had abbreviated itself, even in Lithuania, to a more intimate Abe. Abe Rosenheimer was thirty-three, sallow, thin-cheeked and bearded, with a slightly aquiline nose. He was already growing bald. He was not tall and he stooped. He was a clothing cutter by trade. Since his marriage, nine years before, he had been saving to bring his family over. Only the rapid increase of its numbers had prevented him coming sooner.

Abraham Rosenheimer was rather a silent man and he looked stern. Although he recognized his inferiority in a superior world, he was not without his ambitions. These looked toward a comfortable home, his own chair with a lamp by it, no scrimping about meat at meals and a little money to put by. He had heard stories about fortunes that could be made in America and in his youth they had stirred him. Now he was not much swayed by them. He was fond of his family and he wanted them "well taken care of," but in the world that he knew the rich and the poor were separated by an unscalable barrier. Unless incited temporarily to revolution by fiery acquaintances he was content to hope for a simple living, work not too hard or too long, a a little leisure, tranquillity.

He had a comfortable faith which included the belief that, if a man does his best, he'll usually be able to make a living for his family. "Health is the big thing," he would say, and "The Lord will provide." Outside of his prayer-book, he did little reading. It never occurred to him that he might be interested in the outside world. He knew of the existence of none of the arts. His home and his work were all he had ever thought about.

Mrs. Rosenheimer, whose first name was Minnie, was thirty-one. She was a younger and prettier reproduction of her mother, plump and placid, with a mouth inclined to petulancy.

There were four Rosenheimer children. Yetta was eight, Isaac six, Carrie three and little Emanuel had just had his first birthday. Yetta and Carrie were called by their own first names, but Isaac, in America, almost immediately gave way to Ike and little Emanuel became Mannie. They were much alike, dark-haired, dark-eyed, restless, shy, wondering.

The Rosenheimers had several acquaintances in New York, people from the little village near Grodno who had preceded them to America. Most of these now lived in the Ghetto that was arising on the East Side of New York, and Rosenheimer had thought that his family would go there, too, so as to be near familiar faces. He had written, several months before, to one Abramson, a sort of distant cousin, who had been in America for twelve years. As Abramson had promised to meet them, he decided to rely on Abramson's judgment in finding a home in the city.

Abramson was at Ellis Island and greeted the family with vehement embraces. He seemed amazingly well dressed and at home. He wore a large watchchain and no less than four rings. He introduced his wife, whom he had married since coming to America, though she, too, had come from the old country. She wore silk and carried a parasol.

"I've got a house all picked out for you," he explained in familiar Yiddish. "It isn't in the Ghetto, where some of our friends live, but it's cheap, with lots of comforts and near where you can get work, too."

Any house would have suited the Rosenheimers. They were pitifully anxious to get settled, to rid themselves of the foundationless feeling which had taken possession of them. With eager docility, Yetta carrying Mannie and each of the others carrying a portion of the bundles of wearing apparel and feather comforts which formed their luggage, they followed Abramson to a surface car and to their new home. In their foreign clothes and with their bundles they felt almost as uncomfortable as they had been on shipboard.

The Rosenheimers' new home was in MacDougal Street. They looked with awe on the exterior and pronounced it wonderful. Such a fine building! Of red brick it was! There were three stories. The first story was a stable, the big door open. Little Isaac had to be pulled past the restless horses in front of it. The whole family stood for a moment, drinking in the wonders, then followed Abramson up the stairs. On the second floor several families lived in what the Rosenheimers thought was palatial grandeur. Even their own home was elegant. It consisted of two rooms—the third floor front. They could hardly be convinced that they were to have all that space. There was a stove in the second room and gas fixtures in both of them—and there was a bathroom, with running water, in the general hall! The Rosenheimers didn't see that the paper was falling from the walls and that, where it had been gone for some years, the plaster was falling, too. Nor that the floor was roughly uneven.

"Won't it be too expensive?" asked Rosenheimer. Abramson chuckled. Though he himself was but a trimmer by trade, he was pleased with the rôle of fairy godfather. He liked twirling wonders in the faces of these simple folk. In comparison, he felt himself quite a success, a cosmopolite. Just about Rosenheimer's age, he had small deposits in two savings banks, a three-room apartment, a wife and two American sons, Sam and Morrie. Both were in public school, and both could speak "good English." He patted Rosenheimer on the back jovially.

"You don't need to worry," he said. "A good cutter here in New York don't have to worry. Even a 'greenhorn' makes a living. There's half a dozen places *you* can choose from. I'll tell you all about it, and where to go, tomorrow. Now, we'll go over to my house and have something to eat. Then you'll see how you'll be living in a few years. You can borrow some things from us until you get your own. My wife will be glad to go with Mrs. Rosenheimer and show her where to buy."

The Rosenheimers gave signs of satisfaction as they dropped their bundles and sat down on the empty boxes that stood around, or on the floor. This was something like it! Here they had a fine home in a big brick house, a sure chance of Rosenheimer getting a good job, friends to tell them about things—they had already found their place in New York! Grandma, trembling with excitement, took Mannie in her arms and held him up dramatically.

"See, Mannie, see Mannischen—this is fine—this is the way to live!"

II

THINGS turned out even more miraculously than the Rosenheimers had dared to hope. After only three days Rosenheimer found a job as a pants cutter at the fabulous wages he had heard of. He could not only pay the high rent, twelve dollars a month, he would also have enough left over for food and clothes, and to furnish the home, if they were careful. Maybe, after the house was in order, there would even be a little to put by. Of course it was no use being too happy about it, he told Mrs. Rosenheimer.

"It looks fine now, but you know you can't always tell. It takes a whole lot to feed a big family."

Although secretly delighted, he was solemn and rather silent over his good fortune. Abraham Rosenheimer was a cautious man.

Mrs. Abramson initiated Grandma and Mrs. Rosenheimer into New York buying. It was fascinating, even more so than buying had been at home. There were neighborhood shops where Yiddish was spoken, and already the family was beginning to learn a little English. Mrs. Rosenheimer listened closely to what people said and the children picked up words, playing in the street.

The next weeks were orgies of buying. Not that much was bought, for there wasn't much money and it had to be spent very carefully, but each article meant exploring, looking and haggling. Grandma took the lead in buying—didn't Grandma always do such things? Grandma was only fifty-seven and spry for her age. Didn't she take care of the children and do more than her share of the housework?

Grandma was supremely happy. She liked to buy and she felt that merchants couldn't fool her, even in this strange country. A table was the first thing purchased. It was almost new and quite large. It was pine and bare of finish, but, after Grandma had scrubbed it and scoured it it looked clean and wholesome. It was quite a nice table and only wobbled a little when you leaned on it heavily, for the legs weren't quite even. One was a little loose and Grandma didn't seem able to fasten it. Assisted by Mrs. Rosenheimer and Yetta, she scrubbed the whole flat, so that it equaled the new table in immaculateness. There were families who liked dirt— Grandma had seen them, even in America—but she was glad she didn't belong to one of them.

Then came chairs, each one picked out with infinite care and much sibilant whispering between Grandma, Mrs. Rosenheimer and Mrs. Abramson. There was a rocker, slat-backed, from which most of the slats were missing, though it still rocked "as good as new." The next chair was leather-covered, though the leather was cut through in places, allowing the horse-hair stuffing to protrude. But, as Mrs. Abramson pointed out, this was an advantage, it showed that the filling wasn't an inferior cotton. There were two straight chairs, one with a leatherette seat, nailed on with bright-colored nails, the other with a wicker seat, quite neatly mended. There was a cot for Grandma and a bed for Mr. and Mrs. Rosenheimer and Emanuel. The other children were well and strong and could sleep on the floor, of course. Hadn't they brought fine soft feathers with them?

All of the furniture was second—or third—hand and the previous owners had not treated it with much care. So Grandma got some boxes to help out, and she and the Rosenheimers worked over them, pulling and driving nails. Finally they had a cupboard which held all of the new dishes—almost new, if you don't mind a few hardly noticeable nicked edges—and decorated with fine pink roses. Some of the boxes were still used as chairs, "to help out." One fine, high one did very nicely as an extra table, with a grand piece of brand-new oilcloth, in a marbled pattern, tacked over it. They had a home now.

Grandma and Mrs. Rosenheimer marketed every day at the stores and markets in the neighborhood. Rosenheimer sometimes complained that they used too much money, but, then, he "liked to eat well," The little Rosenheimers grew round and merry.

Grandma and Mr. and Mrs. Rosenheimer, looking at the children and at their two big rooms—all their own and so nicely furnished—could hardly imagine anything finer. Grandma and Rosenheimer were absolutely at peace. But Mrs. Rosenheimer knew that, with more money, there were a lot of things you could buy. She had walked through Washington Square and up Fifth Avenue. She had seen people in fine clothes, people of her own race, too. She didn't have much, after all. Still, most of the time she was content.

Gradually, too, Rosenheimer saw shadows of wealth. He heard rumors of how fortunes were made overnight—his boss now, a few years before, had been a poor boy. ... Nevertheless, smoking his cigarettes and reading his Yiddish paper after his evening meal, or talking with Abramson or one of the men he had met, he was well satisfied with New York as he had found it.

III

As the months passed, the Rosenheimers drank in, unbelievably fast, the details of the city. Already the children were beginning to speak English, not just odd words, here and there, but whole sentences. Already, too, they were beginning to be ashamed of being "greenhorns" and were planning the time when they could say they had been over for years or had been born here. Little Mannie was beginning to talk and everyone said he spoke English without an accent.

Yetta and Ike started to school. Each day they brought home some startling bit of information that the family received and assimilated without an eye-wink. Although most of the men at the shop spoke Yiddish, Rosenheimer was learning English, too. He even spoke, vaguely, about learning to read it and write it, and he began to look over English papers, now and then, interestedly. Mrs. Rosenheimer also showed faint literary leanings and sometimes asked questions about things.

Ike was always eager to tell everything he had learned. In a sharp little voice he would instruct, didactically, anyone within hearing distance. He rather annoyed Rosenheimer, who was not blinded by the virtues of his eldest son. But he was Mrs. Rosenheimer's favorite. She would sit, hands folded across her ample lap, smiling proudly as he unrolled his fathomless knowledge.

"Listen at that boy! Ain't he wonderful, the way he knows so much?" she would exclaim.

Yetta's learning took the form, principally, of wanting things. Each day, it seemed, she could find out something else she didn't have, that belonged to all American children. And, no matter how penniless Rosenheimer had just declared himself to be, unsmilingly and a bit shamefacedly, he would draw pennies out of the depths of the pocket of his shiny trousers.

Only Grandma showed no desire to learn the ways of the new country. She didn't mind picking up a little English, of course, though she'd got along very nicely all of her life without it. Still, in a new country, it didn't hurt to know something about the language. But as for reading— well, Yiddish was good enough for her, though she didn't mind admitting she didn't read Yiddish very easily. Grandma had little use for the printed word.

Each week the Rosenheimers' clothes changed nearer to the prevailing styles of MacDougal Street. Only a few weeks after they arrived Mrs.

Rosenheimer, overcome by her new surroundings, bought, daringly, a lace sailor collar, which she fastened around the neck of her old-world costume. As the months passed, even this failed to satisfy. The dress itself finally disappeared, reappearing as a school frock for Yetta, and Mrs. Rosenheimer wore a modest creation of red plaid worsted which Grandma and she had made, huge sleeves, bell skirt and all, after one they had seen in Washington Square on a "society lady."

Just a year after they arrived in America, Mrs. Rosenheimer discarded her *sheidel*. She even tried to persuade Grandma to leave hers off, but Grandma demurred. There were things you couldn't do decently, even in a new country. Mrs. Rosenheimer made the innovation in a spirit of fear, but when no doom overtook her and she found, in a few weeks, how "stylish" she looked, she never regretted the change. She was wearing curled bangs, good as the next one, before long.

Little Ike had a new suit, bought ready-made, his first bought suit, not long afterwards. The trousers were a bit too long, but surely that was an advantage, for he was growing fast, going on eight. They couldn't call him a "greenhorn" now. He came home, too, with reports of how smart his teacher said he was and of the older boys, unbelievers, whom he had "got ahead of" in school. His shrill voice would grow louder and higher as he would explain to the admiring Mrs. Rosenheimer and Grandma what a fine lad he was getting to be.

Other signs of change now appeared. Scarcely a year had gone by before lace curtains appeared at the two front windows. They were of different patterns, but what of that? They had been cheaper that way, as "samples." By tautly drawn strings, white and stiff they clung, adding a touch of elegance to the abode. Only three months later a couch was added, the former grandeur of its tufted surface not at all dimmed by a few years of wear. Yetta and Carrie slept on it, luxuriously, one at each end. It was a long couch and they were so little.

Then a cupboard for dishes appeared. Grandma bought it from a family that was "selling out." It had glass doors. At least there had been glass doors. One was broken now, but who noticed that? In the corner of the front room, oppposite the couch, it looked very "stylish." And not long afterward there was carpet in the front room, three strips of it, with a red and green pattern. Then, indeed, the Rosenheimers felt that they could, very proudly, "be at home to their friends." They had company now, families of old friends and new, from the Ghetto and from their own neighborhood. And they visited, *en masse*, in return.

There wasn't much money, of course. Rosenheimer was getting good wages, but children eat a lot and beg for pennies between meals. And shoes! But like many men of his race and disposition, Rosenheimer never contributed quite all of his funds to his household. Nor did he take his women into his confidence. He felt that they could not counsel him wisely, which was probably right, for neither Grandma nor Mrs. Rosenheimer was interested in anything outside of their home and their friends. Besides this, he had a natural secrecy, a dislike of talking things over with his family. So, each week, he made an infinitesimal addition to the savings account he had started. He even considered various investments—he knew of men who were buying the tenements in which they lived on wages no bigger than his, living in the basement and taking care of the house outside of working hours. But he felt that he was still too much the "greenhorn" for such enterprises, so he kept on with his small and secret savings.

IV

IN 1897 another member was added to the family. This meant a big expense, a midwife and later a doctor, but Rosenheimer had had a raise by this time—he was, in fact, now a foreman—so the expense was met without difficulty. There was real joy at the arrival of this baby—more than at the coming of any of the previous children. For this was an American baby, and seemed, in some way, to make the whole family more American. The baby was a girl and even the sex seemed satisfactory, though, of course, at every previous addition the Rosenheimers had hoped for a boy.

There was a great discussion, then, about names. Before this, a baby had always been named after some dead ancestor or relative without much ado. It was best to name a child after a relative, but, according to custom, if the name didn't quite suit, you took the initial instead. By some process of reasoning, this was supposed to be naming the child "after" the honored relative. Now the Rosenheimers wanted something grandly American for the new baby. Grandma wanted Dora, after her mother. But Dora didn't sound American enough. Ike suggested Della, but that didn't suit, either. Finally Yetta brought home Dorothy. It was a very stylish name, it seemed, and was finally accepted.

Little Emanuel, aged four, was told that "his nose was out of joint." He cried and felt of it. It seemed quite straight to him. It was. He was a handsome little fellow, and, when Mrs. Rosenheimer took him out with her, folks would stop and ask about him. She was glad when she could answer them in English. And as for Mannie—at four he talked as if no other country than America had ever existed.

Very gradually, Mrs. Rosenheimer grew tired of MacDougal Street. She tried to introduce this dissatisfaction into the rest of the family. Grandma was very happy here. With little shrugs and gestures she decried any further change. Weren't they all getting along finely? Wasn't Rosenheimer near his work? Weren't the children fat and healthy? What could they have better than this—two rooms, running water, gas and everything? Didn't they know people all around them? Rosenheimer was indifferent. Some of his friends, including the Abramsons, had already moved "farther out." Still, he didn't see the use of spending so much money; they were all right where they were. Times were hard; you couldn't tell what might happen. Still, if Minnie had her heart set on it—. The children were ready for any change.

Mrs. Rosenheimer, revolving the matter endlessly in her mind, found many reasons for moving. All of her friends, it seemed, had fled from the noise and dirt of MacDougal Street. On first coming to New York she had been disappointed at not living in the Ghetto over on the East Side. Now, when she visited there, she wondered how she had ever liked it. When she moved she wanted something really fine—and where her friends were, too. She had a good many friends outside of the Ghetto now. On arriving in America she hadn't known MacDougal Street was dirty. She knew it now. And the little Italian children in the neighborhood—oh, they were all right, of course, but—not just whom you'd want your children to play with, exactly. Why, every day Ike would come home with terrible things they had said to him. And their home, which had looked so grand, was old and ugly, too, when compared with those of other people. Of course Grandma liked it, but, after all, Grandma was old-fashioned. Mrs. Rosenheimer discovered, almost in one breath, that her mother belonged to a passing generation, and didn't keep up with the times—that she, herself, really had charge of the household.

Out in East Seventy-seventh Street there were some tenements, not at all like those of MacDougal Street nor the Ghetto, but brand-new, just the same as rich people had. Each flat had a regular kitchen with a sink and running water and a fine new gas stove. The front room had a mirror in it that belonged to the house—and—unbelievably but actually true— there was a bathroom for each family. It had a tub in it, painted white, and a washstand—both with running water—and already there was oil-cloth, in blue and white, on the bathroom floor. The outer halls had gas in them that burned all night—some sort of a law. Those tenements were elegant—that was the way to live.

Rosenheimer got another raise. There was some sort of an organization of cutters, a threatened strike, and then sudden success. Mrs. Rosenheimer never understood much about it, but it meant more money. Now Rosenheimer had no legitimate reason for keeping his family in MacDougal Street.

So he and Mrs. Rosenheimer and Grandma went out to the new tenements and looked around. Mrs. Rosenheimer acted as spokesman, talking with the woman at the renting office, asking questions, pointing things out. At the end of the afternoon Rosenheimer rented one of the four-room flats in a new tenement building.

On the way home, Mrs. Rosenheimer leaned close to her husband:

"Ain't it grand, the way we are going to live now?" she asked.

"If we can pay for it."

"With you doing so well, how you talk!"

"Good enough, but money, these days—"

"Abe, do you want to do something for me?"

"Go on, something more to spend money on."

"Not a cent, Abe. Only, won't you—shave your beard? Moving to a new neighborhood and all. Not for me, but the neighbors should see what an American father the children have got."

Rosenheimer frowned a bit uneasily. Mrs. Rosenheimer didn't refer to it again, but three days later he came home strangely thin and white-looking—his beard gone. Only a little mustache, soft and mixed with red, remained.

Before the Rosenheimers moved they sold the worst of their furniture to the very men from whom they bought it, five years before, taking only the big bed, the table and the couch. It was Mrs. Rosenheimer who had insisted on this.

"Trash we've got, when you compare it to the way others live. We need new things in a fine new flat."

On the day they were moving, Yetta said something. The family were amazed into silence. Yetta was thirteen now, a tall girl, rather plump, with black hair and flashing eyes.

"When we move, let's get rid of some of our name," she said. "I hate it. It's awfully long—Rosenheimer. Nobody ever says it all, anyhow. Let's call ourselves Rosenheim."

"Why, why," muttered her father, finally, "how you talk! Change my name, as if I was a criminal or something?"

"Aw," Yetta pouted, she was her father's favorite and she knew it, "this family of greenhorns make me tired. Rosenheimer—if it was longer you'd like it better. Ike Rosenheimer and Carrie Rosenheimer and Yetta Rosenheimer! It's awful. Leaving off two letters would only help a little—and that's too much for you. Since the Abramsons moved they are Abrams, and you know it. And Sam—do you know what? At school they called him Mac-Dougal because he lived here on this street and he liked it better than Sam, so he's calling himself MacDougal Abrams now. And here, you old-timers—"

"She's right, Mamma," said Ike, "our names are awful."

Mannie didn't say anything. He sucked a great red lollypop. At six one doesn't care much about names. Nor did Carrie, who was eight.

There was a letter-box for each family in the entrance hall of the new tenement building and a space for the name of the family just above it. Maybe Rosenheimer had taken the advice of his children. Perhaps he wrote in large letters and couldn't get all of his name in the space made for it. Anyhow, Rosenheim was announced to the world as the occupant of Flat 52.

V

FLAT 52 was quite as handsome as Mrs. Rosenheim had dreamed it would be. There were four rooms in it. In the parlor was the famous built-in mirror, with a ledge below it to hold ornaments. And, before long, ornaments there were, three big vases. They were got with coupons from the coffee and tea store at the corner—it was a lucky thing all the Rosenheims liked coffee. There was the couch, too, but best of all was the new table. It was brand-new—no one else had ever used it before. Mrs. Rosenheim bought it in Avenue A and was paying for it. weekly out of the household allowance. It was red and shiny and round and each little Rosenheim was warned not to press sticky fingers on it, though it was always full of finger marks.

On the table was a mat of blue plush and on the plush mat was—yes—a book—"Wonders of Natural History." It had been Yetta's birthday present from her father and was quite handsome enough, colored pictures, red binding and all, to grace even this gem of a table. There was a new rug in this room, too, though it was new only to the Rosenheims. There were roses woven right into it and Grandma thought it was the most beautiful thing she had ever seen. She liked to sit and look at it as she rocked.

Yetta, Carrie and Grandma slept in the front room—just the three of them alone in the biggest room. There was a cot, covered with a Turkish spread for the girls and Grandma slept on the couch—no sleeping on the floor any more for this family. So wonderful was the new home that there was a bedroom devoted exclusively to the rites of sleeping. Mr. and Mrs. Rosenheim and Dorothy occupied it. The third room was the diningroom, where Ike and Mannie slept all alone on a cot and weren't afraid. No one slept in the kitchen or bathroom at all. In the dining-room there was a whole "set" of furniture, bought from the family that was moving out, a square table and six chairs. It was lucky Mannie and Dorothy were so little they could sit on others' laps.

The dining-room, with its fine "set," brought the habit of regular meals with it. In MacDougal Street there was a supper-time, of course, but the children weren't always there and the other meals had been rather haphazard, half of the family standing up, likely as not. Now there was a regular breakfast in the morning, everyone sitting down, and early enough for Rosenheim to get to work on time and Yetta and Ike and Carrie to get to school. Lunch was still informal, eaten standing around the kitchen. Supper was a grand meal, everyone sitting down at the same time, the table all set with a tablecloth and dishes, as if it were a party.

It was easy to settle down into the pleasant rhythm of East Seventy-seventh Street. There were big new tenements on each side of the street and before long each member of the family made lots of friends.

Rosenheim didn't have as many friends as the others. He didn't care for them. His hours were long and he was getting into the habit of working, sometimes, at night. It takes a lot of money to pay rent—six dollars every week—and buy clothes and food for a family and save a little, too. Rosenheim didn't complain unless his usual solemn face and prediction of hard times can be called complaining. It never occurred to him that he had anything to complain about. Didn't he have a fine home and a lot to eat, a home grander than he ought to spend the money for, even? When he wasn't busy, he and Abrams and a friend of theirs, sometimes a man named Moses, would play cards long hours at a time, talking in loud, seemingly angry voices and smoking long cigarettes. Or, with coat, collar and shoes off, as he always sat in the house, he would read the paper—he could read English quite easily, but he preferred Yiddish. He didn't talk much and the children were taught "not to worry Papa," when he was at home.

Grandma grew to like the new home in time, though it never seemed quite as pleasant as that in MacDougal Street. She did all of the cooking, of course, and could order the children around as much as she wanted to, though they were good children as a rule, when you let them see who was boss. She would exclaim with clasped hands over the grandeur of things and beg her God that the people from her home town might see "how we live like this." She was always busy. She never learned to speak English well, and though at sixty-two she could drive a bargain as good as ever, she didn't feel quite as comfortable in the nearby shops as she had in MacDougal Street. Gradually her daughter took over the marketing from her.

The spirit of change had reached Mrs. Rosenheim and she did what she could to grasp it. She tried again to persuade Grandma to take off her *sheidel*.

"See, Grandma, these other people. Ain't you as good as them? It ain't nothing to be ashamed of, a *sheidel,* but here in America we do what others do."

But Grandma kept her *sheidel.* She couldn't yield everything to the customs of the unbelievers. She even muttered things about "forgetting your own people."

Mrs. Rosenheim tried to acquire "elegant English." She was very proud of her children because their language was unsullied by accent. But perhaps because she never liked to read and it never occurred to her that she might study, or because her tongue had lost its flexibility, she was never able to conceal her foreignness. She was becoming a little self-satisfied, too, a bit complacent with her own ways, and this may have hindered her progress. The new language issued forth in a strange, twisted form, the "w's" and "v's" transferred, the intonations of the Yiddish always noticeable. She managed to make nearly all of the ordinary grammatical errors of the native and a few pet ones of her own. Her sentences were full of inversions. Her voice, never very low, became louder and louder and the singing intonations more marked as she grew excited. Rosenheim spoke with an accent, too, which he always retained, but his voice was quite low and he soon overcame this strange sing-song of his native tongue. Then, too, Rosenheim never talked very much.

Mrs. Rosenheim bloomed in East Seventy-seventh Street. Her mother did the cooking and Yetta helped with the housework. Even then, with so many children in the house, there was enough to do, but she spent much time in visiting her neighbors, gossiping about her children, the prices of food, other neighbors. Although her family came first, she began to pay more attention to herself, buying clothes that were not absolutely necessary, cheap things that looked fine to her. She became ambitious, too. She found that there was another life not bounded by the tenements and that "other people," the rich part of the world, were not much different outside of their possession of money. Her humility was wearing away. "We're as good as anybody" came to her mind, and was beginning to fertilize. She didn't want to associate with anyone outside of her own group, but she liked to feel that others were not superior. The children, continuing their acquisitiveness, encouraged their mother.

Yetta had her fourteenth birthday soon after the family moved to East Seventy-seventh Street. She began to mature rather rapidly, arranging her hair in an exaggerated following of the fashion and even purchased and wore a pair of corsets. She had a high color and her flashing eyes made her quite attractive. Her mouth was rather wide. Yetta did not speak with a foreign accent, but her voice was a trifle hoarse and was not well modulated. She had a lot to say about nearly everything and delighted in saying it. The niceties of conversation had not been introduced into the Rosenheim family life and most of the things Yetta thought of occurred when someone else was talking. Her favorite method of attracting attention was to interrupt or talk down, in a louder voice, anyone who had the floor. Ike had this pleasant little habit, too, so between them conversation rose in roaring waves of sound.

Yetta felt that many things about her could be improved. She began to criticize things at home—her clothes; her mother's language, which was too full of errors, too singing to suit her daughter; the actions of the younger children. She never liked to read, but she "loved a good time" and was always with a group of girls and boys, laughing and talking.

Ike was much like Yetta, though a bit more serious, more inclined to argument. He could argue over anything, even at twelve. He, too, had definite notions about the upbringing of the younger children and the modernity of the household. He didn't want anyone making fun of the family he belonged to. His own name came in for his disapproval about this time.

He had a fight with a boy named Jim and Jim hit him and called him names. But the cruelest part of Jim's name-calling had been merely to repeat, over and over again, "Ikey Rosenheim, Ikey Rosenheim." For this cruelty Ike had fought Jim and had emerged not entirely victorious, bringing back a black eye and the memory of the derision in the mouth of the enemy.

"I'm going to change my name," Ike announced at supper that night. "I don't care what this family says. You make me sick, naming me Ike. You might have known. This family has terrible names. No wonder people make fun of us. After this I'm—I'm going to be—Harold."

"Oh, no, not Harold," Grandma wailed, with uplifted hands.

"No," Mrs. Rosenheim groaned, "you've got to keep the letter, the 'I.' You were named after your Papa's father."

"There's a lot of good names with 'I,'" Yetta encouraged. So, between them, they found Irving, which seemed satisfactory to everyone. Little Irving, at school, told his teacher that Ike had been a nickname and that the family wanted him called by his own name now. Jim, not satisfied with Irving Rosenheim as a reproach, had to find something else to fight about.

Carrie and Mannie and Dorothy were still too little to bother about names. They begged for pennies for lollypops on sticks, candy apples, licorice and other delicacies that the neighborhood afforded, satisfied to tag after Mrs. Rosenheim as she did the marketing. They were nice children, though of course Dorothy was a little spoiled—the youngest child and always having her own way about everything.

VI

DURING the next year something came up in a business way that caused Rosenheim and Abrams to hold long consultations during many evenings. They nodded together over bits of paper on which there were many figures. Mrs. Rosenheim felt that they had "something in their heads" they weren't telling her about, but, being a dutiful wife—and knowing her husband, and how useless it would have been—she didn't press matters. A few weeks later she found out. E. G. Plotski, it seemed, had owned a small pants factory which occupied half of the third floor of an old loft building in West Seventeenth Street. This Plotski had died, suddenly, leaving no near relatives except a wife. Abrams had heard about the case. Mrs. Plotski couldn't keep up the business alone. If she couldn't "sell out," complete, she was going to give it up and sell the machinery. She had some cousins in a far-Western place called, Abrams believed, Iowa, and was desirous of living with them. If Mrs. Plotski "gave up the business" there was a tremendous loss, it seemed to Abrams and Rosenheim—for Plotski already had operators, customers, "good will." And, with their knowledge of the pants business...

It seemed, indeed, a visitation, as if a whole pants business had descended to them as a direct reward for their long and faithful work.

But Mrs. Plotski had friends, not just in a position to buy the business, it seemed, but quite capable of giving advice about selling it. And herein lay the need of much nodding and figuring. Finally it was settled. Abrams and Rosenheim went to their several banks—it's never safe to put all of your savings in one bank, even if it does look like a fine big one—drew out their savings accounts, for of course they had no checking accounts, and, after the usual legalities had been concluded, were the joint partners of The Acme Pants Company, Men's and Boys' Pants.

After they had signed their names, Marcus L. Abrams and Abraham G. Rosenheim, Rosenheim allowed his stern face to relax into a rather sad smile.

"Good, eh, Marcus? Here, I'm only 'over' seven years and I'm partner in a business already. Of course, we can expect hard times, but, a business ain't anything to be ashamed of."

The family saw Rosenheim's new signature and liked it. Irving wrote it above the letter-box. The G stood for nothing in particular, but Rosenheim had no middle name and of course he ought to have one. It was indeed American. The neighborhood did not notice, it was used to changes.

Abrams and Rosenheim worked all day and most of the night. They "went over the books" with great deliberation. They looked into every minute detail of the business, and wrote numerous letters by hand on the old Acme Pants Company letterheads that they found in Plotski's desk. When this paper was used up they ordered more, retaining the cut of the building at the top but substituting their names for the name of the deceased former owner.

They were very happy over their new business, though you would never have known it by their actions. They always wore long faces.

The factory did well. People liked ready-made pants, it seemed. The two men hurried around seeking new trade, satisfied with as small a profit as possible. They bought job lots of woolens from the factories and did numberless other things to reduce expenses. Rosenheim cut the pants and Abrams was not too proud to do his share of the menial labor. Before another year had passed the whole of the third floor loft belonged to the Acme Pants Company.

Mrs. Rosenheim was proud of her husband. It was mighty fine, these days, to speak of "my husband's factory" to those women whose more unfortunate spouses were forced to exist on mere wages handed them by their overlords. But even this, in time, stopped satisfying. What good does it do for your husband to own a factory if you still live in a tenement in East Seventy-seventh Street? Mrs. Rosenheim knew that her husband was working hard and was nearly always worried oyer money matters, bills to meet, wages to be paid. But, as long as he actually was a manufacturer, an owner of a business, a payer of wages, it was unbelievable that they should live in a tenement. Weren't they as good as anybody? Several months ago the Abrams' had moved. Of course, with only two boys the expenses were less, but what of that? And the Moskowskis—now the Mosses—had moved, too. The Rosenheims had been in the tenement three years and now the neighborhood was filling up with terrible people, straight from the Ghetto—or the old country—and bringing foreign habits with them. It was no place to bring up growing American children.

It was Yetta who precipitated the moving. Although he petted and humored Dorothy, it was his oldest child who was Rosenheim's favorite. Now Yetta tried all of her most endearing tricks.

"Papa," she said, "I'm sixteen. I ought to get out of this neighborhood. Ask Mamma. I'm almost a young lady. I want good things—a fine man like you with a factory shouldn't keep his children in the tenements. All of my crowd are gone. I miss them something awful. You don't want me to go with the—the 'greenhorns' who are moving in around here, do you?"

Similar arguments managed to convince Rosenheim. Anyhow, one night he nodded solemnly and consented to move.

"You women will ruin me yet, with all your spending," he said, but Yetta, tall though she was, jumped on his lap and kissed his thin cheek.

"None of that," he said, in assumed brusqueness, as he pushed her away. "You make a fool of your old Papa, eh? Well, go along and get your fine flat."

Mrs. Rosenheim and Yetta, accompanied by Mrs. and Miss Graham, a recent and becoming transformation of their old friends, the Grabinskis, went apartment hunting. They decided on the Bronx, new and good enough for a manufacturer's family. They had friends there and there were lots of stores. It was a nice neighborhood, Yetta thought, with lots of young people who wore good clothes. She could have a fine time.

No longer were the Rosenheims satisfied with the first apartment shown them. Yetta and her mother had grown critical. Yetta's ambitions had limitations, of course. She didn't aspire to an elevator apartment or anything like that—but she didn't want a tenement. She wanted a big living-room, for she was approaching the beau age and already was going to the theater with MacDougal Adams and Milton Cohn. They visited dozens of apartments, examining the kitchens and the halls, exclaiming over the plumbing. Grandma wanted a big kitchen and she ought to have it, as long as she did most of the cooking. And they had been crowded for years—Yetta didn't want anyone sleeping in the front room, nor even in the dining-room. Young girls do get such notions! Mrs. Rosenheim wanted grand decorations in the lower hall.

After much step-climbing they found their apartment. It was on the fourth floor, rear, of a walk-up apartment, but the rent was forty dollars a month and they dared not pay more. Rosenheim looked dour when the news was broken to him, but, with sad headshaking and remarks about business being bad, he said they might take it.

The entrance hall of the apartment-house was of marble. The letter-boxes were of brass and shining. The stairs leading to the apartment were carpeted. The apartment itself had seven rooms. A few years before the Rosenheims wouldn't have believed an apartment could be so large. Now they all accepted it rather indifferently. Wasn't Rosenheim a factory owner? Didn't some of their friends live just as grandly? The woodwork was shining oak. The floors glittered blondly. Mr. and Mrs. Rosenheim had a bedroom all alone, Grandma shared a tiny cubicle with Dorothy. Yetta and Carrie had their room and there was a room for the boys. All of the rooms had new beds of white enameled iron, fantastically twisted and with big brass knobs.

The Rosenheims got rid of most of their old things at a sale before they left East Seventy-seventh Street. Then Mrs. Rosenheim and Yetta bought things suitable for the grandeur of their new home at an installment house in Sixth Avenue. There was a three-piece parlor set stained to a red imitation of mahogany. The round table had come with them, as had the vases. The dining-room boasted a new "set," a round table that pulled apart and had four extra leaves and sat on a huge pedestal, and eight chairs—two with arms, making one for each of them. There were brand-new rugs, one for each room, most of them in patterns of birds and beasts and flowers in bright colorings, though the front room displayed a gay and exciting "Oriental pattern."

One of the startling changes of the new régime was the name above the letter-box. A simple and chaste A. G. Rosen was announced in Irving's most careful writing. Rosenheim explained that, at the factory, everyone called him Rosen for short and it might make it confusing to keep the old name. The family hailed Rosen joyfully. Surely they were real Americans, now.

VIII

THEY were settled only a few months when Yetta begged for and got—a piano. Shiningly red, it matched the rest of the living-room furniture. It was an upright, of course, and Yetta draped a pale silk scarf embroidered in gold threads, over it, with a vase at either end to hold it in place. Soon she and Carrie were taking lessons from a Mme. Roset of the neighborhood, making half-hours horrible with scales and five-finger exercises.

There were now other forms of art in the household, too. For his birthday the children gave their father enlargements of the photographs of him and their mother. These were "handmade crayons" in grey, with touches of color on lips and cheeks and framed in wide carved oak, trimmed with gold. These were placed side by side above the piano, which stool slightly diagonally in one corner.

The children were growing up. Yetta felt herself quite a young lady and didn't go to school. There was no use going any more—she wasn't going to be a teacher, was she? She had a lovely handwriting, with fine loops at the ends of the "y's" and "g's." It seemed a shame to spend her days in school when there were so many things to do outside. No one tried to persuade her to keep on going. Her father was slightly of the opinion that too much learning wasn't good for a girl anyhow. Men didn't like "smart" girls and Yetta was growing up. If she had wanted to go to school he might have consented, but she didn't. She preferred putting on her best clothes, her hat an exaggerated copy of something she had seen in Broadway and had made after her description at a neighborhood shop, a cheap fur around her neck, and high-heeled shoes. Thus attired, she went walking.

In the mornings she had to help a little with the bed-making, dusting and ironing. But in the afternoons she was free. She'd meet some of "the girls" or "the boys" and drink soda, laughing and giggling over things. She used the latest slang and talked rather loudly. At night there were dances or the crowd would go, in pairs or groups, to the theater, sitting in the gallery, usually, and laughing heartily over the jokes. They were fondest of vaudeville. Yetta was awfully happy when she had enough spending money and a new dress—a bit more exaggerated in style than any of her friends. She couldn't imagine anything finer than the new neighborhood and the new apartment.

Grandma was just a trifle bewildered in the Bronx. She didn't seem to fit in. The children, growing up, were developing unexpected opinions of their own that didn't agree with her ideas. They called her old-fashioned and giggled at her advice. There was plenty to do and Grandma liked housework. But sixty-five isn't young and Grandma had worked hard in her day. Four flights of stairs aren't easy, either, so Grandma didn't go out often. Occasionally, she walked around the neighborhood, not knowing just what to do. Mrs. Rosen did all her own marketing or telephoned for things—there was a telephone in the new apartment. There were a few old friends to go to see, foreign-born women, like herself, and with these she would talk in comfortable Yiddish. But each one lived several blocks away. You didn't talk to strangers in this neighborhood, it seemed, and you could go for weeks and not see anyone you knew. A funny place, America.

Still, there were pleasant things for Grandma—good food and the fun of preparing it, a comfortable home. Mrs. Rosen didn't like to work as well as she used to, so finally she hired a woman who came in, one day a week, to do the washing in the morning and the scrubbing of kitchen and bath in the afternoon. Grandma was quite excited over this innovation. For the first time in her life she could fold her gnarled old hands and watch someone do the work for her.

"They should hear about this back home," she would say. "Abe with a factory and us with seven rooms and a washwoman and all. We've got it lucky, ain't it, Minnie?"

Mrs. Rosen, though annoyed at her mother's simplicity, agreed. Already Mrs. Rosen was planning bigger things. It didn't seem at all impossible to her that some day they might even have a regular servant girl.

Mrs. Rosen was well satisfied, generally. Occasionally she, too, regretted some of the pleasant things that Seventy-seventh Street had meant to her. She had liked the friendly chatter of the neighborhood. Here in the Bronx you had to be "dressed" all the time. In Seventy-seventh Street you could go out in the morning in your house-dress, with a basket, and spend a pleasant hour or so bargaining with the shopkeepers and talking with friends, always meeting little groups you knew. On the steps, in the evening, you could call back and forth. Money was good; she was glad they had it. A servant girl would be fine; it was a lot of work for her and Grandma, cleaning up after five children. But this neighborhood was stylish enough. You knew some of your neighbors here, even if they weren't so friendly. Maybe, after you got better acquainted...

It was nice, having a lot of rooms and new clothes and all that. Mrs. Rosen met new acquaintances and liked them. She played cards in the afternoons now and a few months later joined a euchre club which met every Tuesday afternoon at the homes of its members in turn. There were "refreshments" after the game, cold meat and potato salad, usually, and the prizes were hand-painted china and "honiton lace" centerpieces. Mrs. Rosen won quite an assortment as the months passed.

Irving was getting to be a big boy. He looked a little like his father, thin, a trifle sallow, with a slightly aquilined nose—but much handsomer, his mother thought. His eyes were not strong and quite early he had to wear glasses. He adopted nose-glasses and before he quite got used to them he had formed the habit of tilting his head up, to keep them from falling off. He had rather a sharp chin and wore his black hair straight back and sleek.

When the family moved to the Bronx he was fourteen, had on his first pair of long trousers, and was in the first year of the high school. He was quick in his studies and would argue with his teachers about anything under discussion. He still liked long dissertations at home and had about decided to be a lawyer. In the years that followed he read quite a little, not so much for the love of reading—he had little of that—but from a desire "to keep up with things," so he could discuss and dissect and argue. He liked the theater as he grew older, but preferred serious dramas.

Carrie was quieter than either Yetta or Irving, but she observed a great deal. She liked to spend money, begging it from her parents. "We're rich, why can't I have more things?" she would say, buying unnecessarily expensive ribbons and purses. She liked to correct the family, too, and, when her mother grew vocal and her voice took on the sing-song of her native tongue, Carrie would say, "Don't talk so loud, Mother. We aren't deaf, you know," or "This is America. We try to speak English here." Mrs. Rosen would check herself rather shamefacedly, instead of "calling the child down," as she felt she should have done. Carrie liked expensive clothes and she liked putting them on and taking long walks with just one girl friend, talking quietly. She thought Yetta's crowd awfully loud. Mannie and Dorothy were good-looking little children, still coaxers of pennies and both quite spoiled.

The Acme Pants Company grew, but in spite of its growth none of the family dared suggest any extravagant changes. Rosen spoke too much about hard times for that. And he did worry, too, for with the enlarging of the business came the borrowing of money and notes to meet. He worked at night for weeks at a time and grew thinner. Outside of his usual solemnity he never complained. He enjoyed the business as much for its own sake as for the things he was able to give his family. It was far more interesting and absorbing to him than they were. Even at home his mind was filled with business detail and in the midst of a meal or a friendly discussion his eyes would grow vacant, he would fumble for a pencil and write something down on an envelope. Spare evenings, he played cards with Abrams or Moss or Hammer or fell asleep over his newspaper—an English one, nearly always, now. He still took off his coat in the house and sometimes his collar and tie. It was Carrie who said to him, "Papa, why do you start undressing as soon as you get home?" He always kept on his shoes and sometimes his collar and tie after that.

He never took much part in the family life. Irving bored him. He was not interested in "women's doings," and could ignore whole evenings of conversation about people and clothes. His business was the one thing he cared to talk about—his family knew nothing about business. What was there left? None of them knew or cared anything about world affairs. It isn't likely Rosen would have been interested if they had. So, unconsciously, he drew apart more and more. He paid bills, with a little grumbling. He handed out money when necessary. He greeted all luxuries with something about "hard times." He accepted all innovations with apparent disregard. He was never cross or disagreeable. Everyone was a little quieter when he was at home. Otherwise it was as if he were not there at all.

IX

A YEAR later, when she was eighteen, Yetta became, suddenly, Yvette. The crowd she was going with thought Yetta an awful name, old-fashioned and foreign. And certainly there was nothing foreign about her. She had seen Yvette in a book—and, with the right initial and all—Yvette Rosen sounded fine. After that she frowned at anyone, even old Grandma, if the old name crept in.

The family became more extravagant as the days passed, though not extraordinarily so. But why not? Even Rosen had to admit, grudgingly, that the factory was growing. Little things—Mrs. Rosen had a fine black silk dress, with revers of green satin, lace covered. She bought Grandma a black silk, too, for days when company came in. And Yvette—how that girl did wear out clothes, to parties nearly every night! And Irving wanted "his own money" and was put on an allowance, though he always begged his mother for more before the month was half over. Books cost a lot, it seemed, and you can't be a tightwad with a bunch of fellows. And Carrie had a notion that the family was very rich—when she got new things she wanted the best. Even Mannie and Dorothy needed new things frequently.

In 1906 Irving was graduated, at 18, from the high school. It was a big event for the family. All of them, even Grandma, who didn't go out much, attended the graduation exercises. At the hall they chatted about how fine and smart Irving was until Carrie, who could be very petulant at fifteen, "shushed" them all into silence.

On the way home Mrs. Rosen couldn't help calling her husband's attention to his family—weren't they something to be proud of? To think that only a few years before…

It was Irving who first spoke dissatisfaction with the Bronx apartment. Irving was to enter Columbia University in the fall and he wanted to be a little nearer his school.

"You don't know how it is," he said, one night at dinner. "Everyone laughs at the Bronx. I went to a vaudeville show with Yvette last week, though Heaven knows why she goes to it, and at a mention of the Bronx everyone laughed. It isn't only that. Here we are in a walk-up apartment, when we could have something better. I'm starting—to—to make friends. I've got to make a place for myself. I'm eighteen. When we were younger it didn't make much difference, now we ought to get out of here."

Carrie agreed with him.

"It certainly is terrible here," she said. "I don't like this high school, either. I want to go to a private school. There are several good ones in Harlem and a real fine one on Riverside Drive that I've heard about. Irving is right. You'd think we were poor, the way we live here—no servants or anything. When I meet new girls I'm ashamed to bring them home. Ada is going to private school and Beatrice has moved to Long Island. I don't know anyone around here—but trash and poor people."

Even Mannie, at thirteen, was tired of the Bronx, and Dorothy, at nine, was ready for any change.

The Bronx suited Yvette. She had her crowd here. Still, there was something in what the others were saying. Harlem sounded more stylish certainly. She had friends there, too, and could get acquainted easily enough.

Mrs. Rosen didn't know. She felt, with Yvette, that things were very nice as they were. The old friendliness of East Seventy-seventh Street would never come back, and she, too, had acquaintances in Harlem. It would cost more to live—but didn't they have the money? There could be a servant and new furniture—the children had been hard on the things that had been so shining four years ago. After all, they were rich people, and the children had to have advantages.

Gradually Rosen, grumblingly, was won over. Couldn't he see how terrible it was—all their money, and still living in the Bronx? How could people know he was a success? Their apartment was old-fashioned—that funny tub and only one bathroom for the whole family. And Grandma ought to have a room for herself—with five children there ought to be a servant girl—what was the use of having money if you couldn't get things with it?

Again there was a series of house-huntings. This time Irving accompanied his mother and Yvette. Irving was very critical. Things others pronounced "grand" he didn't like at all. At eighteen he considered himself quite a man. As a coming lawyer he felt that his surroundings should reflect his own glory. What did his folks know about things? Didn't he go to homes they never entered, the Wisels' and the Durham-Levis'? Irving wanted a home with style to it. He hadn't definite ideas about decoration, but it must look fine and big as you came in. He thought they ought to inquire a little about the neighbors—find out if they were just the sort one would want to live near. Their present neighbors certainly were awful.

The new apartment was in West 116th street. The building was large and red, with white stone ornaments. The lower halls were grandly ornamental and a great velvet curtain hung toward the rear. There was an elevator, rather uncertain, with iron grille work in front. That would make it nice for Grandma—she could get out more. The living room had a gas grate and the woodwork was stylishly mission finished.

Followed the usual buying orgy and this, too, Irving consented to attend. The piano came with them, but there was a new parlor set, great heavy pieces of mission, square and dark, with leather cushions. A huge mission davenport was the piece de resistance. The dining room had a brand new "set"—there might be company to dinner—a big table, twelve chairs and a sideboard with a mirrored back. In the bedrooms there were great brass beds, the posts three inches across and large mahogany dressers with "swell fronts," curved generously outward.

In the living room, top, there were fine rugs, "real Orientals" this time, about six small ones, oases of red and blue on the light inlaid floor.

The family admired the lighting fixtures—a cluster of fourteen lights in the living room, to which they added a fancy lamp with a shade composed of bits of colored glass in a floral pattern; in the dining room a great dome of multi-colored glass which hung directly over the table.

Then Mrs. Rosen hired their first maid, though the family referred to her as "the girl." Her name was Marie and she didn't have a very easy life of it. At first Mrs. Rosen and Grandma helped her, but Mrs. Rosen disliked housework increasingly and she didn't want Grandma to work if she didn't. Grandma had always done all the cooking, but as "the girl" learned to prepare the dishes liked by the Rosen family she gradually took over the cooking, too. Then, when "the girl" complained about working too hard a woman was hired for two days each week to do the washing and the heavy cleaning.

Grandma wasn't quite as content as she had been, most likely because she wasn't so busy. Grandma couldn't read English at all and Yiddish very little, even if the children would have allowed a Yiddish paper in the house, now, which is doubtful. Grandma had never had the reading habit, nor, for that matter, any habits of leisure. She had thought that life meant service and now there was nothing to do. It was harder for her to go out because she walked very slowly. There were fewer places to go, fewer friends, fewer Yiddish shops. People would stare, embarrassingly, at Grandma's *sheidel* and Grandma hadn't learned to speak English very well. Mrs. Rosen spoke with an accent, but that was different; people could hardly understand Grandma.

There was always a lot of company in the house and Grandma liked young people, but there was so little to say to them. Unless she knew them awfully well they couldn't understand her, or Yvette or Irving would frown at her attempts at conversation. Everyone smiled at Grandma and shook hands, but that was all—it was more comfortable to stay in her room, usually. There seemed to be fewer old people than there had been. Fewer seemed to live in Harlem, anyhow. In MacDougal Street and even in East 77th Street and the Bronx, Grandma had met old ladies, occasionally, people from her own village and had had long talks with them, interrupted with nods and shakes of the head and tongue duckings. Here it was different. She loved her family, of course, but she didn't seem to fit in. Darning stockings wasn't enough. Of course, Grandma was glad the family was doing so nicely—a fine big apartment with an elevator and a servant girl—and she had two new bonnets and her old one not nearly worn out yet—where did she go to wear it?—and her own room and everything she wanted. And Irving bringing her home candy she liked and Yvette singing for her—Grandma knew she ought to be awfully happy. Yet there seemed to be something—missing—

Mrs. Rosen grew to like the new apartment, though at first it had overawed her a little. But before long she belonged to two card clubs—she had known members of both of them when she lived in the Bronx. She even tried to persuade Rosen to learn euchre or bridge so they could join a club that played in the evening. But Rosen didn't like "ladies' games."

There were some things about the new neighborhood Mrs. Rosen didn't like at all. The neighbors seemed so cold and distant. As if she wanted to know them! Wasn't her husband the owner of a factory—with more money than any of them, more than likely? Yet they minced by her, as if they thought so much of themselves. Well, she could put on airs, too!

That winter Mrs. Rosen went to a beauty parlor for the first time. The women of her set were going, it seemed. It made your hair thicker to have it shampooed and waved, especially when it was starting to get grey. Though it did hurt a little, she grew used to manicures, too, after a while. Mrs. Rosen even considered dieting. But, after a few attempts she gave it up. Just the things she shouldn't eat were the ones she liked best. After all, she was forty-four, though she knew no one would ever guess it, and, if, at that age you are a little plump, who is there to say anything against it? She bought a fur coat that winter, seal, of course, with a great sweep to it and a hat to match, with a curved feather. Now, let one of her neighbors say something! She knew she looked mighty fine—as good as any one in her crowd. Why shouldn't she? Wasn't her husband a well-known manufacturer?

Rosen wasn't quite as busy as he had been, though the Acme Pants Company was getting along splendidly. But with things in good condition there was time to spare. He could have spent more time with his family had he cared to, but it seemed tiresome when he did. Irving annoyed him more than ever with his debates and arguments. In the evening he fell asleep over his paper—he didn't care for other literature except an occasional trade magazine. He still played cards with a few old friends he had made when he first came to America, and who, like himself, had prospered. He kept his coat on in the evenings now or wore the smoking jacket Carrie had given him. What if their friends came in—he had to look nice for their sakes, didn't he? There was a little room, off the living room, which the family spoke of as "Papa's den." There was a couch here, brought over from the Bronx, and a desk. Under pretense of being busy, Rosen would read in there, until he fell asleep.

X

THE next year there was a great change in the Acme Pants Company. An opportunity came almost over night and he and Abrams, after long discussions—at the factory this time—joined the Rex Pants Company, McKensey and Hamberg, partners, and the four formed the Rex Suit Company, Gentlemen's Ready-Tailored Suits. Ready-tailored suits, it seemed, were more in demand every day. The four had capital enough to swing something good and to introduce a new name. Until then, most ready-made suits were mere trade goods. But a few firms had learned the value of a trade name and advertising, and Rosen and Abrams agreed with McKensey and Hamberg that there was room for one more and great possibilities in the idea. They rented an immense loft building and were soon making and selling a line of ready-made suits under the name of the King Brand. They hired an advertising man, giving him an absurdly high salary, an office of his own, with a stenographer and all of that, and agreed to pay exorbitant rates to magazines just for the privilege of a half or a quarter of a page of blank space on which to advertise their wares. A few months later, tall, exquisite young men, in graceful poses, accompanied by impossibly thin young women or sporty dogs looked at you from the magazines under such captivating captions as "King's Suits for the Kings of America" or "Every Inch a King in a King Brand Suit."

Rosen was interested again. Here, expenses were mounting, though profits might mount, too. Now he could figure again, and plan and talk things over with Abrams. Abrams, however, was Abrams no longer. He was Adams, now. He had signed himself Adams when the new firm was organized. Even Rosen's name had changed—he dropped one more let-ter. The indefinite Abraham G. had been altered and he blossomed forth as Abraham Lincoln Rose, to the delight of his children.

Irving was going to Columbia. He had joined a debating club and even his mother had to admit that, at this time, he was pretty much of a bore. He even called his father "Governor" on occasions and twirled a cane on holidays. He was "getting in with fine people" and dined at the homes of new friends, bringing back stories of families who didn't interrupt when you were talking and who had servants who knew how to serve meals. He felt he was going to be quite important and he wanted his family to live up to him.

Carrie was going to a private school—the only kind of school suitable for rich girls. It was in Riverside Drive, and she met some mighty fine girls there. Like Irving, she brought home stories showing the heights of other and the degradation of her own family.

"—We are such rich people and still we never have anything."

Carrie objected to her name, too, it seemed. "Carrie" was such a cheap name. Nobody would know you were rich with a name like that. She was going to be Carolyn after this. Carolyn Rose was a pretty name, wasn't it?

Carolyn loved to spend money. She had decided that the family was really wealthy, that it was all bluff about hard times and saving. She wanted a gold mesh bag and got it before Yvette even knew there were gold bags in the world. Carolyn had a fur coat as expensive as her mother's, but with a smarter, more girlish cut. She disregarded the stupid idea, made up by some one who didn't have the money, probably, that diamonds were for older people, and persuaded her parents to give her a big diamond ring, set in platinum, for her seventeenth birthday.

Yvette's clothes were always a bit loud, too extreme, even cheap looking. Although she paid big prices for them they were still tawdry. Carolyn's tastes were not quiet, but she managed to look "expensive." Her hair was black and sleek and she knew she had "style." She liked collars a bit higher than anyone else wore, when they were high, a bit lower, when low collars came in. She was no slavish follower of fashion, like Yvette. She added a bit of "elegance" to whatever fashion had dared ask for. She liked smooth broadcloth suits, much tailored, for day wear, and elaborate, chiffon evening frocks. She talked with an "accent," but not the kind her mother had. She said "cahnt" when she could remember it, and thought that one ought to have "tone." She had languid airs.

Mannie was growing into a nice child. He was quiet and he started to read when he was just a little fellow. Now you could find him, any time, curled up with a book he'd brought home from school. He didn't care much for out-of-door games. He was the first of the family to have literary leanings, though Dorothy read, too, when she couldn't find anything that pleased her better.

Dorothy was petted and spoiled by the whole family. She got things even before she could think to ask for them. Because there was never anything for her to be cross about the family said she "had a wonderful disposition," though she had a pouting mouth and did not smile very much.

Dorothy was "a little beauty." Although the family kept always with their own race and declared, on all possible occasions, their great pride in it and their aversion to associating with those of other faiths, the thing that delighted them most about Dorothy was, for some unexplainable reason, that everyone said "she looked like a Gentile." Mrs. Rose would repeat to her friends that people had said, "you'd never guess it—just like a Gentile that child looks." Her friends agreed and there was nothing in their minds but cordial congratulation over the fact. Dorothy had lighter hair than the others and grey eyes. She was a slender little thing, quiet, determined, impatient.

"We ought to have an automobile," she said, one day. That was in 1909, before cars had become as much of a necessity as they are now, and Dorothy was only twelve. Two weeks later, after many hugs, her father bought a car, a red one that would hold any five of them. Irving soon learned to drive it and later Carolyn and Dorothy learned, too. Grandma could never be persuaded to enter the car—it didn't look safe to her. Mrs. Rose rode, but it was always sitting stiffly erect with unrelaxed muscles. Rose asked Irivng to drive him places, occasionally, when he was in a hurry. He never liked the automobile except as a convenience.

That year Grandma died. She was sick only a few days and didn't complain even then. The doctor came and fussed over her and finally a nurse came, but Grandma persuaded her daughter to send the nurse away. Grandma seemed quite content to die, and though the family was fond of her, her going did not cause any undue emotion. Mrs. Rose wept loudly at the funeral and Rose looked unusually solemn in the weeks that followed. He had been very fond of Grandma and had appreciated the little things she always loved doing for him. But, after all, as Mrs. Rose would say to her husband, "it ain't as if she was a baby at 72. It ain't as though Mamma ain't had everything money could buy, these last years. A grand life she's had, nothing to do and her own room and all. Many times she spoke of it. It's good we was able to give it to her. She was a good woman, but now she's gone and I can say I ain't got nothing to reproach myself for."

XI

IN 1910, when Yvette was twenty-four, she became engaged to marry MacDougal Adams. Already MacDougal was sales manager for the Rex Suit Company, and he was doing finely. He had grown into a handsome fellow who would be quite fat, one day, if he didn't diet carefully. He was crisply blackhaired, ruddy-faced. He made friends easily and was jovial most of the time. He had no subtleties, but Yvette was not the one to notice. She considered him very modern and liked the way he "caught on to things." Her friends—and the announcement Yvette mailed to the newspapers—spoke of the affair as "a childhood romance," as indeed it was. It pleased the Roses and the Adams, too. They gave a reception at a hall on 125th Street to celebrate the occasion, each of the family inviting their especial friends, with Dorothy and little Helen Nacker to pass flowers to the guests. There was a band behind artificial palms, and waiters in white aprons passed refreshments. Yvette wore a dress of pink and Carrie wore yellow. Carolyn didn't think the party fine enough, and Mannie and Dorothy didn't like it much, either. The rest of the family thought it a successful affair.

Mrs. Rose, Yvette and Carolyn spent the following weeks shopping. Yvette had to have a complete trousseau, starting with table linens and ending with silk stockings. Three months later Yvette and MacDougal were married at the Waldorf, with Carolyn and Maurice Adams as attendants. Only the most intimate friends were invited to the elaborate banquet which followed, though later there was an "informal reception" with much wine. MacDougal had just bought an automobile—black, though Yvette would have preferred a gayer color—and, after a short Atlantic City honeymoon the young couple took a new and elaborate apartment in Central Park West and settled down, with two maids, to domesticity.

"Ain't it grand, Papa?" Mrs. Rose had said to her husband after their first call on the young couple. And even Rose had to agree that even Yvette was getting all that could be expected.

Carolyn was "the young lady of the family," now. She was not as easily satisfied as Yvette had been. She called Yvette's crowd "loudly vulgar," though she was a trifle loud, herself, at times. She raised eyebrows and drew away when fate included her in her sister's parties. She was glad when her sister married—-now she could entertain her loud friends in her own home. Maybe Yvette would even tone down a little; she laughed too loud and had terrible taste in clothes. Her mother talked loudly, too, except when she tried very hard to remember—and it was terrible the way she shrieked and singsonged when she grew excited—but, at least you could remonstrate with her.

The Harlem apartment didn't suit Carolyn at all. Here she was, out of school, nearly twenty—and living in—Harlem. She had gone to a series of morning lectures at one of the hotels and one of the lectures had been on furniture—it seemed all of the things in the Harlem apartment were entirely wrong. Carolyn knew this was true, too. Hadn't she been to other homes, where people knew things? They were rich and had—one maid—and. she didn't know how to wait on the table—and the family treated her as if she were one of them. And Irving talked back to his father, rather impudently, even when company was there, and the car was a sight—she was ashamed to use it. The least they could have was a new car and a chauffeur.

Irving agreed with all of Carolyn's criticisms, excepting those which concerned himself. He was twenty-three, why shouldn't he have things nicer? Dorothy, going on fourteen, also found the Harlem home distasteful.

"A terrible neighborhood," said Dorothy, who became Dorothea, that year. "It's too far from school and we do need a new car. I'm ashamed to tell anyone where I live. I want a big room and my own bath, so I can ask girls to stay all night, if I want to."

Rose sighed, said the family would break him and times were hard. Mrs. Rose sighed, too. Still, Harlem wasn't such a friendly neighborhood—the other couldn't be worse. And with only one girl there was too much for her to do. If they had a man to drive the car and a cook, maybe—

Carolyn went house-hunting alone. She said she'd take the others with her "when she found something." Two weeks later she took her mother and Dorothea to see the new apartment. It was a foregone conclusion with Carolyn that they would take it—just the formality of mailing the lease for her father's signature.

The apartment was on Riverside Drive, in a huge building of cream-colored brick. At the door was a negro uniformed in dark green, and another similarly clad attended the mirrored elevator. The halls had Oriental rugs and were lit and draped with an expensiveness that suited even Carolyn. Of course it was pretty far out on the drive—but it looked rich—and living on the Drive was rather grand, at that. Mrs. Rose was speechless at first, but later the apartment seemed quite satisfying. She liked the ornateness, the grandeur—it was even finer than Yvette's, than any of her friends. Why shouldn't it be, with Abe a partner in a big factory and all—?

The woodwork of the apartment was white enamel. There were little panels in the living room, waiting to be papered, and the dining room had a white enameled plate rail. The lighting fixtures were of the new "inverted" style, on heavy brass chains ending with carved brass holders of white frosted globes. There were French doors of mahogany leading into the living room and dining room, a huge butler's pantry with numerous shelves, a kitchen with a big hooded range and immense white sink, large bed rooms, four baths.

"If—if your Papa will pay for it," Mrs. Rose admitted weakly.

"Oh, he'll pay," said Carolyn, "why shouldn't he—a rich man like him?"

When the men of the family came to see the apartment Irving pronounced it "immense." Mr. Rose looked at the apartment, saw the library that he could have for his own, the big bedroom and bath—and gave in with unexpectedly little persuasion. After all—his friends were living well—why shouldn't he? He was making money—the family might as well spend it. Didn't the way you live show how well you were doing? Not that he was making so much, of course, but, with Yvette married—if Carolyn wanted the apartment—

Mannie and Dorothea were rather indifferent. Still, Mannie was in prep school and cared most about books—even writing a poem occasionally. He was eighteen. At fourteen, Dorothea didn't care about details as long as they were moving. Her new room was nice and big. Still, they ought to have a new car—Dorothea was quite pouty over the old one.

Carolyn took charge of the furnishings of the new apartment. Mrs. Rose, with uplifted hands, declared her ignorance of periods "and such nonsense," but begged her daughter not to spend too much money, "You know your Papa. There's a limit even with him."

Irving gave a long-winded dissertation about what to get and told about a fine apartment he had visited, rather down on the drive—two girls he knew, their father was a criminal lawyer. Carolyn didn't listen very closely. She knew what she wanted.

Accompanied by her most intimate friend, Eloise Morton, daughter of S. G. Morton, the box people (both of Eloise's parents had been born in America), Carolyn visited a number of shops. She called the big stores where Yvette traded "middle class," but she was afraid of the decorating shops and called the things in the windows "junk."

"You might like that old stuff," she said to Eloise, "but I can't see anything to it. Old chairs, stiff and funny—a hundred dollars apiece and then a fake, probably. A whole room full of that doesn't look like any-thing. I like things that show their full value, that you can tell cost a lot of money."

Eloise agreed that her friend had the right idea.

Carolyn didn't allow any mere furniture clerk to suggest or dictate to her. Hadn't she seen a lot of fine homes? Didn't she go to every new show in town and look especially at the stage settings? Hadn't she heard a furniture lecture? Who could advise her?

She didn't want her mother with her, she'd "simply spoil things if she started to talk." Carolyn and Eloise, alone, could give an impression of taste, elegance and riches.

Carolyn decided on Adam furniture for the living room. If the ghosts of the brothers Adam groaned a bit Carolyn was too busy to hear. She liked "sets" for living rooms—didn't everyone have them?—so she choose a great davenport of mahogany with cane sides and back, motifs slightly after some of the Adam designs scattered over the woodwork. The upholstery was rose velour. There were two huge chairs of similar design, one a rocking chair. Other chairs were of cane and mahogany, one a Venetian, one a fireside. There was a great oblong table, too, that Carolyn knew showed good judgment, for it was of "dull antique mahogany." It, too, bore motifs of the house of Adam. There was a floor lamp with a rose shade and two table lamps to match and several pieces of "stylish" painted furniture, factory made. Carolyn looked with scorn on the little rugs that had seemed so fine a few years ago. She chose now an immense Oriental in rose and tan for the living room and a Chinese rug in dark blue to combine with the intricately carved Queen Anne furniture of the dining room.

There were elaborately patterned filet lace curtains throughout the house. Before this Mrs. Rose had always hemmed and hung the curtains. Now Carolyn gave the orders for them. The overdrapes and portieres were of rose velour, heavily lined, and, above the windows were elaborate valances, edged with fringe and wide gold braid. There were blue velour curtains in the dining room.

In the bed rooms Carolyn's imagination had full play. Her parents' room was in mahogany with twin poster beds. Her own room was in ivory, cane inset. Dorothea's was white enameled, painted with blue scenes.

For the walls of the living room, between the panelling, Carolyn chose a scenic paper in grey. On this were to be hung elaborate oil paintings in scalloped gold frames: "A Scene at Twilight," "The Fisherman's Return." In the dining room the paper was in a tapestry effect, red and blue fruit and flowers.

The family moved into the new apartment in October, 1911. The moving was simple for the old furniture was to be sold and professional movers attended to the packing of ornaments and dishes.

Mrs. Rose and Irving were impressed with the effects wrought by Carolyn's taste and her father's money, but it did not take the family long to settle down to the pleasures of life that Riverside Drive opened to them.

XII

MOVING to the Drive, the Roses made the final change in their name. Mannie, usually quiet, was the one to propose it.

"Rose is so—so peculiar," said Mannie. "Anyone could tell it had been something else, Rosen or worse. I'm eighteen and go to college this fall. I'm not going to have a name so—so ordinary. Let's change it to Ross. That's not distinctive, but it isn't queer or foreign. I'm changing my first name just a little, too. I've never been called Emanuel, anyhow. Mannie isn't a name at all. I'm going to register at college as Manning Ross."

There was no letter-box to announce the change, but the elevator man knew that the new occupants of Apartment 31—he wrote the names down with a blurring stub of a pencil to be sure to remember them—were Mr. and Mrs. A. Lincoln Ross, two young Misses Ross and two young men, Irving and Manning.

The family had liked Rose—but there might be something in what Manning had said. But no more changes! Mr. Ross put his foot down, this time. He was meeting important men in business, Gentiles, and he didn't want any more monkey-business about names. Ross was all right and Ross it would have to stay. And it did.

Mrs. Ross took great delight in getting her new servants. It made her feel superior and important, driving up to an employment agent and interviewing prospective retainers. She took Carolyn along for advice and counsel—Carolyn went out a lot and knew about such things.

Carolyn would have liked a retinue, but Ross rebelled—expenses were awful and each servant was another mouth to feed. The old "girl" had got married so they finally chose a cook who was not above helping with other things, a waitress who could combine housework with waiting, and a chauffeur. Besides, the washerwoman would still come in for two days each week.

Soon after the family was settled Mr. Ross bought a big limousine, American made, but one that Carolyn thought looked really expensive. The chauffeur was in uniform, of course. He happened to be a young Irish boy and it seemed to Carolyn, sometimes, that he smiled a bit sarcastically and annoyingly as he held the door open for them, especially after her mother had spoken with an accent or her old sing-song.

Mr. Ross didn't object to the new luxuries. It was much more comfortable driving to the office in the limousine than waiting for Irving or one of the girls to take him or depending on less comfortable modes of transportation. He had more room to himself, too. He liked the way the new cook prepared things—he was getting indigestion and had to be careful about what he ate—though he still remembered with real emotion the pot roasts and fish and stuffed goose that Grandma had delighted to prepare. These new dishes—salads and things like that—everything served separately—you could get used to it—it didn't make much difference—here he was, used to a maid in cap and apron, waiting on table—and Minnie used to it, too, excepting when she forgot and talked to her or reached across the table for things. Still, Minnie meant well, a good woman, rather fat these last years, but a good woman who loved her family—none of this new foolishness some women had, he'd noticed—

Mr. Ross didn't pay much attention to women. He never had. He saw what fine girls his daughters were, that was about all. He couldn't have recognized half a dozen of their best friends, whom he saw constantly at his home, if he had passed them on the street.

His business—that was something. Still, even that didn't keep him busy, the way it used to. This new arrangement, the offices and the factory separated—of course it was for the best. He could always go over to the factory when he wanted to, though there wasn't much need—machinery he didn't understand, everything in such order—with a head for every little department, not to mention the big ones. And, with four partners you couldn't say things as if it were your own business. Mr. Ross was fifty-three, but it hadn't been an easy fifty-three years and things had gone along rather rapidly for a while. Not that he was an old man—far from it.

Still things that had passed seemed pleasanter than they had seemed in the passing—and things to come lacked luster.

This wasn't age—certainly not—he felt as well as he had twenty years ago, practically. Give him some real work to do, you'd find out. But there was so little to do, now. You'd go down to the office about ten and dictate a few letters and potter around with things. You'd examine "swatches" and find that an expert had already given them a chemical analysis. You'd go to luncheon and be careful about what you ate. After luncheon, a little sleepily, you'd dictate more letters, if there were any more and see a few men on business, young upstarts, most likely, or Gentiles who wanted something for nothing—or consult with your partners. Then, you'd drive home after a while and read the paper or listen to Carolyn play on the new player piano or talk with Dorothea, though there wasn't much to talk about. Dinner then, and a game with Adams, though he had rheumatism these last years and wasn't the man he had been. Or Moss would drive over. There was a club, even, if you cared to go to it—a lot of strange men who didn't care anything about you—a club—at least they were of your own race—Dorothea was always asking questions about why the family didn't mix with other people—such notions a child gets—

The Rex Suit Company was still progressing. The great factories were outside New York, but the business offices occupied a whole floor of an office building, each partner with his own mahogany furnished office, with its row of bells and its private stenographers. There was an expert to decide each thing. MacDougal was in the sales department and Maurice, the younger Adams boy, was advertising manager—a big advertising agent had charge of all of the advertising, of course. And what advertising the firm did, too! Double pages in the popular weeklies at thousands of dollars a page. Everyone was familiar with the "Kingly Men." Girls cut them out and mounted them for their rooms. "America's Kings in King's Suits" had been familiar enough to get applause at a musical comedy when it was used to introduce two juveniles. "Every Inch a King for the Kings of Creation" and other well-known slogans ran in letters four feet high above the artist's conception of the "Kingly Man" on the billboards.

Each year there was an ornate catalogue of the styles, "for the Prep Youth," "for the College Man," "for the Younger Set," "for the Older

Fellow." Hundreds of merchants all over the country displayed King Brand signs and carried King Brand suits. The Rex Company had invented half sizes, adjustable models and the giving with each suit of an extra bit of the goods and two extra buttons for mending. There wasn't much you could plan about for the Rex Company. Likely as not, someone else would have thought of it first, anyway.

Mr. Ross was accustomed to meeting men, now. He liked to meet them, in business. He would listen, weigh what they said, learn from them. He never talked much. He always retained his look of severity. He was known as "a crackerjack of a business man," "a man you couldn't put anything over on," but the other partners were good business men, too. There was nothing for Mr. Ross to work for.

Outside of business he had little. His family still seemed apart, yet he would have done anything to have saved them trouble or pain. He liked Yvette because she was frank and lively, but, these last years he liked Dorothea, too, though there was nothing against Carolyn, a fine girl, if she did like to spend money. Minnie was all right—the boys would be, too, when they got a little older and settled down.

Mr. Ross didn't mind listening to the mechanical piano or the Victrola at home, but he did not care for other kinds of music. Concerts made him miserable and fidgety. He saw nothing in them and after several for charity and one visit to the opera he refused to partake of music outside of the home. He had never learned to like reading. He was still content with the daily papers and glanced, occasionally, at a weekly devoted to current events. He knew nothing about art and said so. He didn't want to be bothered with "such notions." Drama of all kinds bored him and even musical comedies entertained him only for a little while. Usually he got to thinking of business in the midst of things and lost all consciousness of what was going on.

Mr. Ross had no social ambitions, so, with no business worries and no outside interests, his days began to drag unpleasantly. He thought often of other days, of "the other side"; when he had been planning to come to America—he was glad that was over, of MacDougal Street, the hard work he had done there, the long hours, the overtime, the little economies so both ends would meet, then the newer tenement, with things a little easier, the beginnings of the factory—those had been real days, staying awake planning to meet bills, figuring to the dollar how to get enough money to pay the "help" and have enough left for living expenses, then Harlem and now Riverside. It was good to have planned and worked. Still, now he was used to his comforts. He liked space and quiet and the car—but, with nothing to do—

Mrs. Ross had long since relaxed her anxiety over her husband. He had never talked business and he seemed just like always, willing to listen to her stories of how she had spent the day. Mrs. Ross was quite content with the Drive. The aloofness of the neighbors, that had been disagreeable to her in Harlem, became one of her own characteristics now. She became more and more aware of her own importance. She had disliked the way "outsiders" and Gentiles had treated her, years before. Now, her last vestige of humbleness gone, she felt herself more than "as good as anyone." Wasn't she Mrs. A. Lincoln Ross, wife of Ross of the Rex Suit Company, a real figure in New York? Didn't she get her picture in the paper when she gave money to charity? Didn't people treat her with respect as soon as they found out who she was? She was frankly fat, but she didn't mind. She had expensive dressmakers and tailors and she thought the results of her toilet satisfactory. After all, she was nearly fifty.

Her voice had toned down, during the years, as had Yvette's. When talking with those she considered important, she even tried to put an elegant swing into her sentences. Usually, though, her voice was accented, ordinary, uninteresting. She still made errors and sometimes quite a lot of sing-song crept in.

In the morning Mrs. Ross attended to her household affairs, giving directions to the servants, ordering her own provisions over the telephone, even planning meals. She looked into the ice-box to see what provisions remained, rubbed fingers across furniture for dust, examined linens. She was a good housekeeper. In the afternoon, with Yvette, whom she found most congenial, or an acquaintance, she went for a drive or shopped. She dropped most of her old friends who had not progressed and she had no sentimental regrets concerning them. A few earlier friends she kept up with, asking them for luncheon or for a drive, with a hint of patronage. Through her daughters she met other women of her own age and circumstances. To these she tried to be pleasant, using her best language and manners. She had no intimacies with these women.

During the second year of the family's residence on the Drive, Mrs. Ross was asked to belong to several committees of important charitable organizations. She joined these gladly and gave generous sums. She liked the society of her own race. She did not feel at home with "outsiders" nor know what to say to them—she felt that they were constantly criticizing her. She had decided social ambitions, however, and wanted Mr. Ross to join a well-known club composed of members of his people. She was proud to know women who, a few years ago, or even now, were she less wealthy, would have ignored her. To the arts she was as indifferent as her husband.

XIII

IRVING was a lawyer now. He had a nice office in one of the newer buildings devoted to professional men, but not much practice. His father found it just as convenient to give him some of the smaller business of the firm as to increase his allowance. When anything important came up Mr. Ross agreed with his partners that it was best to let a better-established lawyer handle the case.

Irving—who became Irwin about this time—could have joined a large firm as a junior member, but he preferred independence. He didn't like to work hard or long and he had heard of the tasks performed by the younger members of big firms. He liked to waste time, browsing around bookstores, walking through the lobbies of hotels, calling on friends. He had a large acquaintance with women and had as many dinner invitations as he could accept. Wasn't he a great catch, a young lawyer with a rich father? And good company.

At twenty-five, Irwin still loved an argument. Although never a great reader, he liked to pose as one, quoting well-known authorities, reading and talking about authors unknown to his hearers. His hair was always immaculately sleeked, though it had just a perceptible wave. He had his favorite manicurist at one of the larger hotels. He smoked an expensive brand of cigarette, carrying them in an elaborate silver and gold case and fitting each one carefully into an extremely long amber cigarette holder before smoking it. He used affected gestures, pounding on a table to emphasize a point he was making. He still wore nose-glasses, now large lensed and tortoise rimmed, and, from habit he held his head too high.

Irwin was proud of his acquaintance with half a dozen actresses of minor importance. These he took to teas, dinners and suppers, talking later as if the engagements had had special significance. He was careful about his acquaintance with other women, choosing those that were, to him, of social importance. He had the same distrust his parents had for those outside of his own race. He never attended services at a synagogue, but to him religion and race were intermingled and he did not attempt to differentiate between them. Since boyhood he had. suffered from prejudice far more than his sisters. He was proud to associate with "outsiders," liked to think he looked and spoke and acted like one of them. But he would never have married a Gentile.

Carolyn was now the liveliest member of the Riverside Drive household. She didn't think much of race and creed. She envied other women in some things, but she thought herself all that was desirable and attractive. She liked best the people of her own race, but she preferred them with American or English accents, appearance and accomplishments. She liked to associate only with people of great wealth. Always gowned a bit ahead of the fashion, perfectly groomed, silky, smooth, crisp, she went to the theater, evenings and matinées, to luncheons and to parties, giggling and laughing, quite moderately, of course, and had a gay time. She loved musical comedy and after-theater suppers. She didn't care for the opera, but even the most serious drama could give her something to giggle about afterwards. Her hair and eyes were dark with something of the Orient about them, but her skin was fairer and clearer than her mother's or Yvette's, her round little nose was always white with powder and her eyebrows narrow and smooth, her lips and cheeks pinkly attractive.

You could see Carolyn almost any fair afternoon, on the Avenue with Eloise or Helen or Mary Louise, stopping in at one little shop for a bit of lingerie, at another for flowers. They spent money with no thought of its value. Most of them could not remember poverty. Those who could found spending the best method of forgetting. Occasionally they met several of "the boys" for tea. When they didn't they bought tea for themselves at

Maillards, usually, or the Plaza. There was always a car waiting and they wore low pumps or slippers and the thinnest of stockings even when the snow was on the ground.

Carolyn "went with" Jack Morton, Eloise's brother. She had met Eloise at the Riverside Drive school. Jack was at Harvard, then, but he was graduated a year later and was "catching on" nicely, in his father's box factory. The Mortons thought the Rosses a step below them socially, for the Mortons were a little farther removed from "the old country." Outside of that, they liked Carolyn. So no one was surprised, when, in 1914, when Carolyn was twenty-three, she announced her engagement to Jack. The Rosses thought Carolyn had "done well," as indeed she had, for Jack Morton was a likable fellow, full of practical jokes and fond of poker playing, but on the whole quite a desirable husband.

Ross gave his daughter a diamond lavalliere for an engagement present, and as Carolyn picked it out herself it was quite glittering. He promised her the furniture for her new apartment as a wedding present. The Mortons gave Carolyn a small car, green, with cushions to match, which she pronounced "a young wonder." They had an engagement "at home" and were married a few months later at one of the newer hotels. Carolyn hoped that it was quite evident to the friends of both families that they were both very wealthy.

The young couple took a three weeks' trip to Florida—Jack couldn't stay away from the business longer than that. Then they went to the Astor, but Carolyn wanted to entertain her friends and a hotel does keep you cooped up so. She and Jack finally decided on a small apartment in a high-priced new building in Park Avenue. They had only one maid to start with for they both preferred eating at restaurants. With the little car you could eat at a different place and go to a show or some place every night.

Without Carolyn the Riverside Drive apartment seemed quiet. Manning went to Harvard for a year, dissatisfied with the unexclusiveness of Columbia.

Dorothea liked school, too, and was now taking a few harmless courses, which gave her something to do, though they didn't satisfy her. Nothing quite pleased Dorothea. She hadn't been satisfied with Carolyn's school—girls of only one creed went there, so narrow. Dorothea said that school was a joke. She had chosen a more expensive school, patronized by daughters of rich men generally. Her new study courses were at Columbia and with private teachers. Mr. Ross didn't like them.

"It isn't as if she had to be a teacher," he said. "A girl can have too much book-learning."

But Dorothea went. She had always been different. Her clothes, for one thing. Couldn't she have had anything she wanted? Look at Carolyn—always dressed like a picture—the family had to admit it, themselves. Even Yvette, though she liked bright colors, was a good dresser. It wasn't as if Dorothea was economical. She spent as much as Carolyn did. Carolyn wore things that "looked expensive," rich broadcloth, elaborate furs—Dorothea preferred rough tweeds. She paid extraordinary sums for little suits that Mrs. Ross thought looked as if she'd got them for twenty dollars in Third Avenue. They were of mixed weaves, in grey or tan and she wore big tailored collars over her coats, not mannish looking or freakish, just plain. She paid fifty dollars for her little round velour hats. She wore heavy gloves and shoes, even when she went out with Carolyn, sleek in white gloves, patent leather pumps and furs. Dorothea paid huge prices for plain little evening frocks which she bought at exclusive little places. Even then she was not satisfied.

Dorothea wore a perpetual little pout—something had always just gone wrong. She spent her time wondering what to do, dipping in "courses" on a variety of subjects, at settlement work, "going with people she didn't have to associate with," her mother thought. Clad in a trim-fitting habit she rode whole mornings in Central Park. She exhibited-funny little Belgian Griffins at shows. She went to benefits and tournaments'. Yet she was always a trifle "put out," a bit bored. Things weren't ever good enough, or quite what she had expected.

For her, twentieth birthday Dorothea asked for and received a new car, a good-looking foreign-made roadster. About time the family had more than one car! She didn't want a chauffeur. Hadn't she been driving as long as she could remember, learning on the old red one? She liked driving the car best of all.

The family, the family's friends, what anyone said or did—all displeased Dorothea. She made sport of Irwin's pet affectations to his face, to her mother's horror. She called Yvette's things "impossible" and made fun of Carolyn's diamonds. She treated her mother as a person of no consequence, never asking her opinion about things. Although she had nothing in common with her father, she made a great fuss over him and he grew to like her better than any other member of his family. She took him out in her car, though he didn't quite enjoy the rides, expecting to be tipped over at. every corner. Carolyn drove perfectly, with the recklessness of a racer.

Dorothea went with "outsiders." She seemed as much at home with members of other races as with her own. She'd bring in unexpected guests, making the family feel ill at ease. While guests were there she'd bring up bits of family history the rest were trying their hardest to keep out of sight.

"Dad," she'd say, "here's someone wants to meet you. He's heard a lot about you … Can you believe that less than twenty-five years ago Dad came to America with no money at all?" then, with a little gesture and a smile, "and now look at him." She'd throw an arm around her father, who, ill at ease, would greet the stranger.

If Mr. Ross had been unsuccessful, he would have looked like any of a thousand of his race whom you can see leaving the shops any evening at the closing hour. But his wealth haloed him. It was impossible to separate him from his money. Thin, stoop-shouldered, solemn, quiet and accented of speech, he stood for success. To Dorothea her father was immensely important. She was the first who had ever made much of him. It embarrassed him—he was a simple old fellow in many ways—but he liked it.

Mrs. Ross thought Dorothea didn't appreciate her.

"It's always her Dad, her Dad," she'd say, "never a word about how I worked when she was small or all I do for her—just Dad this, Dad that— and Irwin don't like—that you're always bringing up old times, about Papa being a cutter. The other night when that fine Miss Tannenheim was here, you said it, when you was talking to that big blond fellow you brought in … "

"You're a dear, Mother," Dorothea would give her mother the tiniest touch of a kiss on her broad cheek, "but Irv's a mess and he knows it.

The Tannenheim person is a cheap old thing with a mean eye and she'll marry him some day, if he isn't watching."

"Dad," said Dorothea, one day. "Let's move. You can't guess how sick I am of Riverside Drive."

"What's the matter? Haven't you got things nice here?"

"Nice—on the Drive?"

"We're always moving, it seems. Only four years ago … "

"I know, Dad. That's just it. A man of your position ought to have a home. Apartments are nothing. This one is simply awful. Riverside Drive is fearfully ordinary, vulgar—don't you think so? Such a cheap collection of newly-rich. Dad, you ought to have your own home in town, anyhow, and something permanent in the country."

XIV

THE idea of a home appealed to Mr. Ross. He felt, now, that he had always wanted a real home. Dorothea called for him in the car and they explored the streets east of Fifth Avenue. Finally, without consulting the rest of the family, Ross bought a three-story house in East Sixty-fifth Street, just off Fifth Avenue.

"Mother will think this is terrible," Dorothea said as she kissed him, "but you and I like it, don't we?' I know it cost an awful lot, Dad, but you can see it's really an investment. After it's made over a bit inside it will do for a family home for years. Imagine you—after all you've done—not having a family home!"

Ross really liked the house. It seemed almost—homelike. The rest of the family were not pleased. The married daughters—of course it was not their affair—but, they wondered if it was just the right thing. Of course, nice people lived in houses, but none of their friends …

"That's why we bought it," said Dorothea.

Irwin "guessed it was all right." Manning was indifferent.

Mrs. Ross held up bejeweled hands and wailed.

"Oh, Dorothea, just as I'm beginning to get into things and can ask people here to a fine apartment on the Drive—an address I can be proud of—and here you buy an old house—I thought, a young girl like you would want things swell—here we've got servants and all——"

"Don't you worry," said Dorothea, "it will be 'swell' enough—awful word. And as for servants—"

The family moved to East Sixty-fifth Street in 1916. Dorothea didn't run around after furniture as those of her family who had chosen furniture before her had done. She turned the whole house over to Miss Lessing, in Madison Avenue. Miss Lessing's corps of exquisitely minded young men came in, looked around, made sketches, brought drapery material and wood finishes, all of which Dorothea examined critically.

"At last we'll have some place we can ask our friends," she said.

The home in East Sixty-fifth Street was rather nice. It was done in English things, mostly, painted walls and rather soft taffetas. There were some big easy chairs that could be pulled around, comfortably, in front of the fireplace. Perhaps because of its seeming simplicity and the plainness of the walls and carpets Mr. Ross liked it more than any home he had ever had. He felt it belonged to him. Mrs. Ross never liked it.

"It's too plain," she said, "nothing to it. No one would believe how much it cost you, Papa. Mrs. Sinsheimer has got an apartment on Park Avenue, just a block from Carolyn. Fourteen rooms. She had a decorator, too, but he got different things than this—gold furniture. It looks like something. We had a fine place on Riverside Drive and Dorothea drags us here, where there ain't even lights enough to see by, at night."

Still, Mrs. Ross found out, from what people said, that there must be something desirable about the new home. She even acquired a bit of the patter Dorothea used, pointing, with something like pride, to "a real Chippendale escritoire, one of the nicest examples in America," and "some Wedgewood placques, three, from an original set of four, you know," and "of course, we are getting old and it's nice we can have a home where we can gather the sort of things we like, as a background."

Irwin "didn't think much of the place, myself," but it was a good idea, the old folks having a home . . he was glad he didn't have to be ashamed of it, though, for his part . . now, that country place Dorothea was talking about . . .

Yes, Dorothea had been talking about a country place. After they were settled in the new home, she continued to talk. They had five servants now—they wouldn't even need two sets—Dad could see now it took that many to run any kind of a house—and they could just shut up the town house in Spring and open it in Fall. All the family could be there, too, Yvette and the new baby, and Carolyn and their husbands… "a real family together. Dad, a permanent family like ours ought to have a decent country place."

The country place was on Long Island, finally. Dorothea picked it out and put the decorations in the hands of the same firm of decorators, who did rather startling things with colored wicker, chintz and tiled floors.

It was near a famous country club, and Dorothea knew, as did the rest of them, that none of the men of her family could ever be admitted. It didn't seem fair to her, of course, and yet… Dad was a great one—there oughtn't to be any place Dad couldn't get into. But Dad didn't care. Though, from things he said, Dorothea knew he had felt things . . expected them. He hadn't even hoped this much of life. Irwin didn't like being left out of things . . and yet, Dorothea, looking at Irwin, hearing him argue in his rather nasal tone, gesturing with his long amber cigarette holder, couldn't blame members of the club, exactly… It wasn't because of Irwin's race . . maybe the members, themselves, weren't so wonderful . . and yet there were her two brothers-in-law, one rather fat, both slow-minded, card-playing, a bit loud and blatant, always bringing money into the conversation . . Yvette, loud, laughing, so heavy, mentally, Carolyn, with her cheap talk of money and spending . . her mother . . it wasn't fair to criticize her, her mother'd had a hard time of it when she was young, and yet…

Dorothea knew that, somehow, the man she liked didn't belong to her race. Hamilton Fournier, now . . of course, if she'd marry him, there be an awful talk, lots of crying and going on about religion . . that sort of thing. She could hear her mother . . she remembered when Freda Moss married,—"He"ll throw it up to you". Yet, if you are proud of your race . . doesn't that . . can you have a thing "thrown up to you" that you are proud of? It was a big problem, too big for Dorothea. She felt that she'd always had everything she wanted . . she could keep on having . .

The family settled down comfortably in the new home, Manning with them. He was going to school in town, now.

Mrs. Ross was getting to like the new home better . . it wasn't Riverside, of course, but people didn't look down on her here. She was even getting in with Mrs. Rosenblatt—now that she lived near her. That crowd—she didn't have their education, but what of it, she was richer than most of them. Who were they, to be so exclusive? Maybe, by next year, if she donated to their Orphan's Nursery Fund . .

Mr. Ross's indigestion seemed a little worse. The doctor came to see him several times each week and he had to be more careful with his diet. There seemed to be less to do at the office. He could retire, of course, but that would take away the only interesting thing he had—the few hours at the office. He even tried outdoor exercise, but after one attempt, he gave up golf as impossible. He gave to organized charities rather liberally and was even appointed on a committee which he attended—he knew it was his money they wanted. He would sit, as he had always sat in the evening, falling asleep over his paper, or bundled up beyond the necessity of the weather, he would climb into the car and spend a few hours with an old friend, or someone would come to see him, playing cards, as always. But a few of the old friends had died, another had moved away . . there had never been many of them. He was just an old man, and lonesome, with nothing interesting to do or think about . . .

XV

MANNING stopped school the year after the family moved into their new home. He had had a year at Harvard and a year or so at art school. Now, nearly twenty-two, he felt that he was a sculptor. His father was disappointed—Manning had started out a nice boy—it did seem that one of the boys . . .

But Manning shrugged sensitive shoulders at anything as crude as the clothing business, even wholesale. His soul was not in such things. And Mr. Ross had to admit that the position of model was about the only one in the establishment that Manning could have filled. Manning went in, rather heavily, for the arts that the rest of the family had neglected. Of course Dorothea read, but Manning thought she skimmed too lightly over real literature. And Irwin—an impossible, material fellow.

Manning wore his hair a trifle long. He talked knowingly of Byzantine enamels and the School of Troyes. He knew Della Robbia and the Della-Cruscans. There was nothing he didn't know about French ivories. He knew how champlevé enamelling differed from other methods . . there were few mysteries for Manning. His personal contributions to Wanty consisted of fantastic heads, influenced slightly by the French of the Fourteenth Century, in bas-relief—very flat relief, of course.

Manning's friends felt they formed a real part of New York's "serious Bohemia." They ate in "unexploited" Greenwich Village restaurants, never complaining about the poorly cooked food, sitting for hours at the bare-painted tables, talking eagerly in the dim candle or lamp light. They expressed disgust when "uptowners" discovered their retreats and sometimes moved elsewhere. You could find them every Saturday and Sunday night in parties of from four to ten, at the Brevoort, sometimes with pretty girls who didn't listen to what they were saying, sometimes with homely little "artistic" ones, hung with soiled embroidered smocks who listened too eagerly, talking of life and art, revolution and undiscovered genius.

There was no question that Manning's father should continue his allowance—there is no money in sincere art these days. Manning knew that even his father must recognize that. Manning spent his summer with the family on Long Island—it was hot in town. But, when one's family is of the bourgeoisie, it does draw one's energy so. In the autumn Manning decided he must have a real studio, some place he could work in and expand, going to "the town house" for week-ends. Having one's family uptown was quite all right, of course—but you couldn't expect an artist to live with them.

Mr. Ross agreed to the studio. He was getting accustomed to Dorothea's friends, unbelievers though they were. He found he could not accept the artistic friends that Manning thought so delightful.

Manning found his studio, finally. The rent was terrific, of course, but the building had been re-built at great expense and was absolutely desirable in location, construction, everything. He furnished it himself in Italian and Spanish renaissance reproduction things. Rather nice! When it was finished—though they probably couldn't "get it," he'd let the family see it.

One Sunday, after a family reunion dinner, Manning announced that his studio was done. If the family liked they might all run down that way—a sort of informal reception . . of course, they probably couldn't understand it all . . .

It was in the Village, of course. Did they think the Village was slumming? Uptown people did. But that's where you'd find real thought, people who accomplished things . . .

"Why, my new studio has real atmosphere"—Manning ran his fingers through his hair as he spoke. "It's in a wonderful old building, magnificent lines and the architect left them all—it's just the inside he's remodeled. I've the third floor front, two magnificent rooms, a huge fireplace, some lovely Italian things . . and the view from the window is so quaint and artistic . . of course you may not understand it . . this family . . it's just a block from Washington Square."

"Why, that's where . ." began Mrs. Ross.

Irwin silenced her.

"Don't begin old times, Mamma. Most of us haven't as long memories as you," he said.

"Come on, now that we're all here, let's go down," Manning went on, "I want you to see something really artistic. A friend of mine, DuBroil—I think you've met him—did me a stunning name plate in copper, just my name, Manning Cuyler Ross. I'm so glad I took Cuyler for a middle name last year. And there is just the single word, 'masks.' I thought it was—rather good. And I've a stunning bit of tapestry on the south wall. Come on—you've got your cars here, we'd better get started—"

It was a pleasant drive. The three cars drew up, almost at once, in front of Manning's studio, as he, in the first car, pointed it out to them.

They made quite a party as they turned out in front of the building—a prosperous American family—Mr. and Mrs. Lincoln Ross, well-dressed, commanding, in their fifties, which isn't old, these days; MacDougal. Adams, plump, pompous; Yvette Ross Adams, in handsome furs and silks; Jack Morton, sleek, black-haired; his always exquisitely gowned wife, Carolyn Ross Morton; Irwin Ross, in a well-fitting cutaway, eyebrows raised inquiringly, chatting alertly; Dorothea Ross, attractive and girlish in rough tan homespun, and Manning Cuyler Ross, their host, pleasantly artistic.

"Here's the place," said Manning. "No elevator, real Bohemia, three flights up, uncarpeted stairs. Come on, Mother."

Mrs. Ross was strangely pale, and on the faces of Yvette and Irwin there were curious shadows. The rest, save for Mr. Ross, were too young to remember. As for him he broke, for the first time in years, into a broad smile. Manning went rattling on.

"This," he proclaimed, "is the way to live! None of your middle-class fripperies. Plain living, high thinking—this is the life!"

They came to the studio at last, and all stood about in silence while Manning explained its charms—the clear light, the plain old woodwork, the lovely view of the square, the remote, old-world atmosphere. In the midst of his oratory Mr. Ross sidled up to Mamma Ross and reached stealthily for her hand.

"Do you remember, Minnie," he whispered, "this room—this old place—those old days—"

"Hush," said Mamma Ross, "the children will hear you."

EVIDENCE

June Gibson

THE slim, green-eyed, pale-haired woman attracted me.
I turned to the woman at my side.
"Is she a lady?" I asked.
"I don't know," said my companion. "Wait until the men arrive."

APOLOGY

Muna Lee

I SAID, I will sing no more,
    For they who should hear are dumb,
And though I sang like the reckless birds,
    No answer would come.

And the leaves made song to my touch,
    And the rain made song to my sight,
And the cloud and the wind made song in my heart
    Ceaselessly, night after night.

I struggled to hold to my word,
    I cried to my will to stand strong,
I vowed I would keep to silence forever
    —And that vow was a song!

THE ETERNAL MASCULINE

Leonora Speyer

P AUL STURGIS looked long and plaintively at the little pile of manuscript which drifted over his nice old Sheraton writing-table.

There lay the unfinished story on which he had been more or less
spasmodically working all the week—his best story, too, he considered—
and visions of its appearance in one of the more pretentious and self-conscious magazines, beyond whose Alpine heights his panting ambitions
sought not to climb, gleamed like a fair landscape before him.

Paul was a lawyer by profession, one of the many quietly successful
ones. The little circle of devoted women-friends, enclosing him like a setting around some rare and greatly prized gem, knew nothing of him as
a lawyer—for although Paul was always gaily loquacious, the "setting"
suspected that it did not know much about *anything* that concerned him
really—but Sybil told Anne "that a man had told Jack that he had heard
Paul passionately pleading the cause of a New Jersey plumber one day in
the courts, while, he, the man, was waiting for his case to come on, and
that it was 'some performance.' "

They knew, too, that Paul wrote for the magazines. Occasionally they
came across a short story of his, in which they sometimes recognized
themselves, more or less fantastically garbed, or some little elaborated
incident in Paul's life—and not very well told, to their surprise, for he was
an unusually good raconteur and they wondered what happened when he
began to write.

Anne brought home a sonnet one day, which she had found—and
surreptitiously taken possession of—among the inevitable pile of back-
numbers on the inevitable table of her dentist's waiting-room. It was a

good sonnet, too,—"as good as gold," Anne said—and the "setting" decided that they liked it very much, and told Paul so.

But on the whole they did not think much of his writing, and as Paul himself seemed to prefer not talking about it, the subject was easily avoided.

He hated criticism of any kind. It hurt him horribly, made him coldly angry, and in that little group of joyously, mercilessly critical young minds, he passed unmolested.

For they had all learned, at one time or another, what "hurting" Paul meant—and how he had been missed as they ate of the bitter fruit of that tree of knowledge and sat alone under its dark branches.

For on these occasions Paul simply disappeared—and it was very difficult to find him again. Anything was better than these vanishings, the setting decided, and so they adapted themselves as well as they could to his debonair self-absorption, his ruthless lack of consideration, his "will-o'-the-wispness," as Anne called it. Paul was "pure pagan," Anne explained—the setting always came to her when in "Paul-troubles,"— again Anne's way of putting it—she *interpreted* him the best, they said.

And they suffered him gladly! They did all the inviting, the telephoning, the ordering of theater-tickets, of supper-tables and taxis. Anne interpreted that it wasn't that Paul was *stingy*, he simply didn't want the *bother*, and he was too busy to be worried with the details; it was enough that he *came*. And they all agreed that no party was in the least what they called worth while, if Paul were not there to make it gloriously, supremely worth while.

Once Sybil "struck," as she announced to her husband hotly. Paul had chucked her at the last minute, *once too often*, she would not stand for it, she was *not* going to ask him to the house again, she was *not* going to Anne to have him explained, she was through, etc., etc.—

"Don't quarrel with Paul; we'll both miss him so," Jack had called to her from the hall, on his way to the office. But she *had* quarreled with him—and Paul had disappeared as usual. It took months to get him back! Always glad to see her when they met, gaily, buoyantly glad, but always just leaving town "on a case" or oppressed with some work that "had to be finished" at home, and a typist coming to help him at eight o'clock.

"I'm sorry, Sybil, but I can't manage it"—and he never could. And perhaps she would meet him that same evening at the theater with Anne; that maddening Anne who had warned her, or with Periwinkle or Madeleine, or worst of all v/ith Mrs. "Gussie" Mainwaring, whom Sybil loathed. And Paul would beam and be so glad to see her, make no excuses and Sybil, no reproach—she wanted him back too much, and as for Jack, he was positively sulking for him!

And one day he returned. She had found his new felt hat, whose untimely loss he had loudly lamented all winter, upon her return to the cottage in the country the following spring. And she had expressed it to him with a neatly-written label tied securely to its immaculate ribbon. It eventually reached him, battered but recognizable, and he wore it, label and all, when he walked in upon them one lovely Sunday morning, remarking that it was hot as Hades in town. Sybil was so glad to see him that she nearly wept, and Jack fell upon his neck and then made three of his wickedest cocktails, which they drank to the strains of "Ridi, Pagliacci" on the gramophone.

Once Anne rang him up at his office to tell him he simply *must* take her to the Russian ballet, as arranged weeks before; Anne had procured the tickets—such good ones, too—after great difficulties, and now Paul announced some work at home that simply had to be finished!

Anne suspected another short story; the last time she had seen him he had told her of an extraordinary scene he had just witnessed in the subway, between two infuriated men and a sobbing woman, evidently the wife of neither, but "something dearer," as Paul described her. He had remarked what a good story it would make and Anne had replied, apropos of nothing at all, "Don't forget we're going to Scheherazade on Thursday!" And they had both roared with laughter.

But Anne didn't laugh as she telephoned him about it. And Paul had suddenly interrupted her to say, "Listen! There's a band in the street! I'm going to hang the telephone out of the window for you to hear!"

There was a pause and then Anne heard the faint, rhythmic strains of a Sousa march. And after a while Paul's voice, excitedly, "Did you get it? We ought to be dancing this minute! Isn't lite hell, Anne! Don't be cross with me, my dear!"

And Anne wasn't. She thought of Sybil's bitter experience and of her own sage advice to her at the time, and so she turned with a very real little pain in her heart, to the next-best companion with whom to share the exotic joys of "Scheherazade."

"I know I'm silly to mind," she whispered to herself as she looked up the telephone numbers of the next-bests, "but there it is—I *do* mind!"

And added as she wrote down the numbers.

"God help the woman that falls in love with Paul Sturgis!"

II

AND now he sat looking at the scattered sheets on his writing-table.

"I could have finished it tonight," he said suddenly in a loud, firm voice. Paul gathered up the manuscript almost tenderly and put it in the drawer of the table. He looked at the clock, and his heart gave a queer little leap. Why had he asked Periwinkle to tea? He hardly knew. Sometimes he wondered if he were falling in love with her. "In love with a girl—? God forbid!" and he touched wood hastily.

At any rate, Periwinkle was coming to tea. Her name was Pervenche, because of a French grandmother, but Paul, not liking his French accent, called her Periwinkle "for short," and called her that, by the way, the first time they met; Anne said once that nobody minded *what* Paul did the first time and if they minded afterwards it was too late.

The setting had demurred a little over Periwinkle. Paul had told Anne she must ask her to dinner.

"But I hardly know her," Anne had weakly objected.

"That doesn't matter," declared Paul, "I've told her about you. She'll love you, Anne. And she's a peach! Thursday and Monday suit her best. Whom shall we ask?"

Poor Anne! She was just convalescing from an acute attack of what she called "bookitis," which meant going seriously into the question of the tradesmen's books, prior to drastic reform, and she had resolved not to have a dinner-party for a month at least. But what could she do?

And the party was certainly a huge success. Periwinkle proved a great addition to the setting, even Madeleine admitted that, as she said good night to Anne.

"What's Paul doing with a *girl,* anyway?" she had disapproved on the telephone when asked to the dinner. "We're all married!"

"Paul says she isn't a bit like a girl," Anne answered happily. "He says she's as young and innocent as we are."

So Madeleine came. And Paul got her to ask them all down to her house on Long Island over Sunday.

He wondered if Periwinkle would mind there being no tea. She never seemed to care much about it herself, although her hands fluttered about her mother's tea table like two expert, administering, bejeweled white birds, every Wednesday from four to six.

He hoped she would not miss her tea, but nothing would have induced him to buy a tea-set and kettle, and all the rest of the paraphernalia! He hated food or the suggestion of food, in his rooms; he did not even break- fast there and certainly never entertained friends, preferring his club, a good restaurant, or better still, their own houses. This he admitted with an engaging frankness when pressed by the setting for an invitation.

"What do you want to come to my squalid little flat for? It's much nicer here!"

His flat wasn't squalid at all and he knew it; he had taken immense pains and spent a good deal of money over it, and the result was thor- oughly satisfactory; but that is how he warded off all possible parties in his rooms.

Not one of Paul's women-friends had ever seen them, but rumors of old prints, Queen Anne furniture and a lacquer cabinet filled with Waterford glass reached them from various reliable sources. It was exasperating.

And then he asked Periwinkle to tea; and she accepted joyfully.

"Oh, Paul, what fun! Of course I'll come! Whom shall we ask? It's *my* party, remember; they're all to understand that!"

"No one's to be asked," he answered. "It's *our* party, just yours and mine."

"Oh," she said, and turned a lovely pink which Paul adored. Then she laughed.

"How disgustingly selfish of us! When we both know how that beloved Anne and Sybil and Madeleine—to say nothing of Mrs.

Gussie—are dying to come! No, no, we must certainly have them, Paul, especially Anne."

"I don't want them," he replied serenely. "I love them but I don't want them, Periwinkle. I only want you. Will you come?"

"I—I'll think about it," she answered.

"Tuesday's a good day," he continued affably, "there's nothing in the courts for me on Tuesday."

"If there were, you'd chuck me, I suppose," she said. And he answered simply, "I'd have to, my dear."

"Or a new story coming," she went on. "I actually believe you'd put me off—provided I said I'd come, which I haven't, *nota bene*—for a new story!"

"There *is* one coming, *nota bene;* what's more, I'm *harassed* about it, I ought not to be thinking about anything else. I'm stuck in the big love-scene, Periwinkle! And I don't care a damn! All I care about is your coming to tea on Tuesday."

"Mother'd be so shocked, Paul. *Do* let's have Anne!"

"Next time, perhaps," he answered quite firmly. "This time, no! Will you come, Winkle?"

"Yes, Paul," said Periwinkle meekly. There was a funny little chirp in her voice as she spoke, she wondered if he had noticed it.

III

She came in quickly, a little shyly and stood in the middle of the room looking about. Paul suddenly remembered he had meant to get some flowers. Her first words broke the thin skim of atmospheric ice with true Periwinkle dash.

"Well, of all the pigs! *What* a sweet place!"

She looked at Paul severely.

"Anne shall know of this!" she announced.

She moved towards the Waterford glass, aloof and sparkling on its shelves.

"And you never wanted us—never missed us!"

"I know now how I've missed you," he answered, "it's wonderful having you here."

He pushed a big chair towards the fire.

"Sit down, you darling Winkle."

"Paul, you *are* the most artistically selfish human being I ever dreamed of! I'm going to take off my hat so that I can lean back and tell you what I really think of you."

"Isn't it a new hat?" he asked with reverent interest.

"*New?*" she echoed. "Why, Paul, I saw that bird of Paradise hatch out of its little French hat-box one hour ago! It's just arrived from Paris! I bought it on my way here! It gave me a great courage, Paul, which Heaven knows I needed when that sinister elevator-girl asked me which floor."

They both contemplated the hat solemnly.

"Bon jour!" said Paul, and placed it respectfully on a fat black satin cushion trimmed with purple chenille and a large bunch of turquoise-blue pears.

"How well my cushion looks, doesn't it?" remarked Periwinkle. "Are the pears very uncomfortable?"

"They haven't complained about anything," said Paul and drew up a little stool close to her chair.

He sat down and laid his head upon her knees simply and naturally. She let him, of course. One always let Paul do these things. Anne had been dropped from the visiting lists of three old friends of her father's because Paul had put his head on her shoulder at a dinner-party. But Anne didn't mind in the least.

"They don't know Paul," was her only comment," and their dinners were a pain anyway."

"Do you think Mr. Sturgis will ever marry?" she had been asked meaningly, after this particular dinner, by one of the shocked ladies who had seen Paul's head, and Paul always claimed that her answer was what caused her name to be erased from the three lists, much more than what he had done to her shoulder! "If one of our husbands dies, he may," Anne said calmly.

Paul's head felt very nice on Periwinkle's knees. His hair was turning gray at the temples, she noticed. How thick it was, how good it smelled. Periwinkle had a curious desire to stroke it. She began to talk lightly of his old prints and the green and white Wedgwood plates running about the room on a little shelf.

"If mother divorces me for coming here today, I think I'll marry you for the sake of those darling old plates," she reflected.

"I wish you would; and I'll give you the plates for a wedding present. Will you marry me, Winkle?"

"No, Paul," said Periwinkle.

"How unkind," he sighed in relieved tones and put his head on her knees again,

"And as I see no signs of tea," she continued, "I'm going to ask for a cigarette to deaden the pangs of hunger."

Paul rose with evident reluctance.

"I was *so* comfortable!" he grumbled, "I wish you wouldn't be so restless!"

He gave her a cigarette and lit one for himself.

"How's the big love-scene?" she asked and blew an expert little ring towards him. "There's a wedding-ring for it!"

Paul groaned.

"They're still floundering about!" he said. "Such a good situation, too! *I* don't know what's the matter with those two people—I simply *can't* make them kiss! They just stand there staring at each other like two fools!"

"*Must* they kiss?" she asked with interest.

"Of course they must!" he cried, looking at her with reproachful eyes.

"But they *won't!* They go on making page after page of ridiculous conversation; I'm sick of them both!"

She looked at him.

"Perhaps it isn't their fault," she said gently, "poor things!"

Paul thought deeply for quite half a minute.

"You mean it's mine," he answered. "Perhaps you're right. I—I have a horror of the melodramatic and lovers are always so melodramatic!"

"And if they are not—they 'stick!' " remarked Periwinkle. "You've read too much Henry James, my friend."

Paul crossed over to the writing table. He opened the drawer and took out his manuscript with great deliberation.

"I think I'll read it to you, Winkle. It's a thing I never do—I hate doing! I don't like criticism—it depresses me! And I certainly never court it. But I'm going to read you the whole darned story—as far as I've gotten. Be as patient—and as kind—as you can!"

There was a glint of two big steel buckles as she crossed her feet comfortably on the stool.

"Read on, Macduff!" she said gaily. "I'm *so* happy, dear Macduff! Oh, Paul, I'm. having a divine time, and I love being read to!"

IV

IT was an involved little story and Periwinkle found it difficult to concentrate upon the plot that seemed to drift like smoke about the characters. Her ear kept wandering to Paul's voice, which took on curious tones and undertones as he read; she liked his intent gray eyes, the whimsical lift of his upper lip, the slim brown hands. Her mind darted in and out of the flow of words like an uneasy humming-bird.

Paul read steadily on. Oh, it wasn't good, it wasn't *any* good, the story! Periwinkle was filled with a kind of panic as she listened. He had told her quite frankly that he didn't like criticism—and she knew what happened when Paul didn't like anything—she was sure, too, that he would see through any forced praise—that dear, dear, over-sensitive Paul! And she began to realize just how dear he was to her.

What should she do? What should she say to him?

"Mother would pronounce this a divine judgment on me for having come," she thought. And now Paul was reading the "big love-scene."

It flashed across her suddenly that she could write this story herself—and much better—she saw so plainly what was wrong, just how she would have built up that toppling structure into swift, sure words!

"And that's all," said Paul, and put the manuscript back into the drawer of the writing-table.

Periwinkle noticed that there was a clock somewhere very near; she had never heard a clock breathe in such a strident, noisy, insistent way, she wondered how Paul could stand it—And the next minute she was in his arms.

She was in his arms and strangely, wonderfully glad to be there; they closed around her like two great gates, shutting out the world of little things that she never wanted to play with any more.

And through the divine unreality of what she knew was a truth still more divine, she listened to a voice against her cheek, Paul's voice that she had always loved so, telling her of his love for her, in abrupt, tender absurd little words that made her even more utterly his.

"Oh, Winkle, darling—we love each other! And we didn't know it! We've fooled about all this time! And we love each other! *Don't we?*"

"Yes, Paul, we love each other."

"Put your arms around me, dear. We adore each other—and we *didn't know it!* Say we adore each other, Winkle!"

"Yes, Paul—we adore each other."

And at last they grew braver and looked into each other's faces, and there they found the light that led them groping, blinded by its brightness, to each other's lips.

Then, as swiftly as she was lifted to the stars, was Periwinkle dashed to earth again.

"The big scene!" said Paul, "I've got it, Winkle! I know how to write it now! Those blessed lovers—I know just what was wrong with them!"

V

SHE had forgotten all about the story. The foolish, badly-written little story! *But Paul had not!* And he was going to write about this miracle— *their* miracle that they had found together—he was going to publish it in a magazine, for anyone to read! Visions of news-stands at the Grand Central Station, at the Ritz-Carlton, at Lexington Avenue and Forty-second Street, rows and rows of magazines all telling of their love, of hers and Paul's great love, rose like a hideous mirage in the stretching desert in which she stood, a mournful traveler, alone. He still held her close.

"How wonderful everything is going to be!" he was saying, and she thought, "I'm dead, broken into little pieces—and he doesn't even know it."

"You see, you darling Winkle, I've always loafed through life, everything was a joke. But now—I love you—kiss me, kiss me—And then we'll ring up Anne and ask her to the wedding!"

What happened after that was always unclear, she could never visualize it in her thoughts. She remembered laughing a high-pitched, ghastly little laugh that seemed to do something to his face, she remembered pushing him away, both hands against his breast, on which she lay no longer; *somebody* said—was it she—it *must* have been, obviously, but what had happened to her voice? "Our honeymoon will make a lovely storm, won't it? *Any* magazine would publish it, I should think!" Again that horrid cackling laugh. *"No, Paul!* You've got the 'big scene'—for one silly little story—they know *how to kiss now,* those blessed lovers!' That's enough, I guess—"

She never knew how she found her way to the street—she had a curious recollection of throwing her Paradise-bird hat out of the taxi window and thinking that he would probably have put that into a story, too—

He had called to her as she slipped through the door, "If you leave me like this, I swear I'll never forgive you!"

And she had answered, "That's a good line for a parting scene!"

VI

THE setting saw little of Paul during the next weeks. And then he telephoned to Anne that he was coming to tea, and arrived with a book of somebody's new poems which he read very beautifully and made brilliant fun of, after a formidable "stinger," Anne-mixed, four large slices of chocolate-cake and countless cigarettes.

He played with the baby, inquiring anxiously why it didn't walk yet, and was Anne *sure* it wasn't paralyzed, which worried her a little for hours afterwards—passionate mother that she was—although she knew it was nonsense; and he insisted upon taking a goldfish out of the Japanese garden, in order to prove that the fluff on top of the baby's head was exactly the same shade of pink-gold, winning his point triumphantly, although at the expense of Anne's best goldfish.

He also made a bet with Sybil, who had been hastily summoned by telephone, to the effect that she would never get her cook back from her sister, to whom she was lent for a dinner-party, the bet consisting of Sybil's platinum and diamond wedding-ring against his dyeing his hair any color she chose.

"Paul was great today," said Anne after he had gone, "but I don't think he's looking well. And he's drinking too many cocktails—although I love him to have them *here* if he *must* have them at all! What a pity Periwinkle is in Atlantic City! Did I tell you I got a handsome post-card of the boardwalk from her the other day?"

"I wonder if Paul is in love with anybody?" remarked Sybil thoughtfully. "He looked just like that when he was running about with Annabel Azore two winters ago—you remember Annabel, and her wonderful trained seals, don't you, Anne?"

"Of course I do; that's the only story of Paul's I ever really liked."

"I wonder if Annabel did?" Sybil rose as she spoke and picked up her muff and gloves. "I do think he ought to buy you a new goldfish. The Japanese garden looks like Asbury Park without it!"

"But he won't," sighed Anne ruefully, "and it cost me five dollars! What color do you intend dyeing his hair? *Do* let me dye it for you, Sybil! You know what a success I made of the baby's winter coat, and I've got heaps of green left over."

<h2 style="text-align:center">VII</h2>

AND then it came!

"You have sent us a very unusual story," wrote the sub-editor of the *Best Monthly,* "and one that gives us much pleasure in publishing. We are including it in our April number. Trusting that you will give us an early opportunity," etc., etc.

Paul read the sub-editor's letter three times. It was an immense comfort to him. A very unusual story!

"It ought to be!" he thought to himself grimly.

Periwinkle—Periwinkle! He had laid his face across the pages of the "big scene" as he re-wrote it—he wasn't sure, but he believed he had wept a little—it was so like her!

He had lost her; she would never come back, he knew; and his face wore the aloof look the setting dreaded so, as he reflected that he *did not want her back.* "You silly little story!" Well, he had the sub-editor's letter to apply to the smart of that, and he was grateful to her in a way, for it was thanks to those ever-remembered words, and to what had come before—remembered, too—that he had had the energy to rewrite the whole story, a thing he had never troubled to do in all his life, and which had certainly improved it enormously.

Still, he did not want her back! She had hurt him too much. He had been intensely relieved to hear that she had left town and he had not seen her since that miserable day. Something of her lingered for weeks about the room. It was not her perfume—he did not know *what* it was—but it drove him to the club-bar too often. He thanked God, he reflected whimsically, that he had not bought a tea-set to remind him of her all his life!

"We wouldn't have been happy together," he kept saying to himself, until it became a kind of parrot-cry squawking at him comfortingly, when the pain for her throbbed through his cold resentment. "Girls aren't human, anyway."

He used to lie awake in the dark repeating over and over to himself, "We wouldn't have been happy together!"

He wondered if she would see the story. Oh, hell—he didn't care!

VIII

THE April number of the *Best Monthly* arrived the last days of March. It had a wonderful cover, all daffodils, and a girl in a blue sweater standing among them, daffodil-colored hair flying in a vividly depicted spring breeze.

Paul's heart beat more quickly as his fingers stumbled over the crisp pages. There it was, "The Big Scene"—yes, he had called it that. He read his name with the unfailing accompanying thrill, he read the story straight through, almost solemnly, an anxious eye on the outlook for possible typographical errors.

When he had finished he smiled, a little wanly. It *was* an "unusual story," the editor of the *Best* was right. God, how sweet Periwinkle was in print!

And suddenly a great longing for her surged through him. He remembered how she had clung, all the warmth of her body glowed against him again, thawing the frozen misery that had chilled his heart all those long weeks. He seemed to hear her voice, the breathless, happy little voice : "Yes, Paul, we adore each other!"

He got up from his chair, something capitulated unconditionally within him; he would *go to* her, kneel to her, implore her to be as she had been when she said, "Yes, Paul, we adore each other!"

What if she refused to see him, what if she were not at home?

He decided that he would telephone. He hated being told that people were not at home; it irritated him; he felt snubbed as he turned away from their closing doors. He couldn't bear Periwinkle not being at home! He must be sure, too, that she would be glad to see him.

He felt a little dizzy as he waited at the telephone. "I'm telephoning Fate," he thought. "I'm telephoning the gods. I'm telephoning Periwinkle!" What a good poem that would make, free-verse of course!

Yes, she was at home. Could he speak to her—never mind about the name; a friend wanted to speak to her.

There was a pause, he heard somebody talking a long way off, somebody whistling, beating a carpet—no, that was his own ridiculous heart—

"Hello! Who is it? This is Miss Middleton, yes—"

And then a strange thing happened. The four walls of his cosy room seemed to topple apart, the earth swung clear of him, and Paul hung in mid-air, clutching the telephone as one would cling to a swaying, creaking branch over an abyss. And something seemed to call from the depths, "Hang up the receiver, you fool! *Or jump!*"

"*Hello—hello—this is 2624—*" It was Periwinkle's voice—and the little chirp was in it—but Paul hung up the receiver.

In one flashing moment of complete self-revelation he realized that he didn't want to speak to her, didn't dare to speak to her. He was afraid of her and all that it would mean if he spoke! He was afraid for his comfortable, self-centered life, his happy-go-lucky, perfectly irresponsible life in the little flat that he had made exactly what he wanted it to be. He didn't want to give it up, to give *anything* up—not even for the bliss of Periwinkle—he didn't want to change, to share—*he didn't want to marry!*

"Your silly little story!" And her face as she said it! He put his hand up to his forehead; it felt wet and he felt faint and sick. With an effort he got up and crossed over to the writing-table, pulled a brandy-flask out of a drawer, put it to his lips, drained it.

"Good God!" he said aloud. A great loneliness came over him all of a sudden and with the loneliness a great longing for Anne.

He would go to her, put his head onto her knee, smoke a thousand cigarettes, drink a thousand stingers! Perhaps he would read her "The Big Scene." He realized perfectly that Anne didn't think much of his stories, but she'd have to like "The Big Scene." It was the best thing he had done and Anne would be the first to see that—dear, clever Anne! He would buy her the biggest bunch of daffodils he could carry and lay them, together with the daffodil-covered *Best*, in her lap, without a word.

"She'll probably drop dead," he thought as he reached for his coat. "I've never done such a thing to Anne, but it's a nice little gesture. Besides, I owe her something for the goldfish. I believe Anne was fond of that goldfish—and I'm fond of Anne."

As he opened the outer door of his flat the telephone rang, long and insistently. Without looking round, he passed out and closed the door behind him.

"We wouldn't have been happy together," he announced to anyone who chose to hear as he ran down the long flights of stairs to the street. He wouldn't ring for the elevator, the new girl got on his nerves; she *would* talk to him. He wished George, the pleasant colored boy who stole things, hadn't been sent away.

THAT SECOND MAN

S. N. Behrman

" *...for, together with, and, as it were behind, so much pleasurable emotion, there is always that other strange second man in me, calm, critical, observant, unmoved, blasé, odious!'*—LORD LEIGHTON : *Letter to his sister.*

I

AS Clark Storrey rang the bell of Courtney's narrow marble house he thought with pleasure of the mournful expression with which, he knew, Courtney would greet him. When Courtney was gay Storrey did not find him amusing but in his fits of depression—lately very frequent with him—there was something, to Storrey, almost jocund. The sag in his plump, pasty cheeks, the little whine that crept into his voice, the limp droop of his big body—the spectacle of Courtney as a forlorn lover, a plump Malvolio, appealed to Storrey's sense of humour, but, more piquantly, to a less amiable sense.

The pleasure he derived from the contemplation of Courtney in his present condition, his own rôle of splendid fellow and good friend, forced him to dissimulate but it lost little of its zest on this account. To think that Courtney—who was a first-rate scientist, master of a hidden vivid world which, he, Storrey, could not enter—was at the mercy of an emotion which made him as abjectly ridiculous as any clerk mooning over a post-card picture of an actress! It vindicated a notion he had long harboured that Courtney, despite his renown, was essentially quite commonplace. The notion of cold superiority that people entertained about him was a myth that Monica had completely melted.

That was pleasing to Courtney, who had always a bit envied and rather despised him. And it was also pleasing to him that before him alone of all people, Courtney made no effort to hide his absurd frailty.

Courtney's telegram had read :

"Must see you at once. Courtney." So, although he was having a good time at the Seldens' house-party, he had decided to come in, especially as pretty Mrs. Morton had volunteered to motor him to town. Courtney must be in a bad way to send him a wire like that; evidently Monica had been unusually definite with him this time ... He hoped not too definite; Courtney mustn't be frightened off. But he felt confident he could patch things up; he smiled again at the thought of how easy it would be for him to restore Courtney's confidence. ...

As he opened the door of the gloomy study his smile disappeared; he advanced into the room wearing an expression of grave concern.

"Just got your wire ... "

Courtney gave him a limp hand and said nothing.

"I was afraid you might be ill—"

"It's Monica. She's refused me."

"Nonsense!"

"She has, I tell you. Point blank."

"You asked her to marry you?"

"I offered her everything—put my life at her feet, my work—" Courtney mopped his brow with a handkerchief he had in his hand.

"I guess I'd better try to forget her," he said miserably.

"Nonsense!" repeated Storrey cheerfully. "But tell me why? Why did she refuse you!"

His voice sounded as though he were quite surprised and not a little indignant.

Courtney made a helpless gesture.

"Doesn't love me."

"Does she love someone else?"

"That's the worst of it. She does."

"Who?"

"Wouldn't tell me. Do you know who it is?"

"Yes. It's no one. It's a lie. She doesn't love anyone."

"What makes you think so?" Eagerness leaped back into his voice and eyes.

Storrey improvised reasons ... He enjoyed the scene: Courtney slumped in a high-backed chair looking very pale and sickly as though he were suffering from indigestion, the long table covered with neatly ordered piles of scientific journals from nearly every country in Europe, abstruse journals filled with curiously patterned figure-formulas covering whole pages.

But Courtney refused to believe, refused to be comforted. Finally Storrey, unable to resist the temptation to be ever so little malicious, said soothingly :

"After all, you have your science, old man."

Courtney responded magnificently to the prod: he turned haggard eyes at Storrey.

"Science! You think science means anything to me now! When I've lost her! I tell you I can't work since I've known her—I can't work. The books that formerly fascinated me, my researches—nothing matters to me now. When I start to do anything and get thinking of her I can't go on. I—I—get a headache," he finished miserably.

Storrey liked to hear Courtney denounce his profession in this way. What an illusion this was of the cold mastery of scientific men! They were as helpless as babies ...

"Of course," said Storrey after a moment; "this is all nonsense. If you want her, really want her, you can get her."

"That's what you always say. You keep telling me that. But it's not true—"

Storrey lit a cigarette.

"No doubt about it. Not in the least—"

Storrey's tone carried conviction. In spite of all Monica had said to him, Courtney felt slightly better already. He began to lift his head.

"But she told me," he began, "last night—"

"A mere child," said Storrey with finality. "Doesn't in the least know what she wants. Won't till after she's married. That's up to you."

"But she's not attracted to me—"

"She doesn't understand you. She has no appreciation of your intellectual gifts."

"It's true. Prohelium means nothing to her."

Prohelium was the name of the new element Courtney had discovered.

"You must make it mean something to her. You must teach her to see how wonderful it is to widen the boundaries of knowledge, the deep mystery and elusiveness of the things you work with, the marvelous delicacy of your experiments. ... "

Courney sighed heavily.

"If I could only talk like you, Storrey!"

"Talk! That's it—talk! By their sensitiveness to mere words women demonstrate their intellectual inferiority—and their right to the vote."

"If she only understood me—as you do!"

"My dear chap—she shall be made to."

"How?"

Storrey lit another cigarette.

"How?" repeated Courtney tensely.

Storrey slid forward comfortably in the dark leather chair till he seemed to be resting on the tip of his spine—a pose, he had read, often assumed by Arthur Balfour.

"Maternal pressure," he replied. "I'll wager you anything a poor poet can pay that Mrs. Gray doesn't know Monica's refused you."

"What if she did?"

"She'd raise Cain. You see Gray-mère—no pun intended, old chap—is desperately afraid—of guess what?"

"What?"

"That Monica will marry *me!*"

Courtney said nothing. But his face went a shade grayer. His plump cheeks hung like dew-laps.

"Of course you see how absurd it is. Monica and I—"

"I wonder you don't marry her," said Courtney a bit breathlessly. "She likes you. She likes you better than me, that's plain." Courney's voice was not without a touch of bitterness.

"Nonsense. She doesn't—really. Fancy my being married to Monica! She'd leave me in six months. By which time I should certainly have left her. Monica couldn't stand the poverty of my ménage and," he laughed bitterly, "neither could I."

"It's strange you're not in love with Monica."

"There speaks the eternal lover. I think it strange you *are* in love with her. She's pretty—I grant you that. But—Great Heavens, man—so young!"

"She is young," said Courtney softly. His voice sounded suddenly like a far, gentle echo.

"And so full of spirits!"

"Isn't she!"

"Her laughter gets on my nerves. Like the constant ringing of chimes."

"Yes," said Courtney. "It is like chimes."

There was a silence.

Courtney seemed lost in tender revery.

Storrey broke into it.

"That's the thing to do," he said. "There's no doubt of it."

"What is?"

"Monica's stepmother must be persuaded that *I* want to marry Monica. She'll never rest then until Monica is married to you."

"What makes you think so?" asked Courtney doubtfully.

"No doubt about it. The old lady is cracked about the idea of having you for a stepson-in-law. Oh, it's not your scientific eminence. It's not even your family, though of course that has something to do with it. It's your money, my friend, your lucre, your multitudinous boodle—"

Courtney lifted a deprecating hand.

"That's what it is, old man. The Grays are mighty hard up—Monica's been dressing shamefully of late."

"She looks better—" said Courtney truculently.

"I know, old man. Niftier in gingham than a fine lady in velvet. How extraordinary, Courtney, that a chit of a girl like Monica can make a man of your eminence talk like a hack writer!"

"I don't like you to talk about Monica that way."

"Why not? She is an impudent minx, isn't she, shallow as a platter? Her lack of appreciation of you proves that."

"She's young. I sometimes think I'm too old for her," he said pathetically.

"You're only thirty-six."

"She's twenty-two. But it's not that alone. She's so gay, full of fun. I can't—prattle, Storrey. I don't follow her small talk..."

"I don't wonder. Her talk is not small. It is infinitesimal. Your microscopic training should help you—"

"I don't do the things she likes, dance, play tennis—you know—"

"You're not a jazz figure, Courtney," admitted Storrey judiciously. "But you'd better marry her. If you don't she'll run away with a tenor or somebody."

"I wish to Heaven I could marry her," groaned Courtney.

"You shall. I'll begin showering attentions on Monica immediately. Poor Mrs. Gray. She'll be frightened to death."

"You're sure about this, Storrey?"

"No doubt of it."

"But if Monica doesn't love me! She told me last night she didn't—never could."

"Just marry her. She'll change her mind."

Courtney rose.

"You know, Storrey," he said, "I used to think—when I thought about it—not often, you understand, until I met Monica—that I'd never marry unless the woman wanted me as much as I wanted her. But that was before I wanted any woman—as I want Monica. I'd marry her on any terms, Storrey. You understand?"

"Of course I understand, old fellow. And you shall. Mighty good thing for Monica, too."

"You really think so?"

"You have only to persist. You'll win her, as the military men say, by attrition. I've got to run now, old man—keep the pot boiling—"

"Forgive me for taking you away from the Seldens. But I just had to see you."

"That's all right, old boy. I was glad of an excuse to get away. Awful bore."

"You always make it so easy for your friends to impose on you," said Courtney earnestly. "No wonder everybody's crazy about you..."

II

STORREY left Courtney's house in singularly good humour. He did not turn down-town, but cut across the avenue into Central Park. He wanted to be out in the cool sunshine, dallying pleasantly with his thoughts.

He walked along buoyantly, swinging his cane, a smile playing about his lips. He was thinking of Courtney's complete and almost pathetic reliance upon him: this man who possessed a knowledge and a skill, a sensitiveness to the hidden forces of nature, that Courtney could not help admiring... Courtney's discovery had brought him the highest fame in scientific circles, he was elected an honorary F. R. S. in England and had even been mentioned for the Nobel prize... And with all this Courtney had inherited an immense fortune from his father.

Courtney had met Monica at a house-party to which his mother had dragged him and the man of science had fallen hopelessly in love at first sight with the beautiful, golden-haired girl, not, Storrey reflected, as a man of the world falls in love, with a certain genial deprecation of his irrationality, but as an awkward schoolboy falls in love.

In Monica's presence Courtney would become tongue-tied; he could do nothing but silently register adoration.... He would sit dumbly staring at her; once when the three of them were having tea together Monica asked Courtney whether he was trying to hypnotize her... She took a certain delight in torturing him; she was always unnecessarily risqué in his presence, would talk of having "affairs" with the blithe ingenuousness of a child prattling of storks.

"When are you and I going to have an affair, Storrey?" she would ask. "You're awfully slow about it..."

Her virginal beauty made her audacities irresistibly piquant, but they hurt Courtney so that he often begged her to stop... An avowed materialist Courtney professed the belief that creation was the result of a fortuitous and not altogether happy combination of circumstances.

"A slight change in the temperature," he was fond of quoting, "and we should have been at the mercy of the ants."

Latterly Storrey had twitted him with his conservatism in the field of morals; was it really so important that Monica should make a fetish of monogamy in view of the Creator's carelessness about more fundamental things?

But Courtney had not pursued the subject, reiterating stubbornly:

"I don't like her to talk that way. Of course I know she wouldn't do anything—well—you know—wrong. She couldn't. She's too pure, too good. But I don't like her to talk that way."

Nevertheless Monica kept on talking that way and Storrey enjoyed Courtney's discomfiture as much as she did. . . . Storrey detested this Puritanism in Courtney; he knew it was the instinct for exclusive possession that made him want to forbid Monica the sharing of even verbal intimacies with others. . . . The girl he wanted for himself must be "as chaste as ice, as pure as snow" . . . It made Storrey indignant to think of it; what right had Courtney to desire for himself alone this beautiful creature full of high spirits and laughter—this desiccated thinking-machine, as intelligent as a mole inside his scientific burrow, but quite helpless and uninteresting once out of it? . . .

Storrey's vindictiveness was partly the result of his envy at Courtney's distinctions, the place he had won for himself in the world: actually he knew that Courtney's activities were not mole-like, but the result of thought-processes as beautifully crystalline as a poem by George Meredith. Storrey's mind was not as superficial as his life and work: which was his tragedy.

The truth was that in an obscure way he was jealous of Courtney: jealous of the place he had won for himself in the intellectual world, jealous of his money, jealous of the fact that he would marry Monica. For of course he would marry Monica. There was no way out of it for her—unless he himself married her . . .

For a moment he toyed with that temptation, the temptation of taking her away from Courtney. Monica was lovely—and really a dear. Storrey liked her better, after all, than any girl he knew. She never really got on his nerves : when she began to bore him she would always know it and say:

"All right, Storrey, I'm leaving."

Moreover there was something quite brave and fine about Monica; Storrey knew that, too. She had been going the pace rather swiftly of late, but chiefly because there was nothing else for her to do.

"We're too poor to refuse invitations, mother and I," she had said to him one day.

And another time, when she described the antics of a gay party she had attended:

"I'd have done anything that night. An antidote to the Genesis-man. He'd spent the afternoon with me."

The sobriquet had been applied to Courtney by Monica after his first attempt to initiate her into modern scientific theories of evolution. He had asked her how she thought it all began and she had replied innocently with the orthodox recital culminating in the Garden of Eve. Courtney, who had taken her quite seriously, brushed away the myth with indulgent superiority and devoted a half hour to the nebular theory.

"So you see, Monica," he had said in conclusion, "it's not true what you've read in the Bible."

"But I like the Bible ever so much better," she had answered quickly; "there's a girl like me in it . . . "

Storrey's smile, which had disappeared as he thought of Courtney's unapproachable eminence, returned as he recalled this recital. She was a demure little witch! It might be the best thing he could do, after all, to marry Monica. He would settle down, quit this awful business of pretending to be something he wasn't, "a snapper up of unconsidered trifles," quit wrapping banal ideas in adroitly turned verse, and get down to brass tacks artistically and actually . . .

He was sick of being tame cat to half the people in New York, sick of playing the good fellow to people he despised . . .

But a moment's consideration and he banished the thought. It was too late to change. He should lead exactly the same sort of life if he married Monica as he led now. He would probably be unfaithful and Monica would probably be jealous . . . No, it was better to continue in his present rôle in life, a spectator who occasionally manipulated a few strings . . .

It would be interesting after all to see Monica and Courtney married. An odd couple. Monica would be bored to death. What would be her revenge?

He repeated the question to himself. . . . His smile deepened.

"How funny!" he exclaimed inwardly. "Poor old Courtney . . . !"

III

WHEN he got to his rooms he found a telephone message from Monica. He was not surprised. The message said: "Very important." That, too, was a cry for help; the second he had received that day. How simple people were, how helpless; they could be turned as easily as a rhyme ... Of course Monica had called him up to tell him that she had refused Courtney, that she had foolishly told her mother about it, that there had been a volcanic scene ... She wanted to get support from him to help her through the crisis. Poor Monica. She would have to succumb ... He thought for a moment of calling her, but decided to wait till she called him again.

He sat down in a great easy chair, pushed a specially prepared arm around so that it made a broad wooden bridge over his knees, reached for a pad and fountain pen and began to write.

He sat slumped down in the chair—he could adjust the angle of the impromptu desk by turning a screw on the side. He always wrote this way; in the same position he assumed when he smoked his after-dinner cigar.

"I wonder if I'd do better work if I really had to earn a living by this stuff," he asked himself. "Probably I'd do better work. Or perhaps I'd just turn out a lot more of the same stuff ... "

Very comfortably Storrey began to write ... a faint smile hovering about his lips as he toyed with the words.... A few nights before, at a dance at the Seldens, he had taken a walk in the moonlight with a girl; they had been dancing and he asked her to go outside with him. They stepped out through the open French windows, crossed the lawn, and walked down a narrow path between high poplars, with the stars quite close, and the moon showing between them ...

It was a most curious moon, red-bronze in colour, wafer-thin, exquisitely curved, like a tiny scimitar, a shaving of a moon. God, Courtney had said, must be a curious person to fashion such a moon, a butcher with artistic leanings. Or was He an artist suffering from a sadistic atavism? Which did she think? The girl thought it was slightly chilly and hadn't they better go back to the ball-room?

They went back to the ball-room.... Storrey put the walk and the talk into a poem. While writing he -struck off several figures that rather pleased him : one was that the tree-tops looked like hedges in the sky between which the stars grew like buttercups. There was a hint of nostalgia, the wavering suggestion of sensuousness as the man and the girl stood for a moment on the brink of understanding, then the sophisticated monologue on the moon breaking the spell! At the end the usual ironic fillip: the mask of convention drawn on with the white gloves, a polite request for a waltz from an ancient dowager ...

Storrey played with his ideas lazily, pared them off, tucked them in. He had written that poem a good many times before. And, when he had nearly finished modeling it, the telephone rang.

Storrey was glad. The interruption was welcome. He had had enough of creation. He reached out and took the 'phone from the tabouret. Monica's voice sounded strained, a bit breathless.

"Hello, kiddie!" he said heartily.

She reproached him for not responding to her message.

"Is it really so important?" he asked.

"Very. I've simply *got* to see you, Storrey."

They made a luncheon engagement. He got together the written sheets and put them into a drawer. He was pleased that he had done some work and that he was going to see Monica. There had been a gravity in her voice today that was quite unusual for her and quite appealing. She must really be upset at the idea of marrying Courtney. One couldn't exactly blame her; Courtney would be forever filling her ears with halting expositions of scientific theory, not because he was interested in her mental development, but that she might have the background to appreciate the splendour of his achievement.

It was absurd, thought Storrey, to think that scientists were less egoists than artists. Their deeper consciousness of the tragic insignificance of man, of the feebleness of his cry amid the vast solitudes of time and space, did not mitigate the tensity of their appetites and vanities. Nor were their minds different from other peoples': they were reputed more rational because, since the problems they attack take longer to solve, they have less leisure for the gratification of instinct. ...

He met Monica in the lounge just off the lobby of the Ritz. Storrey's income was small enough to require husbanding, but he never economized on food. Dining at smart houses had sharpened an instinctive epicureanism. Besides, he liked to be seen at the right places. But today Monica would not lunch in the hotel with him:

"Please," she said. "Let's go to some place quiet. I want to *talk* to you."

"That means," he said lightly, "that you want me to talk to you, to give you advice. I can give you advice here as well as anywhere."

"I want you alone today. We'll meet people we know here. I always meet you in crowds." Already they were walking out of the hotel.

"I know a nice little place in Fifty-first Street," she said. "The dearest old ladies come there to drink iced tea."

"So that's it? You want a setting that will show off your youth."

She looked swiftly at him, smiling with arch gravity.

He had never seen her so subdued. He had never seen her quite so perfect. Sometimes he thought her colouring a bit too vivid, but today she was pale. Her golden hair peeped out from beneath a small toque, two dark-blue bird's wings, shaped like a helmet.

He told her she was looking charming, but she did not seem as pleased as usual at a compliment from him.

"I've read your St. Augustine," she said suddenly. "Most of it."

"I wanted you to read all of it," he said severely.

He had reapproached her the last time for a wicked remark she had made about Courtney and he had told her it was sacrilegious for a girl named after the mother of St. Augustine to talk that way. She had not known that Monica was the name of St. Augustine's mother and she had become greatly interested in the career of the Saint. She wanted to know whether Monica, the Saint's mother, had written anything and Storrey told her that she was not a writer so far as he knew, having more important work to do. But her son had written a rather well-known work called the Confessions and the title had so intrigued Monica that she had made him promise to send her a copy.

"Yes," she said eagerly, "I read it nearly all. I thought it would be dull, but it wasn't, because you know he started off very badly, this saint. He only gets good—when he gets tired. ... Is that it?"

She looked at him questioningly, her eyes quite serious.

"Tell me," she repeated, "I want to know."

"It is difficult, little ingénue, to determine in such cases, whether renunciation or satiety is the cause. But what are such delicate problems to you? If I thought you'd have stopped with the conversion—"

"I know. You wanted me to be just edified. Am I so very wicked?"

"Not wicked. Merely not discriminating."

She pouted.

"Why am I?"

"Because," he said, "the cream of humanity worships you, and you spend your time lunching with a—a footnote."

"What do you mean, a foot-note?" She frowned adorably when she was perplexed.

"A scribbler," he said, borrowing easily from a much-read novel, "is a mere foot-note to reality."

"Oh, but I like foot-notes," she said eagerly. "You know why. Because Once we—a girl I knew at school and myself—got hold of some dry-looking translation of a novel by—oh, I forget—one of those wicked old Romans. Every few seconds or so there were stars in the text and down the bottom of the page there were little paragraphs that really belonged where the stars were. Only they were in Latin! We got a Latin dictionary—Lois and I..."

She chattered on telling of their difficulties with the dictionary... They turned into the restaurant, Monica nodding gaily to the waitresses; she seemed to know them all. They passed through the long dining-room and into an open space in the rear where there were small tables under coloured umbrellas.

"So you see, Storrey, I'm just a light, giddy creature and I love foot-notes. Now what are you going to do about it?"

He did not answer for a moment.

"You're incorrigible, Monica," he said finally.

"I know what you're thinking : that I ought to go in for solider things, heavy text-books. Oh, Storrey, imagine living all your life with a text-book—how bored you'd get!"

"Wouldn't be bad. If you had an occasional foot-note to relieve the monotony."

"I know what you want, Storrey. You want all the fun and none of the responsibility."

He leaned close to her and touched her hand.

"Don't talk like that, kiddie," he said. "I'm terribly fond of you—today."

"Just today!"

"Always."

"Then you might prove it."

"I am proving it."

"If you are, then you'll do me the favour I've come to ask of you."

"What is it?"

"It's such a little thing." She looked at him with troubled eyes. "It's— that you should marry me."

He was astonished. He was astonished because she wasn't laughing, because there was no laughter in her eyes. He was uncomfortable. He was sorry he had come. It was a mistake.

"I'll be ever so good, Storrey, really. I'm fond of you, you know. I won't bother you—ever. I'll just sit in a corner and not make a sound all the time while you write your wonderful poems—"

That was one thing about Monica he didn't entirely like. She really thought his poems wonderful and devoured them as they appeared, like caramels.

Fortunately the waitress came…They ordered consomme and creamed chicken and a salad, leaving the dessert to be decided on later. The waitress disappeared to fetch the consomme.

"What do you say, Storrey?" she resumed. "You see how persistent I am—"

She was smiling now. Storrey solemnly assured her that he would love her for ever and a day but that he would certainly not marry her.

"All right for you!" said Monica and began nibbling a biscuit, quite angry with him.

"The trouble is you don't understand anything about anything," said Storrey.

"The trouble is that you're damn selfish," said Monica. "Yes, you are. You like to go around and be petted by people. You're afraid I'll interfere." Her tone changed suddenly. "But I wouldn't interfere. Really I wouldn't. You could do anything you liked. You see, I know you're really fonder of me than of anyone. Just as I know that I'm fonder of you than I ever shall be of anyone."

"The very young," he said, "especially when female, are subject to obsessions."

"You might think you're so old yourself. You're only thirty … Mother always calls you 'that young fellow Storrey'! … "

Suddenly Monica held an imaginary lorgnette to her eyes and began speaking in a high, strained falsetto : " 'That rather conceited young fellow—er—what's his name—oh, yes, Storrey. Storrey … ! Curious name, very curious. Writes. What? Poetry? You mean verses, my dear, verses. Has anyone ever read them? I'm sure I haven't. No time for such trash, you know—' "

Monica lowered the lorgnette. Her mimicry was delightful.

"Your stepmother is an intelligent woman, Monica. She doesn't even squander her time recklessly."

"Stingy old thing! She wants me to marry that old encyclopedia just because he's rich!"

"You refer to Courtney?"

"You know I do," said Monica savagely. "This shows—how much you like me! You're always playing with me. You're always making fun of me. I ask you to marry me and—instead of being glad—and saying yes—you—you keep me in suspense."

A tear glistened on her eyelash.

"I don't think it's fair of you to ask me to luncheon and take advantage of my absurdly sympathetic nature by threatening to cry. Please remove that teardrop, Monica—unobtrusively …

"Gosh, I am sloppy! I'm sorry, old boy. But I've been jawing with the old lady till I'm half hysterical. Honest, I don't know whether I'm coming or going." She dabbed her eyes furtively with a bit of handkerchief. "Like a manicure at a movie, aren't I, Storrey?" She grimaced.

"You're a dear child, Monica, and I'm terribly in love with you, and to show you that I am I'm going to take you for a drive in the Park in a hansom cab and make you feel ashamed of yourself—"

She clapped her hands joyfully.

"Oh, Storrey!" she gasped ecstatically. "That's just what I've always wanted you to do to me. Is it a promise?"

"You're incorrigible," said Storrey, with decorum.

IV

PEOPLE liked Clark Storrey for various reasons, some because he didn't take himself seriously; others because, though a writer, he was a "regular fellow"; others still because they thought him singularly detached in his judgments of things; and everybody liked him because they thought him a loyal and disinterested friend. Few people understood the true source of these things they deemed his virtues.

It was true, for example, that Storrey did not take himself seriously but that sprang not so much from the absence of conceit in him as from the absolution it offered him from the struggle to attain a perfect and unhackneyed form of expression, from struggle of any sort whatever. If he was a "regular fellow" it was because, among business men and society women, he commanded thereby an adulation other artists would not have yielded him. If he was detached in his judgments it was because it helped him to justify his frailties to see them mirrored in others. The virtue attributed to him by everybody, that he was a loyal friend, was sheer nonsense and he despised the people who believed it. No man manipulated his friends as he did: he got from them everything he wanted, from a yachting cruise in the Mediterranean to the loan of a motor-car, things his luxury-loving soul demanded but that he was too poor to get for himself.

In the hansom with Monica, Storrey thought about these things and, what was unusual with him, he thought about them with a certain compunction. He knew the truth about himself, and now, for the first time, with Monica sitting beside him, her hand resting on his, the knowledge gave him a certain twinge of discomfort.

After all, wasn't he running a serious risk in going on this way? Mightn't he become terribly bored, with a growing sense of emptiness, isolation, stealing up around him? ... No, there was small danger of that: he loved material comforts too much, and, while he had them he could not remain long unhappy ...

He looked at Monica's pure profile. ... Why should he give her up to Courtney? It was ridiculous to give her up to Courtney. If he didn't marry Monica he would never marry anyone; that he knew. To think of her married to Courtney was a little like thinking of her wearing an eternal dead-white mask and hideous clothes. Courtney would not become her ...

And yet he had just been telling her that it was eminently fitting for her to marry Courtney, that he would provide her with the exquisite background her loveliness needed.

"I can't marry him, Storrey, I can't," she was saying.

"He'll be a wonderful husband for you. Just the best. Won't bother you. Spends ages in the laboratory, you know."

"But he'll come back from the laboratory. I'm sure he doesn't sleep in the laboratory."

She looked at him with eyes of unblemished innocence. He patted her cheek. He liked her best when she looked like that ... Why didn't he take her in his arms? Why didn't he kiss her? Why didn't he carry her off and live with her and fashion poems for her? No. That sort of idyl wasn't possible for him. If she were rich—very rich—perhaps. Or if he were. ... But limited means drove people too much together. "I mustn't do it," he kept telling himself.

"I've told mother, you know," said Monica finally, as though she had just remembered something.

"Told her what?"

"That I love you."

"You didn't!"

"Yes," she said tranquilly.

"And what did you say—about me?"

"I told her you loved me, too. And that you had asked me to marry you."

"You impertinent—! How dared you tell such a lie!"

"I'll tell you. I thought that if I told mother that you had asked me that you would be—well—sort of compromised—and you'd *have* to ask me. I'm trying to get it—sort of spread around. Now wait—" She put her hand over his mouth to silence his protest. "You see, I'm doing it for your good. I know that you do love me. I know that you do want to marry me.

I know the reason you haven't asked me yourself is because you think you haven't enough money and that I want all sorts of frivolous things. It's just like you—you're so splendid and always thinking of other people. But you misjudge me, Storrey. I could be most awfully happy on just what you have. And so could you. So I'm just telling everybody that we're engaged..."

"You wretched child! You make me furious with you! But you're not really doing it!"

"Oh, but I am! Isn't it jolly? I'm thinking of sending an announcement to the papers. Of course! That's *just* what I'll do."

"You'll do nothing of the sort."

She laughed joyously.

"I've got you, Storrey. I've got you at last!"

She was maddening...

"You'll do no such thing," he repeated stupidly, not knowing what to say to her.

"Yes, I will. I've told everyone, so it might as well be in the papers."

"You little goose! Don't you see that now you'll have to marry Courtney? Your stepmother despises me. She'll disown you if you don't marry Courtney now. You'll have to marry him because you'll have to marry someone. I certainly shan't. Your stepmother will insist on it—to keep you from marrying me." He was genuinely frightened now.

"But how is she going to keep me from marrying you?"

"She won't have to. I'll disappear. I'll go away. I'll abandon you."

"You wouldn't, Storrey!"

"I won't let you ruin your life..." He didn't want to make that hypocritical speech. But habit was too strong...

"You wouldn't have people say you jilted me? And have them laugh at me...?"

"That's just what I'm going to do," he said fiercely.

Twilight had fallen... In the half-darkness that had descended on them swiftly while they jogged along in the hansom, he saw her lips tremble slightly.

He touched her face with his hands and then drew her to him, kissing her eyes and cheeks and hair ...

She sighed and rested in his arms contentedly, like a tired child. ...

"Oh, Storrey," she whispered, "you make me so happy, Storrey ... "

V

THEY were married in the country on the lawn of Fairview, overlooking the Hudson. Courtney believed in quiet weddings, so there were only a few people, immediate relatives and intimate friends. Storrey was best man.

It was a fine June day. The guests gathered on the terrace in front of the house, chatting and laughing together in little groups of twos and threes. A string orchestra played from a bay window screened with foliage. The long, low-set, rambling house had an air of having settled itself comfortably on the crest of the hill, like an old hen sitting on an egg.

Inside, the Bishop who was to perform the ceremony stood with his back to the great rubble fireplace in the living-room, dressed in full regalia (Courtney's mother was High Church), his surplice blowing in the breeze that swept through the open windows. The Bishop, in a deep, rich voice, was saying things about weddings ...

Storrey felt uncomfortable, nervous, irritated. He walked into the library to smoke a cigarette. Courtney jumped at him from the chair in which he had been sitting:

"I'm frightfully nervous, Storrey!"

Storrey regarded him coldly. An intense dislike of Courtney had taken possession of him.

"I was going to send for you, Storrey," continued Courtney. "I wanted you near me."

"You'd better go in. I think you're wanted inside—"

Storrey found it unbearable to be talking to him.

"Wanted? Already?" He seized Storrey's hand. "All right. But I want you to know that I'll never forget what you've done for me. I owe it all to you. The happiest man in the world—"

He fumbled away, muttering gratitudes ... Storrey, singularly unhappy, walked on through the library and came out on the veranda, encircling the rear of the house ... Well, he'd done it! He'd thrown her away! Why? Why had he done it? Why had he given her up? He did not know ...

A quick picture of Monica rose up before him, as she had been that last time—looking beseechingly at him and saying :

"You wouldn't abandon me, Storrey?"

"Damn him!" His fists clenched as he cursed Courtney under his breath. "Damn him! Damn him!" And after a moment: "What's the matter with you? You're being beastly. You're being sentimental. You're being jealous."

And he repeated to himself over and over the thousand reasons why marriage with Monica was impossible for him. If the whole thing were to do over he would do again exactly what he had done. There was no doubt of it. And yet ...

And yet he could not shake off his mood, the deepening sense he felt that in throwing Monica into Courtney's arms he had repressed the finest impulse he had ever had ... But of course it wasn't that at all. It was jealousy. Plain jealousy. It was that he didn't want Courtney to have her. What had Courtney done to deserve her ... ?

"Damn that fellow," he said to himself, thinking suddenly of Courtney's scientific distinction. "He'll probably discover the Riddle of the Universe some week-end ... "

What was the matter with him? Was he losing his sense of humour? What should he do with Monica on his hands?

It was just like Courtney to be rotten with money. If only he had Courtney's money. What a time he could give Monica with it!

A clear soprano sounded suddenly. ... "Oh, Promise Me ... " Storrey stood by the rail of the veranda, his hands in his pockets, staring off into space ... He would go on forever, he supposed, writing nice little verses to titillate the fancies of middle-aged virgins ... eating other peoples' dinners and being pleasant to everybody. He would probably get fat ... Yes, he would certainly get fat. ... Already his collar was getting too tight for him. ...

What a life! He wished he were blamed well out of it!

Courtney rushed in on him, seized him ...

"For Heaven's sake, Storrey," he almost gasped. "We're all ready—waiting for you. Ten minutes late … "

Storrey addressed a remark to Courtney, which, happily, Courtney did not hear. Then he followed him inside.

VI

THE Bishop was still talking about marriage. He was delivering generalizations to his clients … "It is an honourable estate … " he was assuring them. Did the bishop really believe that? Hadn't he read Shaw?

Then, for the first time, Storrey looked at Monica. She was standing with raised head looking the Bishop square in the eyes. There was something defiant in her bearing, something, too, unconquered and unconquerable.

"She's wonderful," Storrey said to himself. He looked at Courtney. He was standing limply, his big body looking flabbier than ever, his eyes fixed on the ground.

The Bishop's voice rose and fell. He was talking now about sharing things. … Storrey wondered what Monica was thinking. Was she aware of him? Of course she must be. Did she hate him? Would she continue to hate him? Did she understand him now or did she still believe that in renouncing her he was actuated by altruism?

Would they ever resume the old camaraderie? Not for a year, alas, certainly … But, maybe, sometime. Ennui might probably set in. When Courtney's talk about the nebular hypothesis might probably make her feel like jumping out of a window …

Storrey's depression began to lift. … Yes, Courtney might probably try to make an intellectual of Monica, not because he liked intellectual women, but in order to stimulate appreciation of his own achievements. And one day his hesitating expositions might probably drive her into hysterics and she might throw a book at him and run out of the room to be away from him …

And then she might probably telephone to him, Storrey. And he might probably meet her somewhere, perhaps in the old ladies' rendezvous in Fifty-first Street and he might see the desperation in Monica's eyes and he would understand. He would be gentle. He would be silent. He would be comforting. ...

" ... Let him speak now or forever after hold his peace ... " boomed the Bishop.

BENEDICTION

F. Scott Fitzgerald

I

THE Baltimore Station was hot and crowded, so Lois was forced to stand by the telegraph desk for interminable, sticky seconds while a clerk with big front teeth counted and recounted a large lady's day message, to determine whether it contained the innocuous forty-nine words or the fatal fifty-one.

Lois, waiting, decided she wasn't quite sure of the address, so she took the letter out of her bag and ran over it again.

"Darling: *it began*—

"I understand and I'm happier than life ever meant me to be. If I could give you the things you've always been in tune with—but I can't, Lois; we can't marry and we can't lose each other and let all this glorious love end in nothing.

"Until your letter came, dear, I'd been sitting here in the half dark thinking and thinking where I could go and ever forget you; abroad, perhaps, to drift through Italy or Spain and dream away the pain of having lost you where the crumbling ruins of older, mellower civilizations would mirror only the desolation of my heart—and then your letter came.

"Sweetest, bravest girl, if you'll wire me I'll meet you in Wilmington—till then I'll be here just waiting and hoping for every long dream of you to come true.   Howard."

She had read the letter so many times that she knew it word by word, yet it still startled her. In it she found many faint reflections of the man who wrote it—the mingled sweetness and sadness in his dark eyes, the furtive, restless excitement she felt sometimes when he talked to her, his dreamy sensuousness that lulled her mind to sleep. Lois was nineteen and very romantic and curious and courageous.

The large lady and the clerk having compromised on fifty words, Lois took a blank and wrote her telegram. And there were no overtones to the finality of her decision.

It's just destiny—she thought—it's just the way things work out in this blamed world. If cowardice is all that's been holding me back there won't be any more holding back. So we'll just let things take their course, and never be sorry.

The clerk scanned her telegram:

Arrived Baltimore today spend day with my brother meet me Wilmington three P.M. Wednesday Love   *Lois.*

"Fifty-four cents," said the clerk admiringly.

And never be sorry—thought Lois—and never be sorry—

II

TREES filtering light onto dappled grass. Trees like tall, languid ladies with feather fans coquetting airily with the ugly roof of the monastery. Trees like butlers, bending courteously over placid walks and paths. Trees, trees over the hills on either side and scattering out in clumps and lines and woods all through Maryland, delicate lace on the hems of many yellow fields, dark opaque backgrounds for flowered bushes or wild climbing gardens.

Some of the trees were very gay and young, but the monastery trees were older than the monastery which, by true monastic standards, wasn't very old at all. And, as a matter of fact, it wasn't technically called a monastery, but only a seminary; nevertheless it shall be a monastery here despite its Victorian architecture or its Edward VII additions, or even its Woodrow Wilsonian, patented, last-a-century roofing.

Out behind was the farm where half a dozen lay brothers were sweating lustily as they moved with deadly efficiency around the vegetable gardens. To the left, behind a row of elms, was an informal baseball diamond where three novices were being batted out by a fourth, amid great chasings and puffings and blowings. And in front as a great mellow bell boomed the half hour a swarm of black, human leaves were blown over the checker-board of paths under the courteous trees.

Some of these black leaves were very old with cheeks furrowed like the first ripples of a splashed pool. Then there was a scattering of middle-aged leaves whose forms when viewed in profile in their revealing gowns were beginning to be faintly unsymmetrical. These carried thick volumes of Thomas Aquinas and Henry James and Cardinal Mercier and Immanuel Kant and many bulging note-books filled with lecture data.

But most numerous were the young leaves; blonde boys of nineteen with very stern, conscientious expressions; men in the late twenties with a keen self-assurance from having taught out in the world for five years—several hundreds of them, from city and town and country in Maryland and Pennsylvania and Virginia and West Virginia and Delaware.

There were many Americans and some Irish and some tough Irish and a few French, and several Italians and Poles, and they walked informally arm and arm with each other in twos and threes or in long rows, almost universally distinguished by the straight mouth and the considerable chin—for this was the Society of Jesus, founded in Spain five hundred years before by a tough-minded soldier who trained men to hold a breach or a salon, preach a sermon or write a treaty, and do it and not argue...

Lois got out of a bus into the sunshine down by the outer gate. She was nineteen with yellow hair and eyes that people were tactful enough not to call green. When men of talent saw her in a street-car they often furtively produced little stub-pencils and backs of envelopes and tried to sum up that profile or the thing that the eyebrows did to her eyes. Later they looked at their results and usually tore them up with wondering sighs.

Though Lois was very jauntily attired in an expensively appropriate traveling affair, she did not linger to pat out the dust which covered her clothes, but started up the central walk with curious glances at either side. Her face was very eager and expectant, yet she hadn't at all that glorified expression that girls wear when they arrive for a Senior Prom at Princeton or New Haven; still as there were no senior proms here perhaps it didn't matter.

She was wondering what he would look like, whether she'd possibly know him from his picture. In the picture, which hung over her mother's bureau at home; he seemed very young and hollow-cheeked and rather pitiful, with only a well-developed mouth and an ill-fitting probationer's gown to show that he had already made a momentous decision about his life. Of course he had been only nineteen then and now he was thirty-six—didn't look like that at all; in recent snap-shots he was much broader and his hair had grown a little thin—but the impression of her brother she had always retained was that of the big picture. And so she had always been a little sorry for him. What a life for a man! Seventeen years of preparation and he wasn't even a priest yet—wouldn't be for a other year.

Lois had an idea that this was all going to be rather solemn if she let it be. But she was going to give her very best imitation of undiluted sunshine, the imitation she could give even when her head was splitting or when her mother had a nervous breakdown or when she was particularly romantic and curious and courageous. This brother of hers undoubtedly needed cheering up, and he was going to be cheered up, whether he liked it or not.

As she drew near the great, homely front door she saw a man break suddenly away from a group and, pulling up the skirts of his gown, run toward her. He was smiling, she noticed, and he looked very big and— and reliable. She stopped and waited, knew that her heart was beating unusually fast.

"Lois!" he cried, and in a second she was in his arms. She was suddenly trembling.

"Lois!" he cried again, "why, this is wonderful! I can't tell you, Lois, how *much* I've looked forward to this. Why, Lois, you're beautiful!"

Lois gasped.

His voice, though restrained, was vibrant with energy and that odd sort of enveloping personality she had thought that she only of the family possessed.

"I'm mighty glad, too—Kieth."

She flushed, but not unhappily, at this first use of his name.

"Lois—Lois—Lois," he repeated in wonder. "Child, we'll go in here a minute, because I want you to meet the rector and then we'll walk around because I have a thousand things to talk to you about."

His voice became graver. "How's Mother?"

She looked at him for a moment and then said something that she had not intended to say at all, the very sort of thing she had resolved to avoid.

"Oh, Kieth—she's—she's getting worse all the time, every way."

He nodded slowly as if he understood.

"Nervous, well—you can tell me about that later. Now—"

She was in a small study with a large desk, saying something to a little, jovial, white-haired priest who retained her hand for some seconds.

"So this is Lois!"

He said it as if he had heard of her for years.

He entreated her to sit down.

Two other priests arrived enthusiastically and shook hands with her and addressed her as "Kieth's little sister," which she found she didn't mind a bit.

How assured they seemed; she had expected a certain shyness, reserve at least. There were several jokes unintelligible to her, which seemed to delight everyone, and the little Father Rector referred to the trio of them as "dim old monks," which she appreciated, because of course they weren't monks at all. She had a lightning impression that they were especially fond of Kieth—the Father Rector had called him "Kieth" and one of the others had kept a hand on his shoulder all through the conversation. Then she was shaking hands again and promising to come back a little later for some ice-cream, -and smiling and smiling and being rather absurdly happy ... she told herself that it was because Kieth was so delighted in showing her off.

Then she and Kieth were strolling along a path, arm in arm, and he was informing her what an absolute jewel the Father Rector was.

"Lois," he broke off suddenly, "I want to tell you before we go any further how much it means to me to have you come up here. I think it was—mighty sweet of you. I know what a gay time you've been having."

Lois gasped. She was not prepared for this. At first when she had conceived the plan of taking the hot journey down to Baltimore, staying the night with a friend and then coming out to see her brother, she had felt rather consciously virtuous, hoped he wouldn't be priggish or resentful about her not having come before—but walking here with him under the trees seemed such a little thing, and surprisingly a happy thing.

"Why, Kieth," she said quickly, "you know I couldn't have waited a day longer. I saw you when I was five, but of course I didn't remember, and how could I have gone on without practically ever having seen my only brother."

"It was mighty sweet of you, Lois," he repeated.

Lois blushed—he *did* have personality.

"I want you to tell me all about yourself," he said after a pause. "Of course, I have a general idea what you and mother did in Europe those fourteen years, and then we were all so worried, Lois, when you had pneumonia and couldn't come down with mother—let's see, that was two years ago—and then, well, I've seen your name in the papers, but it's all been so unsatisfactory. I haven't known you, Lois."

She found herself analyzing his personality as she analyzed the personality of every man she met. She wondered if the effect of—of intimacy that he gave was bred by his constant repetition of her name. He said it as if he loved the word, as if it had an inherent meaning to him.

"Then you were at school," he continued.

"Yes, at Farmington. Mother wanted me to go to a convent—but I didn't want to."

She cast a side glance at him to see if he would resent this.

But he only nodded slowly.

"Had enough convents abroad, eh?"

"Yes—and Kieth, convents are different there anyway. Here even in the nicest ones there are so many *common* girls."

He nodded again.

"Yes," he agreed, "I suppose there are, and I know how you feel about it. It grated on me here at first, Lois, though I wouldn't say that to anyone but you; we're rather sensitive, you and I, to things like this."

"You mean the men here?"

"Yes, some of them of course were fine, the sort of men I'd always been thrown with, but there were others; a man named Regan, for instance—I hated the fellow, and now he's about the best friend I have. A wonderful character, Lois; you'll meet him later. Sort of man you'd like to have with you in a fight."

Lois was thinking that Kieth was the sort of man she'd like to have with *her* in a fight.

"How did you—how did you first happen to do it?" she asked, rather shyly, "to come here, I mean. Of course mother told me the story about the Pullman car."

"Oh, that—" he looked rather annoyed.

"Tell me that. I'd like to hear you tell it."

"Oh, it's nothing, except what you probably know. It was evening and I'd been riding all day and thinking about—about a hundred things, Lois, and then suddenly I had a sense that someone was sitting across from me, felt that he'd been there for sometime and had a vague idea that he was another traveler. All at once he leaned over toward me and I heard a voice say—'I want you to be a priest, that's what I want.' Well, I jumped up and cried out—'Oh, my God, not that!'—made an idiot of myself before about twenty people; you see there wasn't anyone sitting there at all. A week after that I went to the Jesuit College in Philadelphia and crawled up the last flight of stairs to the rector's office on my hands and knees."

There was another silence and Lois saw that her brother's eyes wore a far away look, that he was staring unseeingly out over the sunny fields. She was stirred by the modulations of his voice and the sudden silence that seemed to flow about him when he finished speaking.

She noticed now that his eyes were of the same fibre as hers, with the green left out, and that his mouth was much gentler, really, than in the picture—or was it that the face had grown up to it lately. He was getting a little bald just on top of his head. She wondered if that was from wearing a hat so much. It seemed awful for a man to grow bald and no one to care about it.

"Were you—pious when you were young, Kieth?" she asked. "You know what I mean. Were you religious? If you don't mind these personal questions."

"Yes," he said with his eyes still far away—and she felt that his intense abstraction was as much a part of his personality as his attention. "Yes, I suppose I was, when I was—sober."

Lois thrilled slightly.

"Did you drink?"

He nodded.

"I was on the way to making a bad hash of things." He smiled and, turning his grey eyes on her, changed the subject.

"Child, tell me about mother. I know it's been awfully hard for you there, lately. I know you've had to sacrifice a lot and put up with a great deal and I want you to know how fine of you I think it is. I feel, Lois, that you're sort of taking the place of both of us there."

Lois thought quickly how little she had sacrificed; how lately she had constantly avoided her nervous, half-invalid mother.

"Youth shouldn't be sacrificed to age, Kieth," she. said steadily.

"I know," he sighed, "and you oughtn't to have the weight on your shoulders, child. I wish I were there to help you."

She saw how quickly he had turned her remark and instantly she knew what this quality was that he gave off. He was *sweet*. Her thoughts went off on a side-track and then she broke the silence with an odd remark.

"Sweetness is hard," she said suddenly.

"What?"

"Nothing," she denied in confusion. "I didn't mean to speak aloud. I was thinking of something—of a conversation with a man named Freddy Kebble."

"Maury Kebble's brother?"

"Yes," she said, rather surprised to think of him having known Maury Kebble. Still there was nothing strange about it. "Well, he and I were talking about sweetness a few weeks ago. Oh, I don't know—I said that a man named Howard—that a man I knew was sweet and he didn't agree with me and we began talking about what sweetness in a man was. He kept telling me I meant a sort of soppy softness, but I knew I didn't—yet I didn't know exactly how to put it. I see now. I meant just the opposite. I suppose real sweetness is a sort of hardness—and strength."

Kieth nodded.

"I see what you mean. I've known old priests who had it."

"I'm talking about young men," she said, rather defiantly.

"Oh!"

They had reached the now deserted baseball diamond and, pointing her to a wooden bench, he sprawled full length on the grass.

"Are these *young* men happy here, Kieth?"

"Don't they look happy, Lois?"

"I suppose so, but those *young* ones, those two we just passed—have they—are they—"

"Are they signed up?" he laughed. "No, but they will be next month."

"Permanently?"

"Yes—unless they break down mentally or physically. Of course, in a discipline like ours a lot drop out."

"But those *boys*. Are they giving up fine chances outside—like you did?"

He nodded.

"Some of them."

"But, Kieth, they don't know what they're doing. They haven't had any experience of what they're missing."

"No, I suppose not."

"It doesn't seem fair. Life has just sort of scared them at first. Do they all come in so *young?*"

"No, some of them have knocked around, led pretty wild lives— Regan, for instance."

"I should think that sort would be better," she said meditatively, "men that had *seen* life."

"No," said Kieth earnestly, "I'm not sure that knocking about gives a man the sort of experience he can communicate to others. Some of the broadest men I've known have been absolutely rigid about themselves. And reformed libertines are a notoriously intolerant class. Don't you think so, Lois?"

She nodded, still meditative, and he continued :

"It seems to me that when one weak person goes to another, it isn't help they want; it's a sort of companionship in guilt, Lois. After you were born, when mother began to get nervous she used to go and weep with a certain Mrs. Comstock. Lord, it used to make me shiver. She said it comforted her, poor old mother. No, I don't think that to help others you've got to show yourself at all. Real help comes from a stronger person whom you respect. And their sympathy is all the bigger because it's impersonal."

"But people want human sympathy," objected Lois. "They want to feel the other person's been tempted."

"Lois, in their hearts they want to feel that the other person's been weak. That's what they mean by human."

"Here in this old monkery, Lois," he continued with a smile, "they try to get all that self-pity and pride in our own wills out of us right at the first. They put us to scrubbing floors—and other things. It's like that idea of saving your life by losing it. You see we sort of feel that the less human a man is, in your sense of human, the better servant he can be to humanity. We carry it out to the end, too. When one of us dies his family can't even have him then. He's buried here under a plain wooden cross with a thousand others."

His tone changed suddenly and he looked at her with a great brightness in his grey eyes.

"But way back in a man's heart there are some things he can't get rid of—and one of them is that I'm awfully in love with my little sister."

With a sudden impulse she knelt beside him in the grass and, leaning over, kissed his forehead.

"You're hard, Kieth," she said, "and I love you for it—and you're sweet."

III

BACK in the reception room Lois met a half dozen more of Kieth's particular friends; there was a young man named Jarvis, rather pale and delicate looking, who, she knew, must be a grandson of old Mrs. Jarvis at home, and she mentally compared this ascetic with a brace of his riotous uncles.

And there was Regan with a scarred face and piercing intent eyes that followed her about the room and often rested on Kieth with something very like worship. She knew then what Kieth had meant about "a good man to have with you in a fight."

He's the missionary type—she thought vaguely—China or something.

"I want Kieth's sister to show us what the shimmy is," demanded one young man with a broad grin.

Lois laughed.

"I'm afraid the Father Rector would send me shimmying out the gate. Besides, I'm not an expert."

"I'm sure it wouldn't be best for Jimmy's soul anyway," said Kieth solemnly. "He's inclined to brood about things like shimmys. They were just starting to do the—maxixe, wasn't it, Jimmy?—when he became a monk and it haunted him his whole first year. You'd see him when he was peeling potatoes, putting his arm around the bucket and making irreligious motions with his feet."

There was a general laugh in which Lois joined.

"An old lady who comes here to Mass sent Kieth this ice-cream," whispered Jarvis under cover of the laugh, "because she'd heard you were coming. It's pretty good, isn't it?"

Lois felt the rims of her eyes growing suddenly red.

IV

THEN half an hour later over in the chapel things suddenly went all wrong. It was several years since Lois had been at Benediction and, at first she was thrilled by the gleaming monstrance with its central spot of white, the air rich and heavy with incense, and the sun shining through the stained glass window of St. Francis Xavier overhead and falling in warm red tracery on the cassock of the man in front of her, but at the first notes of the *O Salutaris Hostia* a heavy weight seemed to descend upon her soul. Kieth was on her right and young Jarvis on her left and she stole uneasy glances at both of them.

What's the matter with me? she thought impatiently.

She looked again. Was there a certain coldness in both their profiles, that she had not noticed before—a pallor about the mouth and a curious set expression in their eyes. She shivered slightly, they were like dead men.

She felt her soul recede suddenly from Kieth's. This was her brother—this, this unnatural person. She caught herself in the act of a little laugh.

"What is the matter with me?"

She passed her hand over her eyes and the weight increased. The incense sickened her and a stray, ragged note from one of the tenors in the choir grated on her ear like the shriek of a slate pencil. She fidgeted and raising her hand to her hair touched her forehead, found moisture on it.

"It's hot in here, hot as the deuce."

Again she repressed a faint laugh and then in an instant the weight upon her heart suddenly diffused into cold fear.

...It was that candle on the altar. It was all wrong—wrong. Why didn't somebody see it. There was something *in* it. There was something coming out of it, taking form and shape above it.

She tried to fight down her rising panic, told herself it was the wick. If the wick wasn't straight candles did something—but they didn't do this! With incalculable rapidity a force was gathering within her, a tremendous, assimilative force, drawing from every sense, every corner of her brain, and as it surged up inside her she felt an enormous, terrified repulsion. She drew her arms in close to her side, away from Kieth and Jarvis.

Something in that candle...she was leaning forward—in another moment she felt she would go forward toward it—didn't anyone see it?...anyone?

"Ugh!"

She felt a space beside her and something told her that Jarvis had gasped and sat down very suddenly...then she was kneeling and as the flaming monstrance slowly left the altar in the hands of the priest, she heard a great rushing noise in her ears—the crash of the bells was like hammer blows...and then in a moment that seemed eternal a great torrent rolled over her heart—there was a shouting there and a lashing as of waves...

...She was calling, felt herself calling for Kieth, her lips mouthing the words that would not come:

"Kieth, Oh, my God! *Kieth!*"

Suddenly she became aware of a new presence, something external, in front of her, consummated and expressed in warm red tracery. Then she knew. It was the window of St. Francis Xavier. Her mind gripped at it, clung to it finally and she felt herself calling again endlessly, impotently—Kieth—Kieth!

Then out of a great stillness came a voice :

"Blessed be God."

With a gradual rumble sounded the response rolling heavily through the chapel—

"Blessed be God."

The words sang instantly in her heart; the incense lay mystically and sweetly peaceful upon the air, and *the candle on the altar went out.*

"Blessed be His Holy Name."

"Blessed be His Holy Name."

Everything blurred into a swinging mist. With a sound half gasp, half cry she rocked on her feet and reeled backward into Kieth's suddenly outstretched arms.

V

"Lie still, child."

She closed her eyes again. She was on the grass outside, pillowed on Kieth's arm, and Regan was dabbing her head with a cold towel.

"I'm all right," she said quietly.

"I know, but just lie still a minute longer. It was too hot in there. Jarvis felt it, too."

She laughed as Regan again touched her gingerly with the towel.

"I'm all right," she repeated.

But though a warm peace was filling her mind and heart she felt oddly broken and chastened as if someone had held her stripped soul up and laughed.

VI

Half an hour later she walked leaning on Kieth's arm down the long central path toward the gate.

"It's been such a short afternoon," he sighed, "and I'm so sorry you were sick, Lois."

"Kieth, I'm feeling fine now, really; I wish you wouldn't worry."

"Poor old child. I didn't realize that Benediction'd be a long service for you after your hot trip out here and all."

She laughed cheerfully.

"I guess the truth is I'm not much used to Benediction. Mass is the limit of my religious exertions."

She paused and then continued quickly :

"I don't want to shock you, Kieth, but I can't tell you how—how *inconvenient* being a Catholic is. It really doesn't seem to apply any more. As far as morals go, some of the wildest boys I know are Catholics. And the brightest boys—I mean the ones who think and read a lot, don't seem to believe in much of anything any more."

"Tell me about it. The bus won't be here for another half hour."

They sat down on a bench by the path.

"For instance Gerald Carter, he's published a novel. He absolutely roars when people mention immortality. And then Howa—well, another man I've known well, lately, who was Phi Beta Kappa at Harvard, says that no intelligent person can believe in Supernatural Christianity. He says Christ was a great socialist, though. Am I shocking you?"

She broke off suddenly.

Kieth smiled.

"You can't shock a monk. He's a professional shock absorber."

"Well," she continued, "that's about all. It seems so—so *narrow.* Church schools, for instance. There's more freedom about things that Catholic people can't see—like birth control."

Kieth winced, almost imperceptibly, but Lois saw it.

"Oh," she said quickly, "everybody talks about everything now."

"It's probably better that way."

'Oh, yes, much better. Well, that's all, Kieth. I just wanted to tell you why I'm a little—lukewarm, at present."

"I'm not shocked, Lois. I understand better than you think. We all go through those times. But I know it'll come out all right, child. There's that gift of faith that we have, you and I, that'll carry us past the bad spots."

He rose as he spoke and they started again down the path.

"I want you to pray for me sometimes, Lois. I think your prayers would be about what I need. Because we've come very close in these few hours, I think."

Her eyes were suddenly shining.

"Oh, we have, we have!" she cried. "I feel closer to you now than to anyone in the world."

He stopped suddenly and indicated the side of the path.

"We might—just a minute—"

It was a pieta, a life-size statue of the Blessed Virgin set within a semicircle of rocks.

Feeling a little self-conscious she dropped on her knees beside him and made an unsuccessful attempt at prayer.

She was only half through when he rose. He took her arm again.

"I wanted to thank Her for letting us have this day together," he said simply.

Lois felt a sudden lump in her throat and she wanted to say something that would tell him how much it had meant to her, too. But she found no words.

"I'll always remember this," he continued, his voice trembling a little—"this summer day with you. It's been just what I expected. You're just what I expected, Lois."

"I'm awfully glad, Kieth."

"You see, when you were little they kept sending me snap-shots of you, first as a baby and then as a child in socks playing on the beach with a pail and shovel, and then suddenly as a wistful little girl with wondering, pure eyes—and I used to build dreams about you. A man has to have something living to cling to. I think, Lois, it was your little white soul I tried to keep near me—even when life was at its loudest and every intellectual idea of God seemed the sheerest mockery, and desire and love and a million things came up to me and said, 'Look here at me! See, I'm Life. You're turning your back on it!' All the way through that shadow, Lois, I could always see your baby soul flitting on ahead of me, very frail and very clear and wonderful."

Lois was crying softly. They had reached the gate and she rested her elbow on it and dabbed furiously at her eyes.

"And then later, child, when you were sick I knelt all one night and asked God to spare you for me—for I knew I wanted more then; He had taught me to want more. I wanted to know you moved and breathed in the same world with me. I saw you growing up, that white innocence of yours changing to a flame and burning to give light to other weaker souls. And then I wanted some day to take your children on my knee and hear them call the crabbed old monk Uncle Kieth."

He seemed to be laughing now as he talked.

"Oh, Lois, Lois, I was asking God for more than I wanted—the letters you'd write me and the place I'd have at your table. I wanted an awful lot, Lois, dear."

"You've got me, Kieth," she sobbed, "you know it, say you know it. Oh, I'm acting like a baby but I didn't think you'd be this way, and I—oh, Kieth—Kieth—"

He took her hand and patted it softly.

"Here's the bus. You'll come again, won't you?"

She put her hands on his cheeks and drawing his head down, pressed her tear-wet face against his.

"Oh, Kieth, brother, some day I'll tell you something—"

He helped her in, saw her take down her handkerchief and smile bravely at him, as the driver flicked his whip and the bus rolled off. Then a thick cloud of dust rose around it and she was gone.

For a few minutes he stood there on the road, his hand on the gate-post, his lips half parted in a smile.

"Lois," he said aloud in a sort of wonder, "Lois, Lois."

Later, some probationers passing noticed him kneeling before the pieta, and coming back after a time found him still there. And he was there until twilight came down and the courteous trees grew garrulous overhead and the crickets took up their burden of song in the dusky grass.

VII

THE first clerk in the telegraph booth in the Baltimore Station whistled through his buck teeth at the second clerk :

"S'matter?"

"See that girl—no, the pretty one with the big black dots on her veil. Too late—she's gone. You missed somep'n."

"What about her?"

"Nothing. 'Cept she's damn good looking. Came in here yesterday and sent a wire to some guy to meet her somewhere. Then a minute ago she came in with a telegram all written out and was standin' there goin' to give it to me when she changed her mind or somep'n and all of a sudden tore it up."

"Hm."

The first clerk came around the counter and picking up the two pieces of paper from the floor put them together idly. The second clerk read them over his shoulder and subconsciously counted the words as he read. There were just thirteen.

This is in the way of a permanent goodbye. I should suggest Italy.

Lois.

"Tore it up, eh?" said the second clerk.

SUMMER THUNDER

Stephen Vincent Benét

I

THE nature of Justice is a thing that has always interested me. I have had more time than most to consider it, perhaps, for I have been a cripple as long as I can remember, and the best the specialists have been able to do for me is to cushion more comfortably my rolling-chair or show the nurse an easier way of lifting me to it from my bed and back again. But reading and the sparkle of thought in the mind, the twisting search of the diver for Truth in the ink-pool of Experience, the dead-leaf quietude of the spirit in the ceaseless millrace of Contemplation—these have been mine inimitably.

Also the sight from each window of this house of the ragged Maine landscape, bitter and starving, where the bones of the rock push through the earth from uneasy spring to thick long winter, white as a bear. Every window alters the picture a little, like various men discussing one woman, but the lines and the strength and the harshness—they are the same forever and ever. I know them by heart like a ballad now, yet like a ballad there is now and then some word of the ground, some feature of the forest of whose meaning I can never be entirely sure. And any pine or hillock can summon generations of shadows and memories to the roll of a phantom drum.

That straggling circle of stones up the slope of the hill, for instance, beside the black tree that looks like a broken Y. There aren't many besides myself who would think of it as a court of Justice—of that Justice we are all of us seeking, I tell you. But I saw a true cause tried there with every circumstance of argument, until judgment was fully given. Not exactly in accordance with our notions of law, perhaps, but the verdict has never been appealed. And it is more than six years this summer since Rafe Batchelder and Lucius Hewitt went up there to plead their cases.

These little stagnant counties of north Maine—they're like a pool that has been dammed too long. Clear on the surface, possibly—looking as easy to read and understand as a sentence set up in capitals—but just stir up the bottom with a stick once or twice and see what comes floating to the surface! The people are inbred, curious; the headstrong, the lively, the heedless moved away from here twenty years ago. You have only to look around you to find as many queer, suppressed, lopsided characters as there are knots in a bad piece of wood. They still seem to have that lean, hard stamina—it's the best thing the Pilgrims gave them, and it dies almost as hard as it lived—but even that is wearing thin in places. Especially over the nerves. Coffee and pie and the frying-pan— the weather and the rocks under the plough—they've forced your native pure-stock American who hadn't the courage to go West right up to the borderline between just "queerness" and insanity, until sometimes he quite forgets and steps over it completely. There are stories in old yellow newspapers and the stilted style of the eighties that make the ways of the House of Atreus seem commonplace. And for myself, I have seen what I have seen.

Rafe Batchelder was a strong man with something wrong in him. It's like looking at a big elm with rot inside it: you may not be sure what the matter is at first, but you are very sure the thing is bound to fall. He had a kind of fair, collie-like good looks—though he was fat for them. But if you ever took hold of his arm or shook hands with him you knew there was iron under the fat.

He was twenty-five or so at the time this happened—quite a prosperous fellow. Brought up on his father's farm here, good with a boat, he had worked at one of the big summer resorts for three years after his father died. The last two winters a New York broker who took a fancy to him had shipped him down to Florida to run his cruising launch. But there had been some trouble or other and now Rafe was back on the farm. Industrious—saved quite a bit of money—had had an offer from one summer resort already (this was March and he had only been back since January)—but he said he was through with working for other people, that he wanted to rest and work for himself. Though what rest he could find in Maine farming—but that wasn't for me to say. At any rate, there he was—you can see some of his fields from the window.

Lucius Hewitt was another kind of flesh entirely, a dark, slight, pleasant little chap. His father had been the village storekeeper and killed himself with patent medicines. So Lucius had hired out to the Batchelders—the old crow of a mother and a slip-shoe niece ran the farm while Rafe was away—and kept his mother and his girl first cousin alive on less than a pine can wring from stones. But the whole Hewitt cottage was as clean and bare as a plate, and the neighbours used to help, as Maine does, with a free hand and a salty tongue.

Everallen Strong, the girl cousin, would wash dishes or help cook in haying time, and they paid her what they could, which wasn't much. Everallen was a singular being. I have never seen anybody who gave quite the same impression of having strayed into the world from a dream.

It was not that she was beautiful, exactly, though I think I have seen her as beautiful as it is permitted a human thing to be; it was that she was separate, that she seemed to have no more connection with the everyday affairs of life than a cloud might have with the turbulence of a city or a crocus with the machinery of a train. Rafe Batchelder, on occasion, convinced you of the existence of positive evil; Everallen made you waver into the belief of a middle world, a world of phantasmagoria, a shadowy borderland of consciousness filled with good elves and nursery tales. She was uniquely alone. I have never beheld another creature like her.

I use the word "creature" advisedly—she seemed as happy in her loneliness, as much apart from crude mankind as wind. She was olive-dusky, slim as a young apple tree. Her eyes were the most distant and yet warmly untroubled things in the world. She was quite nineteen, and Lucius was her friend and counselor by virtue of three more years. To the casual they seemed much the same age. At least Rafe called Lucius "that boy" once when, returning from Florida, he found him working on the Batchelder farm, and, seeing it stung a trifle, took curious pains to do so again.

It had been a set winter and a slow spring, and the pain that comes down on me like a hand now and then had been ungenerously frequent in calling. So, until the ice of the year broke up in a great sluicing thaw at the middle of April, I could only get news by hearsay of the hangman's knot in which these three lives I have talked about were already so crookedly tangled. But Mrs. Ventor, my housekeeper-nurse, would drop me little flakes of gossip now and then through lips pursed up in virtue. The Hewitts had always been friends of hers, and Rafe Batchelder she hated healthily.

"He ain't right," she would throw at me. "He ain't right!"— and then stop when I tried to question her. But one day she went farther. "Ever since that business with the dog—" she deigned to add as a footnote.

By degrees I got the story out of her. It was a common enough tale, God knows, a stray cur, a half-grown lout, a dirty little piece of cruelty done with the causeless ferocity of the stupid. But the way she told it chilled me a little. She ended, her voice drooping into horror.

"And they found the little dog with his throat tore up, in that bunch of trees on the hill there. And they say Rafe did it with—"

But that I dismissed as improbable, as well as certain curious, formless hints at what seemed to taste of ritual sacrifice.

It is true superstition fades slowly from the pastures, and even the scientific farmer says a few words unconsciously now and then that were once propitiation against terror, and goes through certain acts, he knows not why, which, if rooted back to their beginnings, will be found to resemble astonishingly acts of homage to elemental powers, strong and invisible. And Rafe was a reversion to type—and an older type than the Pilgrims.

But I had read fairly widely in folklore in my time, and a circumstance of the kind so doubtfully pointed at occurring under twentieth-century eyes seemed to strain and overpower credulity. So I put the matter out of my mind entirely, with my reasonless dislike of Rafe made a little more reasonable, that was all. It wasn't till I saw him with Everallen that I thought of Mrs. Ventor's hints again.

II

IT was a day in high April, wet and steamy, with the earth a soaking brown under the slush. My chair was wheeled up here to the window. I could see the fence and the path and the slope with the stones beyond.

Everallen came up this way from the Batchelders' with one of those splint-baskets on her arm. She had been doing some work there, I suppose. Her walk was like a grave dance of thistledown; it was plain that she belonged to the Spring. Again in her motions, in the singing toss of her head, I caught the character of something unearthly. She was as happy as a young wave under a cloudless sky—but when Rafe came squelching through the stubble there and crossed over to meet her at the pasture-bars, she sank back into vague earthiness at once; it was as if someone had blown out a flame in her.

She tried to slip by him with a word, but he stopped her. They were both of them utterly unconscious of me—people have got used by this time to thinking of me as just a blank of face at a window, a blank that smiles if you nod to it. But I happen to have practised a little lip-reading for diversion now and then, so I knew more of them than they thought. Though at first I followed their talking unconsciously.

"Wait a minte!" said Rafe. "Where you going?"

"Home." She jerked her head defensively.

"Wait, then. You and me's to have a talk."

Like Apollyon he straddled all across the way.

With an indescribable gesture that made you think of a tired bird, she dropped the basket, clasped her hands on the fence-rail.

"Well?" she said, without turning her head toward him.

He said something I couldn't catch, but her answer was obviously "No."

There followed a rapid interchange of short phrases where I caught only broken words: "Night—the whiny son of a fool—up by the Circle."

Then he turned and said something so slowly and carefully that I received the full impact of the abominable sentence. I hurt my nails on the chair arm. It was as brutal and deliberate as a thrown clod. Along the splintered rail of the fence his hand crept toward hers like a snail, and, like a snail, it was wet and glistening.

She seemed horribly unsure for a moment, weak, shaken, as if the monstrous words were earth crushing down on her. Then all her eeriness came about her like magic.

"No!" she said; and I have never seen such contempt on lips again. She would only waste that much clean speech on him.

And she was walking, not running, walking slowly away from him with his face like the mask of an Indian devil. And she was past the window and round the corner and, for a heart-stopping instant, I thought he would follow. But he just stood and bellowed after her with the anger like dirty scarlet in his voice.

"It'll be yes some day, Everallen! It'll be yes some day, you—" and he ran off suddenly into filth and stopped and stood switching his boot with a twig and glaring, till finally he marched off toward his stable. I was sorry for his horses when I thought of them. Then I sank back slowly in my chair again, and I think I must have fainted for a time. At least what I next remember is Mrs. Ventor bending over me.

I wondered just what I could do. North Maine is not like a city—any charges I could bring—who would believe them? And to whom could I present what evidence there was?

Two days later, when that bearded caricature, the town sheriff, dropped in to talk to me interminably, I hinted to him what I had heard. He was not surprised—that was clear—but we both of us knew the country and the people and he wouldn't take it seriously at all—said Rafe was a loose-mouthed bully, but he'd stopped annoying the girl now and she was keeping out of his way. If he heard any more about it he would take steps, of course—and so on.

Meanwhile, he thought Lucius Hewitt was the best man to stand up to Rafe. I was unconvinced, but didn't say so—I couldn't blame him—he hadn't seen Rafe's face. But, after the manner of mortals, I dreamed and let the matter drift. And for more than a month nothing happened, and I began to think the sheriff must be right.

III

THE third factor, and X of the equation, Lucius Hewitt, did not happen to come within range of my windows till late in May. You have no idea what a curious effect my viewing the story by little snatches of scenes with long gaps between, filled in by the muddy loquacity of Mrs. Ventor, produced. It was like seeing disconnected flashes of a moving picture, lacking titles or explanations, with only naked intuition to set circumstances in their proper relation to each other. But this much I was able to gather in the intervening seven weeks or so.

Rafe was badgering Hewitt intensively. There was a series of petty persecutions. You may have seen a mischievous child prick and plague a perfectly well-disposed and quiet cat till the animal spits and shows claws. It was not a matter of actual physical bullying; Rafe rose over Lucius like a mountain, he could have broken him between his hands. It was more a constant worrying and nagging designed to drive the infuriated gentle man against the stolid violent one—to the former's inevitable destruction. There were stories of meals at the Batchelders that must have salted every mouthful Lucius ate. Rafe hung over him like a weight—he carried Rafe around with him, so to speak, wherever he went, a visible and bowing oppression. And now Rafe had begun to linger by the road in the short twilight and stare at Everallen as she passed.

You may ask, why didn't Lucius go away; take Everallen away?

I think he was making up his mind to it—but this was in the days before Sarajevo—he had no money—his mother was old—where could they go? And people here are more anchored—it's like tearing a plant out of a wall to move them—unless they are unusual people.

Lucius was not at all unusual—a nice lad with the pith of a man in him—that was all. Why didn't he try to marry Everallen, then—for it was obvious by this time that he loved her? It is my idea that he was still in the first stage of love—not yet accustomed to that shock of splendour and awe that comes (and not more than once in the years) when a playmate and companion as known and friendly as bread becomes suddenly something like a burning cloud to gaze upon, and most desirable of all imagined things.

The impact of first love on a soul that has had no tutors is like the first sight of a moonrise over the ocean; it leaves no room for the pure greed of possession. And my eavesdropping on Lucius Hewitt one night showed me that this particular assumption seemed, in its essentials, fairly correct.

He was talking to Mrs. Ventor in the kitchen. I sat reading over there by the lamp. The year had changed—it was one of May's beamy evenings. The door between the rooms was quarter-open for warmth and the companionship of human sound. The first word that came between me and my book was Mrs. Ventor's.

"Why can't you just pick up and leave then, Loosh?" in a tone of stiff concern.

I peeped over the edge of the page. His shadow was all I could see of him. It was bent over like a man in pain.

There was a long mutter of explanation from the shadow.

"Well, *I'd* kill him!" Her voice rose sharply. I could hear the whack of her hand on the bread-board.

The reply came strangely, a desolate whisper.

"Kill him? Sometimes I think I must. Sometimes I think I must."

The calm acceptance of the words evidently shocked her, gave her pause. She resumed less decidedly, in part-satire.

"I'd kill him. They'd never hang you for it, not in this town."

"They'd send me to prison for life, though." The crushed certainty of the words was absolute.

"Then marry Everallen, you dough of a man! Marry Everallen and you can put the law on Rafe if he waits for her and talks to her like you say."

"Marry Everallen? As if it was like I could! As if she'd marry with a thing like me." The shadow wrenched at its fingers.

"Lord, Lord, listen to the boy! As if any man in the world wasn't good enough for a girl Everallen's age! Now if it was a tall, ripe woman like me, Loosh!..." She burst into a cawing laugh.

Hewitt was obviously perturbed.

"Mrs. Ventor—Mrs. Ventor—I didn't—I mean—"

It lent fuel to her creaking mirth. He shrugged his shoulders in a way that seemed foreign, unnatural to him, then went on desperately:

"Besides, Mrs. Ventor, I'm not like her. She's of the woods, she's like the woods. She's like those trees up there—she's strange when you talk to her. And Rafe, he's like that, too, sometimes, and I'm afraid, Mrs. Ventor, I'm afraid...."

Her laugh was shut off like water. He ended on that same blank calmness.

"But I think you're right, Mrs. Ventor. I'll marry her, I'll try to marry her. Marry her and go away, God knows how, after the haying's over. Because, if I don't, I'll kill him or he'll kill me—somehow."

He rose with the tiredness of a man gone old.

"Thanks for the baking powder," he said briefly, and the shadow vanished.

There was more low talking at the back door, but in voices I couldn't catch.

The shadow of Lucius and the quiet words coming from the shadow had impressed me more than any substance could. And his sentence about the likeness between Rafe and Everallen wore a colour of predestined fatality that I trembled at but could not deny. They were atavisms, elementals, both of them—a mere glance showed it clearly. And the play of the dryad and the satyr—to behold which is horror for the human—is as old and as reasonless as death. It was by her very elvish remoteness from the world that Everallen might suddenly be betrayed. Yet if only Lucius Hewitt had courage—and once more I went impotently round the useless circle of thought. Till at last the whole cause seemed a vast delusion, and I opened my book again and started reading.

IV

THERE followed a backwater of some two months, during which, to the surface observer at least, nothing more of any consequence occurred. Then events moved on to their conclusion with the disorderly swiftness of a dream.

Through the two months I considered the case more often than I liked, for, as I say, I was then, as now, examining into the nature of Justice. And there seemed no justice here at all—only the shadow of a man and the sprite of a girl bound fast under a falling sword. And no way of escape was to be seen that did not magnify the tragedy. Doubtless I thought of it strainedly enough—it would not have appeared so hopelessly wrong to the village wiseacres for Everallen to marry Rafe. For it seems that was possible, too, by the gossip Mrs. Ventor brought me. But I could only think of the Black Mass.

It was a sultry night of dying July. Mrs. Ventor had just fetched my coffee.

"Quite a piece of news that's going around the village!" she said hesitantly.

"Yes? What?"

"Loosh Hewitt and that Everallen cousin of his. They're going to get married."

I felt the most inexpressible relief. For weeks I had carried that unjust tangle of lives in my breast as a man bears a secret and mortal disease. And now everything was to be solved and saved in the simplest manner possible!

"He's got a job down Portland way. They're going there the start of September."

My thoughts of what might have happened seemed remembrances of nightmare. The thick, soft air of the evening was as sweet to me as the first touch of driven spray on the lips of a man convalescent from fever. I smiled in the abundance of my content.

"Thank you. I'm glad to know."

Mrs. Ventor was ready to say more, but I wanted to be alone with my reprieve.

I have seldom been so happy as when, in my chair next morning, I tasted over and over again the knowledge of the previous night. Mrs. Ventor had wheeled me to this window. I could sit and look at the long, complacent slope of that hill for hours on hours and be sure no cloud would fall upon it, I thought. No cloud of human will or passion, that is—there were other clouds enough in the hot heavens. The sultriness had only increased with night—and the sky was huddled with cumuli and oppressive—a foretaste of rain was in the air. And the certain coming of the thunderstorm, already brewing far up in the hills, symbolized to me the final breaking of Fate's grip on the men and woman whose entanglement had fascinated me so long.

I glanced up at the circle of stones, a scytheman approached them, mowing. He straightened a moment to wipe the sweat from his face. The diminished and shadowy gesture seemed indefinably familiar. Then I knew him. It was Lucius Hewitt. I wondered how Rafe had taken the news.

Then, as I considered him idly, the man himself passed under the window. The puffy face of a powerful beast looked up at me, smiled. A hand waved. I was surprised into a nod. Why Rafe Batchelder should think me worth a "Good morning!"—but, perhaps he, too, had altered, "seen the light," I thought with a vague reminiscence of tracts. What I could not understand at all was the triumph in his face—a triumph so obvious as to be insolent. It came like a chill upon my idling—but the sunlight was too rare to be so wasted, and my mind slipped back to sunny quiet.

Rafe also carried a scythe. He stopped near the bottom of the hill, spat on his hands, began to mow. The sky grew darker above a fretting wind. The storm would break in half an hour.

After a time it struck me that there was something strange in the way Rafe was mowing. I remembered all the evil I had seen in his face.

Then I saw. Hewitt mowed across the slope of the hill and a little down. Rafe was mowing straight up the slope, the clean path of an arrow. They would meet at the circle of stones.

I glanced around the room desperately. Mrs. Ventor was out; she would not be back for an hour. Both men were good mowers. Within twenty minutes their swathes would cross.

I had always thought it impossible to pray before. For myself I had found it so. But within those twenty minutes I prayed for the cause of Everallen with the strength of unceasing despair. Whether I was heard or not is a thing that you must judge.

Not once did I see the men look at each other as their scythes crept nearer and nearer. There can't have been any sound at all but the soft hiss of the scythes through grass and the sigh of the gathering storm.

Rafe was first at the stones by five yards, and waited. Once he looked down the valley toward this house, shading his eyes—to make sure perhaps that my face was there, a smudge of white against the window, the witness for his acquittal should he need one.

The cloud over the sky was complete. Its center, bearing the tempest, hung astonishingly black above the hill. The dust of the path was splattered with a first few heavy drops of rain. Lucius finished mowing, straightened. He walked slowly toward Rafe, his scythe held clumsily in front of him. It is then that Rafe must have spoken.

I can imagine what things he must have said—and that Everallen's name was one of them. For the bonds that Lucius had put on himself for the last six months broke like strings, and he was crying like a madman and charging at Rafe with a wild, loose hacking of his scythe. Rafe shifted flashingly, dodged the rush as easily as a boxer jerks away from a fist. Lucius plunged past, recovered, almost slipped. Then Rafe came at him, half-dancing, with the ugly agility of a crane, the scythe held poised and quivering like a lunging beak of steel. Lucius gave ground continually. He dared not look to save his footing. He was crowded back between two stones.

Rafe shuttled before him, closed in. It seemed like a figure in a country dance—it was all as unreal as that. Then, with the fury of the desperate, Lucius leaped aside as Rafe swooped and struck. The blade clawed the air and missed, but the staff came full upon Lucius's head. I could hear the *thwack!* in my mind and wondered dully why it didn't reach my ears. Lucius stiffened in his stride for an instant like a man made out of wood. Then he reeled against a stone, hung twitching there, and fell face downward to the ground.

There was no sign from any quarter of the earth, now Cain had killed in self-defense. Rafe looked at the crumple an instant and saw that it did not move. He ran a dozen paces from the stones and stood there waving his arms like an unclean giant of victory.

Thunder slashed across the sky like a ripping cloth, and the rain fell drummingly faster on the yelling lips of his conquest. I saw him sickly and in agony. I saw him skip as he walked, and laugh and shake his long scythe like a metal toy—and then something fierce and thin and incredibly shining reached down out of heaven and struck him.

V

THE rest of it is as simple as flowing water.

They found Lucius there some half an hour after, when he had begun to stir weakly and try to rise. He had no recollection of the struggle, and the char that lightning had made of Rafe they buried as decently as was possible.

Lucius had fever for a month, but Everallen nursed him. They are living down in Portland now—Lucius got a very good job with a shipping concern after his discharge from the army. Two children, a frame house in the suburbs.

It seems strange that people change so much. Lucius is settled, successful—I could tell that the last time I saw them. The village here has never quite forgiven them for daring to go away and be happy—wonders why they so seldom come back. Everallen lost some of her unearthliness with motherhood—but the little girl is an elf from the forest. It gave me a shock when I saw her, the whole tangled play came back so piercingly. They are safe, building safety out of the years, having passed through more torment than most.

And I stay here with my books; and the book that I shall write about Justice. It will be a novel book, that book. For some men think of Justice as Force, causeless Force that drills the chaos of the universe. And to most she is the blind goddess with the balances. But forever now and until I am destroyed, since that hour I sat watching at the window, I have thought of her as thunder—always thunder—summer thunder walking tall between the hills.

THE SATURDAY NIGHT BLUES

Catharine Brody

SOME publicity agent for the antisuffrage organization should have heard Alice Crane Barker tell Mr. Pendleton why she had married. A benign and florid face edged with white hair gave Mr. Pendleton the look of a business-like angel, which further acquaintance bore out. He liked to simulate an angelic—sometimes troublesomely angelic—interest in the affairs of his employees.

Certain eyebrow-raising details had reached him regarding the hasty marriage of Alice Crane Barker. Gus Barker, it appeared, was one of those people who are predestined to go through life on the charge-and-dun plan, and, as no one who had had five minutes' acquaintance with Alice Crane Barker would have suspected her of marrying for love, it was natural that Mr. Pendleton should bluntly hunt for information, much as a doctor hunts for the fallible part of one's back, by administering a series of conversational punches.

"I'll be gosh darned! What makes you women marry for, anyway?" In this way he received Alice Crane's intimation that there was no danger of a collision between her job and her marriage. "If your husband couldn't provide for you, whaddye get married for?"

"For protection," returned Alice Crane equably.

Fortunately the spectacle of Alice Crane Barker, who on occasion presented to the world a surface as smooth and hard and unimpressionable as that of a polished agate, needing protection, moved Mr. Pendleton to give vent to a series of crescendo chuckles. Then his eye lighted on the first letter of the morning's mail and he straightway forgot all about his self-sufficient secretary.

Alice Crane went on looking through the cabinet under "A" for the folder of Acorn & Co., who had just complained of their last shipment.

She moved shapely, square hands, unornamented except for a wedding ring, among the contents of the drawer. Her square, healthy, pale face, with the frank blue eyes and the firm mouth, her flat bright hair, the high-collared crêpe de chine shirtwaist, the assured swing of her hips and the erect carriage of her head—all implied some sly sarcasm lurking in the avowal of her need of a protector, like a pin mischievously hidden in the chair of a schoolmaster.

She had said "protection" on the spur of the moment. It was inadequate to express the mingled considerations which prompted Alice Crane to consent to become Alice Crane Barker. She never hastily o. k.'d a letter for filing or hurriedly ironed a handkerchief, but she married Gus Barker in the wink of an eyelash, on the Monday after the Friday night that she had, after due reflection, decided to cast him out of her mind forever. Saturday made the difference.

Alice Crane lived in one of those out-at-heels brownstone houses which hold their comfortable own among the upstart ten-story white bricks in Central Park West. Gus Parker met her at the door one Friday night. Gus wore clothes impeccably, had a straight profile of which an amber pipe seemed to be an inseparable part, and cropped his hair very close. He affected the athletic type as much as a shipping clerk can.

"I've got another raise," announced Alice Crane, after the preliminary "Hellos."

Gus took his pipe out of his mouth and looked sour. He carried definite news from his old man to the effect that Gus wasn't worth another penny to the firm and wouldn't get one, by gad!

"You women get away with it all right," he said bitterly. "Like the fellow said in the paper, all a girl needs is taking eyes and a giving mouth to get ahead."

He stuck his pipe back in the corner of his mouth.

When a girl has been engaged to a man for an indefinite period and sees every prospect of continuing engaged for a still more indefinite period, the sting of the hornet is more likely to be among her accoutrements than the love-shafts of Cupid.

"Why don't you go into the advice on how to get ahead in business!" sneered Alice Crane. "You've got the main requirement to make a fortune that way. You certainly know what not to do."

They quarreled, disdainfully on Alice Crane's part, resentfully on his.

"What in goodness would I marry you for?" spoke up Alice Crane. "We're not kids of sixteen to be head over heels in love. I can support myself twice as well as you can. I can give myself a good time, everything I need and my freedom into the bargain. Is there anything a man like you can offer a girl like me?"

If the question had been put to a country-store-outfitted Gus at the back door of a farmhouse, he would have scratched his head and gaped. These primordial expressions being taboo in the city, Gus removed his pipe once more and glared.

"I've heard that before," he pronounced, outraged. "Think you got everything, don't you? Just the samee, there'll be a time when you'll give everything just to have a man! I know you women."

The baleful glare of Alice Crane struck and blighted him as the glare of the hot sun withers a violet. His jaw, upon which long years of following-the-leader in work, dress, food and thought had left its mark, the prettified shoulders of the office worker, the narrow waist of the dandy, the surprise-proof eyes of the New Yorker—her glance meaningly swept and obliterated them all.

She stopped at the last button of her gloves, opened the front door and glanced over her shoulder.

"When that time comes, we'll meet again," she snapped.

She slammed the door. It was her adieu, farewell, the "we part forever" of grand opera.

II

No one who knew Alice Crane would be so far misled as to suppose that she wept half the night over what looked like a separation even more interminable than the long engagement. She never even thought of shedding a quiet tear or two in a corner of her immaculate handkerchief, and the idea of dropping them on her pillow would have been distasteful in the extreme. Alice Crane was a scrupulously neat person.

On Saturday morning, however, her smooth bearing was a trifle ruffled. She grumbled at the telephone operator; she grimaced impatiently over Mr. Pendleton's innumerable fussinesses; she wondered audibly with the bookkeeper over the sheerness of the stenographer's georgette waist. In short, Alice Crane was not herself.

At one o'clock she collected her salary, rolled down the top of Mr. Pendleton's desk, slammed her own, dabbed her nose reflectively with a powder-puff before a pocket mirror, jammed on her hat, buttoned her coat briskly, caught the down-going elevator at a run and a shuffle, and stood poised at the head of the stairs in front of the building.

She generally met Gus on Saturday afternoons and had a lingering luncheon with him—latterly she had considered paying her share of the bill. They parted at the door of the restaurant, he to disappear into mysterious masculine haunts with the boys, she to shop or freshen up her dress and her disposition for the evening.

Saturday nights they went to the theater, varying it slightly with vaudeville shows or even motion pictures when the source of Gus's finances was as dry as the Great American. Desert. When that source was profuse as a millionaire's private stock—this happened occasionally during the racing seasons—they finished with a sparing midnight supper in one of the less conspicuous cafés or partook of a before-the-show table d'hôte dinner in one of the less well-known hotels. They quarreled through it all, with sharp irony on Alice Crane's part, with flaring resentfulness on the part of Gus. Yet every Saturday night they went religiously through the same form, ending with final reconciliation at Alice Crane's door.

As she maintained her equilibrium at the head of the stairs in spite of the headlong rush of telegraph boys, brokers' clerks, pimple-faced youths with small eyes, square-chinned youths with hard eyes, and all the other ants that swarm over the anthill of lower Broadway, Alice Crane determined that her amusements would not be curtailed by the absence of Gus Barker. She decided against a matinée in favour of an evening performance of some play. There should be, according to all the laws of nature, more comfort in being alone than with a person who scrapped intolerably.

She planned to have preliminary tea at one of the big hotels in the East Forties, newly built for the growing class of people who have just acquired things—furs, jewels or exquisite women—and like to show them off. She would go alone. She was in no mood to offer excuses or explanations to any of the few girls of her acquaintance.

So Alice Crane hunted up a subterranean cut-rate ticket agency, where she ordered a first balcony seat for a promising musical comedy. She was not in the drama mood, as any self-respecting heroine who had just separated from her lover necessarily would be, but in the musical comedy mood, as any tired business woman after a half-day of grilling office work would be.

"Two?" mumbled the clerk.

"One," said Alice Crane.

"One?" repeated the clerk, and favoured her with a stare out of pale eyes over a debonair nose and a mustache as light as a lemon fizz.

"I said so," she returned frigidly.

"Gee, I just bumped into an iceberg," sang the clerk to his fellow. "How's the weather at your end?"

He added a fatuous wink for Alice. It was not the most opportune opening for what had been planned as a defiantly pleasant day.

At three o'clock, after lunch and some perfunctory shopping, Alice dragged exhausted feet over the heavily carpeted mezzanine floor of the big hotel.

The men who lounged there, revelling in soft armchairs and abundant cigarette trays, looked as if they had stepped out cool and calm and callous from a cellar advertisement. The women who accompanied them were of three classes : lightly rouged, moderately rouged, and expertly made up. The first were the school friends and childhood sweethearts; the second, wives; and the third, by far the larger part, were of a class that toils not nor spins nor has any visible and legal means of support, but manages to put the lilies of the field to envy notwithstanding. Alice, alone, watched them all, envying the women—envying them the quality of their skins, glossy as the coats of exquisitely kept race-horses, envying them the luxurious sheen of their clothes, the splendid appointments of their escorts.

A round-bellied little man with sharp black eyes spoke to a maid who stood and watched from a corner. The maid came and bent over Alice.

"Are you a guest of the hotel, madame?" she murmured suavely.

"Why, no, but I'm waiting here for tea," frowned Alice.

"Then I am sorry, madame, but you cannot wait here. We do not allow unescorted ladies to wait here. There is a special part of the mezzanine floor reserved for ladies."

"But I am waiting here for a friend." "I am sorry, madame, but we do not allow unescorted ladies to wait here," repeated the maid inflexibly. The fat little man never took his sharp eyes off her.

As Alice left, her cheeks burning with the stifling heat of helpless indignation, she saw the maid bend over another girl, who raised a haughty, heavily powdered face. The girl's lips moved in explanation; the maid seemed to insist. Suddenly a man turned the corner and greeted the girl. She exclaimed her relief, while the maid backed away and apologized profusely.

"A man's a woman's card of admission anywhere," thought Alice Crane scornfully. She was too angry to think of having tea, as she went home to prepare for a carefully gay evening as recompense.

III

IT was years since Alice Crane had had occasion to pay her own carfare to the theater district on a Saturday night, and elbow her own way through the peculiar Saturday night throngs, and cling to a strap alone in a car full of Saturday-nighters. The last are in a class by themselves. On week-day evenings a stray caterpillar is noticeable here and there among the butterflies—a man with a clay pipe in his mouth prepared for a dreary night of guarding other people's property or a drab woman bent to her toilsome evening of washing other people's floors. But on Saturday nights these, somehow, disappear. Saturday nights are dedicated to youth—youth rich in money because it has the fulness of the afternoon pay envelope pressing against the pocket, youth rich in time, because it has a whole day of reckless rest before it. This youth comes in pairs.

To Alice Crane it seemed as if the whole heterogeneous universe had evolved into a small world of twos with herself as the one desolate and isolated individual. She was as aloof in the crowded subway as a hermit gazing down from his solitary mountain hut on the gregarious life of a city.

She began idly to classify the groups in the world of twos. From one subway station came the buxom and overdressed damsels of Harlem with their escorts, dark-haired and sharp-eyed, the future dress-goods manufacturers and clothing factory owners of the city. From another came slender, overgrown girls with floppy hats and matter-of-fact voices, with their escorts, blond and square, the furniture salesmen and shoe clerks of the city. And from another, carefully corseted women with costly clothes and still more costly faces and their escorts, smooth-faced, heavy-jowled, the sports, the race-track touts, the gayer fellows of the city.

The theater was even more a hedged-in world of twos. The musical comedy world especially has its twos—to every hero his heroine; to every villain his adventuress; to every chorus girl her chorus man. A girl in a net dress sat on one side of Alice Crane, exchanging futilities with her escort; a girl in a cloth dress sat on the other side, exchanging banalities with hers. And on the stage the Thespian hero and heroine mixed futilities with banalities.

Slightly to the hither part of midnight the Thespian hero gathered his heroine in his arms and, by a kiss on the most intensively rouged portion of her lips, announced that the purpose of the play had been consummated and that the audience might go home with conscience at ease. Young men ploughed a way for their petticoated halves to glide through to the nearest cabaret or perhaps ice-cream parlour, or maybe just the orangeade stand on the corner. Giggling girls moved forward in horizontal line formation. Then came Alice Crane endeavouring to preserve a guiltless air after her intrusion on the Saturday night world of twos.

For the life of her she could not help sidling along in the glaring shade of buildings. Each yellow electric bulb was the cattish eye of a shocked grandma coldly accusing, taunting, unforgiving. She thought two men leaning against a corner building had turned to look at her in the manner of the fat, sharp-eyed hotel detective. Striding away, she passed the subway station and, rather than turn back to face them again, she walked on to Columbus Circle.

By these gradations, we come to "Sandy," for whom in the intervals of taking care of the sparrow and clothing the lily, the Lord provides free pickings either on Columbus Circle or Blackwell's Island.

It was Columbus Circle for Sandy, pickpocket de luxe, tonight, and there he stood in a conveniently darkened corner adjacent to the Subway station, with his hat pulled down low to disclose only the tip of a nose and the stub of a cigar. As if luck had not been generous enough to Sandy that day, it gradually penetrated to the slit of a brain via the slit of an eye that a woman's flat, leather purse lay at his feet. With an agile twist he leaped upon it and began to transfer it to his pocket.

Alice Crane, feeling for an intangible purse and equally intangible carfare, turned back sharply and caught the rebound of Sandy's agility.

"That's my pocketbook," said Alice Crane in mild surprise.

"Go tell it to Sweeney," advised Sandy. There wasn't a sign of a bluecoat within Sandy's line of vision.

"Hand back that purse, or I'll call a policeman."

"You better shut your trap," menaced Sandy.

A few men on their way to the station paused with the vacuous curiosity of New Yorkers. To these Alice Crane appealed.

"Call a policeman, please. He's got my purse."

But they shrugged and stared indolently. It might be so and it mightn't. Besides, it was none of their business.

"But I tell you he has my purse. I can't get home. I haven't any carfare," cried Alice Crane. "Call a policeman. Somebody please call a policeman!"

"Aw, what's your game, sister?" sneered Sandy for the benefit of those within hearing and believing distance.

In the meanwhile he edged closer to the fringe of what had become a fairsized group. There are streets around Columbus Circle bearing the same proportion to it, in point of light, as do the country lanes to the village Main Street. They are convenient for the sudden disappearance of Sandy's kind in moments of dire need.

"You'll not get away with my pocket-book," snapped Alice decisively, and grasped Sandy's arm. He flung it aside and lunged at the crowd, which involuntarily broke. One man with a tardy sense of justice caught him.

"G'wan. Give back the lady's pocket-book."

"Whose got her pocketbook? You let me go."

Shaking the man off, as a mongrel shakes off a flea, Sandy made a dash for the security of the darkened streets. The crowd turned after him instinctively. The same instinct prompted a man with an amber pipe which seemed an indefinable part of his features to halt in his diagonal stroll across the Circle in the path of the fleeing Sandy, and to put out his hands and grab him.

"It's a lady's pocketbook he got," the forerunner of the heated crowd informed him.

"Ah, you shut up! I didn't take no pocketbook," whined Sandy.

Alice Crane came up here, her head down, her throat lumpy with exasperation.

"I dropped it and he picked it up," she gasped.

"I found it over there, and she says it's hers. How do I know it's hers? You let me go or I'll—I'll show you, you big stiff. I'll—"

"Dry up, now. Just give that pocketbook back," ordered the man, and as Alice Crane's head went up in amazement, he nodded reassuringly: "You'll get it back in a minute, Alice."

After Sandy had handed over the purse, receiving a shaking and his release, Alice Crane found herself clinging to Gus Barker's arm in a sub-way train stiflingly full of paired-off couples.

"Gus," she began wildly, "did I say you couldn't give me anything? Forget it! I'll marry you as soon as you say—Sunday, Monday, any time, if you promise one thing. I don't care about the love, honour and obey part, but you must promise to shield and protect me—from ticket sellers, hotel detectives, pickpockets, nasty looks, and the Saturday night blues—Amen."

WOW

W. B. Seabrook

I

ONE summer evening, a sentinel who stood leaning on his spear at the entrance to the Han Ku Pass—for this was many years before the building of the Great Wall—beheld a white-bearded traveler riding toward him, seated cross-legged upon the shoulders of a black ox.

Said the venerable stranger, when he drew near and halted :

"I am an old man, and wish to die peacefully in the mountains which lie to the westward. Permit me, therefore, to depart."

But the sentinel prostrated himself and said, in awe:

"Are you not that great philosopher?"

For he suspected the wayfarer to be none other than Lao-tze, who was reputed the holiest and wisest man in China.

"That may or may not be," replied the stranger, "but I am an old man, wishing to depart from China and die in peace."

At this, the sentinel perceived that he was indeed in the presence of the great Lao-tze, who had sat for more than a hundred years in the shadow of a plum tree, uttering words of such extreme simplicity that no man in the whole world was learned enough to understand their meaning.

So the sentinel threw himself in the ox's path, and cried out.

"I am a poor and ignorant man, but I have heard it said that wisdom is a thing of priceless worth. Spare me, I beg you, ere you depart from China, one word of your great wisdom, which may, perchance, enrich my poverty or make it easier to bear."

Whereupon Lao-tze opened his mouth, and said gravely:

"Wow."

After which he ambled westward in the twilight and disappeared forever from the sight of men.

As for the poor sentinel, he sat dumbly scratching his head, saying over and over to himself in puzzled, uncertain tones, "Wow. Wow! Wow?"

For this absurd monosyllable had precisely the same meaning in ancient Chinese that it has in modern English, which is another way of telling you that it had no meaning at all, and that Lao-tze might just as appropriately have said, "Poo," or "Ba," or "Oh, hum."

But the sentinel, who imagined himself the possessor of some mighty incantation, went about his affairs as one demented, secretly repeating the strange word twenty thousand times a day, expecting with each breath that his wife would suddenly become young and beautiful, or that his hut would be transformed into a palace, or his spear into the ivory baton of a mandarin; until finally the exasperated captain of the guard took note of his strange mooning and muttering and had him beaten on the soles of his feet until he confessed the whole story of his encounter with Lao-tze.

And that was the end of the unhappy sentinel, for he died from the beating, but in due time the captain reported the saying of Lao-tze to the governor of the province, and eventually it reached the ears of the emperor.

II

Now the emperor cared more for the happiness of his subjects than for his own ease, and was accustomed to seek wisdom that he might apply it to better the condition of his people; so when he learned that the great Lao-tze's valedictory to humanity had been "Wow," he called his vizier and bade him consider the mystery.

The vizier engaged in a holy meditation on "Wow" for forty days and nights, after which he returned to the emperor and spoke.

"O Son of Heaven, doubtless it has often chanced that while engaged in the hunt, you have seen two vast companies of lions, arrayed in martial order, maiming and slaying each other in mighty battle."

"Never in my whole life," replied the astonished emperor.

"But surely, then, O Son of Heaven, you have noticed when coursing wolves, how certain of the pack are accustomed to act as slaves and burden bearers for the others."

"You know very well that I have never seen such a sight," answered the emperor, "but what I do see plainly is that my vizier has taken leave of his wits."

"I beg forgiveness, O Son of Heaven," persisted the vizier, "but I am at least convinced that you have observed how certain animals imprison others of their kind in chains and dungeons; how certain ones starve amid plenty; and how all the beasts of the forest, save a divinely favoured few, are compelled to engage in heavy, life-long toil."

"It is with the deepest pain," interjected the emperor in a tone of exquisite politeness, "that I shall now call in the executioner to cut off your honourable head, but I am comforted by the reflection that this will probably cause you only a slight inconvenience, as you seem already to have lost the use of it."

"My poor unworthy head will be too highly honoured, O Son of Heaven, but harken yet once again ere you decree my death. You have never seen such things as I have described, because the animals, whose communication is limited to 'wow,' or 'Baa,' according to their kind, live naturally and simply as God intended; while man, who alone among God's creatures has invented speech to his confusion, is the only being afflicted with wars, prisons, slavery, poverty and sorrow.

"This is the hidden meaning concealed in the mystic utterance of the wise and holy Lao-tze:

"Abolish Language, and man will return to primal simplicity and happiness."

"A most excellent idea, and I forgive you," replied the emperor, "for while the abolition of Language may not accomplish all you say, it will at least put a stop to the incessant chatter and quarrelling of my wives."

So presently heralds were sent throughout all China, with an imperial decree that Language was to be abolished in the empire, beginning with the first day after the Festival of the Full Moon, and that thereafter none might say aught but "Wow," on pain of death.

The people obeyed.

III

AND so there dawned on China an era of simplicity and peace—a Golden Age, in which wars ceased, and industrial bondage and exploitation disappeared, for without spoken or written language they could no longer exist. Desires grew fewer. Each family tilled the soil just sufficiently to supply its own simple wants. Husband and wife, father and son, neighbour and neighbour, dwelt together in harmony and peace, for none said aught but "Wow," and hence all were agreed.

Laws were no longer necessary. Though there were armour and weapons, there was no occasion for donning them. People no longer roved about, for they were everywhere content. Though there were ships and carriages, there was no occasion to use them. Where two villages lay close together, separated only by a little hill, the voices of their cocks and dogs were mutually heard, yet people came to old age and died with no desire to go from one village to the other.

And the emperor, who had grown very old, lived as simply in his palace as his people in their villages, for his empire was no longer a burden on his shoulders, and was governed perfectly because it was not governed at all.

But in the meantime there had been born in a distant village a child with an impediment in his speech, who, as he grew to manhood, endeavored to say "Wow," but could only say "Wo." At first he was ashamed and envious, but later he persuaded himself that his incompetence was a virtue and that his blemish was a mark of superiority, and whenever he heard people saying "Wow," in the contented, old-fashioned way, he would puff out his chest and ostentatiously cry, "Wo," at the top of his voice, until finally he made himself such a nuisance that he was driven out of the village with sticks and stones.

When he arrived in the next village, where they knew nothing of the impediment in his speech, and stood in the market place saying, "Wo, wo, wo," the people arose and would have slain him, when suddenly one of their number, who like the rest had been content to say "Wow" all his life, suddenly took his stand beside the stranger and began to shout vehemently, "Wo! Wo! Wo!" And presently, strange to relate, half the village was imitating him.

Strangest of all, they immediately became discontented, and driven by an irresistible restlessness, abandoned their tranquil firesides and began to wander about the country, as in the old days, traveling in ones and twos and companies, arrogantly clamoring, "Wo, wo," spreading amazement, quarrel and dissension.

All this began in a far-off province, and did not come to the ears of the emperor, who continued to live peacefully year after year in his palace, until one day the door burst open and his ancient vizier appeared, bent with age and exhaustion, covered with dust and sweat.

The emperor was greatly astonished, and uttered an amazed "Wow," for the vizier had departed to his native village nearly a century before, and the emperor had never expected to see him or have need of seeing him again.

"O Son of Heaven," cried the old man in a trembling and unaccustomed voice, "the time for saying 'Wow' has reached an end, for a marvellous thing has come to pass. On the great plain which lies not far beyond the palace walls are two vast armies, armed with scythes and clubs and stones—and they of one army are furiously screaming 'Wow! Wow! Wow!' as if they had gone mad, while they of the other army, with equal fury, are replying 'Wo! Wo! Wo!' Each army is trying to outshout the other, and if they come together in battle the rivers will run red with blood, for their numbers are constantly increasing, and town is arrayed against town, village against village, family against family, brother against brother."

At these strange tidings, the emperor raised himself with difficulty from his couch, and with trembling hands lifted the lid of a massive chest from which he drew the sacred imperial robe of yellow and gold, embroidered with the emblem of the Great Dragon. His vizier's robe of state he also drew forth, and when the two old men had vested themselves in the panoply of power and wisdom, supporting each other, arm in arm, they tottered out of the palace.

When they came to the Yang Shi Bridge, outside the walls, they saw that the waters of the river were running red.

As they stood sorrowing, they heard a confused shouting, and beheld two remnants of the battling armies, the one in pursuit of the other. And it appeared that there would be fresh slaughter at the river's edge. But when the two onrushing bands espied the emperor and his vizier, they gave over flight and pursuit, stopped stockstill, and ceased their shouting.

The aged emperor stepped forward, raising his arms in a gesture that was at once paternal and majestic, and would have spoken. But straightway he was greeted with an angry chorus of "Wows" and "Wos" which were so mingled in the din that they sounded precisely alike to his astonished ears. And shouting thus together, for the moment, at least, in perfect harmony, they seized the emperor and his vizier, tied them together with a huge stone around their necks, and threw them headlong into the crimsoned river. After which, they remembered their former quarrel, and resumed their mutual slaughter.

And when the yellow moon rose, it shone, as of old, upon human strife and fields strewn with the dead, while naught remained of the emperor and the vizier and Lao-tze's holy wisdom save a few empty bubbles floating on a river of blood.

CASTE

Burton Rascoe

I

ERIC SEWARD, having finished the article he was reading, dropped the magazine to the floor, lighted a cigarette, and then, noting for the fiftieth time that the furniture arrangement in the room did not suit him, telephoned the club clerk to send up some one to change it.

"The fellow's absolutely right," he said aloud to the room's vacancy and with vehemence. Eric occasionally permitted himself the pleasure of an audible commitment when no one else was about. The fellow who was absolutely right was Bernard Shaw, and the matter he was absolutely right about was the desirability of giving natural selection a free hand.

If, say (as Shaw in a fashion put it), a mentally and financially solvent young man of mateable physique should, while walking down the street, encounter a comely young woman who was unknown to him and obviously from a different circle from that in which he moved, the young man should, if a vital impulse directed, go straight up to that young woman and claim her for his own.

Eric had seen a young woman on the street that very morning whom he had particularly wanted to claim for his own. It annoyed him to reflect that he had been checked in his impulse by these class distinctions, which, as Shaw revealed, were artificial, and by these conventions, which as Shaw pointed out, were archaic—and by the municipal anti-flirting law, about which Eric had his own opinions.

"Damn outrageous nonsense," he reiterated with equal vehemence and to the same vacancy—having especially in mind the municipal anti-flirting law: "No wonder the race is degenerating. Need more fellows like Shaw to shake them up."

The "them" were visualized for a moment in the back of his mind as a crêpe-draped set of meddling old men who framed—and sent good-looking policewomen on the streets to enforce—a law which was manifestly inimical to the best interests of the race. That they chose well-formed and pretty women and did not identify them as of the constabulary with uniforms and badges, he esteemed as particularly heinous.

His irritation served as a stimulus to literary composition and he was about to address himself to the wording of a protest which should be printed under his full name (if it sounded logical) and under his reversed initials (if he were in doubt about it) in the correspondence column of the leading paper—when he heard a rap at the door.

"Come in!"

Joe, one of the club porters, a blond, squarely built, high-cheek-boned youth, came in and, under Eric's direction, set about moving a lounge and bookshelves, a desk and chairs into a pattern more appealing to Eric's vague æsthetic sensitivity.

"Well, Joe, how's tricks?" asked Eric, when the task was under way.

He had frequently chatted with Joe as man to man (they were of an age) when Joe was engaged in work about his rooms, and he had drawn Joe out on various subjects, one of them being women. Eric's curiosity in this field of research, one is happy to record, was not so limited as his experience.

Eric knew that Joe had two sisters who were tentatively engaged as waitresses downstairs as an experiment while the club waiters were on strike. This information he had come about in a routine sort of way, but his eye had told him that one of these sisters was wholly unattractive, rather blowsy, in fact, and the other quite personable indeed. Eric had, of course, observed this latter sister only cursorily and discreetly but he had remarked an involuntary appreciable difference in the tone and inflection he used when he said, "And I'll have my coffee now, please," to the pretty one and in the tone and inflection he used when he said precisely the same words to the less appetizing sister.

"Fine, sir," answered Joe with that grin which always had secretly annoyed Eric because he could see no occasion for it—he knew Joe was not especially stupid—and which he failed to attribute to embarrassment. The grin made Eric feel uncomfortably conscious that Joe might have something on him, some peccadillo, some observation he had made while piddling about the rooms, which he, Eric, would hate to have generally known … Perhaps Joe had seen the salutation of an unfinished letter lying on the desk; or disapproved of the colour of his pajamas; or thought the things girls had written on their photographs were silly; or had got into his collection of *La Vie Parisienne*. … But perhaps Joe considered him a sly, gay dog and this grin was an admiring tribute to his prowess, hinting at difficult conquests and luxurious bacchanals … Still, that grin was irritating …

On the lapel of Joe's uniform jacket there was a small white feather which had excited Eric's curiosity now going on five months.

Eric again found himself scrutinizing this feather with a nebulous sort of perplexity and wonderment. The first time he had noticed it Eric assumed that it was only a day's vanity on Joe's part. And when Joe kept on wearing it, he decided it must be some kind of identification, like a taxi driver's license tag or a gas collector's badge, proclaiming Joe among his brethren as a member of the porter's union or at all events as a licensed scullion. But he had seen Joe on the street one Sunday, and Joe had had on his best suit, and in the buttonhole the white feather rested conspicuously. And he could not imagine a good-looking young fellow like Joe announcing by his button-hole, as he promenaded on his Sabbatical inspection of ankles, that he was a member in good standing of the porter's union.

He had wanted to ask Joe what the feather was for, but somehow that did not seem the seemly thing to do. He could ask Keith Webster what that dingus on his watchfob was or ask Lancy Savage what the crest meant on his enormous ring; but he couldn't bring himself to ask Joe what that feather was for … Then, what he had just read suddenly occurred to him and simultaneously occurred, "Damn outrageous nonsense!" this time inaudibly.

"Joe, I don't like to seem impertinent. But would you mind telling me what that feather in your lapel signifies?"

"This?" asked Joe, looking at the feather and then at Eric, the while holding the lapel out for easier inspection. "You mean what this feather is for?"

"Yes, if you don't mind telling me."

"White Falcon, sir."

This answer seemed to satisfy Eric for a moment; but it occurred to him that the White Falcon was as great an enigma as the former one. His curiosity had been laid, and then again it hadn't. If he let Joe go, he would be wondering for another four months what a White Falcon is. And certainly no one among his intimates could tell him. Again Shaw gave him courage.

"But, Joe, do you mind telling me what a White Falcon is or are? Is it a fraternity, a sodality, a union, a decoration, a club, an honour society, or an anti-cigarette pledge?"

"*Polska*," answered Joe and grinned, for he knew that Eric would be flattered : Eric had been trying to pick up some stray Polish from him, and, after conscientious drilling had acquired two expressions, "*Polska*" and "*dobjhe-mu-tak*" to a degree which might be called fluency.

"A Polish society?" asked Eric.

"Yes, sir."

"And what do you do?"

"We drill."

"For anything in particular or just to be drilling, like a Knight of Pythias?"

"No, sir, we are going to free Poland."

"Oooey! From whom?" Here, indeed, thought Eric, was an interesting situation, an adventurer right in his own room, in the person of a quite ordinary appearing porter.

"From Russia. We are getting together all over the country soldiers and money to free Poland."

(Forgive me, please, if I have hitherto omitted to record that all this took place a year or so before the war—before the council at Versailles relieved Joe and his compatriots of their noble responsibility. And, too, possibly, I have failed to make it entirely clear that Eric was then a very young man, yet in college, and with a decent allowance.)

"And, do you have meetings and all that sort of thing?"

"Yes, sir. We are going to have one tonight."

"Tonight, tonight, tonight," mumbled Eric more to himself than to Joe.

He was pondering whether he had anything to do that night. Moreover, he was consumed at the moment with an ardent desire to be present at that meeting of men who were going to free Poland from Russia. He fancied it would be like eavesdropping at an anarchist plot to overthrow the government, a dangerous enterprise like spying upon the sinister doings of fiery-eyed assassins. But Eric approved Nietzsche's dictum: "Live dangerously," though he had not to date, unhappily, been afforded a convenient opportunity further to sanction the dictum by deeds.

Possibilities occurred to him in cinematographic order. Even if Joe should consent to smuggle him past the guards, he would, doubtless, have to learn an incredibly difficult set of pass-words in an impossible space of time. And then, if he should fail, instant death! If he blundered by so much as a misplaced consonant or a false guttural, he would be recognized, his throat would be cut, probably, and his body thrown into the river ... There were many things he had wanted to do in life ... His technique with Louis had proved faulty ... He had been delegated to the fraternity convention next June ... Waldron still owed him that money ... He ought to leave a note telling where he was going. His father surely would set an investigation afoot, and his murderers might be discovered, and the plot to free Poland would go up the spout. But that would be little consolation to a young man with a slit throat, floating down the river. Still ... "Live dangerously."

"I suppose it would be quite impossible for you to take me along tonight, wouldn't it?"

"No," and Joe grinned. "You can go 'long if you want to. We dance and have big time. You want to go 'long?"

Eric jumped up and, overjoyed at the prospect of attending a secret meeting to free Poland without any danger to himself, began pumping Joe as to what he would be required to wear, when the thing took place, and where he was to meet Joe.

II

AT eight o'clock Eric stood on the street corner which Joe had designated. To tell the truth, he was a trifle disappointed in the prospects for the evening.

After all, he mused, this plot (it had ineradicably become a plot in his mind), this plot, it seems, is not up to much snuff if any outsider can attend the conclaves without encountering difficulties. But then, one couldn't tell; possibly Joe felt faith in him, entertained a conviction that Eric would not report the meeting to the police. It was a flattering conclusion. He had, no doubt, the type of face that inspires confidence. But was that a wholly desirable trait? Some doctors have it. And doctors are rather to be envied certain secrets. And priests. But weren't there some disadvantages in being the recipient of confessions? . . No matter, Joe had trusted him, and not a word should escape his lips.

He was turning these thoughts over in his mind when he espied Joe crossing the street in his direction. Amazement overcast him when he perceived that Joe was *bringing his sisters along with him!* A fine sort of secret conclave if women were to be tagging along—and the thought died in his mind; for at that moment he remarked that Joe's younger sister was quite unbelievably lovely and that her taste in dress was curious, but irreproachable. Here before him stood a very caressing assembly of crisp starchings and fluffy web laces, black silk hose and black shoes, the pinkest of pink complexion, hair the colour of burnished bronze, a soft flexible mouth, and eyes which it occurred to Eric, though he had never seen a faun, were faun-like, meaning thereby that they were tender and appealing and confiding and whatnot.

And to the other side loomed Theresa, whose physical shortcomings it is unpleasant to recount.

"I see you here, all right," said Joe. This my sister Theresa; that my sister Theka. We catch that car coming yonder."

It seemed not to matter that Joe had forgotten to mention Eric's name because neither of the girls had said a word during the informal formality. Theresa had giggled. Eric was relieved to observe that Theka had not.

After they had boarded the streetcar, Eric was reminded that he did not know Joe's last name and in consequence must perforce, if he mentioned her by name at all, call Theka Theka. And the idea did not displease him. He did not need to be reminded that on this ride he was going to sit by Theka, even if he had to throw Joe and Theresa out of the car. That was a hyperbole which occurred to him; fortunately there was no need to do so, since the feat would have been quite beyond him.

En route Eric had, by way of preliminaries, begun an amiable and spirited and desultory monologue. It was about himself, of course, for his age precluded that. Then for variety he began asking questions. He was puzzled at first that whatever the question Theka answered him only by a nod or shake of the head, looking at him meanwhile with eyes which gave him strange promptings and a smile that he found subtly satisfying.

"The poor child doesn't know any English," he thought, "No, that can't be. She can take orders well enough and explain about the cooking. But maybe, it's only bill-of-fare English. What I am saying is over her head. Still, good God! I can't make conversation out of fillets and chops and cocoa and soup. This is no place to ask her what desserts she would recommend today."

And so he rode the last third of the journey in silence, rather boastful inwardly at having so delectable a creature at his side and wondering what Lancy and Keith would think of her. This line of speculation had carried him so far afield that by the time Joe came forward to tell him that they had reached the meeting hall, he had dismissed Theka altogether.

They climbed two flights of stairs to a large auditorium, wherein was a glorious din of throaty voices, hearty laughter, scraping of chairs and scraping of catgut. At a long table were seated what Eric took to be the leaders in the "plot," the center figure of which was a florid-faced Silenus with a mass of black hair. To his side were several smart young men in light blue uniforms with red and black trimmings. They were not, apparently, plotting at the moment, but were drinking beer out of huge tumblers. Eric presently became aware that the chief plotter was, if not drunk, at all events in an expressive mood. At intervals he would bawl, "*Vivat Polska!*" in a most disturbing basso profundo. And the entire gathering would take it up.

On a platform in the rear of the room some fifty girls in khaki uniform sat at prim attention, not a little self-conscious. Since Eric saw no men, except the officers, in uniform, he wondered, not unwarrantably, if the women were going to free Poland from Russia. Joe, who had disappeared, came back with four large glasses of beer, which Theresa and Theka and Eric and himself thereupon drank, Eric with a trifle of uneasiness.

While Joe was returning the empty glasses, a violent bedlam broke loose to be concluded by leaving a large floor space vacant, after which the orchestra began a waltz.

Eric watched the others dance for a moment—balloon-busted women and thickset mien,—and he beckoned to Theka. The music was somewhat different from that he had been used to, but he managed decently even from the first and Theka followed him with surprising grace. Consciousness of his step was succeeded by consciousness that there snuggled to him a soft bundle of warm femininity and a tingling took place within him. They ended the dance reluctantly.

Eric gave silent thanks when events made it unnecessary to relinquish Theka to take into his arms the unpretty Theresa. The four of them stood in a corner while a pale young man with a falsetto voice announced something which Eric later divined to be a drill by the girls. These martially clad young women executed their maneuvers with skill and Eric found it pleasant entertainment : there were curves which struck him as exceptionally symmetrical.

In the periodic general scramble which followed the drill as it had followed the dance, Eric gazed about the room and suddenly felt his pulse increase. For, coming toward him, was what he was instantly convinced was the most beautiful girl he had ever laid eyes on. She was dark, lithe, self-assured, with lips that were puckered bits of scarlet velvet and eyes whose glance was a caress. She passed near him and he stared after her. Then, turning to Joe abruptly, he asked:

"Who is that pretty girl, Joe? I should like to meet her."

At that moment he lost whatever answer Joe gave him, because his left hand, which was resting on a chair back, was grasped by a soft hand in a convulsive grip. He turned and looked into eyes in which were mingled despair and the tremulous hope of desperation. They were eyes in which moistless tears lurked—and adoration. They were Theka's.

"Come," she said quickly, "Weel you please, come queek wif me. For a moment, please."

She hurried on out of the door ahead of him and he followed, followed her down the first flight of stairs to the landing. There she waited for him in the dim light. She put her hands on his shoulders and grasped the lapels of his coat.

"Come, walk wif me, please. You weel not meet that girl tonight, weel you? Not tonight, please. I ask you, not tonight. Any night, tomorrow night, not tonight. Tell me, please you weel not, weel you? She ees no good. She got husband already. She got playnta fellows. She ees engaged. Her sweetheart a beeg man. He keel you queek like that."

This incoherent and inconsistent speech dumfounded Eric. He had never been beseeched that way before in his life, nor had any woman ever looked at him in such a manner. He felt tenderness and compassion and even love; but, it occurred to him, that this was not inevitably the sort of place to show it, with other people likely to descend upon him at any moment or some late comer to encounter them on the steps. He took her arm, patted her shoulder, and led her down into the street. The building was at an intersection of streets, one of which was a well-lighted suburban business thoroughfare and the other was less well lighted. He directed her into the latter.

Theka clung to his arm and began shortly.

"Leesen. I luf you, I luf you, I luf you. Only tonight, mebbe, but I luf you. You be mine, tonight, won't you. My fella, please. You don't want to see that other girl tonight, do you? Tell me no. Please tell me no. You breck my heart eef you spik to her. I luf you."

The entreaty died into a plaint and then into an almost inaudible sob.

Eric was visibly and pertinently affected. He hastily considered what was best to be done under the circumstances and decided that it would not be amiss if he put his arms around the girl and reassured her—and, if this venture was successful, he might kiss her.

The which he presently did. And when her soft, moist lips touched his and clung there Eric experienced those physiological phenomena which mankind has immemoriably accounted among its most exquisite pleasures, and which, in the springtime of youth, one does not grow weary of repeating, provided the variety is sufficient. At all events, Eric's faculties soon assembled in cogitable order, which enabled him to a sense of the awkwardness of being encountered while kissing a passively limp figure in the middle of the sidewalk. A policeman was turning the corner.

***

"No, sir, I can get the girls home all right."

"Well, thank you, Joe, for a very delightful evening."

Eric lifted his hat, whistled lightly as he walked to the corner, and hailed a taxicab.

III

THAT night Eric lay awake all of half an hour, pondering lost opportunities, unpropitious circumstances and kindred regrets and fell at last asleep, happy in the memory of the suffusing warmth of Theka's lips.

The next morning he was up early. He took a very hot bath. And then he took a very cold one. He examined twelve shirts and eight ties, and, after some deliberation, decided upon his blue cheviot suit. Then he spent an unconscionable time in shaving and dressing. A timidity and a cold fear seized him as he closed the door behind him and strode toward the elevator. His hand trembled as he pressed the button.

"The grill, sir?" asked the elevator operator, hesitating a moment at that floor.

"No. All the way down." Eric had decided to breakfast at the hotel across the street.

In the lobby he met Lancy Savage.

"Hello! How are you, old boy? Just going up for a bite of breakfast. Eaten yet?"

Eric answered in the negative before he had time to check himself, and then, wishing that morning, of all mornings, to avoid the grill, he said, "I was just thinking of eating across the street. Just for a change."

"Nonsense. Come on upstairs. Eats here are as good as any you can get elsewhere, and you can sign your check."

And two minutes later Eric was following Lancy to a table.

Theka was not to be seen, and Eric sat down with a greater feeling of easiness, and with a comforting hope.

When, however, he had looked over the card, he glanced up and saw Theka emerging from the swinging doors which led to the kitchen. She bore a laden tray in front of her. She looked serene and bright and pretty; but, somehow, Eric wished she weren't there. She served adroitly at the table and, having finished that task, looked about for more stomachs to conquer. She espied Lancy and Eric at the table and came tripping daintily, unswervingly toward them. Eric looked only long enough to observe that there was coolness and remoteness and a business-like servility in her manner.

In a moment she was hovering over Eric's shoulder. Her hand reached out to flip away a crumb in front of Eric. He was appalled an hour later when he recalled that he had wanted nothing so much as to grasp that hand.

"Have you ordered, sir?"

RUBIES IN CRYSTAL

Grace H. Flandrau

I

THERE was something about his morning coat that was so intensely like him. She had not known anyone before she married, at least not well, who wore one. In Westport they mostly didn't.

When he asked her to marry him it was as unthinkable to her, as it would have been to Westport, that she should refuse. As soon refuse God, or George Washington if he should come back to earth. He was the wonder and admiration of the town. He was a diplomat and had known kings and queens. A real diplomat, not a bad political joke, and he had made elaborate studies in Paris when other boys as rich as he would have gone to the devil on Broadway.

But that was long before—long before he chose, whimsically, to spend a summer in the village of his birth. After years of disdain a Scarth had returned to Westport.

He brought servants and reopened the old house. He was all that Westport could have expected. He was grave and courtly, quiet and at the same time grand. His clothes partook of his incredible perfection. So did his morals, although it is possible that Westport, in extolling them, experienced a certain disappointment here. After all, a man who has lived so long in foreign cities—Westport, however, concealed its dissatisfaction and acclaimed the fact that he even went to church. Every Sunday his discreet bald spot reflected the ruby light of the Scarth memorial window from one corner of the Scarth pew, and his flawless morning coat exuded sanctity.

That he should have chosen Lily was, faintly, a second disappointment. When we create deities, we expect them to repay us with disdain. The least they can do is to despise us, else we are cheated of our reverence. Westport couldn't see why he had done it, with all his money and the kings and queens. Lily was nice enough, pretty in a simple Westport way, with yellow curls. But that was all. Lily sometimes wondered too, especially after they were married. It didn't even seem to be the yellow curls, at least not to any indecorous extent. Tilden was as decorous in pajamas as in a morning coat.

At any rate he did ask her to marry him. And when Lily gave her gold head and twenty years into his exalted keeping the town certainly hoped she appreciated the honor done her.

II

THE legation windows were open, and floods and floods of gay, foreign sunshine poured into the high-ceilinged room. They were entertaining at luncheon for the new Italian. Tilden had been stepping about in his morning coat for an hour arranging the flowers and the place cards. He would know to the last subtle distinction where each guest should sit, rank upon rank. He went about his business, not breathing hard—Tilden never breathed hard—but with a consecrated earnestness. She thought she had never seen such clean fingernails, clean and white and even—of course he never committed the vulgarity of polishing them. He smelled faintly of toilet vinegar, he wore white gaiters and a white line around his waistcoat. His morning coat fitted beyond belief. He was really quite bald.

She stood looking down the table. Filet lace and a Dresden epergne with fruit and flowers. The Dresden piece only used in the daytime, silver at night. The bewildering sunshine caught and twinkling in the ruby red of the Bohemian wine glasses. Ruby red, ruby red light, glowing hotter than the ruby light through the Scarth memorial window. "In memoriam, Zacariah Phineas Scarth, Sarah Deborah Scarth"; then the Doxology, "Praise God from whom—" A smell of varnish and lilies, and pretty soon the Sunday gravy and sweet potatoes. Westport.

No, this was another ruby light, dancing in the wine glasses where it belonged. Ah, and the smell of mimosa flowers, sweet, sweet! On her right would sit Amiotti, on her left the nice old Frenchman. Then Madame Cusac, then de Palma. Over there, Mme. de Palma, and next—next— Her heart did a giddy swerve. Something caught her breath. Intoxicating became the mimosa and the orange flower sweetness of the freesias blooming in the Dresden epergne. She was dizzy with the giddy, singing sunshine rioting in glass and silver.

She stepped through the French window onto a small balcony of graystone overlooking the street. An old woman passed with a basket of flowers strapped to her back, bright little bunches tied together in hard knots and a string of little dead birds over one arm.

"Niña, roses and beautiful gardenias—cheap, cheap! Or some little birds to breakfast on—Niña!"

The sky blue, a snowy breeze from the mountain, and the smell of sunshine on hot flowers. Presently, presently he would come, he would be there!

The sun shone straight on Tilden's bald spot, but not into his eyes. You couldn't imagine it shining into his eyes at a diplomatic luncheon. Or anything happening to him. About him all things would be perfect. He was talking gravely and pleasantly, leaning first to this side, then to that. Lily too was talking and laughing, not too much. He had told her to be restrained. But it was hard to be restrained today, knowing what she knew. Knowing the whole monstrous, gallant, shameless sweetness of what she knew. Hard to be restrained when she was drunk, drunk, drunk.

"What is it, eh, eh? What is it that's going on in that charming head?" squeaked old Piroigne, dean of the corps and soon to be retired. He quizzed her, looking into her eyes, taking advantage of his pose of old man. She knew that her eyes were too bright, too dazzling.

"Nothing, dear Baron, nothing."

"Nothing, eh? That's what women always say. I've seen it before in my life," he sighed. "*Sacré tonnere,* what a thing it is to get old! What a damnable thing!"

He turned away from her querulously. Poor old thing! Was it awful to get old? She didn't know. It had nothing to do with her.

III

THEY looked at each other but four times during lunch. Once when they sat down. How gay and caressing his eyes were, at once humble and daring. Again when the fish went out—ah, she had not eaten any of it! She could not eat food today. Then a non-committal glance over the *salade*. Why so noncommittal? Had anything happened? Where things no longer as they had been? No, she had found his eyes again, just now. They were hungry, almost stern. She was comforted. Tilden was talking.

"No, just for a few days. We're leaving tomorrow. Goncourt thinks there may be some quail."

Tilden was going away. He was going off with three or four colleagues into the country. Had that been in the back of her mind all during luncheon? She wondered. She had not consciously thought of it. She was glad that *he* had heard it that way. She would have been ashamed to tell him outright. But why should he know? Why did she wish him to know it? What did she want? She, the wife of Tilden Scarth, wife of the *chargé*. It was monstrous. She was a monstrous woman. What would all these so fine and proper people say if they had any idea?

But there had been really nothing, not so much as a word. Just the knowledge, pulsing back and forth between him and her like crackling, diabolical lightning.

IV

THEY took coffee on the inner balcony, hanging over the courtyard. A balcony smothered round with thick plants, shaded by a gay awning, red and white. It was cool in spite of the blazing sun. The fountain cooled it and that breeze from the hills. And as though the smell of the orange blossoms were not enough, a wanton, drooping, yellow, depraved mimosa set a trap for the very angels in Paradise with its enchanted fragrance.

In continental fashion the men joined the women for coffee. She poured it from the small silver coffee pot with the hot handle. Every little figure in the wrought silver stood out today, startlingly plain. It was as though she had never seen them before—sweet little figures, how sweet they were! Also the thick, brown coffee, strong and aromatic. Her hands trembled a little and the egg shell cups rattled on their saucers.

He was just inside the yellow salon talking to Piroigne. Short, straight nose and full lips. And he wasn't too big. His smile was caressing, even with Piroigne. Caressing eyes and smile—gay, debonair, intoxicating he was, like the county, like this life so undreamed of in Westport! Even Piroigne was captivated. She could see his hand on the young man's knee. She was jealous.

They had met only three times. Once at the opera. She had seen him across the foyer. He was looking at her. She knew he would come. He came swiftly and spoke to her hostess.

"This is Diego, Lily. Mrs. Scarth has heard the Ravallos speak," and so on.

He bowed low, appraising, adoring. In the instant of his greeting he seemed to observe, lovingly, all of her, her golden hair, her ankles, her smooth breast. Next at a tea. There were vague, breathless words on a sofa about—who knows what they were about? Nothing. His arm touched hers as they sat. Accidentally, of course. Of course if he had known it he would have moved. If she had thought he knew it she would have moved. But she did not think so and she did not move. It was too sweet.

They talked and their words were like nothing or like some nondescript thing flung over a hot-bed under which little, fragrant plants were springing up quickly. The very next day she met him on the street. She had been sure when she went out she would meet him. A smile and a question in his eyes, something reverential and impudent, and he passed by, leaving her heart pounding hard thumps that jarred the back of her neck.

The luncheon today was an accident, a fated accident. Someone had failed at the last moment. Tilden said :

"I wonder who we can get, that is, whom. Awkward at the very last—"

She said, "I wonder." Irrationally, as they never had him, she thought, "Tilden will now suggest Diego."

He did. A person, he said, of no importance, but possible. And Diego had come. Soon they would say something to each other. What she did not know. Or perhaps they wouldn't say it. Mysterious raptures would envelop them beyond the scope of speech. Nor was she thinking of caresses. Not thinking of them.

It was the French ministress who brought it about. "Will you dine with us tomorrow, child, since you are to be alone?"

"Thank you, Madame, I will come with pleasure."

"Until then, *chère petite*. As you see, I am leaving Piriogne behind for bridge." And to Diego who stood near her, hat in hand, "May I set you down somewhere, Monsieur?"

"I thank you, my own car is here."

Then they were alone. From the salon came the voices of the players—"Three spades—no, never Burgundy—*Voyons, voyons*—my trick, I think—" The sunlight poured in upon them and lay in still, dazzling pools on the red Turkey carpet and marquetry floor. A tall footman crossed the hall silently behind them with a tray of liqueurs—the dregs of mint and brandy gleaming like emeralds and blood red rubies in the stems of the small glasses. Silently he disappeared. Her gold hair blazed in the sunlight and the pearl gray of her dress dissolved—ethereal.

"Yellow hair," he murmured, "we who are dark must love it. Oh, it is beautiful!"

She raised her charged eyes to his. Unspoken things grew loud between them. Upon its perfect sound came a thin belated tinkle of speech, late because emotion had outrun it. Speech lagged along, dotting the i's. But breathless, worshipful:

"Tomorrow night—afterward? At the little gate—at eleven? At twelve?"

Terrified, she whispered back, "At twelve."

Oh Westport! Oh, horror! Oh, rubies dissolved in crystal and stained glass!

NOT GUILTY

Llewelyn Powys

N O, I have never deceived a living man but, by Jove! I came near doing so on one occasion.

I was staying in a Swiss sanatorium, in one of those colossal oblong buildings fretted with balconies that look so square and incongruous on the mountainside. Life in such places is intolerable.

Day after day I did nothing and thought of nothing; one was in the world and yet not in the world, forsaken, abandoned, on its topmost ledge. It is in these huge hospitals for the rich that half the degenerates of Europe congregate, hoping to eke out an ebbing and worthless vitality. With such people as companions my existence was insufferable. If I went for a walk there was never anything to be seen, the landscape was always the same—fir trees and perpetual snow-covered mountains— that was all. As for the Swiss peasantry—I loathed them; they seemed to me to spend all their time smoking monstrous pipes, yodelling grotesquely and leading from chalet to chalet ridiculous mouse-coloured cows.

Yet even in sanatoriums there may still be found one consolation— for women also, luckily for us, sometimes fall sick. I was not seriously ill and had good prospects of returning to England for the summer months; yet, even so, I cast my eye round for some girl who might enliven the wretchedness of my exile.

I had reached that moment in a young man's life when the desire for amourous adventure is overwhelming, when he can think of nothing else and is ready to follow up any acquaintanceship that seems at all promising.

Well, one day, as I was resting on a green sanatorium seat half-way along the mountain path, another Englishman came up and seated himself at my side. He, poor devil, was very ill. How he had managed to walk so far I don't know : report said that he suffered from a weak heart and might die at any time. After a fit of coughing he told me he had just received a letter from his wife, saying she was coming to him. He could speak only in a whisper because the disease had attacked his throat, but even so I seemed to detect in his utterance that particular kind of pride which belongs to a man who has secured for himself a beautiful and superior woman.

He himself was not a gentleman. He had made his money by manufacturing boots—brown boots—which he had always assured us were the best in the market.

We treated him abominably, with the silent insolence which the upper classes adopt toward inferiors who happen to stray amongst them. He was made to feel out of it, I can tell you.

When I was introduced to his wife I certainly thought her an amazing person. I shall never forget the look in her eyes as we shook hands—a look that seemed to estimate my capacity for giving her diversion—a look provocative, defiant, and at the same time ironic. She belonged to the spoilt pussy-cat type, to the type of women who have no soul and who strangle men daily with languid caresses.

That very evening when "her old man," as she called him, had gone to bed, we sat talking together in the Vestibule. She had evidently taken a fancy to me, for she was extraordinary gracious.

"I know your thoughts," her eyes seemed to say. "You find me attractive—very well then, be bold and treacherous and you shall have me." Even to this day I recall the intoxicating aura of her presence, dressed as she was in silk of Prussian blue that rustled at her least movement and had about it the faint, delicious fragrance of a lady's toilet.

As the days passed I fell more and more under her spell : the tedium of my life vanished—vanished, as it always does vanish, when one is attracted by a woman. She completely fascinated me. Her feminine wit, her chance expressions, her lovely attitudes—I could not resist them.

You know how the personality of a clever woman finds expression for itself in all the petty incidents of daily life. It was so with her—she was always charming. At meal times I would sometimes look across to her table, but with laughing eyes she always contrived to hide behind a vase of tulips. I can never see these flowers in the beds at home without thinking of her exquisite and perfidious beauty.

The manufacturer was obviously flattered by the impression his wife had made and would ask me up to his rooms to drink coffee and liqueurs before we settled down to our afternoon's rest. He used on these occasions to make pathetic efforts to forget the misery of his predicament, but all the time as he whispered and laughed his features wore that curious harassed expression which I have noticed before on the faces of dying consumptives.

I have seen scores of consumptives like him. They become unaccountably preoccupied, their souls seem to sling to the remotest corners of their bodies, reappearing only at the rarest intervals to wave wild, supplicating hands out of the windows of their eyes. His wife would often rally him and call him stupid because of his depression. Her incapacity to understand the bitterness of his situation was a constant astonishment to me. It is no joke for a man who has lived only for the world and its ways suddenly to find himself dying, to realize all in a moment the ghastly and fatal conditions which regulate human existence.

Yet the slightest allusions to the graver aspects of his case were deliberately and persistently ignored. One day after luncheon she asked me up to coffee as usual. Her husband had not been down that morning and she assured me that my presence would cheer him up.

"His temper and temperature are both out of order," she added with a laugh.

I opened the lift door and we ascended together, getting out at the third *étage* and walking down the corridor to my friend's room. We opened the double doors and found it empty. Thinking he might have gone out on to the balcony, she called his name. There was no answer. A friend of his occupied a room opposite and we concluded that he was paying him a visit.

It was the first time we had been in the room alone with each other.

Our eyes met. I touched her hand; she did not take it away. I took her into my arms; she did not resist. Except for the sound of our kisses we were absolutely silent—silent with that strange half-human silence that overtakes lovers when for the first time they abandon themselves.

Then suddenly, in the midst of those tremulous and passionate embraces, I experienced an uncanny sensation of there being another presence in the room with us—I was sure of it! I was convinced we were not alone!

I turned my head.

The doors leading on to my balcony were ajar and through the narrow open space I could see the end of my friend's couch. Judge, then, of my horror, on catching sight of one of the well-known brown boots! He had been there all the time and had perhaps been a witness of our illicit love! What were we to do?

My companion rose and went toward the balcony. From the hard lines on her pretty face I understood that she meant to brazen it out. She pulled open the doors.

"Now!" she said, and there was mocking cruelty in her voice. "Now, that we and the coffee are ready I'll call in my old man."

But she need not have been facetious, she need have said nothing, for her old man was dead!

THE HISTORY OF A PRODIGY

Lewis Mumford

I

I DREAMED about Tempe's baby long before it was born; indeed, long before anyone knew who the baby's father would be. It was manifest from the way that Tempe used to fondle cats, stroke little ornaments, and cuddle the urchins on the street who mistook her for a moving picture star whose name has long vanished from the screen—it seemed plain, I say, from these little indications that Tempe would some day espouse motherhood—joyfully.

This is not to imply that she was the sort of stolid, capacious-bosomed girl who one usually characterizes as "motherly." In those days—what a long time back a decade seems!—Tempe was the embodiment of lithe, mischievous, spirited girlhood, and as the cabarets were having a great vogue and the tango was vanishing reluctantly before the fox-trot, she gave herself over desperately to a round of parties, dances, teas, suppers, and automobile excursions with the miscellaneous riffraff that dropped into our studio. In 1910 Tempe was one of three models I used to illustrate Haddon Richard's serial, "The Battered Moth," and she towered above the other two girls for the reason that Tempe was Tempe, and not merely a model.

To say that Tempe was Tempe is to say that she was a prodigy. I had been acquainted with her, in a casual, friendly way, since her childhood, and I never knew of anyone who combined so many disconcerting excellences. Her beauty, even at the age of ten, was something I prefer not to describe : there is an early portrait by Sir Whiteing Wendy at the

Corcoran Gallery in Washington, in his habitual Gainsborough manner, and at the other extreme, much later in date, is my series of cover designs and illustrations, chiefly for the Megalopolitan Magazine, which portray her after she had budded into adolescence. In spite of Sir Whiteing's densely opulent background and my own infernal superficiality, there is no mistaking Tempe's unique loveliness; and a certain freshness you will find in my portrayal of the July Tennis Girl, the August Swimming Girl, and the September Canoeing Girl derives from the fact that she had a furious capability at all of these sports. Never could I scrutinize Tempe's physique without recalling some lines of Whitman about a splendid motherhood: one felt that, adequately mated, a new race of gods might issue from her womb. Her constitution was of granite, and many a morning she came into my studio to pose for the better part of a day with open eyes whose perfect violet clarity concealed the fact that she had slept for perhaps three hours the night before.

Why Tempe should have preferred to be a model instead of continuing as an actress I have never been quite able to fathom. Ever since the age of five she had been in the public gaze, and I suppose that had a great deal to do with it. Back in 1905 she was the leading child actress in Sir William Kirkie's "The Way to Wonderland." This was her last engagement prior to the wise retirement from the stage that punctuated her growing period. Some time when she was fifteen, she once told me, the late Mr. Charles Frohman had addressed a letter to her mother in which he offered to take Tempe back again under his wing and push her to the front of Broadway with all possible speed. In her fear of being forced back into a profession she had come to loathe, Tempe had become criminally desperate, and had opened and read and finally burned this portentous letter, and a subsequent note of inquiry, before her mother had a chance to get hold of either.

Tempe's mother, a softly aggressive woman, with a tendency to cackle, was hugely proud of her daughter's career, and when one visited their home, as one occasionally did (for, after all, Tempe was Tempe!), one noted that reminiscences, photographs, or clippings were strictly taboo in Tempe's presence. Tempe hated her past with an intensity that caused one no little curiosity, and she kept it buried with an assiduity one could

not possibly mistake for sham. It was only the happy accident of her occasional absence that gave her mother the opportunity to impart to me any
of Tempe's history.

Tempe's excellences were not merely physical. She composed verse
that had a tinkling charm which Henry Cuyler Bunner might have
envied, and her drawings—for she drew, too—showed a talent that was at
least susceptible of cultivation. As a child her mind was swift, accurate,
and forthright. Her mother had had a theory about withholding from her
the smattering of A B C's that is imparted to children at a tender age, and
lo and behold! she had actually learned to read and spell by deciphering,
through tenacious questioneering, the big-lettered advertisements that
she encountered in street cars and billboards.

That was Tempe all over in the days when I knew her best; an eager,
restless, prying, insatiably adventurous creature, as intractable as a filly
that has never felt the bit in her mouth—a perpetual challenge to all that
was stodgy and settled and respectable. Before she was eighteen she had
been engaged to be married at least four times, to my knowledge, so keen
was her desire to experiment; and each engagement was finally broken,
so fearful was she, apparently, that her period of experiment might come
to an end.

II

I MUST not make believe that Tempe retained through the decade that
followed her turn into adolescence all the qualities for which I have given
evidence, in their pristine state. The endless round of distractions into
which she threw herself—a hectic life as she herself used to call it—had
the inevitable effect of making her a little hard and perhaps more than
a little superficial. Her cleverness became a sort of patter; she grew glib,
and her mind became more and more circuitous : in short, she told lies.
Her lies were usually attempts to reconcile the high premises upon which
she conducted her friendships with the rough affronts she delivered them
from day to day. With me she developed a very jolly comradeship indeed,
and we used to tramp around the city occasionally, when the day's work
was done, and talk about all sorts of abstruse matters for hour upon
hour—there was a time when we read Plato together!—but more than

once she threw over an engagement with me for the sake of (I am using her own pat words again) a more hectic evening.

Perhaps Mr. Owen Johnson had Tempe in mind when he wrote "The Salamander," a popular novel that was talked about during that sex craze we had a few years ago. At any rate, Tempe was a sort of salamander in the closing days of this period, and some of us wondered whether she would get married or—burnt. As a matter of fact, she passed through the whole round of experience physically unscathed, but for the fact that she developed scales. Alas! I grieve to confess that she developed spiritual scales.

There was an interval when her face became a little drawn and strained and white, and she rouged too heavily and talked too volubly in order, as it were, to cover it up—and shortly after that her engagement was announced in the usual copper-plate and starched paper.

The event was a shock, for all our guesses had gone wrong. I had conceived that Tempe might, in a fit of compassion, run away with some poor devil of a serious artist to live for a while in an attic off Fourth. Street, or that she might, as a relief from the basically penurious life she was leading, fasten herself in wedlock temporarily to some more or less vacuous millionaire. Tempe did neither; her fiancé was an earnest young business man who practised physical culture, read the *Saturday Evening Post*, and thought that womanhood ought to be protected.

When the marriage took place I was spending a preoccupied year in Nevada. I got back to discover that Tempe had accompanied her husband to Pittsburgh (of all places!) and had taken up residence in one of those hard and bright little suburbs on the Ohio River which shine like occasional diamonds in the long chain of cinders that stretches along the banks. At intervals I wrote her amiable, discursive letters, and the silence with which they were greeted only plagued me to repeat them. Then at last she wrote me a spear-headed little note in which she reminded me of her marriage and insisted that, while she still held me in the highest regard, she could not carry on a correspondence of which her husband, she was sure, would disapprove. The only thing about this note that reminded me of Tempe was the handwriting, and even that was a little changed.

I rationalized my chagrin by developing a series of corrosive witticisms on the general theme of marriage. And presently I forgot Tempe, except to wonder about her babies. The suburban life she had embraced was manifestly favourable to babies.

III

So nine years passed. I made calculations and allowances, and decided that Tempe must have at least four children. Curiously, I heard nothing which permitted me to correct my figures until one day this spring Hilliard Brown, the automobile designer, stopped me in front of the Library and asked me whether I had heard that Tempe was in town.

"I met her by accident," he explained. "She asked after you and said perhaps you would like to see her."

I have nothing important to tell about our meeting. Tempe was not present, even in the flesh. In her stead was a tall woman of some thirty-two, with a blank face whose babyish outlines only heightened the effects of her age. There was an improvised crib in the sitting room of her mother's flat, and a little six-months-old child whose blue eyes were filled with serious amazement was uneasily sitting up in it. The baby charitably distracted my attention from Tempe—from the person who used to be Tempe—for the greater part of my visit, and I hope I managed to conceal the shock of disillusion with a show of idiotic geniality. Some lingering fragment of the old Tempe must have caught the shadow of disappointment in my eyes, however, for she made one or two essays at explanation.

"I have become quite calm and reserved," she said, "not wild, the way I used to be. James and I have a lovely house that overlooks the Ohio, not far from the golf links; I draw a great deal; and of course we have a car. James isn't artistic, you know, and the car is quite a bond between us. Now we have the baby. We really didn't need a baby: James is very steady and he likes his home. The baby is a dear, but somehow I cannot get enthusiastic about him."

"He's a very lively and intelligent little beggar," I hazarded.

"Yes," answered Tempe, "but I hope he won't get too intelligent. I don't want him to be an infant prodigy."

Tempe's mother, who has had many disappointments, and who was never reconciled to Tempe's mediocre marriage, said something caustic about the impossibility of rearing a prodigy from such parents. "He really can't help being stupid," said Tempe's mother to me, with a smile in which raillery played second fiddle to truth. Tempe's eyes narrowed and her face became hard?

"Oh, I hope he *will* be stupid," Tempe exclaimed. "I want him to be— *quite stupid.*"

When I left I wondered whether it was the old Tempe or the new Tempe that had uttered this wish.

THE BLISSFUL INTERLUDE

Myron Brinig

I

ALPHEUS PARR looks far better in death than he ever did in life, and his widow is in Reno. Only it isn't necessary that she should be there, now...

I've just come away from Parr's home, where, in the living room, resting solemnly on two high-backed chairs, is his coffin. It's just an ordinary coffin, black and awesome and horribly comfortable; but lying in it with his toes turned toward heaven, Alpheus looks extraordinary. With the whitest of sheets wrapped about his cumbersome body, his hair carefully brushed to cover the bald spot and his eyes closed, Alpheus looks almost dignified. Curious, isn't it, that a man whose greatest ambition in life was to attain dignity, should accidentally stumble upon it in death? But Alpheus was ever a stumbler, a buffoon, so one more stumble matters very little. Peace to your bones, Alpheus Parr, and it is my respectful hope that in whatever place you have re-opened your eyes, there are souls more sympathetic and kindly than those on this planet which you have now so happily forsworn!

It was at Harvard that I first met Alpheus. I used to observe him waddling shyly from the chapel to the Romance languages. He attained the languages but never got within miles of Romance—although he deluded himself into thinking he had reached that Arcadia after his marriage to Cora. Just a delusion...

There was something about Parr that attracted a comfortable pity in my being. He was forever looking into other men's eyes with that hang-down expression of his that seemed to say, "Oh, take me up, do! I'm not at all a bad fellow when you get to know me!" But Alpheus was never taken up; he was doomed from the cradle to be a gentleman-in-waiting— a dank, clumsy gentleman with moist, begging eyes.

In company with my room-mate, Ross Kemp, a leader in all sorts of college activities, I was walking across the campus one day when Alpheus hove, like a storm-tossed brig, into sight. From a distance of five yards, I could feel Parr's eyes upon us, begging some kind of acknowledgement. Passing abreast of us he gurgled something that sounded like "Hello," though it may have been any other word in the English language. It was all very awkward and pathetic—like an intoxicated man trying to sing a hymn. After he had passed us—I am certain that he did not look back—I turned to my room-mate and asked who the peculiar fellow was.

"Oh, don't you know?" answered Ross, as if the subject weren't of great importance. "That's Alpheus Parr. Funny looking fish, isn't it? They say he's a leetle bit loco upstairs. *I* don't know. Anyway, he's an unhealthy looking bounder."

Perhaps I did not realize it at the time, but Ross's references to Parr prejudiced me extremely in the awkward fellow's favor. "Leetle bit loco?" My interest was strangely, acutely aroused. "Unhealthy?" I resolved to investigate the funny looking fish.

The opportunity presented itself shortly after.

Parr was going to, or coming from some class and his arms were loaded down with books and papers. Men of his type always have great difficulties with objects they are carrying, particularly when the objects are many and of uneven size. As usual, upon seeing me, Parr began to experience unusual emotions—for I was one of the popular ones of the University—and in his efforts to appear harmless and agreeable dropped several books to the ground. I stooped and returned them to him. For a few moments he wrestled with his burdens, physical and of the spirit; then he managed to gurgle, "Thank you."

"Not at all," I returned. "Going my way? Perhaps I can help you."

His soft cowed looking eyes had grown moist with an exceptional experience.

"Would it be any trouble for you—I mean—" he floundered.

He seemed all at sea. I acted promptly and relieved him of some of his books. Then, fitting my stride to his more ungainly one, I began an extraordinary acquaintance. For some minutes he had no words to express his gratitude. Then he turned towards me, quite overcome, and mumbled :

"I hate to put you to all this bother."

"You're not putting me to any bother," I snapped back at him, for now I was beginning to understand why the others shunned him.

We said not another word until we arrived outside his rooms—a surprisingly dignified looking house for so undignified a chap. By the steps we halted, and I was afraid lest he drop the books again in his confusion. At the time I thought him an awkward ass, but now I know that he was debating with himself whether or not I would consider it an insult if he asked me in. Imagine that! I solved his momentous problem for him by preceding him up the flight of steps. He must have followed me joyously.

His rooms, I thought, were exceptionally well and tastefully furnished. Evidently, Parr's family had money. I remember seating myself in a comfortable chair without invitation—how superior undergraduates can be!—and calmly lighting a cigarette. Parr, having disposed somehow of his books and papers stood uncertainly in the center of the room looking at the ceiling. From top to bottom he was sloppy with the sloppiness of the soft and abnormally self-conscious. His features were sloppy, his hands were huge and damp looking, and his clothes had a dissipated, stale look.

"Nice place you have here," I began in a self-satisfied way.

"Ya, yep. It's not so much," acknowledged Parr still gazing at the ceiling.

I picked up a book lying on the table. Moore's "Memoires of My Dead Life."

"Moore," I remarked, not without a trace of surprise. "Smooth style that fellow has."

"Oh, so you've re—," began Parr. "Hasn't he? Lovely... Style... lovely... Have you seen my Keats?"

"No," I invited. "Where?"

It took Parr an unaccountably long time to bring his body into accord with his promises, but presently he was showing me a fine set of the poet's work. And he was talking intelligently about the poems! "Loco?" Certainly not. "Funny fish," maybe. But certainly not "loco." Only a buffoon...

It is extraordinary how articulate shy people can be at times. Inside the hour I was possessed of practically all his history. And I was beginning to piece Alpheus together. His father was a publisher of some note among the excessively high-browed, but his mother was dead. He hadn't cared about coming to Harvard particularly. He had felt that he would be out of place in the slender hipped, athletic atmosphere of college... but to please his father...

"I'm so funny," said Alpheus getting his foot caught in the rug. "I wish I was different. No one seems to like me... "

I got up to go. His cumbersome, moist manners were beginning to wear on me. If he would only have exercised that seal-like body of his! If he would only have put on running trunks and set those flabby legs of his in motion!

"You'll come again?" he begged of me at the door.

"Yes, thanks," I accepted a trifle wearily and looked away from his worshipful eyes... Outside the air was so crisp, and there was a haunting smell of woodsmoke.

II

I CONTINUED to see Parr on and off for the rest of my college career. After I left Harvard, I lost touch with him for two years, and when I thought of him at all it was rather like a soiled page in a neglected book. It was at a Fifth Avenue art gallery that we met again. It was there that Alpheus met Cora Lear for the first time. Cora is a sort of relative of mine—a third or fourth cousin I believe. Why on earth she happened to be viewing an exhibition of art, I can't for the life of me remember. At any rate, there she was at my elbow, pretending an interest in nudes in and out of the bath.

In order that there may be no misunderstanding, I must say at once, that Cora herself, in the nude, must be a stunning creature. She's the blazing sort of woman and it's easy to catch fire from her. A noted French artist has called her the most beautiful woman in America—mind you, not the world, and hence his statement carries some weight. Certainly, she whipped Parr's craving spirit cruelly. Optically, therefore, Cora was very much at home in Fifth Avenue art galleries. Spiritually, she should have been at her kennels.

One of the numerous newly sprung psychoanalysts once told Cora that she would never love any man as much as she loved her dogs. She had a dozen of them, I believe, ranging from one of those absurd toy poodles to a gigantic St. Bernard. She never walked out but there was a dog by her side, and she never fell asleep properly without that St. Bernard somewhere in the vicinity. I believe she would have slept with the dog but for the fact that he took up so much room. I believe she included Giant in her prayers—Giant was the St. Bernard's name. He's dead now, and there's a great shaggy granite tombstone to mark the place where he lies. Alpheus will hardly have one as impressive.

But to get back to the art gallery. Cora and I stopped to look at one of the whitest of the nudes emerging from a nondescript bath-tub. What a figure! One of those cool, white nudes that seem a thousand worlds away from the way of all flesh. There was a spiritual beauty about the figure in the painting, a cruelty of far-away beauty. She had moved Alpheus Parr to tears. I heard someone sniffling at my elbow, and looking about vexatiously, I beheld a familiar profile, a profile that seemed to have oozed down from its proper proportions.

"Alpheus Parr," I mumbled.

He did not hear me—how could he so far away from me?

"Stop that idiot, will you?" Cora commanded me.

Naturally, she could not abide anyone, particularly a foolish looking man, moved to tears by a piece of canvas with paint on it. For a moment, I feared that Cora would treat Alpheus roughly, so I touched him on the shoulder. He looked at me uncomprehendingly.

"Well, well, Parr, fancy meeting you here!" I said warmly.

Then he remembered.

"You!" he gasped.

I reached for his hand and shook it. In my grasp it felt like a mess of warm dough. Hands ought to be educated.

I turned to Cora—Oh, she shouldn't have been there—and introduced her. She took to him at once and shook his hand in the same way she shakes a paw. "Parr? Parr? Where have I seen your name?"

Of course this was a little bit too much for Alpheus. A beautiful nude and then the most beautiful woman a French artist has seen in America! The wonder of it all was that he didn't go mad on the spot. "Where? Where?" she petted him. Oh, these dog women!

Words came to Alpheus at last.

"On a book, maybe," he managed to say.

"A book?" asked Cora. "Then you are an author?"

Alpheus looked pleased to the verge of pain.

"I'm a publisher," he acquainted her.

Cora should have quit there; she should have left him to his nude on canvas. These shy men become a trifle mad when they meet up with substantial ideals.

"Now I remember," said Cora. "I believe you are the publisher of that remarkable book, 'A Dog's World.' I'm sure you are."

When Alpheus admitted to this, Cora seemed to forget my existence. It was—well, preposterous. Never one had encouraged Alpheus to such a degree in such a short space of time. As for Alpheus, he must have been inwardly hysterical with the wonder of it all. Cora invited him to tea on the spot, and I had to help him into the car. Unaided, he would hardly have been able to manage it all. Cora evidently understood the man. How, under the sun, I had not the faintest idea. Now, I know.

His life was like a day that begins with a thickly depressing drizzle; in the late afternoon the sky opens his great blue eyes with a look of sublime bewilderment; and then the sun steps out from behind a cloud with a golden unexpectedness. Cora was as dazzling as she was unexpected. He lay back against the cushions of the limousine hardly daring to look at her for fear that a cloud would suddenly cover her and she would disappear again into the long dreary morning.

We came, at last, to her home, a large, rambling growth in the suburbs, and she led us out into the garden, rather crowded with lilac bushes and dogs. The dogs welcomed her vociferously and they sniffed at Alpheus kindly as if they had known him all their lives. He made several awkward attempts to pat them, and they jumped up and licked his face and hands. He had a way with them.

Presently, the favorite of the kennels, Giant, was led out to us. He was no longer young and nimble. He came slowly and reluctantly, and his eyes ran—for joy of seeing his mistress, presumably. Cora introduced him to Alpheus very gravely; Giant held out a nonchalant paw and Alpheus shook it with something approaching enthusiasm.

"Nice doggie," he murmured vacuously. "Nice doggie."

"He's twelve years old," Cora informed us. "He keeps his figure remarkably. But I'm having trouble with his food. He hasn't the appetite that he had."

Alpheus murmured something unintelligible in response. What did it matter whether or not Giant had an appetite! Lucky dog to be so frequently in the presence of his mistress. Alpheus sipped his tea as if he were in the Garden of Eden rather than a garden of dogs. He probably saw himself alone with Cora in a far-away land. She was the center. There were no dogs—at least they weren't conspicuous; only himself and herself—with probably the whitest nude, the finest set of Keats and a Chopin Nocturne thrown in for good measure.

"I'm so attached to Giant. If he should die, I believe I'd go crazy," Cora was saying.

"But he will die some day," I informed my third or fourth cousin. I thought her slightly ridiculous.

Cora at once became amazingly unstrung. She upset her cup of tea on Parr's frock coat.

"I'm so sorry! Awfully clumsy of me!" she apologized.

"Oh … It's nothing," said Alpheus looking at her with his life in his eyes. He seemed greatly honored that the tea she had been drinking was on his frock coat. Something to take away with him.

"I'm so attached to Giant, you see," she explained. "I can't bear the thought of his being dead. The dog is part of my life."

"I understand," said Parr with a ridiculous reverence. Of course he did no such thing. The man was simply stretching himself in the sunlight—warm, gorgeous sunlight. I doubt if he realized he was living the experience. He must have felt that the next moment someone would wake him, and he would look out, and it would be cloudy and blue and tragic.

I finally led him away. Before taking his leave, he promised to come again in a few days when the three of them, Cora, Giant and himself, would go out for a stroll together. On the way back to town, he spoke only once. I told him that I thought the winter we had just been through had been unusually mild. He said, "Beautiful," and closed his eyes. I was glad to leave him at his apartment. He waddled away without even saying good-night.

I beheld the unusual spectacle of Alpheus Parr in love.

III

"SHE treats me abominably," Ross Kemp complained to me several days later at the club. "Perhaps she doesn't love me, but she might respect me as much as she does her dogs."

"Are you really in love with Cora!" I asked my old room-mate. "If you are, I feel dreadfully sorry for you."

"I am in love with her," Ross emphasized. "And please keep your pity to yourself!"

I retreated behind my newspaper.

"She is amazing!" Ross re-commenced. "This afternoon we had arranged to go to a matinee together. I bought the tickets—had a hard time getting them; the play's a success—and went out to get her. Well, I might have known! She wasn't in. The housekeeper told me that she was out strolling with that damn dog, and a man. After I had got the tickets, too. Don't you think—"

"A man?" I inquired from behind my newspaper.

"Yes. Mr. Parr or Carr or something."

"Ah," I said, putting aside my newspaper. "You mean Alpheus Parr."

"There, that's it," affirmed Kemp. "Who is he, anyway? Where did she meet him?"

"Why Ross, you must remember Parr? That fellow at Harvard who was so out of things? Parr, the publisher?"

"That—boor!" Ross flung a half-smoked cigarette at the ash-tray and missed. "Why should she go out walking with him? Why, I can't imagine…He's not bearable. But then, what do you expect of a woman who worships dogs?"

"That's just it, Ross," I told him. "Don't expect anything of Cora. She's the strangest girl in the world. Born that way. You just fall out of love with her, Ross, as quickly as you can. Go and take that engineering job in Central America, or wherever it is, and forget about her." And then I resumed my newspaper.

"You don't understand," observed Ross. Straight and handsome and clean as a man could be! Dear old Ross! That bridge of his that spans the Amazon ... And not only that. A man who used to win debating matches and football games at Harvard. A man with a future; the best friend in the world. And here, she had gone out strolling with a twelve-year-old St. Bernard and a clown with baggy trousers! Well, well ...

"Perhaps I had better go down to Central America." Ross was bending over my chair and his voice sounded as if he wanted me to argue him out of it.

Instead, I said, "By all means, Ross! And by the time you've come back, she'll be ready to jump at you!"

V

THREE months later, Cora and Alpheus were married. The outcome of that strange courtship shocked me, but Alpheus must have been the most shocked of all. In a few miraculous months to be lifted out of the slough of morbid ineptitude to the heights of glorious romance is enough to make any man wake sensitively to the downright goodness of human existence. But life if not one, it is a series of awakenings, and tomorrow we may open our eyes to tragedy.

Those same qualities in Alpheus Parr that others found repugnant drew Cora irresistibly. Those gaping uncertainties of manner, the gawky shyness, the weakness of his features, the sloppiness of dress, in short, the whole impossibility of his excuse for counting himself acceptable in most eyes, made Cora fall in love with him. After that first stroll together Alpheus became her slave; never a man lived who worshipped a woman so absolutely. He lost no opportunity to make himself useful to her; there was something irrevocable about the way he answered her moods. And he wanted nothing in return but just the small favor of looking at her—looking, and treasuring every aspect of her beauty. What must have been his divine bewilderment when she suggested marriage! His gratitude must have wrung his very soul.

Not that she hadn't encouraged him. She used to take him out into the garden and feed him tea and cakes while she fed the dogs bones and chocolates. And when she was absent in town, it was Alpheus who watched jealously over the dogs until her return. To his especial care she gave Giant. The two, dog and man, became inseparable—although I am sure Alpheus would not have felt the least spark of interest in the dog had the mistress been other than she was. I often beheld the ludicrous spectacle of Giant and Alpheus walking along the road, putting up with each other because their mistress so willed it!

"Really," I remember saying to Cora one day after having met the two on the road, "I can't for the life of me understand what you see in the man. And Ross eating out his heart in Central America!"

Cora got quite angry with me that day, and her anger is the snappish kind. "You are insulting Alph—Mr. Parr I won't have it. Do you hear?"

I had never seen her in precisely that mood before, and I was amazed at the instantly summoned venom. Cora has always been a study to me; now I was bewildered by a new facet she showed me. She was an infinitude of perversities—men fell in love with her and she fell in love with dogs.

Alpheus reappeared at that moment, and Cora became her usual self again.

"Did you have a nice walk, you two? I'm so glad you like each other! Come, let's go out into the garden, and I'll have something hot for the both of you."

Giant wagged his tail in an emotional manner and Alpheus grinned down at his shoes. Parr was certainly coming along in Cora's estimation, for she included very few mortals in the same breath with Giant. I saw them enter the garden, the woman moving briskly in front, the man and animal following with muffled exclamations of appreciation. I felt an almost uncontrollable desire to laugh until I was blue in the face. Instead, I scowled and left them abruptly.

Then one morning, Giant turned in his tail and died. It was awfully unusual and inconvenient. Cora achieved the epochal and cried. The dog lay stretched out, immensely still, amazingly cold, in Cora's bedroom. When he refused to stir, Cora called shrilly for her servants, and they came, but nothing could be done about it. Dead dogs are as dead as dead people. In a way, their lack of life is even more emphatic than the lack in humans, because one expects death from the higher animals, whereas in the lesser there is something radically different about it.

"He's dead! He's dead! What shall I do?" Cora demanded of her servants.

After a few minutes, the gardener suggested that she might bury him.

"What!" cried Cora. But the gardener was correct as things turned out. He had to be buried sooner or later, and the sooner the better. Cora began to realize this after an hour or so. She summoned Alpheus to the telephone and ordered him to be at the funeral the next day. No one else came to Cora's mind. No one else could. The dog had become inextricably linked up with the man.

Cora had the gardener procure a casket with silver handles, and inside Giant was laid with his sapphire studded collar and his various wraps. The journey to the cemetery was solemn. The casket was placed on the floor of the limousine, and the two mourners sat in silence. Halfway out, Cora asked Alpheus to take her hand, and he obeyed. She looked up into his eyes sadly.

Upon that instant he ceased to think of the dead dog. But then, the dog had always been a background for him. It was always Cora in his eyes. Cora was the beginning and the end. Whatever she chose to do was as right as the sun and the rain and the stars.

On the way back from the cemetery Alpheus accompanied her to the monument works where she arranged for the shaggy granite stone that now marks the place of Giant's ashes. Then the two motored back to the house in the suburbs and secluded themselves. The house must have seemed curiously empty to her at first. But as the days passed the ache of Giant lessened. In his death was the triumph of Alpheus Parr. When the dog had lived he was secondary. Now that there was no Giant, he became the favorite slave of the household—to Cora he made up for that which had been taken from her. More and more of his time was taken up with that extraordinary woman … And they were married.

V

Ross Kemp had departed for Central America a man of uncertain capabilities and wavering will. He returned, true steel. From an indefinite, undecided boy, he had developed into a genuinely strong power, a man of determination. Months of battling alone and overcoming the most stubborn difficulties had turned the trick. When he grasped my hand in the club, I felt the contact of a grim sureness gripping me. Of course I had always vaguely realized that Ross had the makings, but the surprise of his matured assurance was none the less disturbing. I felt securely carried away.

"Man of deeds, how are you? You've the zip and flash of a brand new locomotive!"

"Thanks," he answered. "Well, I've come back to marry Cora. Is she ready to jump at me?"

"You've come—really?"

"Good God, how I've longed for her!" he grumbled.

This was really very good! "Cora is already married," I told him. "Hadn't you heard?"

He let go of my hand very suddenly, and I felt like a swimmer must, who abruptly realizes a discouraging case of cramp. "Married? No. No, I hadn't heard that. Whom did she marry?"

"Alpheus Parr." The name caused me a certain degree of nausea. If I could only have laughed!

"Who is Alpheus Parr?"

Curious how Ross kept forgetting that man! "You remember Ross, surely? The publisher? That peculiar chap ... "

"Oh ... Well ... "

"Well, Cora married him, Ross."

"What for!"

VI

It was funny to see Cora leading that husband of hers about town—that peculiar personality who had succeeded into the place left vacant by a St. Bernard. She showed him everywhere, not the least abashed, and though everyone grinned behind their backs, she continued to lead. It wouldn't have made the least difference to Cora if they had grinned directly at her. And Alpheus wore that expression of plaintive adoration in his eyes. It was obvious that he, himself, did not understand "what for." It was enough for him to realize the *actuality* of it. Someone had pushed him to the peak. He was there, sniffing the air of the heights, a trifle dazed, perhaps, but what of that?

Extraordinary personalities, Cora and Alpheus—there is hardly any explaining them. It's like trying to explain a beaver mothering a blind puppy—a rare occurrence, but not without the bounds of probability since it has been known to happen. Now it is only necessary to lift the gate and enter in the ruthless, stabilizing force, Ross Kemp, and you have the divine comedy, complete.

I do not know exactly where Ross met Cora again, but wherever it was, the rekindled sparks of passion must have flown merrily. There can be no doubt in my mind now, that Ross returned from Central America at the propitious moment. Cora was beginning to tire of Alpheus. There had been moments when that husband of hers must have demanded something of herself—and Giant had never demanded anything of that especial kind. How Alpheus could have so far forgotten himself, is a mystery. But perhaps there was something in him that had gotten the upper hand, for the time being, something of the animal in every man that demands its purple nights. Alpheus had been caught napping on the heights, and his wife had shaken him rather roughly. Cora allowed her household pets unusual freedom, but when it came to licking off the table plates.

The novelty of Alpheus was beginning to wear off, but he, of course, did not understand the change. His eyes begged forgiveness from her every moment of the day, but Cora had become wary. He tried to make it up to her with jewels and flowers, and succeeded in irritating her the more. He ought to have known his place.

It was at a dinner dance given by Ross's mother to celebrate his return from Central America that the definite break between them came. Alpheus was the duck out of water at these affairs, and this particular event was no exception. The party found him at his incomparable worst. He seemed deplorably at variance with his evening clothes, his hands and his feet. These things had not irritated Cora before, but tonight, the conquering hero, Ross, happened to be sitting at her elbow. And Ross was in his particular glory. Beside him, Alpheus appeared a preposterous imitation, a caricature. Cora was obviously ill at ease with her husband, and gave herself up to Ross's conversation. I noticed that Alpheus looked relieved to find that his wife was having an interesting evening—boredom had been becoming frequent with her. Public gatherings always filled him with terror, and at them, he spent most of his time pretending an interest in the furniture.

Alpheus never danced, and for a long time Cora had abstained because she had lost interest. But at Mrs. Kemp's affair she re-entered into the exercise with Ross as partner. I observed them moving gracefully across the floor, and it seemed quite natural for them to be so close together. It must have been then that Cora succumbed to the greater realities. Probably the strength of Kemp's arms awakened Cora's somnolent desires after so many years. In such a splendid creature as Cora, sex is bound to come out sooner or later, and unfortunately for Alpheus, it came later.

Toward the close of the evening, they disappeared from the floor, and did not re-appear again until "Home Sweet Home." Alpheus, meanwhile, had been making some half-hearted attempts to find his wife, and had looked everywhere but in the green-house. If he had entered there, he would have been considerably shocked. As it happened, I had been the one to come upon Cora and Ross kissing away all of the obstacles in the world. Well, Cora had fallen in love three years too late. Out in the hall I collided with Alpheus, and it came over me all of a heap that he was Cora's husband. It took me a few minutes to pull myself together again.

"Did you find her?" Alpheus asked sleepily.

"No—yes, she'll be here directly." I hoped to God they would.

Presently, Cora and Ross made their belated appearance, and we were all bundled into that historic limousine of hers. She looked younger than she had in months and Ross seemed strangely at ease. I remembered his, "I've come back to marry her" and stole a glance at Alpheus. He sat alone in one corner, raising his eyes now and again to the splendid vision of his wife. She had never looked more beautiful.

When we reached the house in the suburbs, Alpheus got out of the car first and stood beside the door offering his hand to Cora. She made as if to descend, then seeing Alpheus for the first time in several hours, drew back involuntarily and motioned Ross with her eyes to get out first. And it was he who assisted her out and let his firm brown hand linger with a tender authority upon her arm. I saw Alpheus following them obsequiously up the steps, across the threshold ...

VII

FROM what Cora has since written me—her letters are distressingly frank—and from what I know of Parr's character, I have been able to reconstruct, bit by bit, that last dreadful evening. For five months Cora -had been flaunting her new discovery of love in everybody's face. Only Alpheus misunderstood. The woman had mesmerized him when she married him, so it is easy to understand his blindness. He was frankly glad that Ross had returned to "entertain my wife—I'm afraid I'm such a bore." It is small wonder then that his awakening should be so piercingly tragic.

After dinner, Cora came down, dressed for traveling, and informed her husband very coolly that she was leaving him forever. They were in the dining-room, and Alpheus dropped a log into the fireplace with such vehemence that the sparks flew up and bit his cheeks.

"What did you say, dear?" he asked, still looking into the fire. There is something about a fire that robs the very moment of its cruel contours.

"I'm going to Reno tonight, Alpheus. I've bought my ticket. I'm not coming back. I'm going to marry Ross-Kemp."

Alpheus turned about slowly so that he faced his wife. He dreaded to look into her eyes, but when he did he knew it was all over, ended—this unutterably blissful interlude.

"Cora ... "

"I never loved you, Alpheus. You must know why I married you."

He opened his mouth but said nothing. There was a collision of far-off planets sounding in his ears.

"I love Ross, Alpheus," she said with terrific candour. "If he wanted to kill me, I'd let him."

"You—you don't love me, Cora!"

"No. Look out! The flames will burn your coat."

The pitiful expression in his eyes! "Then why did you marry me, Cora?"

"You ask and ask! Can't you keep quiet? You're such a noisy old fellow. Your eyes—they're just like Giant's. After he died, I had to have someone around me to remind me of the dog." She went up to him and began patting him on the head. "You have the kindest eyes in the world, Alpheus— so sweet and pleading—like dear old Giant's. Now run off to bed, dear fellow, and be thankful you're rid of me." Then the maid brought down her bag, and she left the house. Alpheus was alone. Far off, a dog howled, howled, howled…

"Cora!" he screamed. "Cora! Cora!"

The maid reappeared in the door with a very frightened face. "She's gone, and she said for you to go to bed, sir. Will you, sir?"

He said nothing. He merely stood in the center of the room, swaying slightly. The maid disappeared.

He merely stood. It must have been an hour later that he went to the library table and removed something from one of the drawers. Then, without hat or overcoat, he went out of the house. He walked and walked. There was a bench. He sat down mechanically. It was a bright evening. The moon shone.

A mongrel cur came up to him and sniffed his heels. The moon shone into the dog's eyes—sweet and pleading. Alpheus remembered swiftly as a falling comet. The cur looked up at him as if begging a caress.

"Oh!" sobbed Alpheus. He removed the gun quickly and fired into the dog's eyes. Then he pressed the muzzle to his temple. There must have been an instant of remembering the most amazing happiness…Keats and Chopin and her…then nothing at all.

***

With the whitest of sheets wrapped about his cumbersome body, his hair carefully brushed to cover the bald spot, and his eyes closed, Alpheus looks almost dignified. Curious, isn't it, that a man whose greatest ambition in life was to attain dignity should accidentally stumble upon it in death?

THE RENUNCIATORY GESTURE

Mabel McElliott

ALL her life she had practised it—the gesture.

It had begun, this "play acting," when she was very, very small indeed. She remembered darting guiltily away from the mirror in her mother's room at the sound of a warning footstep in the hall. Draped in a shawl, her mother's best hat sliding giddily down her shining, freckled little forehead, she had been practising it.

The Renunciatory Gesture.

That, at least, was what she had called it after she grew up.

Then she knew it was only fun to draw her turquoise ring grandly from her finger, strike a haughty attitude (observing herself meantime in the mirror) and say, to an imaginary suitor:

"This is the end ... " or

"Take it, please," ... or

"Everything is over between us."

Small as she was, she had greedily sampled the books of romance which their limited library afforded; and this was one of the dramatic bits she had treasured for herself from the frayed pages of some old novel by the Duchess, perhaps; or Laura Jean Libby; or Rosa Nouchette Carey. She really could not say where she had read it first.

At fourteen she still played the game. Time did not seem to dull its charm. Then she had been violently and silently in love with the somber dark-haired boy down the street : the one who wore a tiny red cap when he played baseball, and whistled "Cheyenne, Cheyenne, Hop on My Pony" when he went to the store for his mother.

She used to sit happily in the dark, of nights, watching the light that streamed from the window of his house. And sometimes, when dreams palled, she would practise the gesture again. She would pretend she was twenty…and beautiful.

It was not easy to imagine, the beautiful part, but she managed it somehow. Yes, her freckles somehow miraculously effaced…her painfully straight hair a glory of tumbled curls…her eyes "strangely sweet and blue as cornflower" (that was another book phrase)…she would charm the somber one.

She would be lovely in a frock of pale yellow, and come dancing down a dark old staircase into a room sweet with firelight and flowers. He would be there, at the foot of the stairs. Awed by her beauty, he would gasp out broken phrases of adoration. Would press upon her a ring…"with a single glittering stone in it."

She would stand there, tense, for a moment. Would look at him with great, mysterious eyes.

Then she would put it back into his hand with a gesture of ineffable pity.

"Take it please," she would murmur, in tones of incredible sweetness.

"Is there someone else?" the boy would ask, with a note of bitterness in his voice.

She would nod her head slowly in assent…

That was as far as she ever got with that particular day dream. When she had got to that point, she would begin all over again—pale yellow frock and all. But sometimes the frock would be mauve. Or pale blue. Or ladyslipper pink. She varied that part of it. And sometimes she would be carrying an armful of flowers, which she would drop in surprise, as she caught sight of him.

When she was sixteen, the dream changed. There was a violinist who led the orchestra in the stock company theater near her home. He had been there a long time before she noticed him. She had been absorbed in dreams…

She had not actually observed him until one memorable afternoon when he had risen in his place in the pit to play a solo. It had been, she remembered, that poignantly sentimental, "Believe Me, If All Those Endearing Young Charms." (Because it was St. Patrick's Day, probably.)

At any rate, she had been bewitched by the dragging loveliness as the notes dripped from his violin. She had noticed, for the first time, that he was young and astonishingly good-looking; that he had fair hair and a cleft chin and keen blue eyes. That he looked more like a rising young business man than the leader of an unimportant orchestra in an unimportant outlying theatre.

She had been in a highly impressionable state, helped along, probably, by the romantic tenor of the drama the company presented that day; and she had fallen for him with all her heart.

Yes, after that he had been, in her dreams, the Hero. The superman to whom she paid homage. Then she had begun again to practise the gesture upon *him*.

He would ask her to marry him ... In gentle, flowery, fervent language, he would attempt to press upon her the boon of his manly devotion.

She would sigh ... turn her head delicately (like a lily on its stem) and accept. Later the Gesture would come into play ... this after he had offended in some way—negligence—or lack of understanding—or something ...

Then she would put the ring back into his hand, gently ... but finally—

Yes, all her life she had planned this, this *coup d'etat.*

All her life she had been waiting, subconsciously, for this triumphant moment.

Now it was no good ... no earthly use.

All her rehearsals had been in vain.

As she stood in the dreary, smoky dawn of an August morning, looking wearily down the dim cañon of the street, she realized that her chance had come, and that somehow she was being cheated of it.

Cheated in a fashion that was wickedly unfair.

She looked with distaste at her husband, sleeping heavily on the untidy davenport bed. At the ugly room. The old-fashioned grate was littered with cigarette ashes. The remnants of their midnight supper, over which they had drearily quarreled, stared at her from the dim table in the kitchenette, beyond.

Yes, she was being cheated of her Moment, even as she had been cheated of life and romance.

She was leaving him. Clearing out for good and all. This was the time to put to use, in a real drama, the gesture she had perfected through years of dreaming.

But she could not. Could not toss her head … turn it slowly on her slim throat … press into his limp palm the jewels he had given her.

The irony of it struck her as she paused before the streaked mirror to put a final pathetic touch to her cheap hat.

She could not give back her wedding ring.

He had pawned it the night before.

THE SECRET OF SUCCESS

Donald Ogden Stewart

I

THE young man in search of employment came at last to the inner shrine in that temple of Modern Business known as the Ellsworth Products Co. As he stood hesitating at the portals, one of the high priests advanced to meet him, chanting the greeting of his order.

"Mr. Ellsworth is a very busy man. A *very* busy man," he droned, and at each pronouncement of the name "Ellsworth" the heads of the seven stenographic vestals in the office were reverently bowed.

Five times that morning in five outer offices had the young man been told that Mr. Ellsworth was a very busy man; five times had his letter of introduction carried him through the efficient obstacles which guard the inner temple from the eyes of infidel unbelievers. And now, his pilgrimage ended, for the sixth and last time he gave his name—Richard Kennedy, his business—an interview with the president regarding employment, his credentials—a letter of introduction from one of Mr. Ellsworth's friends.

While this letter was being examined, young Kennedy reverently surveyed the temple.

At one end was a huge mahogany door—the entrance to the throne room. His gaze fell next upon the seven virgins, busy at their consecrated stenographic tasks. One glance at these maidens told him that he was indeed on holy ground, for they were of such loveliness as belongs only in the offices of high executives. Kennedy had already, in the course of his pilgrimage, noted the significant business fact that standards of office furnishings and stenographic beauty increase progressively as one ascends in the scale of executive rank—exemplified in the present instance by the impressive early Georgian hangings and late Ziegfeldian typists of this office as contrasted with the plain chaste furniture and plainer, chaster stenographers of the lower departments.

"Sit down, Mr. Kennedy," said the president's private secretary, "Mr. Ellsworth is a very busy man."

Young Kennedy obediently took the designated chair outside the throne room door, from behind which he could hear at intervals a faint swishing noise. He idly wondered as to its cause, and one heretical thought which occurred to him before he could check himself was that it sounded somewhat like the noise made by the swinging of a golf club.

His eye fell upon a magazine lying on a nearby desk. *Efficiency* it was called, *Efficiency—The Journal of Success*. He picked it up and was soon deeply engrossed in a fascinating article concerning a business man of Tacoma, Wash., who had actually eliminated twelve minutes wasted time per clerk per day by the masterful ingenuity of having the fountain pens of his employees filled each evening by the night watchman.

The next article, entitled "How I Make Men Like Me," was by Abraham Nussbaum, sales manager for the Sutco Tire Co., illustrated with graphic and convincing photographs of Mr. Nussbaum caught in the very act of making men like him. "The secret of my success," confessed Mr. Nussbaum, "is personality. Personality and pep—that's the stuff, boys!" And farther on in the article he gave this advice : "Radiate magnetism! Envelop your customer with your personality. Practise at home before a mirror until you are sure that everything about you radiates personal magnetism."

Young Kennedy looked around for a mirror, but before he had time for any practise in the radiation of personal magnetism, the private secretary announced that Mr. Ellsworth was ready to see him.

The swishing noise had ceased; all was silent behind the mahogany door. The high priest took the young man by the arm. A bell was struck, the seven vestals bowed their heads, the door swung open, and the worshipper beheld the Great Man seated on his throne. He stepped forward, trembling; the door closed behind him.

Richard Kennedy stood alone before the president of the Ellsworth Manufacturing Co.

"Well, young man—" and President Ellsworth directed at Kennedy those keen eyes which, as described in the April number of *Efficiency*, seem to "look right through you."

"Yes, sir," said young Kennedy. And then he added, by way of explanation, "Yes, sir."

"Well, young man—what do you want?"

The idea of wanting anything suddenly seemed so incredibly blasphemous to the young man that for a moment he was silent. Then he ventured to give his name, his request for employment and his letter of introduction.

Mr. Ellsworth adjusted an impressive pair of gold-rimmed eyeglasses to his nose and gravely examined the letter with that shrewd, keen glance which had so impressed the interviewer for *Efficiency*. His shrewd, keen comment, "You want a job, young man?" after he had finished the letter asking that young Kennedy be given a chance, showed that he had instantly grasped the fundamentals of the situation.

"Yes, sir," replied Kennedy, adding, apologetically, "I'm just out of college."

President Ellsworth took off his eyeglasses. There was an impressive silence. Finally the Great Man gravely clipped the end off a cigar, lighted it slowly, and spoke:

"Young man, when I first came to this city, I didn't have a cent. Not a penny."

He paused and closed his eyes to let the full significance of this fact sink in upon young Kennedy.

"Young man, listen to me."

The room was hushed. The smoke from President Ellsworth's cigar gradually settled around his head, covering him as with a cloud. Outside the building all noise of traffic had ceased. The sky was darkened. Suddenly there came a terrific clap of thunder, and from the cloud surrounding President Ellsworth was heard a voice saying:

"Young man, there are three rules for business success. The first of these is 'Don't watch the clock,' the second 'Don't be afraid of getting your hands dirty,' and the third 'Work just a little harder than the other man.' "

As he finished, the cloud ascended and President Ellsworth sank back exhausted.

The young man, overcome with emotion, could not speak. It was one of those rare moments in which words are superfluous; his heart overflowed with joy that he, of all people, had been chosen to be the recipient of the Great Man's secret of success.

It was Mr. Ellsworth who finally broke the silence.

"You will report to Mr. Augustus in Department 12 on Monday morning."

The young man's eyes shone with gratitude as he thanked his patron. A bell rang, the door opened, and with bowed head he backed out of the presence of the Great Man.

II

THE following Monday he who had miraculously received the three commandments descended from Mount Sinai and went to work as clerk No. 4 in Section No. 8 of Department No. 12 of the Ellsworth Products Co. at a salary of $15 per week. Inasmuch as Richard had never been good at penmanship or long division, this was probably considerably more than he at first merited.

At the commencement of his business career, in fact, on the very first morning, the young man came perilously near damnation; forgetting, in a moment of weakness, the first commandment, Richard was just on the point of *looking at the clock* when he remembered. It was indeed a narrow escape, and he shuddered for weeks afterward every time he thought of it.

The second commandment also caused him a great deal of real worry at first for, in spite of all his efforts, his hands were often quite clean.

The observance of the third and last commandment, "Work harder than the other man," didn't seem quite so difficult; in fact, in Richard's department, it was almost suspiciously easy.

After a few weeks Richard's hard work combined with his college education began to have its effect on his superiors, and sometimes he was entrusted with the addition of three and four columns of figures—a responsibility which the young man assumed with a modesty and capability which greatly pleased the older heads.

Richard did not spend his evenings in idle pleasure, either, as did the young men who had not been so fortunate as to have been entrusted with the three secrets of success. He subscribed for the Benjamin Franklin course in business administration, and after reading fourteen books he was quite ready to take an executive position in any business. He knew what caused panics and just how to prevent them; he learned that the cost of labor and materials was apt to increase periodically provided that some other factors did not cause a decrease.

So they made him a clerk in the filing department and he was entrusted with the stamping of the word "Filed," with the date, on every letter.

This promotion did not, however, make Richard conceited, and his innate modesty won him many friends among the other employees with whom he was quite popular as soon as it became known that he was a friend of Mr. Ellsworth's.

One day, after Richard had been working for six months as filing clerk, he conceived an efficient idea for saving time. This was no less revolutionary a scheme than to cease stamping both the word "Filed" and the date, and simply imprint the latter in a certain definite place which would, of course, signify that the correspondence had been filed on that date. Richard worked hard in perfecting this idea; he figured out that it would eliminate 302 movements of the clerk's arm in a day, which, allowing for Sundays, holidays and half days on Saturdays, would mean the saving of 87,580 movements per arm per clerk per annum.

When his idea was finally ready he took it to his immediate superior, Mr. Wilkes.

"That's all right," said Mr. Wilkes, for he believed in encouraging young men, up to a certain extent, "but the Routine Book says that the correspondence must be distinctly stamped 'Filed.'"

"But—" began Richard, and at that the patient Mr. Wilkes took down the Routine Book and pointed to the exact page, section and paragraph which supported his contention. This closed the argument.

Or rather, it would have closed the argument had Richard been a less ambitious young man.

But the more he thought about his idea the more efficient it seemed; he discovered also that in his previous figuring he had not allowed for the fact that the clerks worked overtime and all day Saturday during the winter months, which made his net total of saved-clerk-arm-movements per person per annum 92,365 instead of 87,580.

Fortified thus with an additional argument, this young Luther bravely contemplated nailing his thesis to the door of no less a person than president Ellsworth himself, but in several attempts he got no nearer that sacred portal than the office of the second assistant general manager, who coldly imparted to him the not entirely unknown fact that Mr. Ellsworth was a very busy man.

Then in his hour of despair Richard remembered Abraham Nussbaum—the sales-manager who had so successfully radiated personal magnetism in the pages of the *Efficiency* magazine. Three hours a night for the next five nights young Kennedy spent in front of a tall mirror, with a copy of Nussbaum's article on "How I Make Men Like Me" spread out before him; on the morning of the sixth day he was ready to try his skill. Behold—a magnetic smile at breakfast and the waitress forgot to charge him for heavy cream on his corn flakes; another smile, through the window of the café, and a street sweeper outside ran in and embraced him. This last was rather embarrassing, and Richard deliberately shut off as much of the magnetism as possible until he could reach the office. But he was so charged with personality that four newsboys, two beggars, a plumber and a traffic policeman followed him to the door of his office, overpoweringly attracted to this magnetic young man.

In the office his progress to the throne of president Ellsworth was triumphal; managers, secretaries, stenographers—all instantly liked him and made way before his "Nussbaum" smile. But as he stood alone before the president all of young Kennedy's magnetism was promptly short circuited by the Great Man's patriarchal impressiveness.

"Well, young man," said Mr. Ellsworth, fumbling among the papers on his desk.

"Yes, sir," said he, "I am Richard Kennedy, sir. I have a plan which I have worked out for eliminating a great deal of unnecessary work in the clerical department, sir. It will save 92,365 movements of a clerk's arm in one year—and in ten years—"

During this speech the president had continued the search among his papers.

Suddenly he fixed his shrewd, keen gaze on young Kennedy and said "Humm."

Then, before Richard could reply to this, the Great Man pressed a button and a stenographer appeared.

"Miss Meyers," said the president, "did you see a little leather note-book of mine?"

There was a minute's silence. Richard trembled as he thought of the portentous possibilities of those notes—undoubtedly his complete record with the Ellsworth Products Co.

The fatal little book was found and handed to Mr. Ellsworth. Young Kennedy, in dumb suspense, watched the features of the Great Man for any sign of hope. At last the president shook his head sadly and muttered, "I ought to have had an 84 easily. Six strokes on number twelve—a par 3 hole—six—"

He looked up and saw young Kennedy. The shrewd, keen look returned instantly to his impressive features which, in the previous moment of forgetfulness, had carelessly become quite human.

"Well, young man?" he said.

"Why, sir," replied Kennedy in stubborn desperation, "I want to tell you about my plan for saving waste time in the clerical department."

President Ellsworth took off his gold-rimmed eyeglasses and listened thoughtfully as Kennedy unfolded his scheme.

When the young man had finished he sat lost in deep thought for some time, before he gave his answer.

"Young man," he said at last, "when I first came to this city I didn't have a cent. Not a penny."

He paused and closed his eyes to let the full significance of this fact sink in upon Kennedy before he resumed.

"Young man, there are three rules for business success. The first of these is 'Don't watch the clock'; the second, 'Don't be afraid of getting your hands dirty'; and the third, 'Work just a little harder than the other man.'"

The Great Man paused—then added :

"I hope that answers your question, young man."

"Yes, sir," said Kennedy gratefully as he bowed out of the room. "Thank you very much, sir."

III

KENNEDY returned from his second pilgrimage to the Oracle greatly strengthened in his resolve to keep holy the three commandments on which hang all the laws of the profits. He realized more than ever before that it takes time and hard work to win true success. At the office he set to his task with added zeal; in the evenings he pored over his new correspondence course in Modern Business which guaranteed executive ability and a handsome set of nine books for $65.

But after a few months more he began to grow restless. He felt that possibly he wasn't getting ahead as fast as he should; somehow there wasn't at all the old thrill in adding figures, initialing correspondence and in being efficient.

Furthermore, there had been a distressing visit to a Vocational Expert. While perusing his beloved *Efficiency* magazine one evening, his attention had been caught by a full page advertisement which demanded, in big type, "Young Man, Are You in the Right Job?" Under this was a photograph which Kennedy supposed at first to be a horrible example of a young man *not* in the right job; more careful study showed it to be Morris Stuttgart, A.B., Vocational Expert, who for $25 would analyze your character and advise you at once as to your real life work.

So Kennedy called on Mr. Stuttgart and after sitting for half an hour in a strong light while the expert analyzed his character, he got a headache and the information that he had an unmistakable aptitude for a musical career. He thanked Mr. Stuttgart, paid his $25, and lay awake that night wondering why his parents had let him drop his piano lessons.

The next noon he sat at his desk, trying to concentrate on the chapter in his business course concerning "How to Write Effective Business Letters to Japan and China," when Mr. Fisher sat down beside him to pick his teeth. Mr. Fisher was a kindly chief clerk who sported three 18 karat molars and a 14 karat watch charm, the latter a present from his fellow clerks on the anniversary of his Twentieth Year with the Ellsworth Products Co.

"Well, Kennedy, what's new? Aren't married yet, are you?"

This was Mr. Fisher's daily question; Kennedy's daily answer was: "Well, not yet, Mr. Fisher. Can't get a girl to take me. How's Mrs. Fisher today?"

Kennedy had a sincere interest in the domestic welfare of his fellow employees, and never faltered in his daily enthusiasm over the latest photo of the wife and kiddies.

Mr. Fisher shook his head mournfully.

"She had a bad night again with her stomach."

Mrs. Fisher's stomach was a subject on which the whole office got minute daily reports. Then he added, "What are you reading?"

"Why, it's the Dearborn Business Course. Pretty good, but I guess you can't get much out of books. It's the hard, practical experience that counts, isn't it?"

Kennedy possessed the modest attitude of assumed contempt toward mere book learning which college men diplomatically employ when speaking to those who are unfortunate enough to have Henry Ford's cultural background.

"Well, the Dearborn course is all right. Not as good perhaps as some others," replied Mr. Fisher, mentioning three or four names.

"What, you've taken all those correspondence courses, Mr. Fisher?" said the amazed young man.

Here was something wrong; surely Mr. Fisher couldn't have absorbed all that knowledge as to how to be an executive and still remain a chief clerk.

"Oh, sure, I've read them all," was the answer.

"Well, tell me, have most of the clerks here taken the course?" asked the young man.

"Sure," was the surprising answer. "Long ago."

"Well, then, how about Mr. Schmidt?" The mystified young man mentioned the name of one of the highest officials; probably some handicap had kept the clerks from being executives; quite likely they had been "clock watchers" or even worse, afraid of getting their hands dirty.

"Oh, Mr. Schmidt?" said Mr. Fisher. "Well, that's different. You see, he married Mr. Ellsworth's oldest daughter. Certainly a dandy fellow, too—Mr. Schmidt. Calls me Ed—always joshing me about my kids." And Mr. Fisher chuckled reminiscently.

"Oh," said young Kennedy. "He married Mr. Ellsworth's daughter. I see. And how about Mr. Spencer, the vice-president?"

It was Mr. Spencer who had patted Richard several times approvingly on the back when he had found the young man studying during the noon hour.

"Spencer—say, there's a regular man," replied Mr. Fisher. "Nothing stuck-up about him. He asked Bertha and I to his wedding—married Kitty Ellsworth, you know—the old man's second daughter. My, it was some swell wedding, I'll tell the world."

"Yes," said the young man. "It must have been."

Then there came to him the vision of J. D. Ellsworth battling his sturdy way from poor boy to president.

"But," he said to Mr. Fisher, "but, how about Mr. Ellsworth? He came to this city without a cent, and by following three rules he won his way to the top. Told me so himself."

"Yes, sirree!" said Mr. Fisher. "That's just what he did. I can remember when he first came. I was his boss for a while. Used to say to him, 'John, do this now,' or 'John, hurry up.' There wasn't any 'Ellsworth Products Co.' then. It all belonged to old Walter Kinnard, and when he died it went to his daughter Ethel. I guess you've met her—"

"Why, no—where?" said young Kennedy.

"She's Mrs. J. D. Ellsworth, the old man's wife, you know," was the answer.

The door of the office opened suddenly and young Kennedy looked up at the sound of a woman's laugh. A plain young girl swept by them and passed into the inner sanctum.

"Say, isn't she a beauty?" whispered Mr. Fisher with awe in his voice.

"Why, no—I wouldn't pick her out of a crowd." The young man listlessly surveyed the book on business efficiency.

"Don't you know who she is?" said Mr. Fisher.

"Why, some stenographer, I suppose," replied Kennedy.

"She's Ellworth's youngest daughter, Grace," said Mr. Fisher in the same tone of voice with which he would have mentioned the deity or John D. Rockefeller.

"What? Ellsworth's got another daughter?" cried the young man, clutching Fisher's arm.

"Sure."

"Married?"

"No—just nineteen."

"Oh," said young Kennedy.

IV

So he married her.

V

THIRTY-FIVE years later a trembling young man stood in the impressive office of Richard Kennedy, President of the Kennedy (formerly the Ellsworth) Products Co.

"Yes, sir," he said eagerly to Mr. Kennedy. "I want to show you that a college man can start at the bottom and work up."

President Kennedy took off his gold rimmed eyeglasses.

"Young man," he said, lighting a cigar, "when I first came to this city I didn't have a penny. Not a cent."

He paused and closed his eyes to let the full significance of this fact sink in upon the young man.

"But I made three rules which I always followed. They are the secret of success."

"Yes, sir," said the youth, eagerly.

"The first rule is, 'Don't watch the clock'; the second, 'Don't be afraid of getting your hands dirty'; and the third, 'Always work just a little harder than the other man.'"

THE MERRY-GO-ROUND

Julia M. Peterkin

I

AWHITE man came from nobody knew where with a merry-go-round and set it up in the vacant lot across from the village depot. Every evening when work on the plantations was over the gay music sounded clear in the still air, and the darkies flocked down to the village and rode out all the money they had. Then they stayed on a while to listen to the merry tunes.

Flaming gasoline torches lighted the tent, and fiery looking bay and black and gray horses rocked and challenged riders to come try them; and gilded chariots shone bright.

The man's name was Carson. He was white, for his skin was fair, but no such white man had ever been in these parts before. Except for his white skin he seemed black as any of the folks that rode on the merry-go-round.

Maum Mary Parker cooked his meals and took them to his tent. He offered to go to her house to eat, but she refused to allow this.

"No, I rudder fetch yo' victuals here to yo'," she said.

He offered to pay her well if she'd let him sleep in the soft looking, quilt-covered bed that he could see through the open window.

"No," she said, "No white man ain' nebber yet sleep in no bed o' mine, an' I know I ain' gwine sta't wid you."

He laughed and spat on the ground.

"All right, Aunty, but my money's good as anybody's. I'm sure it's as good as any these white folks round here's got, if they've got any."

"You eat yo' dinner; I'm waitin' on dem t'ings, an' keep yo' mout' off my white folks."

He laughed again.

"Some folks, eh?"

II

JESSE WEEKS worked at the oil mill for good wages. He was strong as a mule and muscled like an ox. He was well fed, for Maum Mary fed him, and besides her good meals he often carried sweet potatoes to the mill and dipped them in the smoking hot oil that dripped from the press. Nothing in the world was better, except sometimes ash cake dipped in that same hot oil for gravy.

Jesse worked at the press ten hours a day, then went home to Maum Mary's, washed up, dressed, and was ready to take Meta, Maum Mary's daughter, to a dance or a party. Now they rode on the merry-go-round every night. One night they'd choose a chariot; another night white horses side by side. Meta sat modestly sidewise as she had seen white ladies sit on real horses. Another night they'd ride bay horses, or black.

They'd be married Thanksgiving with a big wedding. Maum Mary was already saving up eggs for the cakes. For 'twas something in these days to raise a girl and marry her off without anybody's ever having said anything against her.

The first time Carson smiled at Meta she was confused. She dropped a curtsy in return and said respectfully,

"Good evenin', sir."

He laughed, looking at her with bold, appraising eyes.

The next night when Jesse left Meta and went over to the parcher to buy a sack of peanuts, Carson walked over by her and said with a smile.

"You look like you're scared to speak to me. What's the matter with you? Is he got you under the hack?" indicating Jesse, who was returning.

"No, sir," answered Meta in an embarrassed way. She was not altogether certain of his words, for his r's rolled strangely.

Next morning Meta went to the village store, and Carson was lounging on the counter inside.

"Won't you have a dope?" he asked her.

The clerk glanced up at him quickly, but Meta appeared not to hear, and nothing more was said.

When the girl stepped out of the door, Carson got down off the counter and stood in the door and watched her cross the railroad track, then on the path up the hill.

Maum Mary was late getting the clothes in off the line that evening. The washing was a big one.

"Meta, you run on an' take da' white man's supper to him. I ain' likes to sen' yo', but jus' leab de dishes wid him till in de mornin', an' hurry on back."

Carson took the pan from the girl and untied the white cloth that covered it. Chicken, biscuits, hominy, gravy.

"Your ma is some cook, girl. I'll get fat staying here. But what makes you treat me so cold?"

Meta turned away and started home.

"Ma say she'll git de dishes in de mornin'."

"Hold on, what's your hurry? I've got a book of tickets here for you to ride out. Wait a minute, let me get 'em for you."

But Meta was gone.

III

JESSE cut a step or two to the jazzy music, then asked Meta gaily, a little later,

"What'll we ride tonight?"

"Le's ride one o' them gol' chariots. I declare tha's de sweetes' ridin' I ever ride," declared Meta in her gentle voice.

When the ride was over and a pair of horses had been tried to see which was really the better, Jesse went to the parcher for peanuts. Carson saw him go and came at once to where Meta stood waiting.

"What made you run off so? Whyn't you wait and get the tickets? You must think I want to eat you or something. Why, a girl like you—"

He didn't finish his sentence, for Jesse landed a terrific blow on his jaw, and followed it quickly with another.

A crowd gathered around them uncertain what to do. "You all lef' Jesse 'lone, he knows what he d' do. Dat ain' no white gentleman." One of the older men watched the fight with interest until Carson was soundly beaten, then he took Jesse's arm in a firm grip.

"You done gi' him enough, Jesse. Quit now."

Meta's voice was full of excitement as they walked home up the hill.

"I'm sho glad you done it, Jesse, but I was dat scared!"

But Maum Mary shook her head in disapproval.

"You better mine, boy. It don' do to trifle wid strange white men."

Next morning, before day, somebody knocked on the door of the shed-room where Jesse slept. He jumped up quickly, for the gasoline torches had made him dream of fire. Maybe the oil mill was afire!

He opened the door, saying excitedly,

"What you want?"

Carson's pistol gleamed in the starlight.

"Gawd!" said Jesse at it flashed and he fell, shot through, in the doorway.

The stillness was rent with the shrieks of Meta and Maum Mary. The news spread like wild-fire—Carson had shot Jesse. By dawn, hundreds of negroes filled the village street. Men and women were armed with hoes and rakes, axes and guns. Where was Carson? He was not in the tent where he slept.

The clerk in the village store had already dressed and gone downstairs, from the room where he slept, to the telephone. When he got Central, he said.

"Will you please telephone all the gentlemen around here and tell them that this merry-go-round fellow down here has shot Jesse Weeks? The niggers are pretty well stirred up, and they'd all better come help me get him off on the eight o'clock train."

By sunrise one of the plantation owners on horseback, with a gun on his shoulder, came riding down the hill into the village.

"What are all you niggers doin' here this time o' day?" he asked as he rode through the crowd.

"Good mornin', Cap'n," they answered politely and touched their hats.

"You'd better go on home, all of you. If Sheriff Hill has to come up here this mornin' there'll be trouble for somebody."

There were indistinct mutterings as he hitched his horse to a tree in front of the store and went upstairs to the clerk's room. Soon three more gentlemen rode up, hitched their horses and went upstairs, then two more. At last, nine horses were hitched outside.

Maum Hannah cooked for the clerk upstairs and lived in a cabin back of the store. She came out of her door with a great pot of steaming coffee that left a trail of fragrance behind it.

"One o' you niggers come open dis door fo' me," she commanded.

When it was done she went up the stairs talking to herself.

The eight o'clock train blew at the river bridge three miles away. There was a hush. Then steps sounded on the stairway, slow steady steps. Ten men came down—no, eleven. In the hollow square they formed at the door was a man with his hat pulled down over his eyes. Another man joined them, the village policeman. He was black, but he upheld the law whenever it was possible.

They walked slowly across the street to the depot, as with the dead, and reached it just as the train stopped. Two men stepped aboard; then Carson; then two more. The train started and the four men got off the rear end of it.

"Looks like you-all are having a picnic out here," said the conductor to the others who were standing outside.

"No, nothing like that," one of them answered.

The white men mounted their horses and rode up the hill toward home. The black people stood around talking in low tones. One of them came over to the policeman and talked a minute, and the policeman walked on down the street in another direction. Soon there was a shout and the tent over the merry-go-round was in flames. Horses and chariots stood still and burned to charred wood, they that had been so gay and swift!

IV

CARSON left the train at the first large station it reached. He went to the station lunch counter, got a sandwich and a cup of coffee, then went across the street where he saw a sign "Board and Lodging." He took a room and went to bed.

When he awoke, the day was almost over. A new moon showed clear through the window. He stretched his limbs, yawned, then got up and washed his face in the china basin. He looked in the glass at his bruised cheek, smoothed his hair with his hands, put on his coat and went downstairs to the sidewalk.

With his hands in his pockets, he looked around. A cotton mill was over on the hill beyond the depot. Not far from it was a large tent. It was no merry-go-round tent. He'd go take a look at it.

He walked through its open door and a red-faced, stockily built man with a black moustache greeted him.

"Well, brother, how do you do?"

Carson's quick eyes took in the Bible on the table, the organ on one side, the hymn books.

"I'm down and out," he answered gloomily. "I thought I'd come talk to you."

"That's right, that's right. Cast your burden on the Lord, brother, it's the only way to salvation."

"But I'm out of a job," said Carson.

"Well, according to John 6:27, 'Labor not for the meat that perisheth.' What's your business, brother?"

Carson hesitated.

"I wish I could get work here with you. I'm mighty handy with a tent. You ought to see me take one down and put it up."

"You know anything about music?"

"I know it from A to Z," Carson answered confidently.

"I've been thinking about getting a regular fellow to go around and help me, but collections haven't been much lately."

"I tell you," said Carson. "You try me. I'll work for my board till you see if I give satisfaction. You won't be out anything much that way."

"How about them gas lights; can you light them?"

"Just watch me."

That night Carson rose from the congregation and gave a remarkable testimony of his salvation from sin. Next morning he practised faithfully on the organ until he could play a number of the hymns to be sung during the services.

"That's right, you got to put pep in 'em," approved the preacher.

Carson soon developed into a fine exhorter, and followed the sermons with a moving appeal to sinners to turn from sin. It was a steadier business than his former one; more exciting, too.

* * *

Jesse did not die. He's only crippled. He has crutches, and drags both feet together when he walks. He makes baskets and fish traps and chair bottoms out of split hickory.

Meta and Maum Mary take in washing still, and all together they make a living. Maum Mary is careful to take a part of their earnings to pay the preacher.

"Preachers is de servants ob Gawd, Meta, we 'bliged to take care of 'em or de worl' 'ud git too full o' sin."

JUST HIM AND HER

Ruth Suckow

I

"**W**HO lives in that little house at the edge of town across from the cemetery?"

"Oh, that's where the Lew Daveys live."

"Just the old folks?"

"Yes. Just him and her."

***

This was one of the oldest houses in Plum Branch.

It stood close to the ground and leaned forward a little. It was of a gray, aged, indeterminate color. It had small-paned windows that gave out a saddish light. The porch floor sloped toward the ground and was broken at the edges. The posts were thin with an insert of lattice-work. An old buggy seat stood on the porch. No one but an old couple would be living in such a house.

There was a gray picket fence around the lawn, but not around the garden that sloped south to the straggling grassy road that went only as far as the hilly pasture across from the house. Lilac bushes grew so close to this fence that the leaves pushed between the pickets. There was no gate, but a scraggly cedar tree on each side the opening like a gate post. A clump of tall pines grew in one corner of the lawn, and, underneath, a mass of bluebells standing like a pool of blue water. There were flowering bushes close to the house wall and a lily-of-the-valley bed near the porch, in a corner. In the backyard stood plum trees with smoke-black branches strangely wind-blown and now a delicate froth of greenish-white bloom.

The house was on the outskirts of town. A red-brown clay road went past it and died out in a few grassy wagon tracks at the fence of Glissendorf's pasture. The Plum Branch cemetery was up this road a little way. The white tombstones were set thick among blackish evergreens where birds were always busy. Just across from the house, a hill pasture rose in an emerald-green mound. It was sprinkled with buttercups. A little brown path was cut around it. A wooden gate fastened with an old wire gave entrance. A reddish-colored dilapidated wagon stood in the grass at the foot of the hill. Plum Branch, the creek, was beyond the hill in a limestone gully.

II

THE Lew Daveys had come to Plum Branch among the early settlers; but now not many people seemed to know them. They were retired farmers. Mr. Davey had a team and did a little hauling and his own gardening. He still owned a farm west of town. They lived on the rent—on a little of it. Most of it they saved.

Some of the ladies in the Congregational church—Mrs. Sperry, Mrs. Kuehnle, Edie Robbins—always took pains to think of Mrs. Davey, to ask her to Missionary meetings and to solicit her for church suppers, to speak to her at church. But she went out very little.

They both did go to church, however, every Sunday morning, and sat at the side in the fifth row from the front. People sometimes asked who that old couple were who always sat in the fifth row. "He" was short and stocky, but now he began to look very frail—hollowed out between the big bones. He had a short rough beard. "She" had a grayish sad indeterminate face like the face of her house. She wore an old dark blue suit with gathered sleeves, a small black hat with a bunch of black ribbon at the side, and gray cotton gloves.

They never made much response when the minister shook hands with them after church. They never seemed to make much response to anything. There was a kind of emptiness in their faces—yet not stupidity. As if they had lived on so long without exactly meaning to, and couldn't make much of it. In church, their gnarled, misshapen hands, with the skin stretched tight over the knuckle bones and hollow and wrinkled between, lay with a kind of mournful patience in their laps. They had worked hard all their lives. Now there was no need.

The air of their house was clean, and yet there was something mouldy about it. The rooms were scrubbed, but that could not lighten the dark, old-fashioned look of the brown-painted woodwork and cupboards and the dark-gray rag rugs with threads of red. Everything was aired religiously, but there could be no freshness in the look of the orange plush on the parlor chairs and settee, the brown-and-red calico cushion on the lounge, the red-checkered table cloth, the little old ornaments and pictures in walnut or silvered frames, the dark wall paper. The plants, too, growing in tin cans wrapped in crêpe paper—the geraniums, the ferns, the cactus, the dark-red foliage, the red lilies.

It was strange to step into this house in its out-of-the-way setting and sense the old left-over life lingering on in it.

It seemed as if they must always have been living in this house, but really it was not so long. When the children were gone they had stayed on at the farm for a few years and then rented it and moved into town, as most farmers did. They said they were getting along and it was time to take some comfort in life.

Their farm was out on the Sand Spring road just off the highway— a grayish, rain-stained house like this, shaded with bushes, with fowls straggling over the yard and the needle-matted ground under the grove of evergreens. It had never been a rich farm, but they had made "enough."

They had had a big family. The pictures of all the children were in the blue, plush-covered album with the steel clasps on the center-table.

The one of Levi, the oldest, was a wedding picture. It had been taken at the old photographer's in Adamsville, where all the wedding couples used to go. It had a background of blurry trees done in charcoal work on a big screen, and in front of this the bride was sitting on an artificial stump, with the groom standing beside her. The bride was one of the Liebes. She had a broad German face with a fringe of light hair straight across it, and she wore a white basque strained tightly across her big breast and hips. Levi had curly hair and a curly mustache and a sour, dubious look. They had moved out to Nebraska and Levi had died of cancer of the stomach. "She" had married again.

The next two children, Edwin and Lily, had died in infancy. They had no pictures—only two black memorial cards with their names and dates and verses of Scripture, with two doves bearing open Bibles, in gold. They were buried out in the little Sand Spring cemetery, hardly used any more, where the old slabs of white were now toppling over the sunken, grass-covered mounds under the sad-creaking evergreens.

Luella, the oldest girl, now lived in Diagonal, in the southern part of the State. Her husband had a vulcanizing works. In her picture she had a slight wildflower prettiness—small features under frizzled bangs—but she was now scrawny, overworked, bitter-tongued, with a great brood of children and "nothing to do with." She wrote home occasionally on scraps of yellowish scratch paper torn from the children's tablets, and sometimes the old lady made little nightgowns for the youngest of the children.

Sam, the next boy, was a farmer. He did not write, but sometimes he brought his whole family in the car and stopped over for Sunday dinner.

Achsia, the favorite daughter—they always called her Axie—lived close by in Adamsville, the county seat. Her mother used to go often to see her, but now she seldom did. She said she was getting so she hated to go places. Axie still wrote, and the children wrote. Axie was fat and dark, rather pop-eyed. She had a good, sentimental heart and had always been kind to the old folks.

John had died of tuberculosis when he was twenty-seven. In the picture it could be seen that he was of a more delicate mould than the others—his nose thin, temples slightly hollowed, thoughtful eyes. There was a ghastly enlarged picture of him in a silvered frame on the parlor wall with all the life retouched out of it. His tombstone in the family lot could be seen just beyond the Soldiers' Monument in the cemetery.

Walter had gone West and had a fruit farm now in Oregon. They seldom heard from him. Or from Barney, who had not turned out well, and was still unsettled—going to a place and then tearing up and leaving almost as soon as he got there. The last they had heard of him he had been working at the docks in New Orleans. He was separated from his wife, whom the old people had never seen.

These were all that were left to them.

They knew a few old people around town, but not well. They had never had time to get acquainted with folks. Sometimes "she" drove out into the country to see the Old Lady Finley, who was living with her daughter. "He" went down to the store occasionally and hung around with the other old fellows who sat on the bench under the awning until the sun got around that way.

They still got up at five or halfpast every morning. "He" started the fire in the cook stove and "she" made the breakfast of fried eggs or buckwheat cakes that was just what they had always had. They ate at the kitchen table, silently, the old man bent over the table and shoveling in his food, the old lady jumping up to wait on him as in the old days when she had had the men to feed.

Then he went out to hoe a little in the garden. You could see his bowed, gnarly figure in the faded shirt and overalls, moving slowly, with a strange sad significance, over the soft earth-brown of the plowed field— the green pastures beyond, and the blossoming plum trees that scented the May air.

But he couldn't do much any more. He had tried to trim up the plum trees this spring, but had suddenly grown dizzy up there where the thin, black branches criss-crossed against the blue sky, and had almost "had a fall."

He was not even going to do hauling this spring. He liked to feed the two big horses in the barn that smelled of hay and manure. All the stock he had now, and he had always been good to his stock. The horses were fed up so, the men in town said, that they were too lazy to pull a load.

Then there were errands "she" could send him on downtown. He did most of the trading and still handled all the money. "She" was careful how she used up stamps and crochet cotton, for she hated to ask him for more. Their money lay in the Plum Branch Bank, ready to be distributed among the children when they were gone.

The old man was not unhappy working out in his garden. He liked the smell of the soil. But it was so small, so no account, after the farm. He had a feeling of being lost, somehow, "let down."

"She" was better off. Her work had never seemed to count for as much as his. It had not brought in the money. But it had lasted better. It fit into the new place. She still had a house to look after, and time to do it right at last. She did everything herself—washing, ironing, baking, cleaning, sewing.

And then there were her plants. She had always been a great hand for plants, but had never had much time for them on the farm. She had red foliage plants and cactus and red King lilies. She tended the plants in the afternoon when all the housework was "done up" and no one could reproach her.

Then she did crotcheting and knitting, although her eyes were giving out. Now she was working on a crotcheted filet yoke for Axie's Marguerite's graduating clothes. She always had some work in hand in the flowered silk bag that Marguerite had made for her.

Still, this was not much after her work with that big family—every minute full. Sometimes when she sat down to her fancy work, quite contentedly, in the afternoon, a feeling of guilt would come over her. It would seem as if there were something she ought to be doing. Then she too would feel lost, sitting there in her little cane-seated rocker by the dining-room window, looking out beyond the pines to the white stones in the cemetery.

The children—all gone. None of them needed her any more. None of them had seemed to need her very long. Except John. He had needed her. He used to sit in the big rocker by the west window in the farm house, reading the magazines that the minister brought out to him. He used to call for her when she was out on the place at work. She felt closer now to John, in his lone grave in the cemetery just down the road a little way, than to the others. There was something she still could do for John. She could care for his grave, plant it with pansies, put on it her choicest flowers. She took a kind of strange, sad pride in its order and beauty.

She had never had much time to give to the children when they were small. As soon as they were grown they had married and left her. Each other was all these two had left.

III

THEY did not talk much. They never had. When they did, it was in a dry, faintly sarcastic tone. They would have been ashamed to show affection. They would not have thought it becoming in old folks.

Besides, what they felt was not affection. It was a feeling of belonging. The only things on earth to which they were still of use were each other. To each other, they were not left over, and lingering on. "He" locked the doors and made all safe as he had always done. He tinkered around and made things a little handier for her. He went for the mail and bought in the milk and got her medicine for her at the doctor's. "She" mended his clothes and kept him tidy, saw to his comfort, cooked the food that he could eat. Each felt a kind of deep, unspoken reliance on the other, and their age that was setting them apart from everything else was pulling them together. No one else knew what they had been through. No one else understood.

In these spring evenings, "she" sat out on the buggy seat on the porch and "he" on the step below her, staring ahead of them—at the line of the green hill pasture against the sky, at the unused road beyond the fence. "He" might say—"Corn's goin' in late this year"—or "she"—"Who's that I see going into the cemetery just now? Looked like it might be Haller's folks." The sky deepened to cool dark blue; a little moon hung over the plum trees. The thick green grass was wet; sent up a fresh night odor. The old wagon stood sad, forlorn, at the foot of the hill. "Well, might's well go to bed—I s'pose. D'you put the hoe in the barn?"—

They got up and went into the warm, dark house, lit a lamp in the small downstairs bedroom, undressed, climbed into the old pine bedstead. Neither would have thought of going without the other, somehow.

The pale light from the window that they never opened until June silvered their thin, hollow faces and lay like frost on their hair.

But they were feeble now. The life was running out. Axie said she had them on her mind. She even wrote a letter to Sam about them in her childish, sentimental hand without any capital letters. She kept meaning to run over to Plum Branch. But somehow she never got there.

The minister could see it when he went to call. He was glad to meet George Horton on the street so that he could say what was in his mind—"I went over to the Lew Daveys' this afternoon. You know, they're getting pretty feeble. I'm afraid the old man won't last much longer."

They knew it themselves in a kind of way. They gave up one thing after another—going to church, trips to town. When they sat, a kind of silence seemed to muffle them in.

But it was the old lady who went first. Before the bluebells were gone, before she could see how many plums there would be on the trees that year, before the yellow and purple pansies were out on the lot in the cemetery. She was sick only a few days. Axie was there. The man wandered about the place, stood in the barn, sat out on the old buggy seat. She was unconscious most of the time. But just at the last she seemed to give him a look—full of a kind of mute, intense meaning.

The old man seemed to "take it" better than they had feared. He was quiet and docile; he hardly spoke. He let Axie lead him about at the funeral, washed and brushed, in his best black clothes.

"I don't know as Pa ever seemed to make over her much," Axie said to Sam, "but he'll miss her just the same."

Afterward they looked about the place for him and finally found him sitting out on the cistern by the side wall where some white violets grew. He did not seem to be grieving—only sitting with his hands on his knees. They felt relieved; they could hardly have said why.

Axie put her arms around him. "Come on into the house with us, don't you want to, Pa?"

He let her lead him in. They went into the dining-room, that seemed pitiful and useless now. Axie sat down on the lounge beside him and took his hand. Sam went creaking solemnly up to the rocker.

"Pa, I'm going to stay with you tonight," Axie said, "and until I've got things all looked after. But after that I got to go back. I got the children, you know. Don't you want to come back with me, Pa?"

She stroked his hand. Sam did not dare to look at them—he stared at an old faded photograph of the farm that hung behind the stove.

"Why, yes," the old man said vacantly. "I guess I might do that."

"I'd love to have you, Pa," Axie's voice shook with relief. "Just think how the children will like it." She kissed his hand. He did not notice her.

"Well," Sam said, rising, "I suppose me and the missus had better be starting if we're going to get back. Goodbye, Pa." He shook hands awkwardly.

"Goodbye. Goodbye."

The old man went to bed when Axie told him to that night. The next day he was just the same. He went about the place, stood a little while here and a little while there, sat out on the cistern again. There was a vacancy in his eyes. He did not seem to be thinking or feeling much.

The next day at twilight Axie went into the dining-room to speak to him. He was not there—but she could see him in the parlor, in the plush chair by the window, a queer place for him to sit. But there was a stillness—she knew before she called out "Pa!" and went up to him, that he was gone.

"Just like that," she told her husband tearfully. "I left him while I went out to the kitchen, and when I came back he was already gone!"

$$* * *$$

People in Plum Branch had not thought very much about it when the old lady died. They had only said, "I hear the Old Lady Davey died this morning." But they talked of the old man's death, the women in their houses, the men in the Post Office and the depot and the store.

"Yes, sir, that was a queer thing. There didn't seem to be anything special the matter with him—no sickness, you could say. It just seemed as if when *she* went *he* wanted to go too. Couldn't keep on without her. Didn't know what to do with himself, they'd been together so long. I've known of other old couples like that."

SUCH A PRETTY LITTLE PICTURE

Dorothy Parker

MR. WHEELOCK was clipping the hedge. He did not dislike doing it. If it had not been for the faintly sickish odor of the privet bloom, he would definitely have enjoyed it. The new shears were so sharp and bright, there was such a gratifying sense of something done as the young green stems snapped off and the expanse of tidy, square hedge-top lengthened. There was a lot of work to be done on it. It should have been attended to a week ago, but this was the first day that Mr. Wheelock had been able to get back from the city before dinnertime.

Clipping the hedge was one of the few domestic duties that Mr. Wheelock could be trusted with. He was notoriously poor at doing anything around the house. All the suburb knew about it. It was the source of all Mrs. Wheelock's jokes. Her most popular anecdote was of how, the past winter, he had gone out and hired a man to take care of the furnace, after a seven-years' losing struggle with it. She had an admirable memory, and often as she had related the story, she never dropped a word of it. Even now, in the late summer, she could hardly tell it for laughing.

When they were first married, Mr. Wheelock had lent himself to the fun. He had even posed as being more inefficient than he really was, to make the joke better. But he had tired of his helplessness, as a topic of conversation. All the men of Mrs. Wheelock's acquaintance, her cousins, her brother-in-law, the boys she went to high school with, the neighbors' husbands, were adepts at putting up a shelf, at repairing a lock, or making a shirtwaist box. Mr. Wheelock had begun to feel that there was something rather effeminate about his lack of interest in such things.

He had wanted to answer his wife, lately, when she enlivened some neighbor's dinner table with tales of his inadequacy with hammer and wrench. He had wanted to cry, "All right, suppose I'm not any good at things like that. What of it?"

He had played with the idea, had tried to imagine how his voice would sound, uttering the words. But he could think of no further argument for his case than that "What of it?" And he was a little relieved, somehow, at being able to find nothing stronger. It made it reassuringly impossible to go through with the plan of answering his wife's public railleries.

Mrs. Wheelock sat, now, on the spotless porch of the neat stucco house. Beside her was a pile of her husband's shirts and drawers, the price-tags still on them. She was going over all the buttons before he wore the garments, sewing them on more firmly. Mrs. Wheelock never waited for a button to come off, before sewing it on. She worked with quick, decided movements, compressing her lips each time the thread made a slight resistance to her deft jerks.

She was not a tall woman, and since the birth of her child she had gone over from a delicate plumpness to a settled stockiness. Her brown hair, though abundant, grew in an uncertain line about her forehead. It was her habit to put it up in curlers at night, but the crimps never came out in the right place. It was arranged with perfect neatness, yet it suggested that it had been done up and got over with as quickly as possible. Passionately clean, she was always redolent of the germicidal soap she used so vigorously. She was wont to tell people, somewhat redundantly, that she never employed any sort of cosmetics. She had unlimited contempt for women who sought to reduce their weight by dieting, cutting from their menus such nourishing items as cream and puddings and cereals.

Adelaide Wheelock's friends—and she had many of them—said of her that there was no nonsense about her. They and she regarded it as a compliment.

Sister, the Wheelocks' five-year-old daughter, played quietly in the gravel path that divided the tiny lawn. She had been known as Sister since her birth, and her mother still laid plans for a brother for her. Sister's baby carriage stood waiting in the cellar, her baby clothes were stacked expectantly away in bureau drawers. But raises were infrequent at the advertising agency where Mr. Wheelock was employed, and his present salary had barely caught up to the cost of their living. They could not conscientiously regard themselves as being able to afford a son. Both Mr. and Mrs. Wheelock keenly felt his guilt in keeping the bassinet empty.

Sister was not a pretty child, though her features were straight, and her eyes would one day be handsome. The left one turned slightly in toward the nose, now, when she looked in a certain direction; they would operate as soon as she was seven. Her hair was pale and limp, and her color bad. She was a delicate little girl. Not fragile in a picturesque way, but the kind of child that must be always undergoing treatment for its teeth and its throat and obscure things in its nose. She had lately had her adenoids removed, and she was still using squares of surgical gauze instead of handkerchiefs. Both she and her mother somehow felt that these gave her a sort of prestige.

She was additionally handicapped by her frocks, which her mother bought a size or so too large, with a view to Sister's growing into them— an expectation which seemed never to be realized, for her skirts were always too long, and the shoulders of her little dresses came halfway down to her thin elbows. Yet, even discounting the unfortunate way she was dressed, you could tell, in some way, that she was never going to wear any kind of clothes well.

Mr. Wheelock glanced at her now and then as he clipped. He had never felt any fierce thrills of father-love for the child. He had been disappointed in her when she was a pale, large-headed baby, smelling of stale milk and warm rubber. Sister made him feel ill at ease, vaguely irritated him. He had had no share in her training; Mrs. Wheelock was so competent a parent that she took the places of both of them. When Sister came to him to ask his permission to do something, he always told her to wait and ask her mother about it.

He regarded himself as having the usual paternal affection for his daughter. There were times, indeed, when she had tugged sharply at his heart—when he had waited in the corridor outside the operating room; when she was still under the anesthetic, and lay little and white and helpless on her high hospital bed; once when he had accidentally closed a door upon her thumb. But from the first he had nearly acknowledged to himself that he did not like Sister as a person.

Sister was not a whining child, despite her poor health. She had always been sensible and well-mannered, amenable about talking to visitors, rigorously unselfish. She never got into trouble, like other children. She did not care much for other children. She had heard herself described as being "old-fashioned," and she knew she was delicate, and she felt that these attributes rather set her above them. Besides, they were rough and careless of their bodily wellbeing.

Sister was exquisitely cautious of her safety. Grass, she knew, was often apt to be damp in the late afternoon, so she was careful now to stay right in the middle of the gravel path, sitting on a folded newspaper and playing one of her mysterious games with three petunias that she had been allowed to pick. Mrs. Wheelock never had to speak to her twice about keeping off wet grass, or wearing her rubbers, or putting on her jacket if a breeze sprang up. Sister was an immediately obedient child, always.

II

MRS. WHEELOCK looked up from her sewing and spoke to her husband. Her voice was high and clear, resolutely good-humored. From her habit of calling instructions from her upstairs window to Sister playing on the porch below, she spoke always a little louder than was necessary.

"Daddy," she said.

She had called him Daddy since some eight months before Sister was born. She and the child had the same trick of calling his name and then waiting until he signified that he was attending before they went on with what they wanted to say.

Mr. Wheelock stopped clipping, straightened himself and turned toward her.

"Daddy," she went on, thus reassured, "I saw Mr. Ince down at the post office today when Sister and I went down to get the ten o'clock mail—there wasn't much, just a card for me from Grace Williams from that place they go to up on Cape Cod, and an advertisement from some department store or other about their summer fur sale (as if I cared!), and a circular for you from the bank. I opened it; I knew you wouldn't mind.

"Anyway, I just thought I'd tackle Mr. Ince first as last about getting in our cordwood. He didn't see me at first—though I'll bet he really saw me and pretended not to—but I ran right after him. 'Oh, Mr. Ince!' I said. 'Why, hello, Mrs. Wheelock,' he said, and then he asked for you, and I told him you were finely, and everything. Then I said, 'Now, Mr. Ince,' I said, 'how about getting in that cordwood of ours?" And he said, 'Well, Mrs. Wheelock,' he said, 'I'll get it in soon's I can, but I'm short of help right now,' he said.

"Short of help! Of course I couldn't say anything, but I guess he could tell from the way I looked at him how much I believed it. I just said, 'All right, Mr. Ince, but don't you forget us. There may be a cold snap coming on,' I said, 'and we'll be wanting a fire in the living-room. Don't you forget us,' I said, and he said, no, he wouldn't.

"If that wood isn't here by Monday, I think you ought to do something about it, Daddy. There's no sense in all this putting it off, and putting it off. First thing you know there'll be a cold snap coming on, and we'll be wanting a fire in the living-room, and there we'll be! You'll be sure and 'tend to it, won't you, Daddy? I'll remind you again Monday, if I can think of it, but there are so many things!"

Mr. Wheelock nodded and turned back to his clipping—and his thoughts. They were thoughts that had occupied much of his leisure lately. After dinner, when Adelaide was sewing or arguing with the maid, he found himself letting his magazine fall face downward on his knee, while he rolled the same idea round and round in his mind. He had got so that he looked forward, through the day, to losing himself in it. He had rather welcomed the hedgeclipping; you can clip and think at the same time.

It had started with a story that he had picked up somewhere. He couldn't recall whether he had heard it or had read it—that was probably it, he thought, he had run across it in the back pages of some comic paper that someone had left on the train.

It was about a man who lived in a suburb. Every morning he had gone to the city on the 8:12, sitting in the same seat in the same car, and every evening he had gone home to his wife on the 5:17, sitting in the same seat in the same car. He had done this for twenty years of his life. And then one night he didn't come home. He never went back to his office any more. He just never turned up again.

The last man to see him was the conductor on the 5:17.

"He come down the platform at the Grand Central," the man reported, "just like he done every night since I been working on this road. He put one foot on the step, and then he stopped sudden, and he said 'Oh, hell,' and he took his foot off of the step and walked away. And that's the last anybody see of him."

Curious how that story took hold of Mr. Wheelock's fancy. He had started thinking of it as a mildly humorous anecdote; he had come to accept it as fact. He did not think the man's sitting in the same seat in the same car need have been stressed so much. That seemed unimportant. He thought long about the man's wife, wondered what suburb he had lived in. He loved to play with the thing, to try to feel what the man felt before he took his foot off the car's step. He never concerned himself with speculations as to where the man had disappeared, how he had spent the rest of his life. Mr. Wheelock was absorbed in that moment when he had said "Oh, hell," and walked off. "Oh, hell" seemed to Mr. Wheelock a fine thing for him to have said, a perfect summary of the situation.

He tried thinking of himself in the man's place. But no, he would have done it from the other end. That was the real way to do it.

Some summer evening like this, say, when Adelaide was sewing on buttons, up on the porch, and Sister was playing somewhere about. A pleasant, quiet evening it must be, with the shadows lying long on the street that led from their house to the station. He would put down the garden shears, or the hose, or whatever he happened to be puttering with—not throw the thing down, you know, just put it quietly aside—and walk out of the gate and down the street, and that would be the last they'd see of him. He would time it so that he'd just make the 6:03 for the city comfortably.

He did not go ahead with it from there, much. He was not especially anxious to leave the advertising agency forever. He did not particularly dislike his work. He had been an advertising solicitor since he had gone to work at all, and he worked hard at his job and, aside from that, didn't think about it much one way or the other.

It seemed to Mr. Wheelock that before he had got hold of the "Oh, hell" story he had never thought about anything much, one way or the other. But he would have to disappear from the office, too, that was certain. It would spoil everything to turn up there again. He thought dimly of taking a train going West, after the 6:03 got him to the Grand Central Terminal—he might go to Buffalo, say, or perhaps Chicago. Better just let that part take care of itself and go back to dwell on the moment when it would sweep over him that he was going to do it, when he would put down the shears and walk out the gate—

The "Oh, hell" rather troubled him. Mr. Wheelock felt that he would like to retain that; it completed the gesture so beautifully. But he didn't quite know to whom he should say it.

He might stop in at the post office on his way to the station and say it to the postmaster; but the postmaster would probably think he was only annoyed at there being no mail for him. Nor would the conductor of the 6:03, a train Mr. Wheelock never used, take the right interest in it. Of course the real thing to do would be to say it to Adelaide just before he laid down the shears. But somehow Mr. Wheelock could not make that scene come very clear in his imagination.

III

"Daddy," Mrs. Wheelock said briskly.

He stopped clipping, and faced her.

"Daddy," she related, "I saw Doctor Mann's automobile going by the house this morning—he was going to have a look at Mr. Warren, his rheumatism's getting along nicely—and I called him in a minute, to look us over."

She screwed up her face, winked, and nodded vehemently several times in the direction of the absorbed Sister, to indicate that she was the subject of the discourse.

"He said we were going ahead finely," she resumed, when she was sure that he had caught the idea. "Said there was no need for those t-o-n-s-i-l-s to c-o-m-e o-u-t. But I thought, soon's it gets a little cooler, some time next month, we'd just run in to the city and let Doctor Sturges have a look at us. I'd rather be on the safe side."

"But Doctor Lytton said it wasn't necessary, and those doctors at the hospital, and now Doctor Mann, that's known her since she was a baby," suggested Mr. Wheelock.

"I know, I know," replied his wife. "But I'd rather be on the safe side."

Mr. Wheelock went back to his hedge.

Oh, of course he couldn't do it; he never seriously thought he could, for a minute. Of course he couldn't. He wouldn't have the shadow of an excuse for doing it. Adelaide was a sterling woman, an utterly faithful wife, an almost slavish mother. She ran his house economically and efficiently. She harried the suburban trades people into giving them dependable service, drilled the succession of poorly paid, poorly trained maids, cheerfully did the thousand fussy little things that go with the running of a house. She looked after his clothes, gave him medicine when she thought he needed it, oversaw the preparation of every meal that was set before him; they were not especially inspirational meals, but the food was always nourishing and, as a general thing, fairly well cooked. She never lost her temper, she was never depressed, never ill.

Not the shadow of an excuse. People would know that, and so they would invent an excuse for him. They would say there must be another woman.

Mr. Wheelock frowned, and snipped at an obstinate young twig. Good Lord, the last thing he wanted was another woman. What he wanted was that moment when he realized he could do it, when he would lay down the shears—

Oh, of course he couldn't; he knew that as well as anybody. What would they do, Adelaide and Sister? The house wasn't even paid for yet, and there would be that operation on Sister's eye in a couple of years. But the house would be all paid up by next March. And there was always that well-to-do brother-in-law of Adelaide's, the one who, for all his means, put up every shelf in that great big house with his own hands.

Decent people didn't just go away and leave their wives and families that way. All right, suppose you weren't decent; what of it? Here was Adelaide planning what she was going to do when it got a little cooler, next month. She was always planning ahead, always confident that things would go on just the same. Naturally, Mr. Wheelock realized that he couldn't do it, as well as the next one. But there was no harm in fooling around with the idea. Would you say the "Oh, hell" now, before you laid down the shears, or right after? How would it be to turn at the gate and say it?

Mr. and Mrs. Fred Coles came down the street arm-in-arm, from their neat stucco house on the corner.

"See they've got you working hard, eh?" cried Mr. Coles genially, as they paused abreast of the hedge.

Mr. Wheelock laughed politely, marking time for an answer.

"That's right," he evolved.

Mrs. Wheelock looked up from her work, shading her eyes with her thim-bled hand against the long rays of the low sun.

"Yes, we finally got Daddy to do a little work," she called brightly. "But Sister and I are staying right here to watch over him, for fear he might cut his little self with the shears."

There was general laughter, in which Sister joined. She had risen punctiliously at the approach of the older people, and she was looking politely at their eyes, as she had been taught.

"And how is my great big girl?" asked Mrs. Coles, gazing fondly at the child.

"Oh, much better," Mrs. Wheelock answered for her. "Doctor Mann says we are going ahead finely. I saw his automobile passing the house this morning—he was going to see Mr. Warren, his rheumatism's coming along nicely—and I called him in a minute to look us over."

She did the wink and the nods, at Sister's back. Mr. and Mrs. Coles nodded shrewdly back at her.

"He said there's no need for those t-o-n-s-i-l-s to c-o-m-e o-u-t," Mrs. Wheelock called. "But I thought, soon's it gets a little cooler, some time next month, we'd just run in to the city and let Doctor Sturges have a look at us. I was telling Daddy, 'I'd rather be on the safe side,' I said."

"Yes, it's better to be on the safe side," agreed Mrs. Coles, and her husband nodded again, sagely this time. She took his arm, and they moved slowly off.

"Been a lovely day, hasn't it?" she said over her shoulder, fearful of having left too abruptly. "Fred and I are taking a little constitutional before supper."

"Oh, taking a little constitutional?" cried Mrs. Wheelock, laughing.
Mrs. Coles laughed also, three or four bars.

"Yes, just taking a little constitutional before supper," she called back.

Sister, weary of her game, mounted the porch, whimpering a little.
Mrs. Wheelock put aside her sewing, and took the tired child in her lap.
The sun's last rays touched her brown hair, making it a shimmering gold.
Her small, sharp face, the thick lines of her figure were in shadow as she
bent over the little girl. Sister's head was hidden on her mother's shoulder,
the folds of her rumpled white frock followed her limp, relaxed little body.

The lovely light was kind to the cheap, hurriedly built stucco house,
to the clean gravel path, and the bits of closely cut lawn. It was gracious,
too, to Mr. Wheelock's tall, lean figure as he bent to work on the last few
inches of unclipped hedge.

Twenty years, he thought. The man in the story went through with it
for twenty years. He must have been a man along around forty-five, most
likely. Mr. Wheelock was thirty-seven. Eight years. It's a long time, eight
years is. You could easily get so you could say that final "Oh, hell," even to
Adelaide, in eight years. It probably wouldn't take more than four for you
to know that you could do it. No, not more than two. ...

Mrs. Coles paused at the corner of the street and looked back at the
Wheelocks' house. The last of the light lingered on the mother and child
group on the porch, gently touched the tall, white-clad figure of the husband and father as he went up to them, his work done.

Mrs. Coles was a large, soft woman, barren, and addicted to sentiment.

"Look, Fred; just turn around and look at that," she said to her husband. She looked again, sighing luxuriously. "Such a pretty little picture!"

THE GREEN ELEPHANT

Dashiell Hammett

I

JOE SHUPE stood in the doorway of the square-faced office building—his body tilted slantwise so that one thin shoulder, lodged against the gray stone, helped his crossed legs hold him up—looking without interest into the street.

He had stepped into the vestibule to roll a cigarette out of reach of the boisterous wind that romped along Riverside avenue, and he had remained there because he had nothing better to do. In fact, he had nothing else to do just now. Tomorrow he would revisit the employment offices—a matter of a few blocks' walk along Main and Trent avenues, with brief digressions into one or two of the intersecting streets—for the fifth consecutive day; perhaps to be rewarded by a job, perhaps to hear reiterations of the now familiar "nothing in your line today." But the time for that next pilgrimage to the shrines of Industry, through which he might reach the comparative paradise of employment, was still some twenty hours away; so Joe Shupe loitered in the doorway, and dull thoughts began to crawl around in his little round head.

He thought of the Swede first, with distaste. The Swede—he was a Dane, but the distinction was too subtle for Joe—had come down to the city from a Lost Creek lumber camp with money in his pockets and faith in his fellows. When the men came together and formed their brief friendship only fifty dollars remained of the Swede's tangible wealth. Joe got that by a crude and hoary subterfuge with which even a timber-beast from Lost Creek should have been familiar. What became of the

466

swindled Swede's faith is not a matter of record. Joe had not given *that* a thought; and had his attention been called to it he probably would have been unable to see in it anything but further evidence of the Swede's unfitness for the possession of money.

But what was vital to Joe Shupe was that, inspired by the ease with which he had gained the fifty dollars, he had deserted the polished counter over which for eight hours each day he had shoved pies and sandwiches and coffee, and had set out to live by his wits. But the fifty dollars had soon dribbled away, the Swede had had no successors; and now Joe Shupe was beset with the necessity of finding employment again.

Joe's fault, as Doc Haire had once pointed out, was that he was an unskilled laborer in the world of crime, and therefore had to content himself with stealing whatever came to hand—a slipshod and generally unsatisfactory method. As the same authority had often declared: "Making a living on the mace ain't duck soup! Take half these guys you hear telling the world what wonders they are at puffing boxes, knocking over joints, and the rest of the lays—not a half of 'em makes three meals a day at it! Then what chance has a guy that ain't got no regular racket, but's got to trust to luck, got? Huh?"

But Joe Shupe had disregarded this advice, and even the oracle's own example. For Doc Haire, although priding himself upon being the most altogether efficient house-burglar in the Northwest, was not above shipping out into the Couer d'Alenes now and then to repair his finances by a few weeks work in the mines. Joe realized the Doc had been right; that he himself was not equipped to dig through the protecting surfaces with which mankind armored its wealth; that the Swede's advent had been a fortuitous episode and a recurrence could not be expected now. He blamed the Swede now. . . .

A commotion in the street interrupted Joe Shupe's unaccustomed introspection.

Across the street two automobiles were twisting and turning, backing and halting, in clumsy dance figures. Men began to run back and forth between them. A tall man in a black overcoat stood up in one of the cars and began shooting with a small-caliber pistol at indeterminate targets. Weapons appeared in the other automobiles, and in the hands of men in the street between the two machines. Spectators scrambled into doorways. From down the street a policeman was running heavily, tugging at his hip, and trying to free his wrist from an entangling coat-tail. A man was running across the street toward Joe's doorway, a black gladstone bag swinging at his side. As the man's foot touched the curb he fell forward, sprawling half in the gutter half on the sidewalk. The bag left his hand and slid across the pavement—balancing itself nicely as a boy on skates—to Joe's feet.

The wisdom of Doc Haire went for nothing. With no thought for the economics of thievery, the amenities of specialization, Joe Shupe followed his bent. He picked up the bag, passed through the revolving door into the lobby of the building, turned a corner, followed a corridor, and at length came to a smaller door, through which he reached an alley. The alley gave to another street and a street-car that had paused to avoid a truck. Joe climbed into the car and found a seat.

Thus far Joe Shupe had been guided by pure instinct, and—granting that to touch the bag at all were judicious—had acted deftly and with beautiful precision. But now his conscious brain caught up with him as it were, and resumed its dominion over him. He began to wonder what he had let himself in for, whether his prize were worth the risk its possession had entailed, just how great that risk might be. He became excited, his pulse throbbed, singing in his temples, and his mouth went dry. He had a vision of innumerable policemen, packed in taxicabs like pullets in crates, racing dizzily to intercept him.

He got to the street four blocks from where he had boarded the street car, and only a suspicion that the conductor was watching him persuaded him to cling to the bag. He would have preferred leaving it inconspicuously between the seats, to be found in the car barn. He walked rapidly away from the car line, turning thankfully each corner the city put in his path, until he came to another row of car tracks. He stayed on the second car for six blocks, and then wound circuitously through the streets again, finally coming to the hotel in which he had room.

A towel covering the keyhole, the blind down over the one narrow window, Joe Shupe put the bag on his bed and set about opening it. It was securely locked, but with his knife he attacked a leather side, making a ragged slit through which he looked into depths of green paper.

"Holy hell!" his gaping mouth exclaimed. "All the money in the world!"

II

He straightened abruptly, listening, while his small brown eyes looked suspiciously around the room. Tiptoeing to the door, he listened again; unlocked the door quickly and flung it open; searched the dark hall. Then he returned to the black bag. Enlarging the opening, he dumped and raked his spoils out on the bed: a mound of grey-green paper—a bushel of it—neatly divided into little soft, paper-gartered bricks. Thousands, hundreds, tens, twenties, fifties! For a long minute he stood open-mouthed, spellbound, panting; then he hastily covered the pile of currency with one of the shabby grey blankets on the bed, and dropped weakly down beside it.

Presently the desire to know the amount of his loot penetrated Joe's stupefaction and he set about counting the money. He counted slowly and with difficulty, taking one package of bills out of its hiding place at a time and stowing it under another blanket when he had finished with it. He counted each package he handled, bill by bill, ignoring the figures printed on the manilla wrappers. At fifty thousand he stopped, estimating that he had handled one-third of the pile. The emotional seething within him, together with the effort the unaccustomed addition required of his brain, had by then driven his curiosity away.

His mind, freed of its mathematical burden, was attacked by an alarming thought. The manager of the hotel, who was his own clerk, had seen Joe come in with the bag; and while the bag was not unusual in appearance, nevertheless, any black bag would attract both eyes and speculation after the evening papers were read. Joe decided that he would have to get out of the hotel, after which the bag would have to be disposed of.

Laboriously, and at the cost of two large blisters, he hacked at the bag with his dull knife and bent it until, wrapped in an old newspaper, it made a small and unassuming bundle. Then he distributed the money about his person, stuffing his pockets and even putting some of the bills inside his shirt. He looked at his reflection in the mirror when he had finished, and the result was very unsatisfactory: he presented a decidedly and humorously padded appearance.

That would not do. He dragged his battered valise from under the bed and put the money into it, under his few clothes.

There was no delay about his departure from the hotel: it was of the type where all bills are payable in advance. He passed four rubbish cans before he could summon the courage to get rid of the fragments of the bag, but he boldly dropped them into the fifth; after which he walked— almost scuttled—for ten minutes, turning corners and slipping through alleys, until he was positive he was not being watched.

At a hotel across the city from his last home he secured a room and went up to it immediately. Behind drawn blinds, masked keyhole, and closed transom, he took the money out again. He had intended finishing his counting—the flight across the city having rekindled his desire to know the extent of his wealth—but when he found that he had bunched it, had put already counted with uncounted, and thought of the immensity of the task, he gave it up. Counting was a "tough job," and the afternoon papers would tell him how much he had.

He wanted to look at the money, to feast his eyes upon it, to caress his fingers with it, but its abundance made him uneasy, frightened him even, notwithstanding that it was safe here from prying eyes. There was too much of it. It unnerved him. A thousand dollars, or perhaps even ten thousand, would have filled him with wild joy, but this bale. . . . Furtively, he put it back in the valise.

For the first time now he thought of it not as money,—a thing in itself,—but as money—potential women, cards, liquor, idleness, everything! It took his breath for the instant—the thought of the things the world held for him now! And he realized that he was wasting time, that these things were abroad, beckoning, while he stood in his room dreaming of them. He opened the valise and took out a double handful of the bills, cramming them into his pockets.

On the steps descending from the office to the street he halted abruptly. A hotel of this sort—or any other—was certainly no place to leave a hundred and fifty thousand dollars unguarded. A fine chump he would be to leave it behind and have it stolen!

He hurried back to his room and, scarcely pausing to renew his former precautions, sprang to the valise. The money was still there. Then he sat down and tried to think of some way by which the money could be protected during his absence. He was hungry—he had not eaten since morning—but he could not leave the money. He found a piece of heavy paper, wrapped the money in it and lashed it securely, making a large but inconspicuous bundle—laundry, perhaps.

On the street newsboys were shouting extras. Joe bought a paper, folded it carefully so that its headlines were out of sight, and went to a restaurant on First avenue. He sat at a table back in one corner, with his bundle on the floor and his feet on the bundle. Then with elaborate nonchalance he spread the paper before him and read of the daylight hold-up in which $250,000 had ben taken from an automobile belonging to the Fourth National Bank. $250,000! He grabbed the bundle from the floor, knocking his forehead noisily against the table in his haste, and put it in his lap. Then he reddened with swift self-consciousness, paled apprehensively, and yawned exaggeratedly. After assuring himself that none of the other men in the restaurant had noted his peculiar behavior, he turned his attention to the newspaper again, and read the story of the robbery.

Five of the bandits had been caught in the very act, the paper said, and two of them were seriously wounded. The bandits, who, according to the paper, must have had information concerning the unusually large shipment from some friend on the inside, had bungled their approach, bringing their own automobile to rest too far from their victim's for the greatest efficiency. Nevertheless, the sixth bandit had made away with the money. As was to be expected, the bandits denied that there was a sixth, but the disappearance of the money testified irrefragably to his existence.

From the restaurant Joe went to a saloon on Howard street, bought two bottles of white liquor, and took them to his room. He had decided that he would have to remain indoors that night: he couldn't walk around with $250,000 under his arm. Suppose some flaw in the paper should suddenly succumb to the strain upon it? Or he should drop the bundle? Or someone should bump heavily into it?

He fidgeted about the room for hours, pondering his problem with all the concentration of which his dull mind was capable. He opened one of the bottles that he had brought, but he set it aside untasted: he could not risk drinking until he had safeguarded the money. It was too great a responsibility to be mixed with alcohol. The temptations of women and cards and the rest did not bother him now; time enough for them when the money was safe. He couldn't leave the money in his room, and he couldn't carry it to any of the places he knew, or to any place at all, for that matter.

III

He slept little that night, and by morning had made no headway against his problem. He thought of banking the money, but dismissed the thought as absurd: he couldn't walk into a bank a day or so after a widely advertised robbery and open an account with a bale of currency. He even thought of finding some secluded spot where he could bury it; but that seemed still more ridiculous. A few shovels of dirt was not sufficient protection. He might buy or rent a house and conceal the money on his own premises; but there were fires to consider, and what might serve as a hiding place for a few hundred dollars wouldn't do for many thousand: he must have an absolutely safe plan, one that would be safe in every respect and would admit of no possible loophole through which the money could vanish. He knew half a dozen men who could have told him what to do; but which of them could he trust where $250,000 was concerned?

When he was giddy from too much smoking on an empty stomach, he packed his valise again and left the hotel. A day of uneasiness and restlessness, with the valise ever in his hand or under his foot, brought no counsel. The grey-green incubus that his battered bag housed benumbed him, handicapped by his never-agile imagination. His nerves began to send little fluttering messages—forerunners of panic—to his brain.

Leaving a restaurant that evening he encountered Doc Haire himself.

"Hullo, Joe! Going away?"

Joe looked down at the valise in his hand.

"Yes," he said.

That was it! Why hadn't he thought of it before! In another city, at some distance from the scene of the robbery, none of the restrictions that oppressed him in Spokane would be present. Seattle, Portland, San Francisco, Los Angeles, the East!

Although he had paid for a berth, Joe Shupe did not occupy it; but sat all night in a day couch. At the last moment he had realized that the ways of sleeping-cars were unknown to him—perhaps one was required to surrender one's hand baggage. Joe did not know, but he did know that the money in his valise was not going to leave his hands until he had found a securer place for it. So he dozed uncomfortably through the ride over the Cascades, sprawled over two seats in the smoking-car, leaning against the valise.

In Seattle he gained no more liberty than he had had in Spokane. He had purposed to open an account with each bank in the city, distributing his wealth widely in cautious amounts; and for two days he tried to carry out his plan. But his nervous legs simply would not carry him through the door of a bank. There was something too austere, too official, too all-knowing, about the very architecture of these financial institutions, and there was no telling what complications, what questioning, awaited a man inside.

A fear of being bereft of his wealth by more cunning thieves—and he admitted frankly now that there might he many such—began to obsess him, and kept him out of dance-hall, pool-room, gambling-house, and saloon. From anyone who addressed even the most casual of sentences to him he fled headlong. On his first day in Seattle he bought a complete equipment of bright and gaudy clothes, but he wore them for only half an hour. He felt that they gave him an altogether too affluent appearance, and would certainly attract the attention of thieves in droves; so he put them away in his valise, and thereafter wore his old clothes.

At night now he slept with the valise in bed beside him, one of his arms bent over it in a protecting embrace that was not unlike a bridegroom's, waking now and then with the fear that someone was tugging at it. And every night it was a different hotel. He changed his lodgings each day, afraid of the curiosity his habit of always carrying the valise might arouse if he stayed too long in any one hotel.

Such intelligence as he was ordinarily in possession of was by this time completely submerged beneath the panic in which he lived. He went aimlessly about the city, a shabby man with the look of a harried rabbit in his furtive eyes, destinationless, without purpose, filled with forebodings that were now powerless except to deepen the torpor in his head.

A senseless routine filled his days. At eight or eight-thirty in the morning he would leave the hotel where he had slept, eat his breakfast at a nearby lunch-room, and then walk—down Second to Yessler Way, to Fourth, to Pike—or perhaps as far as Stewart—to Second, to Yessler Way, to Fourth....

Sometimes he would desert his beat to sit for an hour or more on one of the green iron benches around the totem in Pioneer Square, staring vacantly at the street, his valise either at his side or beneath his feet. Presently, goaded by an obscure disquietude, he would get up abruptly and go back to his promenade along Yessler Way to Fourth, to Pike, to Second, to Yessler Way, to.... When he thought of food he ate meagerly at the nearest restaurant, but often he forgot to eat all day.

His nights were more vivid; with darkness his brain shook off some of its numbness and become sensitive to pain. Lying in the dark, always in a strange room, he would be filled with wild fears whose anarchic chaos amounted to delirium. Only in his dreams did he see things clearly. His brief and widely spaced naps brought him distinct, sharply etched pictures in which invariably he was robbed of his money, usually to the accompaniment of physical violence in its most unlovely forms.

The end was inevitable. In a larger city Joe Shupe might have gone on until his mentality had wasted away entirely and he collapsed. But Seattle is not large enough to smother the identities of its inhabitants: strangers' faces become familiar: one becomes accustomed to meeting the man in the brown derby somewhere in the vicinity of the post-office, and the red-haired girl with the grapes on her hat somewhere along Pine Street between noon and one o'clock; and looks for the slim youth with the remarkable moustache, expecting to pass him on the street at least twice during the course of the day. And so it was that two Prohibition enforcement officers came to recognize Joe Shupe and his battered valise and his air of dazed fear.

They didn't take him very seriously at first, until, quite by accident, they grew aware of his custom of changing his address each night. Then one day, when they had nothing special on hand and when the memory of reprimands they had received from their superiors for not frequently enough "showing results" was fresh, they met Joe on the street. For two hours they shadowed him—up Fourth to Pike, to Second, to Yessler Way. ... On the third round-trip confusion and chagrin sent the officers to accost Joe.

"I ain't done nothing!" Joe told them, hugging the valise to his wasted body with both arms. "You leave me be!"

One of the officers said something that Joe did not understand—he was beyond comprehending anything by now—but tears came from his red-rimmed eyes and ran down the hollows of his cheeks.

"You leave me be!" he repeated.

Then, still clasping the valise to his bosom, he turned and ran down the street. The officers easily overtook him.

Joe Shupe's story of how he had come into possession of the stolen quarter-million was received by everyone—police, press and public— with a great deal of merriment. But, now that the responsibility for the money's safety rested with the Seattle police, he slept soundly that night, as well as those that followed; and when he appeared in the courtroom in Spokane two weeks later, to plead futilely that he was not one of the men who had held up the Fourth National Bank's automobile, he was his normal self again, both physically and mentally.

www.ingramcontent.com/pod-product-compliance
Lightning Source LLC
Chambersburg PA
CBHW022236020726
47496CB00004B/937